Praise from Ireland for *Racing the Moon:*

'The twins' often fraught relationship is credibly drawn, as is their emotional development . . . Another of the book's strengths is its strong sense of place, particularly in the scenes set in Dublin'
The Irish Times

'An engaging book, not least for its *roman a clef* tendencies; its asides on Irish life . . . the occasional aphorism . . . the imagery'
Sunday Tribune

'Mastery of the foibles and weaknesses of corporate and political Ireland'
Irish Independent

D0774034

Also by Terry Prone

Blood Brothers, Soul Sisters

About the author

Terry Prone has written several non-fiction bestsellers
and in 1994 published a collection of short stories,
Blood Brothers, Soul Sisters, described by David Marcus as
'possibly the best short story debut by an Irish writer in the
past ten years'. Terry Prone is Managing Director of Carr
Communications, a PR firm; she is married to
consultant Tom Savage and has one son, Anton.

Racing the Moon

Terry Prone

CORONET BOOKS
Hodder & Stoughton

ISBN 0 340 72853 1

Printed and bound in Great Britain by
Mackays of Chatham plc, Chatham, Kent

Hodder and Stoughton
A division of Hodder Headline PLC
338 Euston Road
London NW1 3BH

For the real Amanda Nelligan

ACKNOWLEDGEMENTS

Stephen Cullen, Brenda O'Hanlon, Donal Cronin, Anne Foley, Frank Sweeney and Frances Fitzgerald read the manuscript and offered helpful advice. Mark Bruce of the Sun Bark Hunting Lodge, Custer, South Dakota, was generous in his expertise, as – on a rather different theme – was Deirdre Purcell. Some friends with special expertise advised on aspects of thsir area of knowledge and, although I may not name them, I am deeply grateful to them. No thanks is sufficient for Kate Cruise O'Brien, Gerard Kenny and Neasa Kane. One steadfast academic provided reading, titling, defence and rescue services. He gets tenure . . .

CHAPTER ONE

Sunset and puddled shadows.
Two children in silhouette against the slanted evening light.
All concentration as they release the day's catch of pinkeens.
That was how their parents always remembered them as toddlers.
Together.
Moving and thinking as one.
Moving and thinking as one.
Until their fourth birthday.

That birthday separated Sophia and Darcy, silencing one and making a leader of the other. Their parents gave them bicycles as birthday presents, when they had half-learned to cycle on bikes belonging to neighbours' children. It was Sophia who spotted that it was tougher to pedal up the hill outside their house than down it. But it was Darcy who decided that if you started at the top of the hill, it might be easiest of all. She tried it out immediately, heading off down the hill with windsong in her ears, hair flying, a cool breeze whipping in under her cardigan, euphoria building as she went.

The counterpoint to the euphoria came swiftly in the physical comeuppance of hitting the lamppost at the end of the road at top speed, the bike crashing and in mad metal venom attacking her, handlebars bright with pink plastic ramming into her small mouth, crunch-tearing teeth from bone and into tongue, mouth all swollen to burst with blood and broken bits, the pedal strangling her ankle, the chain wrapped around soft pants legs and the tidal wave of pain following three heartbeats later.

Two saw it. Sophia took off at a run down the hill, ditching her bike in one dexterous throw into the front garden as she passed. Pat Rice, glancing into the street from his bedroom, watched Darcy's progress with out-loud protest:

'That kid is going too fast on that bi – what's she *at* – Oh, lovey, you don't know how to use the brakes – ' and he was running down the stairs of his house before the collision was consummated. He picked the child up before the back wheel of the bike stopped spinning, dragging his pristine handkerchief out of his trouser pocket and swamping the child's face in it as the other twin arrived, wide-eyed and wide-mouthed at the instantaneous change from white fold-starched cotton to red, *red* limp dribbling wetness, Darcy's eyes goggling over it. He upped Darcy onto the crooks of his arms, running with her, Sophia trailing. The twins' mother, Colette, was half-way down the path when Pat Rice rounded the gate-post, carrying a mass of blood with flailing arms and legs, for the handkerchief had drowned and overflowed in Darcy's blood. Colette backed up, had the door open and directed the neighbour into the kitchen.

'On the table, on the table,' she said, and tore the heavy hanky off Darcy's face. A ruined mouth opened in a bubbling scream.

'I'll get my car,' Pat Rice said, and was gone. Holding Darcy in position with one hand, Colette reached to the sink and soaked a towel in cold water, dragging it back and spilling it into Darcy's mouth, sitting her up and squeezing water into her mouth at the same time.

'Spit it all out,' she told her daughter.

'Sophia?'

A small white face came up over the edge of the table.

'I want you to run straight in next door to Mrs Clifton and tell her what's happened. Say that I'm going to the hospital and can you stay with her, and come to the door quickly so I can see you're all right.'

Sophia opened her mouth to protest at not being taken to the hospital but something in her mother's face made the protest die at source and she ran out the front door, ducked under the fence in the side passage, and was knocking at Mrs Clifton's door as Colette and Pat Rice were going down the front path. Again in dumb-show enforced by Darcy's screams, which were uniform on in-breath and out-breath, Colette could see Meg Clifton taking in Sophia's message, hugging her and giving a 'Go on, don't delay, everything'll be fine' gesture to Colette.

At the hospital, Darcy was taken from her mother's arms and into rooms of people who told her to hold still and were cross with her when she didn't, because their X-ray machine would not take pictures of her if she moved. They asked her questions and couldn't understand her answers, which was just as well, since they were unrelated to the questions and mostly consisted of pleas for no pain, for her mother, for it not to have happened, to be left alone and for someone to take away the fear.

Then they put her on an ice-cold metal trolley and took her into another room where there were white and green monsters that talked from behind faces of fabric that crinkled with their movements and some of them had glasses on above the fabric. The biggest one told her to put out her tongue and when she cried – because her tongue was a great solid obstruction in her mouth that didn't do anything it normally did – snip-snipped a scissors in the air and told her if she didn't put it out he would have to cut it off. Some of them laughed. One of the ones who had laughed touched her on the arm and said he didn't mean it, but then the big one got very cross and said, 'Hold her steady.' Big hands circled her arms and shoulders and knees and ankles and the big fabric face came at her with pointed grabbing things and a huge needle with black thread and even though the other pain had been bigger than she was, this pain stewed her down to a nothing that they talked over while they tortured.

When they wheeled her out of that room, her mother was standing with her father. Darcy grabbed them so tightly they could not peel her fingers away, because she was afraid that the fabric-face monsters would come back and do more pain to her.

'She'll be fine,' the voice of the biggest monster said behind her, and she screamed all over again, trying to tell her mother and father that he had said he would cut her tongue out, baffled with betrayal when her father was grateful to the figure behind her. At least they didn't give her back to the fabric-face monster, but carried her to her father's car. Pat Rice had evaporated the way figures in nightmares often do, but – the thought made her cry again – he would probably come and kill her for bleeding all over his nice clean hanky and his trousers.

'She'll be asleep before we get home,' Robert told his white-faced wife. She nodded at the windscreen in front of her, thinking: he feels this would not have happened had I been watching all the time.

'Honey,' he said, changing gear and patting her gently on the knee at more or less the same time. 'Honey, accidents happen to children. No point in trying to blame yourself.'

That's true, he thought, but still, you'd think on the first day of them being on the bikes, she could have found the time to watch them. Denying to himself that he had thought the thought, he could not know that Colette knew he had thought it and agreed with it.

First thing the following morning, Sophia was up examining Darcy, who looked, if anything, worse than the previous night. Her face was darkened on its lower half by a purple-navy staining which gave her the look of a heavy-set dark man who not only hadn't shaved for days, but – because one of her eyes was half-closed by swelling – had a lewd winking comment to make on the world. Darcy examined her sister as fixedly as her sister was examining her.

'Your bike is all right,' Sophia said. (Darcy wanted to know if the fabric-face monsters were going to come back.)

'Some of the spokes got bent, but Daddy straightened them all out and it's lovely again.' (Darcy wanted to know was she in trouble for ruining everybody's day.)

'I'll be able to show you how the brakes work, so it'll

never happen again.' (Darcy wanted to know if the birthday cake had been given away the previous night.)

'Did you eat all the cake?' Darcy asked. What came out of her mouth was a woofling stuffed nonsense that hurt her and terrified her twin. Sophia was reversing out of the door to get away from it when their mother came into the room and went down on her knees in front of the damaged child.

'The good news is that you get jelly for breakfast,' Colette said. 'With ice-cream if you'd like. The bad news is that you look *dreadful*. I would have to laugh because otherwise I'd be frightened of you.' She sat back on her heels, looking doubtful. 'I'd be scared you'd do something awful to me. You wouldn't, would you?'

Darcy shook her head and discovered that nodding was less painful than shaking from side to side, so she changed the head-shake to a nod.

'You *would* do something awful to me?'

Darcy held the sides of her face to indicate pain. Colette trailed a gentle finger across her forehead.

'It doesn't hurt up there, sure it doesn't? But it begins to hurt down here,' she said, the finger touching the bruised cheekbones, 'and down here it's really really bad. Inside your mouth, it feels so dreadful you can't believe it.'

Watching this, Sophia found a new role. She would be Darcy's interpreter. Listening to the bubbling bolstered eruptions of sound coming from Darcy's mouth very carefully, she could usually figure the essentials of Darcy's messages so she began to lead Darcy by the hand and point out to others the more interesting aspects of her case.

Pat Rice dropped to his hunkers in the doorway when he saw the twins. 'Ah, *sweetheart*,' he said to Darcy. 'Ah, love.'

She roared a communication at him which had no consonents whatever in it.

'She's *really* sorry for ruining your hanky,' Sophia said.

'Divil take the hankie, for God's sake,' said Pat Rice.

Darcy blurted again.

13

'And your suit,' Sophia said.

'Listen, you mind yourself and concentrate on getting better,' Pat Rice said. Darcy nodded. She was pleased to discover how often nodding paid off in conversational terms.

'She had twelve stitches in her tongue,' Sophia said, over her shoulder, as she led Darcy away. 'Twelve. *Stitches*.'

Darcy looked at her in horror, not having known this.

'Sall right,' Sophia said, patting the hand she was holding in race memory of every grandmother who ever lived. 'Sall over now.'

From that day it was Sophia who owned the narrative of the twins' days.

'We were down at the swimming pool,' she would announce. 'Darcy and me and the whole class were in the pool and they had a big rope to hang on to with big floaters so it wouldn't go under when you leaned on it, the rope, and Mr Gurney was showing us how to kick.'

Which was about the size of it, Darcy had to acknowledge.

'This is my twin sister, Darcy,' Sophia would announce with a half-turn to the left like a man on television introducing the singers. 'She was in an accident and she can't talk properly, but she will.'

That more or less wrapped Darcy up. Relationship: twin sister to the normal, pretty one. Drama: accident. Consequences: can't speak. Light at the end of the tunnel: but she will. When Sophia was doing this riff for nuns and priests or people who were old, she would add 'Please God' at the end of it.

Because of this little introduction, Darcy not only did not *have* to speak; she could sustain her invalid prestige only by *not* speaking. If she opened her ravaged mouth, what came out was so far from Sophia's neat diction that hearers were almost physically jolted by it. Sophia, meantime, developed the status of a trial-size Florence Nightingale.

For the first time, Darcy began to be conscious of the advantages and disadvantages of being a twin. On the positive side, Sophia was very good at understanding what Darcy was saying, so it was often helpful to have her around as an interpreter. On the negative side, Darcy realised that she was the second-class twin. Not talking gave her more time to observe and to learn the language of eyes, as newcomers met Sophia, enchanted by her pretty politeness, and then encountered this bigger, lumpier twin locked in sullen silence.

'And this is your *twin*,' they would say, their tone diluting its enthusiasm.

'Your *big* twin,' some of them would add, as if giving a bouquet to Sophia. Darcy would stand there, inflating, she would feel, into a figure of hulk and bulk and gross inferiority.

When they both went to ballet class, the situation worsened. The ballet teacher quickly spotted Sophia's instinctive grace and was equally speedy in viewing the heftier twin as a write-off, in terms of what the teacher always referred to as 'The Dawnce'. So, in their last year in primary school, Sophia was the star of the concert given for parents, and Darcy was in the back row of the chorus.

This seemed a great injustice to one of the twins. A few nights after the concert, Sophia talked to her parents about it. It wasn't fair, she pointed out, that Darcy was in the chorus, because she had a lovely singing voice. It wasn't fair that people always talked first to Sophia and only then to Darcy, as if she were stupid. It might *make* her stupid, being talked to like that, Sophia said.

'Sophia has a point,' Robert King said to Colette that evening. 'It would be good for Darcy to have something to shine at.'

'She shines pretty well at silence,' Colette said.

'Silence has no practical use,' Robert said impatiently. Colette, who thought silence had great practical use, decided not to fight him on the point.

'Has Darcy any interests?' her father asked.

'Horses,' Colette said.

'Horses?'

15

'Horses. Ponies. Stables. Did you never look at the line of books over her bed?'

Robert King shook his head.

'Anything to do with horses, she loves reading,' Colette told him.

'In that case,' Robert King said. 'We must make sure she takes up horse riding when she goes to secondary school in the autumn.'

CHAPTER TWO

Darcy looked at her horse and her horse looked at her.

'What's his name?'

'Ginger.'

The horse was black-and-white like a dalmatian.

'Ginger?' she said in a glad-to-meet-you voice to the horse. The horse ignored her, put its head down and began to eat grass.

'Get on, would you?' the instructor demanded.

Darcy summoned up a careless smile, bounded up the three steps, threw her right leg over the saddle and – unstuck by the slipperiness – fell off on the other side. Her black helmet hat slid around her head, choking her on its strap. She shoved the hat back where it was supposed to be, dusted her behind as casually as she could, and walked up the steps again. This time she managed to stay on long enough to get her feet into the stirrups and be handed the reins.

Horses, she knew from her many books about them, fitted in between your legs like pillows. You had only to squeeze them gently – the very lightness of your squeeze was the measure of your skill as a rider – and they would respond to your every half-finished thought.

This horse was some awful exception. Sitting on Ginger was like sitting on the roof of a double-decker bus. You were three miles off the ground. Your two legs were stretched out on either side of you so that the only question was how soon you were going to split up the middle of your body. No muscle below Darcy's waist was capable of squeezing this double-decker called Ginger. Ginger shifted from haunch to haunch and Darcy faced the possibility of a second involuntary dismount before she ever left the stables.

The others started to move away on their horses. Ginger moved in solidarity with the others. The pain between

Darcy's legs, which had subsided to a turbid throb, screeched into searing stabs as she tried to raise her bottom off the saddle at each step.

'No trotting yet,' the instructor said. She looked at Darcy as if she expected her to urge Ginger into a headlong gallop. As far as Darcy was concerned, the hippy amble Ginger had opted for was more than headlong enough. The ground was as far away as if she were in an upstairs window, except upstairs windows weren't slidy under your trousers and hot to the touch. She could hear her classmates talking among themselves. For all she knew they were including her in their conversation but she was too busy praying silently to Ginger. Be a good horse, please be a good horse and don't do anything bad.

The others led the way. Ginger halted and decided to eat grass. Darcy slid wildly forward over the horse's neck, losing the reins. The instructor came back on her horse and pulled the reins up, handing them to Darcy with a look of unveiled contempt. The leather was wet from horse-spit. Ginger had been eating the reins as well as the grass.

Darcy tweaked the left-hand side of the reins. Nothing happened. She tweaked again. Nothing. Irritated, Darcy gave the left-hand rein a hard, long pull. Ginger came up out of the grass and twisted his head around like a snake, to look at Darcy with one huge eye. Darcy pulled the other side and the horse looked straight ahead. Emboldened by this, Darcy decided that it was possible that she would eventually learn to handle this animal.

'OK, *now* trot,' the instructor ordered.

Ginger, freshly fuelled by grass intake, leaped into enthusiastic action, his huge back humping and straightening out, spearing Darcy afresh.

At this point her trousers split from knee to knee. Ginger's vast rump lifted her and she was airborne. All she saw was mercifully disappearing bottom of horse. Gravity took over and pulled her groundwards, her torn trousers flapping like a flag of surrender. She landed squarely in the middle of the worn pathway, where the ground was hardest. The blow reverberated along her spine up into her hair. In an instant, it was clear to her. She would be in a wheelchair for the rest of her life. Like Clara in *Heidi*.

'Get up. Get back on.'

The instructor had Ginger by the reins and was holding the black-and-white horse alongside her own chestnut. She looked down at Darcy.

'No,' said Darcy.

'What do you mean, no?'

'No,' said Darcy.

'Get up.'

'No.'

'Get *up!*'

'*No!* Shag off!'

Darcy got to her feet. Each bone and muscle shrieked.

'This is serious, Darcy,' the instructor said. 'You have to get up again, right now. If you don't, you will never be able to again. It always happens. If you don't get back up straight away, you get a mental block.'

'Good.'

Darcy turned back the way she had come, hauling her hat off.

'*Darcy?*'

Darcy stopped. 'Would you care to suggest *how* I would get up on that half-arsed horse out here in the middle of nowhere when I couldn't get up on the shagger back at the stable where I had the advantage of a frigging great flight of farting *stairs*? Anyway, I'm not going to. Ever. So I have a mental block – great. So I will never ride another horse as long as I live – hooray. So I am a coward and a weakling and a worm – yeah. But I am a one-piece worm. A few minutes ago, I thought I was going to be a ten-piece worm. I do not propose to look a gift horse in the arsehole or anywhere else, ever again and Goodbye Ginger.'

It was the longest speech anyone had ever heard from her.

When Darcy woke the following morning, stiff as an arthritic old man, bruised from thigh to shoulder, she didn't have to totter into school to face the ironic plaudits of her peers because it was Saturday. She did have to face Sophia's directive sympathy, however.

'You're very bruised,' Sophia said.

'It's very frustrating the way I always get bruised on my arse,' Darcy said, twisting to get a view in the mirror. 'I never have bruises in noticeable glamorous places. I never get a black eye, for example. I've always wanted a black eye and I've always wanted to faint.'

'The soreness would be gone by next Friday,' said Sophia, sticking to the point, her voice heavy with meaning.

Darcy dressed in silence.

'You should really give it another go,' Sophia said.

'No, I really shouldn't give it another go,' Darcy replied, tying her hair back.

'But what are the bruises *for*, then?'

'Bruises aren't for anything. Bruises are just bruises.'

Sophia shook her head.

'Symptoms all have a purpose.'

'Listen, if I want Da's words of wisdom, I can go next door and get them from him direct, you know?'

'But he's right. Every sore muscle means you're gaining strength.'

'Bullshit.'

'Oh, *charming*.'

'Sophia, I have one sore muscle from knee to knee,' Darcy said, standing bowlegged. 'Tell me how I gain by having a stronger crotch. Tell me I am going to be better at surviving Life's Great Challenges because of the ironclad strength of my private parts. Tell me that the world is going to envy me as I waddle along like two brackets trying to keep my thighs from touching because they are so inflamed you'd think scalding water got thrown on me.'

Sophia winced in sympathy. Her own hand had a raw place after much recent work with a tennis racquet. She could imagine how much sorer Darcy's thighs must be.

'Did you show the sore place to Dad? He is a doctor, you know.'

Darcy blinded her with a look. 'Listen, kiddo, it's bad enough having to be lectured by you without being lectured by him, too.'

'I'm not lecturing you.'

'Yeah, you are.'

'It's no benefit to me, you know.'

'Right. It's for my own good.'

'Well, it *is* for your own good. If you walk away from something like this, it's an opportunity missed. You can build up – '

' – character. Come on, give me the character-building bit – '

'*Yes*, character, and sneering doesn't make it not true.'

Darcy could feel words boiling at the back of her mouth as in the days when her tongue wouldn't work. I hate you, you priggish perfect piss-artist, went the words. I wish I wasn't stuck in the same room, the same family. I wish you'd never been born, you dreadful walking Good Example that converts me into a pudding-faced failure. I hate the fact that everybody loves you and admires you. If you were somebody else's sister, it would be fine. If you were my sister, only not my twin, it would be grand. But because you are my twin, I'm a loser where you're a winner. Even after weeks in the new school, teachers automatically call me Sophia because they think of you first. They never, *ever*, call you Darcy. Just being this close to you swells me up and makes me think thoughts I'll go to hell for thinking. You love me and that's probably why I hate you more than anybody else in the world and I want to hug you as well and cry.

'I'm sorry,' said Sophia in a small voice. 'It's just that you know so much about horses from all your books. It seems a waste of years of reading and studying, almost, not to become a good rider.'

'But just reading the books might be enough,' Darcy said desperately. 'It doesn't have to *lead* to anything.'

Her sister nodded in a way that suggested tolerant disagreement. Darcy wondered how long it would take her, given a dressing-gown cord and a bit of determined pulling, to choke Sophia into cross-eyed, tongue-extended suffocation.

She'd noticed this a lot recently; that she was spending a lot of time imagining ways of smothering Sophia.

The week after Darcy and Ginger parted company, Margaret Graham, the twins' English teacher, set the class the task of writing an essay about their parents.

'You don't have to do any research,' she explained. 'That's why you can sit down today and have the essay finished before the bell rings. The title is very simple: My Father. I want three pages from each of you.'

When the English teacher came to the essays from the King twins, Darcy's was so filled with crossing-out, additions and amendments that Miss Graham opted for Sophia's beautiful handwriting first.

My Father
My father is Dr Robert King and he is the Head of Pathology at Angelus Hospital in Ballsbridge.

A pathologist is qualified to study the causes of diseases and how a particular disease may change the structure and function of an organ within the body. Pathologists do this by means of microscopic examination of tissues. This is called a biopsy. In some instances, it requires surgery. Some materials, such as bone marrow, are aspirated by a special needle. Pathologists also utilise X-rays and analyse body fluids.

A German pathologist discovered the first antibiotics. A professor of Pathology at Oxford won the Nobel prize for work on penicillin, and an American pathologist won the same prize for discovering that eating liver helps people with pernicious anaemia.

The pathology department in Angelus Hospital employs five people and has its own laboratory. My father, as head of the department, contributes to discussions within the hospital as to whether or not a particular operation was effective or a particular approach should be tried.

My father also has to give testimony at inquests.

When he is not working, my father spends a lot of time at home. He reads extensively and is a fine gardener. He also has an interest in sport.

Sophia King

My Father

My father is mostly noises. He keeps his change in his left-hand pocket (he is left-handed) and he jingles it, usually in time to something he's singing. When he's sorting things out or even just setting the table, he goes Tuk Tuk Tuk in his mouth and when he's really bothered about something he closes his mouth when he's doing it so you can hear it from inside his cheeks. Noises tell you how he's feeling. When he's mad he breathes through his nose and keeps his mouth closed. He doesn't like answering the front door, and when he has to, or the phone, he whistles a particular little tune that he never whistles any other time, although he whistles a lot when he's in good humour.

When he's going to sneeze, he sucks in his breath really slowly across his throat so he gets a kind of reverse voice and then there's maybe five seconds of complete silence and then he roars out a sneeze as if he was shouting at you in a rage: *Aaahch*. At the weekend he always has tools in the back pocket of his trousers, a screwdriver and a chisel or a hammer, and they make a noise and also he's always doing noisy things like clipping the hedge or mowing the lawn or digging with the metal of his spade against stones. He whistles as well, and he's able to do a great musical saw whistle.

In the back garden he loves sweeping the concrete bit with the yard brush, which is like a nail brush only bigger, not soft like the brush in the kitchen, and it makes a great brushy busy noise and bubbles any water that's there.

When my mother or sister go to sleep, they go quiet, but my father gets even noisier. He snores so loudly and in such a sort of deep voice, you'd think it must be hurting him to do it, and if you poke him to stop it, he shudders all over and does a kind of oinking with his mouth. But he always looks so shy and frightened if you wake him by poking him that I don't like to do it no matter how noisy he is. Sometimes it's very funny because he stops snoring when his head is back, but his breath comes down out through his mouth in a sad whistling sound like a train going far away.

He blows his nose like a trumpet. When he's doing things like driving the car, he talks out loud all the time to other drivers, telling them off. I asked him once if he did this when we are not in the car with him, and he said he did not know he did it when we *are* in the car with him, so how could he know about when we are not?

When he's thinking he runs the back of his fingernails across the front end of his teeth and because his fingernails are ridgy, this gives a tiny bimpity bimp noise you can hear if you're very close to him. At work, he wears a white coat that has starch in it and it makes a noise against itself.
Darcy King

Margaret Graham showed the two essays to another English teacher, a nun, who read the two of them carefully, then looked up. The lay teacher looked at her expectantly.

'What do I think? I would have thought it very obvious. Sophia has much greater clarity, much better ordering of information, much better grammar and much better syntax. Not to mention,' the nun went on, scraping what looked like impacted chocolate off one of Darcy's pages, 'not to mention having less of the almost agricultural filth that seems to distinguish her sister's presentation of her thoughts.'

Margaret Graham looked so crestfallen that the nun, who had been a teacher for nigh on twenty years, was moved to sympathy.

'Margaret, if you want to pat yourself on the back for teaching English so they get good marks in their exams and get their arts degrees, you teach them to write like Sophia. The Darcys of this world are just for fun.'

She handed the essays back, noting impatiently that the other woman looked even more pale and enervated than normal. The older teacher figured the younger to be a sufferer from depression and made a mental note to ask somebody knowledgeable about it.

Meanwhile, Sophia King guessed correctly that the teacher was likely, sooner or later, to require the class to do an essay on their mother, so she did some research. When the essay was duly demanded, her offering was as detailed as a curriculum vitae.

My Mother
My mother's name is Colette King.

She went to school in Galway and then in Dublin, where her family moved because her father was a teacher.

My mother is five feet six in height and of slender build. She has light brown hair with a wave in it. She has never worked outside the home, although she has on occasion considered getting a job.

She met my father when he was a student, and they married after he became a doctor. She says she would prefer to be married to a pathologist, such as my father, rather than be a family doctor's (GP) wife, since family doctors are on call day and night and very often their wives work as their nurses or receptionists or general assistants. My mother would not like that at all.

My mother describes herself as an 'emotional pacifist', because she never gets into arguments with people. Some- times, even when she disagrees with people, she stays silent rather than engage in discussion.

My mother enters a lot of competitions and frequently wins prizes. If a manufacturer is running a competition, my mother will stock up on that particular product in order to have a lot of entry forms, and then she will consult with the rest of the family about what slogan would be the best. Last summer she won a swinging hammock with a canopy over it. She never reads the paper although she buys it every evening for my father. She knits and makes clothes. She used to play the piano, but says that she is out of practice. She is a good cook, particularly of pastry.
Sophia King

When Sophia showed the essay to her mother, her mother laughed at the beginning.

'It sounds like a police report,' she said. 'Of slender build . . . '

Sophia, taking offence at this, went to take back the essay, but her mother waved her away. 'No,' she said. 'I subjected myself to your research. I want to see how faithfully you've quoted me.'

She read in silence for a few minutes, then began to smile to herself.

'What's funny?' Sophia asked desperately. There was no intentional humour in the essay.

'I'm amused by what you left out. You have the "emotional pacifist" bit in but you left out where I said I came from a family where screaming insults and drunken reproaches were par for the course, where sobriety meant sulking and where my own mother specialised in melodramatically reproachful sighs you could neither contradict nor argue with. Found guilty by a sigh, I was. On a daily basis. You left all that out.'

'I see no reason why Miss Graham should know details

like that.'

'You're right. You're right.'

Darcy's essay on her mother lacked any research and was handed over only under protest.

My Mother

My mother is like a streetlamp. She has no curiosity about you except for the things you want to tell her. One day I was sorry for telling her something that wasn't that important really, and she said it was her job to be told more than just important things and I thought that's the same as the streetlamp, it is its job to be leaned against and ignored and even for dogs to pee on it. You give directions to your place that way, you say 'Our house is at the third streetlamp on the left.' But also a light gives you a very unpleasant look at your own self, you can see pimples and blackheads. My mother sometimes looks at me. And it's as if I can see myself more clearly.

My mother does not do things like go out that much and when we go home from school she is usually there. She doesn't come to where we are. We go to her. She does things while you talk to her, like wash clothes or knit, and it makes it very easy to tell her things. Now and again I sit down beside her and I don't say anything and she doesn't say anything. If I am unhappy, I know she knows and doesn't need to say anything and after a while I can go back to ordinary things just as if she had said a whole lot of consoling things to me. Even though my father is a doctor, when either of us is injured it is my mother who does bandaging and disinfecting. When everything is finished, she just stands there with Dettol and the tin of Band Aid and you go off playing, but she's there if you want to go back and say thank you but half the time you don't. She doesn't mind, in fact she looks sort of surprised when you do.

My mother plays the piano and it's like she has a series of songs in her head. Because you know, like you know at the end of a track on an LP what's going to be next, what one she's going to play next. I used to love it when I was a very small child, because she had me convinced that down on the left hand side of the piano was where the tigers were kept and she'd touch the furthest away keys very softly and you could hear the growling. But she stopped it when I began to think (as a very small child only) that the tigers would come out of the piano at night and eat me.

There is a programme on the radio called Hospitals Requests and it annoys me because there are always letters from people asking for a record to be played for the best mother in the world, and I hate it because mine is.
Darcy King

Sophia had an acute sense of entitlement. Being popular, liked by teachers, approved of by adults and surrounded by challenging but achievable expectations seemed to her as natural as the blonde hair she had been born with.

If she had reservations about her success rate thus far, those reservations were that her very popularity and success, in class, at subjects like mathematics, seemed likely to put Darcy at a disadvantage. She regarded Darcy as more intelligent than herself, and saw it as her duty to make Darcy toe the line and deliver on her God-given potential. Darcy's stony opposition to her best efforts made her feel ineffectual, and since Sophia believed that all feelings of emotional discomfort were symptoms of unaddressed personal failing, she decided that the best way to explore all the possibilities was to start keeping a diary. Then, as the second year of secondary school ground on, both twins read *The Diary of Anne Frank*.

Darcy thought the surrounding circumstances of the eventual death of the writer were very sad, but went off Anne Frank three-quarters through the book, when Anne and Peter had their embryonic relationship.

'That's a let-down,' Darcy said. 'God, she could have done better than *him*.'

'She couldn't, actually,' Colette said. 'Two families living in secret in a hidden annex don't really have that much choice when it comes to having relationships.'

'I thought it was very romantic,' Sophia said.

'*Romantic*,' Darcy said, as if it were a dirty word.

'Well, I did. She began to discover things about him.'

'She began to *make up* things about him, because there was nothing better on offer, that's what she began to do,' Darcy said. 'He was a dull hoor in the beginning of the book and he was a dull hoor when she fell in love with him, she was just putting her imaginings around him to make him seem more than he was.'

Sophia got totally distracted at this point, torn between the desire to tick Darcy off for swearing and the realisation that her mother would probably interpret such a ticking-off (as would Darcy) as a currying of parental favour. She was torn too between disapproval of the description and interest that Darcy pronounced the word that way. Sophia had always assumed that 'whore' was pronounced the way it was spelled. She now wondered if the whorls on people's fingerprints were pronounced 'hoorls'. Darcy, expecting more of a fight from her sister, continued.

'I think the book would have been much more interesting if she'd *never* got involved with that Peter. It just made her like everybody else, like she *had* to fall in love.'

'The call of the raging hormone,' their mother said helpfully.

'Anyway,' Sophia said, as if this followed, 'I'm going to start keeping a diary.'

'What kind of diary?' The question came from their mother.

'How do you mean, what kind of a diary?'

'Well, it could be a "meet Darcy at 4.00" kind of diary, or a diary like Anne Frank's, where you examine what's happening in your life.'

'Oh, an Anne Frank diary.'

'Good. I'll buy you the right kind of journal-book.'

'Why is it good?' Darcy asked. Here was yet another bus she had missed.

Her mother replied, 'Writing things down is a useful discipline. It makes you see things differently. It forces you to examine things that you do by reflex. I think it may also be a woman's duty. Women are the record-keepers, the letter-writers, the card-senders. Without women, we would be a society without a written trace.'

The following day Colette gave Sophia a notebook the size and shape of a substantial hardback novel, with a padded cover that looked like watered silk. The notebook had its own satin ribbon and a loop of stiffened moiré to hold a pen. Pausing only to get out-loud family agreement that nobody of any class or honour would ever read anybody else's diary, Sophia departed for her shared bedroom, where she cleared a space on the dressing-table for the diary – a space it and its successors were to occupy for years to come.

28 September 1982

I plan to use this diary to improve myself, because diaries are sad when they record the lives of people who make no progress and who are as bad at the end when they die as in the beginning. I am:

14 years of age

5'5"in height

8st 5lbs (Which I think is my ideal weight, although I could go as high as nine stone and still be within the average for my height, but I prefer to be this weight.)

Blood group AB

My best subjects in school, in order of the most recent tests, are: English, History, Maths, Geography, French

I have to work harder in Latin but I probably work as hard as there is any point to working in

Art. I am very different to my sister Darcy. Darcy is much heavier than I am. My father says people should leave girls our age alone about weight; that there is plenty of time for being thin when you are fully grown and a danger of anorexia nervosa, which is a slimming disease where young girls (mainly) diet until they are starving. Darcy says: 'There are two chances I will develop anorexia'. (By 'two chances', she is referring to a phrase a lot of people use. They say, 'there are two chances that X', meaning 'Slim and F--- all.' But Darcy does not use the full expression.)

Which brings me to something I have to think about. Darcy swears a lot and has twice got into trouble in school over it, although our parents do not know this. I think maybe she swears as a way of contrasting herself with me, but when I said this to her she was furious and called me an unqualified f---ing psychoanalyst.

I think perhaps she is right, but I do not like it in school when I am compared to her, because I always feel that the people doing the comparing do not know what she is really like.

Sometimes I think that not even our parents understand Darcy the way I do, knowing how clever and good she is. In fact, that worries me, because Darcy seems to have decided that she is not clever or outstanding and that what she should do is always be good for a laugh. This is a pity because she should not have to make people laugh. She could do anything.

My parents never let other people compare my sister and myself, but I think it is important that I observe what is different about us so that I can learn things from Darcy and improve myself. It would be silly not to use this journal so that at the end of every month I could look at it and check am I any better than I was a month previously. Or maybe a month is too short a time, but we can see.

Action: learn one new word every day. My new word for today is: *iterate*. Definition: to repeat, to utter or to do a second time.

CHAPTER THREE

The twins' English teacher, Margaret Graham, had long, elegant hands and feet – like the painting of Miss Horniman in the Abbey, her mother had once said to Margaret's father, not thinking Margaret could hear the pair of them as they came in from the theatre and a few drinks in the Plough.

'Another bloody spinster,' her father remarked, and her mother hushed him, saying there was no such thing any more and he shouldn't be making himself out to be more old-fashioned than he really was.

She was not another bloody spinster, Margaret thought, as she lay in bed that night and made up her mind to move into a flat the following day (which she did). Or, if a spinster, she was not a virgin, having at that point slept with three men. The first was a fellow student in college, and she had gone to bed with him to see if this would make her feel less like a foreigner in her own land and generation. She closed her eyes in the dark and clenched her teeth and he bucked and sweated and spasmed in her as if electrocuted and then fell asleep, his shrivelled penis trailing slug-shine across the pallor of her thigh.

She gathered her belongings and walked for six miles, afraid that a taxi man would smell the overwhelming chlorine smell of sex off her. At home, she could not shower because the noise would have disturbed her parents' sleep. She spent hour after hour in the bathroom, washing and wringing out a face cloth in TCP, the smell of it, redolent of childhood grazes, making her cry for someone to mind her and make it better.

The second sexual encounter happened because she did not know the difference between flirting and wit, nor between hospitality and intent. The man was well-read and talked dirty with a zest that mesmerised her. He brought her to dinner, which she thought was social and he thought was preparatory, and at a certain point it would have required a greater decisiveness and confidence than she possessed to break out of his assumptions and go home alone. He was a thoughtful and sensuous lover and caused her huge misery, because his lovemaking was lengthy and selfless.

In his efforts to please and arouse her he brought her first through embarrassment, then humiliation and finally to a gratitude for the ending of it so unconcealed that he took it for satisfaction. Because he was a man of warmth and uncomplicated sensuality, he regarded the encounter as pleasurable and complete and made no further overtures, moving effortlessly into a casual acquaintanceship. Margaret read this as a rejection she must have deserved.

Her third lover was as flinching and over-protective of her as she was of him and afterwards wept with gratitude because, he told her, he was usually attracted to men and maybe this was an indication that he wasn't gay.

Her three lovers were a movement in the symphony that played around her all the time. In the foreground were her students. She hated and feared them. Hated them because she feared them.

By the middle of the year the King twins turned up in her class, the terror and hatred had become a logic, an intent. Only the logistics of the suicide mattered. She did it by hanging herself from the bannisters in the first week of the school holidays.

The impact on the school was lessened by the fact that Margaret Graham had connected only fitfully with individuals on staff and with the student body. Rumours of the suicide details circulated with both relish and nausea. Darcy, hearing some of them, felt guilty because Miss Graham had been kind to her.

At the beginning of the next term, another teacher came to her and handed her a fat manila envelope.

'Duke University in the United States was in touch with

Miss Graham a month before she died. She was once there for a year on a scholarship. They are doing some kind of research about relationships, an observation of a selected set of individuals in different countries over several years, to see how their relationships form and break up. This graduate student gets in touch with six students in different countries, and they write back and forth as long as they want to and eventually they'll publish the thing, selecting some quotations from the people who have participated. Complete anonymity. This graduate student contacted Margaret Graham and asked her to suggest a student who would do it from Ireland.'

'OK,' Darcy said, dying to get out of the room, as discomfited as the teacher was by the task allocated by the dead Margaret Graham.

The teacher was getting back into her stride, as if thinking about her next class were already clicking her into staccato sureties.

'You'd write letters to this person. Margaret Graham seemed very sure that by doing it in some way you could achieve something for yourself, I don't know, maybe I should have been paying more attention.' (The teacher's tone said: but did I know she was going to die, like a reproach to me?)

'Yes?'

'Well, I'm not going to check up on you or anything. It's out of my hands now and I don't want to hear anything more about it. Is that clear?'

That night, Darcy took all of the documentation out of the manila envelope and spread it out. There was general brochure material about Duke University. Then there was some sort of semi-legal document which seemed to be an assurance that her privacy would in no way be infringed by participation in this study. Since this required her signature, she put it on top of the brochures. Then there was a letter.

May 7 1982

Dear Student

This is to invite you to participate in a long-term study of relationships being conducted by the Department of Psychology at this university, under the supervision of Professor Ladislas Dusinski. The twin themes of the study will be approached in different ways. A formal set of questionnaires will be administered in a number of countries to a statistically valid cross-section of young people at particular intervals, and it is anticipated that this element of the study may, depending upon the initial results, be repeated indefinitely, to provide an audit of the sexual and relationship behavior of teen subjects in different cultures at different points in time.

The second element of the study will involve an informal but structured correspondence between a number of graduate students, of whom the undersigned is one, and fewer than a half-dozen (per graduate student) students in other countries, this correspondence to allow for the collection of anecdotal material for illustrative purposes in the event of the publication of an account of the study for a wider audience, should the material merit such wider publication.

Although observations which you might make in corresponding with me might in due course be published, no identification other than your age, sex and nationality would accompany the quotations chosen. In addition, in the event of publication, your specific permission would be sought for the use of any material which might carry any potential to reveal your identity to any reader.

All the students approached to take part in this study have been selected through teachers who believe that the correspondence involved would not be so onerous as to make unacceptable inroads on normal study or leisure time. It is anticipated that the frequency of letters in the initial months, during which key information would be elicited and registered, would greatly diminish as time goes on, and that in some subsequent years, contact might be as infrequent as quarterly or less.

Any expenses, such as those involved in responding to questionnaires, will be reimbursed to participants, who will also receive an *ex gratia* payment of $100 during each year in which the study continues.

If you are willing to participate in this study, perhaps you would confirm this in writing (air mail, please) to:

A. C. Brookstone
5345 Tradewinds Ave., #283
Fort Attic
Missouri, MO 33003

Thanking you in anticipation
A. C. Brookstone

Darcy thought the letter was bad enough but when she read the contract-type document headed *Study Protocols* she was cowed by its more active and dogmatic formality. This study seemed to impose more rules than joining a convent. She must not send a photograph to A. C. Brookstone, nor must A. C. Brookstone send a photograph to her.

'Why the hell would I want to send a photograph to some old fart in a university in the US?' Darcy asked out loud.

Sophia, who was filling in her diary at the time, looked reproving. Darcy silently read on. She was not to publish any of the correspondence. She was not to use it for broadcasting purposes. She was not to seek the judgement of A. C. Brookstone on any behavior (sic) pattern revealed in her correspondence.

This, she could see, was going to be tedious beyond belief. However, since Margaret Graham had wished it on her and then committed suicide, Darcy decided that there must be something very important about the task. Unsheathing her good pen, she wrote her first response as neatly as she could.

17 Glanmire Park
Raheny
Dublin 5
Ireland
7 October 1982

Dear A. C. Brookstone

It would help if you were human and had a sex. Or even a gender. I don't believe any human was *ever* called A. C. Like, your mother used to say 'must get you off to sleep, now, A. C.'? I know we have to be impersonal and all that stuff, but I actually find it very difficult – or would over a period of time – to write to someone that sounds like an inanimate object or a program in a computer.

I think you are a man, but I may already be breaking the rules of this study – maybe trying to find out what sex you are is illegal the way sending a picture would be. Don't worry. I do not feel frustrated over not sending you a picture. In fact, I would rather die than send you a picture (of me, I mean).

I have read all of the stuff that came in your envelope, and I am sending back the form I had to sign. Yes, I will correspond unless as things go on I find I cannot answer questions or something like that. I am fourteen. I don't have much 'behaviour' of any kind done at this stage. I'm not going to bore you telling you a whole load of things about me that don't fit into a professor's filing systems, so I will leave it up to you to tell me what you need to know.

Yours sincerely

Darcy King

PS Just in case it invalidates anything, I am a twin.

Three weeks later, a reply arrived.

A. C. Brookstone

5345 Tradewinds Ave., #283

Fort Attic

Missouri, MO 33003

28 October 1982

Dear Ms King

Thank you for your letter of the 7th.

We are delighted that you will be able to take part in the study.

I will take the issues raised in your letter one by one.

I am male and my full name is Alexander Carbine Brookstone. The graduate students who are undertaking the correspondence aspect of the study, including myself, may err on the side of formality in writing style, bearing in mind that our respondents may be revealing factors concerning themselves and their most intimate relationships which are sensitive and private.

You indicate that you are relieved that you do not have to submit a photograph of yourself. This brings me to the first area we would like you to address in your response to this letter: your view of yourself. I note that you are a twin. Please indicate in your letter why you envision this as an issue.

In addition, perhaps, in your response and using your own words, you could elucidate on these areas:

1 Your level of sexual experience to date.
2 Your level of understanding of matters sexual and your sources of information for same.
3 Your expectations from relationships.

Please give time and thought to your response.

Yours

A. C. Brookstone

By the time Darcy got around to writing a reply to this one, school had broken up for the Christmas holidays.

17 Glanmire Park
Raheny
Dublin 5
Thursday 23 December 1982

Dear A. C. Brookstone

Could I call you by your initials, or something? I can't imagine that starting a letter Dear A. C. would be over-familiar. Might be better, though, to call you A. C. B. because A. C. sounds like electricity. (AC/DC, you know? That's one of the odd things about being part of this study. It isn't just that I am writing about what I might be thinking about anyway, in the area of sex, it is that knowing I have to write about it makes me think about it much more often and so I am doubly aware of the sexual connotations of phrases like AC/DC. I also, to be perfectly honest, get a charge out of writing down phrases like 'sexual connotations' as if I were cool.)

Carbine? I thought I was bad with my Confirmation name. I chose Perpetua. She was an early Christian that got ate by lions. I wonder, if you get eaten by lions, how long it hurts? (The teacher who

40

put me in for this study committed suicide by hanging and I often wonder how long it hurt her.)

Anyway, I am blithering. My view of myself. My view of myself always starts with my weight. I am fat. (I couldn't say that out loud, even in a room on my own.) Eleven stone four pounds, and at 5'6" I should be about nine stone four pounds. I am a heap.

Because I am a heap, I have to be funnier, kinder, nicer, harder-working, neater etc. etc. than thin people, which I haven't yet managed. I am conscious that you probably want deep stuff, and I should stop just being trivial, but the problem is that when you're a heap, you're not entitled to sensitivities and vulnerabilities and deep thoughts. No heroine is ever fat. Hedda Gabler isn't fat, and neither is Lady Macbeth or Ophelia or Jo in *Little Women*. Snow White and Cinderella and Beauty and the Beast are all tiny-waisted little wankers without jowls.

The only place fat people are allowed is as light (you should pardon the pun) relief. Billy Bunter. Or gouty old farts in Rowland cartoons fallen back off their chairs showing their knickers and their roly thighs. O God.

I have decided that after Christmas I am going to go on a diet. I am now fourteen and I think my father's idea that if anybody under twenty goes on a diet they will immediately get raging anorexia is a load of cobblers. I would *love* to have anorexia. My God, to have people trying to tempt me to have a little taste of cheesecake or just a couple of chips . . . I don't think I am unselfish enough to develop anorexia.

But I am going to go on a diet after Christmas – nobody ever went on a diet *before* Christmas.

Me and Sophia are not identical twins. If we were identical twins, maybe I'd have the right genes.

Being a two-cell twin is the worst possible thing from my point of view. I raised it because I thought maybe doing a study like this, you'd have to take both people.

Your first question is about my level of sexual experience to date. Simple answer. Zero. Nada. Nothing. Negative quantity. I am unkissed, untouched by human hand – or anything else belonging to a human. I suppose in the States they are making out in the backs of Oldsmobiles from the time they are ten, but forget that in Ireland. Well, forget that in our family.

Your second question is my sources of information and my level of understanding. My level of understanding is fantastic. I could get an A in the Leaving Cert for it. My parents have this Open Question policy – you ask it, they give you a straight answer to it. I knew about where babies come from long before anybody in my class in school did.

It's like electricity and fuses and so forth: I know all the explanations but I still expect to get blown up or stuck to the ground. With sex, I know all about erections and orgasms (although I've never had to write down the words before) and sperm and spermatozwhatever the way the end of that word is spelt, but I cannot see how it would be anything but disgusting. Putting a penis that's used 99 per cent of the time for peeing with into someone else is a puke idea and when I think about French kissing, I get that cold quiet feeling you get just before you have to throw up.

This may just mean that I am lesbian. I have twice got crushes on teachers in school, although I would never have described them as crushes at the time, but I am trying to analyse myself so I suppose that's what they were.

I don't think my sister gets crushes. I sometimes think my sister and I are like the difference between a good swimmer in a pool and a water-wing kid. You know the way good swimmers go in and they know where they're going and they swim in a straight line? Sophia is like that, but I'm like a kid in water-wings going in all sorts of different directions.

My expectations are non-existent.Even if someone did fancy me, which they're never going to, I would be too embarrassed to do anything until I was thin.

I hope you have a very happy Christmas or if you are Jewish, a happy Channukah.

Darcy King

PS Why don't you call me Darcy?

5345 Tradewinds Ave., #283
Fort Attic
Missouri, MO 33003
18 January 1983

Dear Darcy

I appreciate your good wishes for Christmas and was amused by the possibility of somebody named Carbine being Jewish. The name was chosen by my father.

One of the legends he likes to tell is of a man long ago in the army here who was recalcitrant and difficult as a private. Various punishments failed to change his performance until, eventually, he was put into a 4' X 4' corrugated iron box out in the open near the barracks, which would have been somewhere in the deep south. Normally, after twelve hours in the box, soldiers would emerge subdued and willing to apologise and strive to fit in better. But when this man Williams emerged from the box, he was more entrenched in his opposition to authority than ever. His superiors made the decision that more time in the box might change his mind, and they put him in it for the longest confinement inflicted on any soldier to that point: a full week.

Williams was unable to sit down or lie down, but he was also unable to stand up, so when he was finally released, he could not walk for several days and was extremely ill. The experience did not change him greatly, but his superiors were wary of taking this 'cruel and unusual' punishment any further. His colleagues later asked him how he had sustained the agony and he told them that he had not been in the box at all. He had been so concentrated on working out the mechanics of a new gun which he planned to build that he had not paid much attention to the discomfort of his physical surroundings. The gun he later built, based on the planning he had done while confined in the box, was called the carbine rifle, because his name was Carbine Williams. Hence my father named me after him. (My father is a member of the NRA. We go hunting together).

As you can see, I will certainly address you as Darcy if you prefer this form of address. I am not familiar with it as a woman's name.

Your letter was very detailed and helpful. Please clarify/confirm the following points:

1 11 stone 4 pounds is 158 pounds.
2 You refer to yourself as a 'heap'. A heap of what? I assume this is a shortened reference to a longer illustrative phrase.
3 You are not sharing your letters regarding this study with your sister. No, the study is not examining any issues related to twins, although I have a long-standing interest in such work.
4 The teachers in school you had 'crushes' on were female?

5   Do you date? What is the typical age of dating
    in Ireland and where are the preferred venues?
    Yours sincerely
    A. C. B.

17 Glanmire Park
Raheny
Dublin 5
Sunday 6 March 1983

Dear A. C. B.

Just in case you were about to work up to asking
me about sexual fantasies, let me tell you I don't
have enough brain cells to devote to sexual fantasies.
My brain cells are all busy with food fantasies
because I've been on a diet. Crispy golden chips,
one end dipped in tomato sauce. With battered fried
Brie. And then six of my mother's delicate tender
pancakes with castor sugar and lemon juice and
cream. Cornflakes and sugar and cream. Ten orange
creams, the long pointy dark ones out of the middle
of the Black Magic box. (And that's just for
breakfast!)

I have been staying at 1,000 calories a day since
January and life is not worth living. I can't sleep,
I'm so hungry and when I do go to sleep, I have
nightmares that start off as wonderful dreams where
people are forcing sandwiches (egg, mayonnaise and
really soft white bread) on me and I eat them and
then get into a panic because I've blown the diet
and I'm going to swell up all over again, not that I
have *un*swollen that much, but I have lost nearly a
stone and people have noticed. There is no pleasure
in them noticing because they say things like, 'Yes,
you were really getting a bit on the heavy side' or 'I
had noticed you were putting on a lot of weight'
and since I thought that by wearing loose things it
wouldn't show that much, I now feel retrospectively

ashamed. The reason I am looking forward to St Patrick's Day so much is that I can come off the diet on that day. (Also Easter, but Easter feels like it's six hundred years away.) I have the whole day's eating planned and I will probably put on half a ton. I was so worked up about going on a diet after Christmas that I ate during Christmas more than I ever did and was heavier than I said to you in my last letter starting the bloody diet.

I was also roasted more than the goddamn turkey because I had to throw cardigans over everything. My father has not noticed me losing weight, but he has noticed I'm not wearing cardigans as much and he keeps telling me I'm going to get pneumonia. Can you imagine a doctor telling you you'd get pneumonia for taking off a cardigan? It's probably just as well he doesn't deal with real patients.

Your question regarding a big heap. Heap of what? No. Heap. Full Stop. That's what they call girls like me. Older people say, 'She's a fine girl' as if it was a compliment. Bloody eejits call you a big girl. You're supposed to think they mean height. Nobody ever describes you as a big girl if you are five ten and thin. Then you are willowy or something.

My twin sister who (mercifully) you don't want to know about, who is so kind she makes my teeth curl, my sister who is kind like the Crusaders were kind (take this Christianity or else we'll cut your goolies off), my sister who is naturally and sweetly kind from the depths of her own beauty, says I am splendid and Junoesque. My father talks of puppy fat and I may stab him as he sleeps.

I said to my mother (having read your letter, although I didn't let her see it), that no man was ever going to fancy me because I am fat and she said that if that was the case, it was a wonder the human race hadn't died out years ago, because all through history it was sexy to be fat and she went and got a picture to show me, *Déjeuner sur l'Herbe* I think it was called, and it was *seriously* weird, with these people sitting around a field and one great lardy white beef-to-the-heels like a Mullingar heifer woman sitting in the middle of them stark naked.

I don't know what my mother thought she was proving, but she didn't. My mother does that a lot. It's not that she barks up the wrong trees. She barks up things that aren't trees at all. It's very interesting to watch when it isn't your tree.

Anyway, I am thinner and all hail St Patrick.

I was thinking about your earlier question about my sources of information, and it struck me that it might be relevant to tell you that in this house, first of all, there are books here on everything and one of the things my father has a bee in his bonnet about is looking things up.

Anyway, we have books about sex. (Waah, shock horror.) Kiddy books with a little square boy and a little square girl and it explains what happens and vaginas and so forth.

(Why are all the words for sex so awful? Words for food are lovely: hot chocolate, warm scones, french fried potatoes, sautéed onions. But 'vagina'? It sounds like a punishment. Do that again and I'll vagina you. Penis is worse, because it reminds you of pee all the time.)

We also have books where the things stand up(!). That was unintentional. What I mean is that you open the book and the details stand up so you can see how they work. We have two of those kinds of books.

One is about the reproductive system of the human being and the other is about Hansel and Gretel, and in my view Hansel and G. beat the shit out of the reproductive system, because they are nice little kids and the chocolate house is wonderful, and also you can, by opening and closing the book, push the bad witch into the oven again and again and I find there are days when I want to imagine that little witch as all sorts of people from school, particularly a clever pouch of poison called Sister Jennifer, which is an awful waste of a sweet name, but that's not relevant. (Names are important, though. That's why I don't like all your initials. They make you sound like a bakery.) The thing is, though, that the reproductive organs book tells you more than you could ever want to know about how it all works.

I'm running out of time because we have a test at the end of the week and I should be studying Latin, which I truly hate. Is it any wonder it died out? Not fast enough!

Why are you interested in twins?

How the hell do I know when people date? Everybody tells lies so much I don't know what to believe. If you were to listen to what the girls in my class say, half of them have been hard at it since they were seven. You go to dances at the local cricket club, which is the pits and I don't go. Or you meet fellas from the local school – there's a putrid coffee house on the way home. My parents basically disapprove of the whole thing. It's 'get your exams first and then you can get into all that stuff and certainly none of it in term time'. But we are the exceptions, which may make you want to strike me from your study. Do I care? Not when St Patrick's day is coming up, with:

French bread hot and crusty with butter and jam
Bewley's sticky buns
Fry's Chocolate Cream bars
Lentil soup
2 choc ices
Etc.
I don't honestly give a toss.
Happy Patrick's Day!

5345 Trailwinds Ave., #283
Fort Attic
Missouri, MO 33003
Thursday 5 May 1983

Dear Darcy

Before your school breaks up for summer, you might send me some thoughts about the impact on boy/girl relationships of the long vacation. If this is not on, perhaps you would make some notes during the summer and communicate with me in the fall?

I will be working in Seattle during the summer, but you should continue to address any correspondence to the normal address.

Yours sincerely

A. C. B.

7 Glanmire Park
Raheny
Dublin 5
Tuesday 14 June 1983

Dear Initials

This is going to be short. I am a failure. I never got back on my diet after St Patrick's Day and am as fat as ever. So my summer 'vacation' is not going to be exactly full of gorgeous hunks in the Gaeltacht falling over themselves to get off with me.

Seattle is cold, isn't it?

Bet you don't know what the Gaeltacht is.

See you in the autumn. (That's the proper word for 'fall'.)

Mind yourself

Darcy

CHAPTER FOUR

The summer they were fifteen, what forced them further apart was the Gaeltacht. Neither of them wanted to go, but Sophia felt they should.

'I'm not satisfied with the sound of my Irish,' she told her parents over breakfast one Saturday morning. 'My grammar and my understanding are good and my teacher expects me to do well in the Inter, but my *blas* isn't great.'

Darcy, who had decided that high fibre was the answer to all her problems, was eating her way doggedly through All-Bran. It tasted like sugared matchsticks.

'I think one should be able to speak one's native language,' Sophia added.

'Darcy?' her father prompted.

'What?'

'What do you feel about this?'

You mean 'what does *one* feel,' don't you? Darcy thought. One frankly doesn't give a shit about one's native language and one doesn't see how a *blas* is going to make a hell of a difference to one's later life one way or t'other. When one goes into Dunnes Stores, can you see one asking for All-Bran in Irish?

'Darcy,' her mother said. 'The Gaeltacht. In July. Do you want to go?'

'Would I have to be in the same house as Sophia?'

The atmosphere around the table chilled. Darcy could feel, as if the tiny hairs on her arms were antennae, that her father was getting livid. Into the gap, like the marines, rode Sophia.

'It's not a house, Darcy. It's a sort of dormitory in a place that's a college during the winter months. But we wouldn't even have to be on the same floor. I already asked about that because I think it would be better if we were separated.'

51

Robert looked startled.

'We're not going to learn much from each other's Irish,' Sophia continued, 'even if we were to try very hard to talk Irish to each other. We'd be better separated if we're really going to gain from the experience.'

Robert looked mistrustfully at Darcy, who widened her eyes and nodded as if Sophia had expressed her own thoughts better than she could.

'So I get to send a cheque for ninety-eight quid to this guy in Spiddal and decide whether your father and I will go on a cruise or head for New York for the duration,' Colette said, taking out her cheque book.

Sophia and Darcy looked equally dismayed. Robert, his anger forgotten, twinkled at them. 'You have a problem with your mother and me taking a holiday on the first occasion we get rid of the two of you for a whole month?'

The possibility that her parents might be away from home when she was immured in the Gaeltacht made things worse for Darcy, who dreaded the trip and made no secret of her misery. Sophia found herself half-apologising, half-encouraging. 'It's not going to be that bad,' she told her twin. 'Aileen's going and so is Siobhán.'

'Thanks,' Darcy said with heavy irony. '*There's* an attraction. Drag myself across the benighted country through the bloody Bog of bloody Allen to a place where they probably have no plumbing and the nearest sweet shop is six light years away and they talk nothing but Irish and put a notch on your stick every time you break out into *Béarla* – and the big attraction is Aileen, who bores the knickers off me at home. Oh, thank you, thank you, thank you, Sophia. Really. My gratitude passes all bounds.'

'I'm not responsible, you know.'

'Well, if you're not responsible, why are you trying to sell me on it?'

'I just think it will be good for the two of us.'

'Yeah, that's the problem, isn't it. The two of us.'

'Sorry?'

'Don't be. You didn't choose to be born a twin any more than I did.'

'What's being a twin got to do with it?'

'Listen, if I were on my own, I could say "Thanks, but no thanks". I could say "Pass on the self-improvement". I could say "*Go raibh maith agat agus póg mo thóin.*" I could persuade them that it wasn't exactly vital that I learn to speak a language that is never going to be worth a damn to me. But joined at the hip to little Miss Sunshine, little Cailín Glé-gheal, I'm screwed, aren't I?'

'I'm sorry.'

'No, you're not.'

'How do you know?'

'I know. You think once I get there I'll like it.'

'Well you might, if you took a positive attitude.'

'I took the most positive attitude in the world to horse-riding and I didn't like *that* when I got up close.'

'Well, you know what I think about that.'

'Yes, Sophia, I know what you think about that. I know what you think about bloody everything. Life is a challenge to make lists about and people are projects. If you're not able to mark yourself better out of ten today than you were yesterday, you should be discontinued.'

Darcy was flinging the past year's schoolbooks into a carton as she spoke. Sophia was sitting on her own bed, watching. Darcy sensed her sister's consternation.

'Oh, Sophia, *don't* pull the silent-upon-a-peak-in-Darien bit, for Chrissake.'

'I don't know what you mean.'

'*I don't know what you mean,*' Darcy mimicked in a die-away voice, the back of her right hand clapped theatrically to her forehead. She grabbed the carton of books and humped them out on to the landing, then came back and continued to tidy her belongings with ferocity.

'I won't tolerate that from you.'

Sophia's voice was quite different. Darcy stopped and looked at her.

'I have never in my life imitated you to be cruel, or mocked you in that kind of way and you should be ashamed of doing it to me.'

'Oh, come *on*, Sophia – I – '

'No, I *won't* come on. I don't mock you. I don't set out to be cruel to you. I don't criticise you. I don't find fault with you.'

'You're *always* telling me things I should – '

'I see potential in you that you're too self-absorbed to see for yourself and I tell you when you should be doing something about it, yes, and you should be grateful that you have someone who sees that potential.'

'Self-absorbed?'

'Yes. You think just because you criticise yourself and get the criticism in before anybody else does that it means you are selfless and modest and – and it doesn't.'

Darcy sat down in silence on the other side of Sophia's bed, stunned and fascinated.

'You think I have no feelings,' Sophia went on. Darcy started to disagree, but was silenced by the quiet force of her sister's repetition.

'You think I have no feelings. You think you are the only one who experiences defeats and humiliations.'

'I think you are popular and successful a – '

'You don't know the first thing about me and, after fifteen years, I deserve better from you than that you'd box me into a – a – ' Sophia shook her head as if to free herself of the verbal tangle she was in. 'What does it matter if outsiders like me? It's still *right* to be kind to people and to try to improve yourself. There is nothing wrong in liking the Irish language or making an effort to pronounce it right.'

'Sophia, I was just trying to say that – '

'You were just trying to make yourself out to be better than I am. I'm the one who makes lists and regards myself as a project – '

'Well, you do – '

'I'm not stupid, Darcy.'

'Jesus, I never said you were stupid.'

'I am not stupid. If I make lists, it's for a reason. When you write something down, the chances of you remembering it and acting on it are greater than if you just make pie-in-the-sky resolutions.'

Darcy opened her mouth, only to find there was no space into which to speak.

'And don't decide to take that personally,' Sophia was going on. 'Because if you decide that I'm just saying you make pie-in-the-sky resolutions, that'll allow you to go off in a corner and console yourself that here is yet another person who doesn't realise the unorthodox, freewheeling, deeply sensitive and artistic person Darcy King really is. And you'll be wrong, because I probably know all those things a heck of a lot better than you do. Yes, I do regard myself as a project. I think I was given talents. If you get talents given to you, you shouldn't just say "Oh, if the wind is in the right direction and I feel like it at the time, I might use those talents". Talents are like muscles, they atrophy if you don't use them systematically. I can't tell you how much it hurts me and how much I reject and resent the way you portray me as a limited, systems-driven mechanical person because I am not, not, *not* that kind of person.'

Darcy found herself breathing very quietly, as if any noise from her side of the bed would cause something to crack apart. She wanted to apologise, to argue, and above all to touch Sophia. Put a warm palm on the slender forearm. Hug her. Even reach out to her tight-clenched hands, knuckles whiter than the pale skin. Sophia pulled the tense hands apart and flattened them on her knees.

'If you touch me,' she said more calmly, 'I shall spit.'

Both of them noted – Sophia with fleeting pleasure, Darcy with slightly hysterical amusement – the use of the word 'shall'. It sounded like a free sample from BBC Radio 4 – the Home Service, as their mother called it.

'I won't touch you.'

'Good.'

The two of them sat, knees separated by about twelve inches, in a frozen silence.

'You wouldn't, maybe, tell me what it would be safe for me to do?' Darcy asked. Sophia looked at her, suspiciously.

'No, seriously,' Darcy said. 'I don't know. Do I apologise or just go flush myself down the loo or what?'

Sophia stood up and went to the small window in the room and looked out. Wouldn't I love to be thin enough to silhouette myself like people do in films in a window, Darcy thought. See, came the following thought: she's right. My every thought is self-referential.

'I think we should make the best we can out of the Gaeltacht,' Sophia said, as formally as someone drawing up terms of treaty. 'If you would like, I will pack for you.'

'No, I – ' Darcy stopped, breathed deeply, and started again. 'I would appreciate that. Thank you.'

'Not at all.'

Sophia did the packing for the two of them, and Darcy noticed her twin pushing an Irish language novel called *Sláinte an Domhain* by one D. de Róiste into her own duffel bag.

The train journey to the west was about the best part of it. A poker school was set up in one of the carriages, and Sophia, who was a very good poker player, won three pounds fifty before they crossed the Shannon.

The train journey took three hours. The ensuing bus journey seemed to take as long again before they arrived at the *óstán*. The man who greeted them (in Irish) called out their names and added something.

'What did he say?' Darcy asked Sophia.

'He said I'm on the second floor and you're on the third floor.'

'Ask him if there's a lift.'

'You ask him.'

'I don't know my own name, for Chrissake, I'm so tired after that bus and I sure as hell don't know the Irish for lift. You ask him.'

Sophia asked him. A glow of disbelieving delight broke across the man's honest countenance at the very idea that lithe fifteen-year-olds would want a lift or that an *óstán* would have such a frivolous machine.

'Oh shit,' Darcy muttered under her breath. 'Three storeys for four weeks.'

The man was in full flow. Glancing blows of his meaning got through to Darcy. They were to be up each morning at seven and they didn't need to set clocks because someone would come and wake them. They would be in bed, lights out, each night by ten, except on Saturday night. Because on Saturday night the man said, looking gleeful, as if sharing a delightful secret with them, on Saturday night, there was a *céilí* and they would all go to the *céilí*. Everybody went to the *céilí* ('I want three volunteers, you, you and you,' Darcy muttered). Use of the Irish language, and *only* of the Irish language was to start immediately, the man went on. Anybody caught breaking this rule three times would be sent home. ('Très bien,' Darcy muttered, but more quietly this time.) The man invited them to climb the stairs and find their respective dormitories.

The stairs were metal. One hundred and twenty Dublin teenagers climbing them sounded like the invasion of a battalion wearing suits of armour. Under cover of the noise, Darcy spoke to Sophia.

'I'm not going to be able to stick this, you know, even if I really really try.'

'*Nílim chun Béarla a labhart leat.*'

'Oh, Jesus, Sophia, not on the frigging first night.'

'*Sin iad na rialacha.*'

'Yeah, and *is mise* your *deirfiúr*, in case you'd forgotten.'

At this point, Sophia and those sharing her dormitory peeled off and the girls sharing Darcy's sleeping quarters climbed the third flight of stairs. They stood at the top, winded, taking in all of the signs of institutional living. The curve where the walls met the floor, typical of every orphanage and hospital built in Ireland from the 1930s to the 1970s. The speckled imitation-marble walls. The high echoing ceilings and the old two-pin sockets in the walls.

Having got their second wind, the group made their way into their own dormitory. Long rows of bunks along each of the two walls. Foot of bunk facing foot of bunk across a four-foot divide like old black-and-white pictures of pre-war British hospitals. Heavily darned sheets with stuck-on labels carrying letters and numbers. Stained coverlets, no blankets.

'*Cá bhuil an leithreas?*' Darcy asked the man as he came puffing up the corridor after them. He pointed.

In the communal toilets, Darcy tried the hot tap. It coughed repeatedly but no water came out of it, hot or cold. She tried the cold tap. It coughed, then spat ice-cold water. Green. Maybe, she thought, maybe if I let it run, it'll stop being green and go clear.

The lights went out. The bed was freezing. Darcy kicked her legs up and down a hundred times to try to get her circulation going.

'*Bí ciúin,*' someone said, so long after Darcy had stopped that it was obvious it had taken them ages to come up with the Irish for 'belt up'.

I am *ciúin*, Darcy thought resentfully. It's only my feet are making noise. Her legs were briefly heated, then got cold again.

Probably, she decided, she was so cold because she needed nourishment. There was a Caramac and a Cadbury's Rum-and-Butter bar in her bag. She slid over to the side of the bed and groped in the dark for the locker, trying to remember which side it opened from. Left to right, she decided, and popped it. The noise stilled the general movements within the dormitory as the others worked out what it was. She decided that if she counted to one hundred, they would get all relaxed and go off to sleep again. At fifty, she aborted the count and began to grope through her bag, the noise amplified by the tinniness of the locker.

'*Cad tá ar súil agat?*' someone asked.

Mind your own business, Darcy thought. She went for the Rum-and-Butter first. She lay on her back and ate her way through it in the dark, piece by piece.

'*Tá duine éigin ag ithe rud milis,*" a furious voice said.

'Oh, shut up and let's get to sleep.'

'Someone's eating chocolate. I can smell it.'

'So can I.'

'For *ages.*'

'God, this hour of the night.'

'*As Gaeilge, led thoil.*'

'Oh, piss off, on our first night.'

'I'll tell.'

'Off you go and tell right now and I hope it makes you feel great.'

'Betcha it's Fatso King.'

'Darcy?'

There was a silence, which Darcy could have filled with denial, except that her mouth was clogged with chocolate, because she had not thought of bringing a glass of water to the locker. She breathed evenly and heavily through her nose to convince them that she was asleep.

'Of course it's Darcy, who else?'

'No sharing, you notice.'

'Jesus, nobody but Darcy would want to eat chocolate in the middle of the night in the middle of the Gaeltacht.'

'Why don't you have a full-scale debate about it and keep us awake all night?'

There was silence for a few minutes, during which Darcy quietly slid the Caramac up under her pillow. She was now so thirsty that she couldn't eat it.

She had to have water, she decided. She dropped down to explore the floor, collided with her bedside locker and overturned it in a cacophony of metal noises, clutching it to try to minimise its continuing echoes. This time the responses were all in English.

'Oh, what's wrong?'

'I'll kill you, whoever you are. I mean, I will *kill* you. I was dead asleep.'

'It's OK. It's OK. Go back to sleep. It was an accident.'

'It's *not* fucking OK.'

'Oh, shag off, stop making a production out of it. I said I was sorry.'

'Looking for more chocolate to feed your face, were you?'

Darcy righted the locker noisily. At this point, she no longer cared about anything except getting to the bathroom. Knocking into the ends of other people's beds, she progressed to the door and made her way down the lino corridor to the toilets, where she drank water from the tap before going back to bed.

As the night wore on, the girls who had been woken by Darcy's engagement with the locker one by one felt the need to go to the toilet themselves, so there was a muffled traffic for the whole night, which kept all but the heaviest sleepers awake. For the first time ever, Darcy failed to sleep until half past five of a cold dawn. At seven, a teacher arrived, yelled encouragement and grabbed the barred ends of each bed to shake the sleepers awake.

This place will be the death of me, Darcy thought, stumbling to the bathroom again. When she got back to the bedroom, one of the other girls pointed to the floor beside her bed.

'Didn't feel up to eating it all, did you not, Darcy?'

The Caramac had fallen from under her pillow and was sitting in full view.

The Irish-speaking teacher came back, roaring enthusiastic instructions as to how they might reach the eating room.

When they found it, the key element was huge tin jugs. There were huge tin jugs of diluted orange juice, huge tin jugs of pale porridge, huge tin jugs of rust-coloured tea, huge tin jugs of purplish coffee.

In rows on the tables were small bowls, dusted to a depth of half an inch with cornflakes. Lining up a huge tin jug of milk over one of these small bowls was like trying to land a 747 on a hearth-rug. Milk went everywhere.

Sophia arrived clutching an orange. Darcy sidled up to her.

'Where'd you get the orange?'

'*Bhí sé im' mhála.*'

'Oh, you worked it out that there would be no food worth eating?'

'*Gaeilge,*' Sophia said, and walked away to a table to join members of her dormitory. They all seemed well-slept and in high good humour, whereas Darcy's companions of the night were hung-over, exhausted and filled with hate for each other, particularly for Darcy.

The morning consisted of classroom work – grammar and reading – actively contributed to by people like Sophia, survived resentfully by Darcy's dorm.

Lunch was white gelatinous soup with a faintly green cast to it, but without any flavour. Darcy watched her sister across the room. Sophia tried the soup. After three tentative spoonfuls, she quietly pushed it to one side and drank a glass of milk. Imitating her, Darcy tried three spoonfuls. The slimy texture of the soup made her gag. She hated milk, so sat in silence watching other students not only eating the soup but having second helpings. Never mind, she thought. There will be a main course.

There was. Sausages. Hundreds of under-cooked sausages with fat tasselly ends were piled on big oval plates in the middle of each table. Darcy took two, shiny with grease, and sliced them. In cross-section, she decided, they were worse. You could see the lumpy gristly bits.

The jelly, when it came, was a determined cherry colour and had spoonfuls of what looked and tasted like soup on top. Darcy scooped the soup to one side and ate the jelly in desperation. There wasn't much that you could do to jelly that made it very different from any jelly you had experienced in a previous life.

Sophia came up beside her and talked quietly but slowly in Irish.

'*Arís?*' Darcy said, not having understood.

After three repetitions, she got it. Between three and four they were free and could go into the nearest village. Sophia was suggesting that the two of them stock up on fruit and packaged orange juice, to ensure that they got their vitamins. Maybe tomatoes, too. Cheese would not keep in their lockers. Darcy thanked her so miserably that Sophia said something encouraging.

'Sophia, more power to you and thank you for trying, but *nothing* will make me tolerate this place for a month, I'd rather be dead.'

The teacher came up behind Darcy, demanded her name and ostentatiously noted that she had broken the rules by speaking English. Sophia looked ashamed.

That afternoon, Darcy in the local shop spent half the money she had brought with her. She didn't ask for anything in either Irish or English. She simply pointed to what she wanted: a packet of Nice biscuits, four packets of salt-and-vinegar crisps, a bag of iced caramels, a bag of chocolate éclairs, a six-pack of 7UP, a packet of Cream Crackers, a half-pound of butter, three tomatoes and a packet of salt. When it came to tea-time, she went to the dormitory rather than to the eating room. Having climbed the three flights of stairs, she discovered that the dormitory was locked. Rather than go back and join the others, she sat on the top step of the stairs and spread out the food she had brought.

She searched around for something sharp enough to cut the tomato, even gave the serrated doubled-over edge of the crisps a try as a makeshift knife, then abandoned the bag and bit into it instead. The tomato, ripe and warmed by a day in her bag, exploded, sending tiny yellow seeds into her hair, ears and all over her blouse.

She ate it anyway, sluicing salt on to it from the hugely oversized packet she had been forced to buy because salt seemed to come in nothing smaller. She held a Cream Cracker underneath the tomato to catch the worst of its drips. She ate the tomatoes, half the Cream Crackers (digging one into the softened butter and using it to spread the butter on another cracker) and two packets of crisps in an indiscriminate gorging without pleasure.

Then she had two cans of 7Up and half the Nice biscuits. Because she had butter left over, she tried some on the biscuits but decided it did not greatly improve them. When eight or nine Nice were gone out of the packet, so that one end of it was open and empty, she put her nose in and sniffed the sugary coconut scent of it for a long time. She tidied up most of the food and leaned against the wall, regretting that she had no book to read. She sucked iced caramels for a while, knowing they would give her mouth ulcers.

The following day, after lunch, Darcy found Sophia and told her she was getting out. Sophia insisted on speaking Irish and told her she couldn't, that she would be ashamed for the rest of her life. Darcy told her, in English, that being ashamed for the rest of your life was a better option than being miserable for the remaining twenty-eight days of this July. Sophia invoked their parents, the church, Darcy's future progress as a human being and common decency, although she had to break into English for that phrase. Darcy sat through it all in silence and then said she was going anyway. Sophia asked her if she had enough money and wished her – with strange formality and still in Irish – a safe journey.

Darcy headed for the administrative office of the óstán, where the teacher who had already noted that she was talking English looked up disapprovingly.

'I need to use a phone,' Darcy said.

The teacher took out the notebook.

'That was two,' Darcy said. 'This is three. Three strikes and I'm out, right? Lemme make the phone call and you won't even have to make any more notes about me.'

When her mother answered the phone, Darcy burst into tears.

'OK, let's get it clear, you're not hurt?' her mother asked calmly. No, Darcy managed to snuffle.

'Sophia's not hurt?'

Another negative snuffle.

'Neither of you are sick?'

No, Darcy said, getting her tears under control. She was just a failure and wanted to come home. Now. Please.

'You're homesick?'

The word brought on the tears again. Oh, yes, Darcy said. She was so *home*sick.

'A few more days would kill?'

Yes, she swore. She knew how silly it seemed. She knew how furious her father would be. Sophia had already told her off, she knew it all, but please, could she just be a failure and come home? Please?

There was a long silence at the other end.

'Hang on a minute,' Colette said.

Darcy waited fearfully.

'There's a bus at 2.15 from the village, can you make that?'

Yes, Darcy gasped joyously. Of course she could.

'It'll connect with the train out of Galway at 4.15. I'll meet you at the station. Get going.'

Colette put the phone down. Darcy didn't. She held and hugged it as a link to comfort and connectedness and relief. Then she put it down quietly and offered to pay the teacher, who shrugged with contempt and turned his back on her. Don't waste your energy, Darcy thought with a stab of returning spirit. You ain't a gaoler any more and I ain't your prisoner. My ma has sprung me, you sanctimonious note-taking spy, and you can take your little criticisms of me and put them where whatever animal it was put whatever he put.

When Robert King arrived home that evening, Colette told him quickly.

'And you allowed it?'

'I should have said "stay, suffer"?'

'Oh, Colette, every child that's ever gone to the Gaeltacht goes through this phase.'

'Well, Darcy isn't every child.'

'What about "Hello Mudda, Hello Fadda"?'

'What about it?'

'The weather changes, things begin to look up.'

'And if it didn't?'

'Oh, it always does.'

'Anyway, she's about passing Athlone right now, so there's not much point in revisiting the decision.'

'Very bad for her, you know.'

'Sophia's already told her all that.'

'How do you mean?'

'Sophia argued with her and tried to make her see sense.'

'Oh, so you do think it would make sense for her to stay?'

'I don't think anything. That's what Sophia said. Sophia also told her you'd be furious with her.'

'Not *furious*. Just – '

'Just vastly disappointed.'

'Yes. Is there anything wrong with that?'

'No.'

'Well, *is* there?'

'No.'

Silence.

'I mean, why *shouldn't* I be disappointed?'

'No why. I'm not sure what effect it will have, but you're certainly entitled to be disappointed.'

'This is a missed opportunity.'

'Yes.'

'She'll probably never be fluent in Irish.'

'That's true and that's a pity.'

'And she will have got out of a difficult situation without facing up to it.'

'That's true too. Question is, will she learn something from the experience?'

'How could she learn something from running away?'

Silence.

'She should know how disappointed we are in her.'

'She does.'

'But we should sit her down and tell her.'

'I won't.'

'Why not?'

'Because she already knows.'

'But she should know that we have standards in this house and that she has failed to live up to them.'

'Jesus, Robert, this isn't the army.'

'That's below the belt.'

'If you sit her down and give her all this heavy stuff about standards and failures, she's going to be soaked in disapproval and she's not going to feel loved.'

'Of course we love her. But – '

'But a little less because of this failure?'

'Love is always influenced by the behaviour of the loved one.'

'Love should be unconditional.'

'So it doesn't affect your love for her that our few days away are buggered?'

'No. Although I was looking forward to it.'

'So if she turns into a drug addict, you're still going to love her?'

'Yes. Are you not?'

'And say if she has kids and abuses them. Are you going to love her then?'

'Say if she causes world war three, why don't you?'

'It's a legitimate question.'

'No, it's not. You have a miserable ashamed teenager coming back all on her own on a train, knowing – *saying* – that she's a failure, knowing and saying that you're going to be desperately disappointed with her, and you're working out how much you'll love her less if she becomes a child-batterer.'

Robert King went silent and announced, after tea, that he was going for a walk. Colette said, in a voice of determined cheerfulness, that she would pick up Darcy and see him later.

'I might go to bed early,' he said.

'Good idea,' she said calmly and went to collect the failure off the train.

CHAPTER FIVE

Darcy's defection from the Gaeltacht gave both twins their first real experience of separation, and Darcy her first experience of an alarm clock.

'Why do you want to get up, anyway?' her mother asked.

'I'm going to get a summer job.'

'People who want summer jobs have the arrangements made by Easter,' her father said. Darcy nodded humbly. She had decided that her father was going to spend a considerable time giving her overt and covert digs about being a failure and that she should silently absorb each and every last dig as a form of penance.

The following day Darcy went into town and got a job in Hardware and Floor Coverings at Goggins.

After a week in the job, Darcy wrote to Sophia about it.

Sunday 10 July 1983

Dear Sophia

You wouldn't believe how good I am at selling things. There's an arrangement here that you get point nought nought nought one of ten per cent of the sale price as a commission. It's such a small proportion that nobody had even bothered to tell me about it, so you can imagine how charmed I was when they handed me seven pounds eighty pence on top of my week's wages. I couldn't believe it. Neither could the senior girl in the department, who is a living bitch with an arse like a shelf and legs like milk bottles. Also a distinct lack of shoulder. It's like she got melted below her neck. All her blouses have a sort of empty peak where her shoulders should fit into them. Her name is

Hazel and I was told to watch her for the first few days and all would be well. So I did. Sophia, she is the phoniest phoney you have ever met.

She clasps her hands at boob level and hovers around customers. If they as much as lift the corner of a doormat, she's over telling them that the colour is very fashionable this year and it will save their carpet so much wear and tear.

She gave me a book about this. The technique is called 'sales by assumption'. The book says when customers come back with a complaint, you have to do these things:

Smile

Disarm

Restate

So when someone comes in and says your effing clothespegs failed and all my clothes fell in the muck and my wife's size 83 drawers flew off on the wind and wrapped themselves around the head of a passing motorcyclist and he ran over a blind old lady's guide dog and got killed himself, you smile at him. Can you imagine?

Having right royally pissed off this person, you then disarm them. That means saying 'I know just how you feel.' Of course, if *your* wife's size 83 drawers have never caused a fatal accident, it's bloody amazing if you know just how he feels, but the claim is supposed to disarm him.

Then you restate his problem to him. Like: 'I hear what you're saying. You're telling me that our clothes pegs failed and your wife's size 83 etc. etc.'

Now I had this man who came in the other day and he was very self-conscious because he said his wife was in bed too upset to come in and deal with it herself, even though she had bought the coal scuttle from us the previous week. He said that she had bought the coal scuttle because they were having a very important dinner party.

He had been promoted. They had this new house. She had put champagne carpeting all over the ground floor. I didn't know what champagne carpeting was, but it's sort of off-white, apparently.

So she feeds the guests. They are impressed to death. They gather around the fire to have a post-prandial whatsit. She lifts the coal scuttle, all shiny brass, and the bottom falls out of it. Half a ton of good Polish coal comes out, most of it raining down on the outstretched, cream-cashmere-trousered legs of a female guest. Trousers ruined. Ankles cut and bruised. The rest of it comes down on the carpet, and champagne it isn't any more. His wife's social début at a higher level is shat upon and she doesn't think she's going to live.

So I listened to all this and then I said, 'Jesus'. And he said, 'My thoughts exactly,' and sort of laughed. I didn't know what to do, so I said, 'I can't grasp this. Tell it to me again,' and in telling it to me, he began to remember funny things the other guests had said. At the end of it, we were both in stitches and the other customers looked as if they wanted to buy whatever had been so beneficial to this man. Eventually he asked me what were we going to do about it, and I said I didn't really think sending him home with a replacement was going to make his wife into a happy little unit, and he said, no he didn't think so either.

So then I said why didn't we get Young Mr Goggin to deliver the replacement and the company's apologies personally? The customer thought this was nifty, and went off. (Talking about 'Young Mr Goggin' is me being singular about something very plural. Old Goggin was as prolific as a rabbit

70

and there are nine Young Goggins, about seven and a half of them working here for the summer. One of them drives the delivery truck and if he puts on a sports jacket looks quite respectable, so he became 'young Mr Goggin' for the day and placated the woman and all is well.)

I am saving up my bonus and my wages because I am on a diet. Did you know that it takes up more calories to digest a hard-boiled egg than are actually *in* a hard-boiled egg? You have eighty calories in an egg so you can eat ten in a day, eight hundred, and come out thinner. Not that you could really eat ten eggs a day – not that even *I* could eat ten eggs a day, but I am starving most of the day and eating three, boiled to bullets, in the evening. I feel like Paul Newman in that film where he ate about a million eggs in one go, do you remember?

So how is the Gaeltacht? Did everybody sympathise with you for having such a crap sister? Are you homesick at all?

Love
Darcy

The reply came four days later.

Dear Darcy

This should reach you at the same time as Mam and Dad receive a missive from me. I am not going to duplicate items in this letter which are in that one. Please get them to tell you anything you might be interested in.

I'm not surprised that you would be a good saleswoman. I think the best salespeople are not the ones who are pushing the company's products at you, they are the ones who are almost in league with you *against* the company, and that is typical of you.

The *céilí* is fun and I have three boyfriends. One of them you would like. He is in Belvedere and he is on their rugby team, so he has big shoulders and a thick neck. He does very good impressions of politicians. His name is Gregory but he is known as Greg. He has a friend named Nicholas, who is quiet, but Greg says Nicholas is a wonderful musician and a composer. The third boy I like is from Galway and his name is Ruaidhrí. His Irish seems to me to be perfect, and really I think he is here because his parents are gone to France and he doesn't get on with them at the moment.

I miss you.

It is coming close to ten and the lights will be going out soon, so I had better sign off.

Much love
Sophia

Accustomed to trying to establish standards of behaviour for Darcy and to rescuing her from a series of disasters, Sophia felt like a too-young mother given a welcome holiday from motherhood.

'We're going to have a picnic on the beach on Saturday night,' Ruaidhrí told her one Thursday in Irish. 'You coming in to Spiddal to buy beer?'

'No, I am not. Beer?'

'Not much alcohol in beer. You'd think I was asking you to buy meths.'

'Why are you asking me?'

'You're tall.'

'So?'

'So you'll pass for 18.'

'I don't see – '

'They'll sell you beer. They won't sell a six-pack to a midget like Aileen.'

'I'm not buying beer.'

'Why not?

'I'm just not, that's all.'

'But give me a good reason.'

'I don't think people here to learn Irish should be getting drunk.'

'How about people who already know Irish – they OK?'

Sophia smiled at him. They were sitting on a high bank overlooking the beach. 'Do you swim?' he asked her.

'Of course she swims,' Greg's voice said from behind them. He and Nicholas dropped on either side of Sophia and Ruaidhrí. Nicholas gave Sophia one of his long sideways conspiratorial smiles. Something had convinced Nicholas that almost all life's human problems could be solved by beaming in an amused way at the weeper or attacker or rival.

'Ruaidhrí, as a gobshite from the benighted arsehole of the country, you wouldn't know about middle-class Dublin doctors' daughters and their skills,' Greg began. He was very good-looking, she thought. Much better in the looks department than Ruaidhrí, but Ruaidhrí had a sinewy harsh-freckled carelessness to him that she liked.

'The Dublin doctor's daughter is a species unto herself,' Greg continued loudly, for the benefit of the other two. 'She not only learns to do athletics or maybe ballet, she not only learns to do tennis, or in some schools hockey . . . she learns to do all of them technically perfectly. Right, Sophia?'

'I swim very well,' she admitted.

'I'm gonna report the whole lot of you,' Nicholas said lazily, lying back and upturning his slightly pimpled face to the sun. 'Talking *Béarla*. Ye have no shame.'

'None,' Greg said. 'That's why we're here. Nobody watching us would think we'd talk English to this linguistic throwback here.'

Ruaidhrí swiped at him. The two of them rolled off the bank and wrestled in the sand. Nicholas kicked them.

'I'm going back up,' Sophia said, 'and no, I am *not* buying beer,' she told Ruaidhrí.

Greg and Nicholas did instant sit-ups.

'Beer?'

'For Saturday,' Ruaidhrí said dismissively. 'After the *céilí.*'

'Where?' Greg demanded.

'Out here. Bonfire. Potatoes. Sausages. Beer.'

'Yeah!'

'Even if you won't buy the beer, you'll be there, won't you?' Nicholas asked Sophia.

'No, I won't. You lot are going to be expelled – '

'Like Darcy,' Greg said quickly.

' – *not* like Darcy, and I'm not taking that risk.'

'You know something?' Greg said. 'Maybe we should get the Darcy one back. Maybe she'd have a bit of go in her, you know?'

'Oh, she certainly has go in her,' Sophia replied. 'Too much go, probably. You'd like her.'

'What's she look like?'

'You'll see when you meet her some time.'

Sophia walked back up towards the *óstán* with Ruaidhrí, who was singing under his breath.

'*Níos airde,*' Sophia said.

He began to sing, unselfconsciously, out loud.

Sé fáth mo bhuartha nach bhfaighim cead cuirte,
Sa ngleanntán uaigneach ina mbíonn mo ghrá . . . '

She listened, catching some of the meaning, until he came to the end, half-conducting himself through the final words.

'*An bhuil tú in ann an seinm sin a múint domsa?*'

He corrected her gently. '*An bhuil tú in ann an t-amhrán sin a mhúineadh domsa?*'

She repeated it after him.

'Of course. Now.'

'Oh, not now, some time, just.'

'Why some time? What's wrong with now?'

Always resistant to impulse, Sophia glanced about her.

74

There were lots of other students within earshot. He did a 'so what?' gesture and she felt suddenly embarrassed at her own unwillingness.

'OK. Now.'

It was not a path they were standing on as much as a beaten-out trail, grass flattened, sand impacted by generations of young feet. He faced her in the middle of it and sang the first verse to her. Haltingly, she sang it after him. Her voice was high and clear, his rough and powerful.

Other students began to gather around, to mock, but something about the uncomplicated concentration of the two singers silenced them. A few – including Nicholas, who had followed them at a distance – hummed the notes Sophia was being taught, or whispered the words to themselves.

'*Anois. Ar aghaidh leat.*'

'*Ón tús?*'

'*Sea.*'

Sophia took a deep breath and closed her eyes. Her voice was edged with unsureness, each meaning given the particular vibrancy of new understanding.

> *. . . Ní bheidh orm brón ná duifean croí*
> *Ach mé bheith pósta le mo mhíle stóirín,*
> *'S mo láimh go bródúil ar a brollach mín . . .*

When she finished, there was silence, and she opened her eyes.

Ruaidhrí gave her a long considered nod. Yes, the nod said. Good, the nod said. Beautiful, the nod said. He glanced around him with an air of contained threat, and a few people murmured compliments. 'One of the great love songs,' he said to her.

On the third weekend the weather forecast was good. Greg announced this on the Friday evening.

'Tomorrow night,' he said, gesturing at the sands in front

of them, 'tomorrow night this beach is going to be a seething swarm of sun, sand and sex. *Seething*, I'm not joking you.'

'I have no idea about sand and sex, but it'll be a miracle if there's sun at night,' Sophia pointed out.

'OK,' Greg said agreeably. 'Sausages, sand and sex.'

'Your chances are better with sausages than sex,' Ruaidhrí told him.

'*What?*'

'I don't think you're getting it at all,' Ruaidhrí said. 'If you *were* getting it, why would you be trailing Beethoven here with you everywhere?'

'Oh, Jesus, Mozart if you must, not fucking Beethoven,' Nicholas said, surprisingly stung by the description.

'Beethoven travels with me,' Greg told him as if imparting a state secret, 'to protect the women of Spiddal from my rampant, insatiable, ineffable – '

' – impregnable?' suggested Nicholas.

'Absolutely. That too.'

'What?' Sophia asked.

'What what?'

'Your rampant, insatiable, unspeakable *what?*'

'Lust.'

'Oh, that's a relief.'

'Without Beethoven here, nobody would be safe. Nobody,' Greg said, advancing on Sophia. Ruaidhrí reddened and stood up.

'Bit of the old possessives surfacing here,' Nicholas warned Greg.

'There is *no* possessiveness and nothing like that,' Sophia said, gathering her cardigan and giving indications that she was heading back to the *óstán*. 'If you're going to risk your time here by being on the beach tomorrow night, good luck to you.'

'We bring you back a sausage?' Nicholas offered.

'No. If you're bringing me back something, bring me back a potato.'

The following night, after the *céilí*, Sophia sat on her bed at midnight, wishing she had brought her journal with her. If she could write in the diary, she thought, she could put guide-ropes around what was happening to her. She missed Darcy because Darcy was funny but also because Darcy's constant presence and her own need to be both protective and directive of her twin provided a safe membrane around her own life. Here in the Gaeltacht she was free-floating, with the liberty a high wind gives to the leaves it scoops and scatters.

She felt as if her fences had been taken away, her borders breached. It was, she thought, quite ridiculous that she should be wasting so much good learning time thinking about a young man from the west she had met less than three weeks ago, and might never see again. Trite stuff. The equivalent of a shipboard romance. It didn't happen to people like her, and she must find a way to recover her personal essence so that she became again the 'her' that it didn't happen to.

The other girls began to arrive and undress for bed, swapping supplies, like toothpaste, which were by now running low in some lockers. Eventually the lights went out. No moon poked cold quiet light through the long windows as on other nights. In the dark, Sophia lay there, listening for laughter from the beach, but it was too far away.

'Sophia . . . Shhh!'

The whisper was right beside her. The 'shhh' to silence her startled gasp. Someone was crouched beside her bed.

'What is it?'

'Someone outside for you.'

'What?'

'Out*side*. The window at the fire escape.'

Sophia slid out of bed and crept to the door. Opened it. Closed it behind her. Darkness in the corridor outside, a slightly lesser darkness. Shape at the window. The window half up.

'Who is it?'

'Who the hell d'you think it is?'

'Ruaidhrí?'

'That's me.'

She dropped to her knees so that their faces were at a level, he on the outside in the cooler air. Instinctively, they spoke in Irish.

'What are you at?'

'You ordered a potato, Madam.'

In the darkness, he produced a bundle. Looking and touching, she found it like a knitted bird's nest. One egg. The nest his wound-around jumper. The egg a warm potato.

'Salt, even,' he said with a flourish. She could begin to make out that the skin at the top of the potato was completely black.

'I should complain to the management,' she said.

'Why?'

'Burned.'

'Rubbish. You've never eaten a spud done in the ashes of a sand bonfire. Eat it.'

'You wouldn't like to suggest how?'

'Oh, right.'

Another flourish. She moved her hand along the window-sill and suddenly his warm, dry, strong, hand was fastening her smaller hand around something. A plastic teaspoon. For a moment, she thought about thanking him and taking the potato somewhere else to eat it, but eating on her own with him watching somehow had an extra appropriateness. She split the blackened skin and began to spoon the contents.

'Well?'

'Gosh, it's wonderful. It's quite different.'

'Not going to complain to the management?'

She fed him a spoonful of it, then took another spoonful. Soon the skin was hollow.

'I'll take it away with me.'

'It was really lovely. You're half-mad, you know that?'

'No.'

'Nothing else explains this.'

'C'mere till I explain it.'

He tilted her chin and kissed her, holding her face. The first brushing of their closed lips was a beginning and only a beginning. Her eyes closed and his hand slid from the edge of her face to her neck, stroked under the pale hair, traced the line of her collar bone, palming in under her nightdress to the roundness of her shoulder. He smelled of the sea and of the bonfire. They were bathed in a stunned silence and physical content.

'Greg said he wanted some credit.'

'For what?'

'He stopped Beethoven eating the last spud, 'cause he knew I wanted it for you.'

'Did he?'

'Stop Beethoven?'

'No. Know you wanted it for me?'

''Course he did.'

'You told him?'

'I told everybody. Beethoven just didn't give a shit.'

'He'd eat it and then smile at you.'

'If he ate it, he wouldn't be capable of smiling for a month. I'd make sure of that.'

Her knees were getting sore and cold. She tried to peer over the windowsill.

'What are you at?'

'Trying to see are you kneeling on that hard fire escape.'

'Yes I am.'

'Here, put your jumper under your knees.'

'Thank you.'

'You'll have to go, you know.'

'Mmmm. Who was the girl I sent for you?'

'Aileen.'

'She nearly shit a brick when I hissed at her from here.'

'She shares a desk with Darcy in school. My sister.'

79

'I know who Darcy is. Will you tell her?'

'Tell who?'

'Darcy?'

'Tell her what?'

'About us.'

'What about us?'

'That you met a wild man in the west that loves you.'

This is not happening, her thoughts said. Or if it is, it is a lie. This is a pretence, and he is playing on my naïveté. Are you naïve if you know yourself to be naïve? Or innocent if you start to think about things in this way? You can't be insane if you believe yourself to be insane. He probably does this every summer and there's some girl like me who believes it is a first, it is unique.

'A wild man from the west,' she repeated, filling time.

'That loves you,' he completed, deadly serious, pulling her face to a couple of inches away from his in the near-darkness. 'That *loves* you.'

Her face went from side to side in his strong hands.

'That loves you,' he said again, wearing her contradictions down with the repetition.

'That loves you, loves you, loves you,' he said, singing it like a prayer, an incantation, a mantra.

She wanted to trot out the denials to him. I am fifteen. This doesn't happen. This is silly. (Not silly, a more condemning word was needed.) But she looked at him in darkness: the pale face, sooted in shadow. She traced the darkened space below his brows. The harsh hooded face of a peasant beaten by the weather and years and dulled expectations was hidden there behind the fullness of his youth.

'That loves you,' he said, his fingers on the softness of her mouth.

'Loves you,' she whispered, taking comfort from the possibility that he might think it a shortened repetition of what he had said, not a statement.

'Say it.'

'That loves you.'

'Say it, all of it.'

'I love you.'

His hands held her face so hard her cheeks bunched around her mouth, pursing it the way a child purses its mouth for a kiss.

'My girl,' he said and kissed the mouth. 'My love.'

'You must go,' she whispered.

'I must. There is tomorrow.'

'Tomorrow and tomorrow and tomorrow.'

He retrieved his jumper from under his knees and bent to kiss her again.

'Sleep well.'

'You must be joking.'

'I am.'

The fire escape vibrated as he went down and she sensed him waving at her from the car park. Instinctively she waved back, slid the window down and went back into the dormitory, moving with effortless quiet to her own bed.

After Mass the following morning, Ruaidhrí was there outside the church to claim her, silent and calm in a way that aged him by a decade. Last week, he was a student, a teenager. This week, he was a man, a man without need of commonality with his peers, a man stepping into the moves of mating like an animal reaching its prime. The smart-ass comments of the others fell away from him like straw brushed off trouser legs. He took her arm and they walked to the beach.

'We have an hour,' she said, knowing the schedule.

'We have much more than an hour,' he said, 'but maybe not today.'

'I go home on Sunday next.'

'You do.'

He said it as if it were an irrelevant detail, sketching a move with an imaginary hurley stick. She sat and watched him. The air promised the warmth of midsummer by noon.

The tide was way out.

'On Saturday, you have to come to the beach after the *céilí*,' he said over his shoulder. 'Last night. No room service with spuds. Take out only.'

'You'd make a great waiter.'

'Oh, no,' he said, suddenly serious, with no compunction about contradicting her. 'I will be a great TV director.'

'Why?'

'Because I'll work like hell and I'm – '

'No. Why do you want to be that?'

'Because,' he said, eyes slaty with angry determination, 'television is diluting and poisoning this place. Krauss calls it "linguistic nerve gas". Linguistic nerve gas for the Gaeltacht. For all Irish speakers.'

He was silent.

'I know Irish is important,' she said, not knowing who Krauss was, and trying for her normal confident tone, '*very* important – '

'It's the only thing that's important,' he told her, voice flat. 'The only thing. Without it, we aren't Irish. Without it, we don't exist. We could lose religion, we could lose industries, we could lose – oh, millions of things. Lose the language, lose it as a living thing, there's nothing.'

She was frightened by the vehemence.

'But we'll have television here and great programmes and roll back the soap opera shite, and I will make those programmes. There is money out there,' he said, pointing back inland. She worked out that he meant Europe.

'There's money out there. They talk about pluralism and diversity and minority languages and cultures and I will go over there and get them to put money into a TV station here.'

She was only fifteen and in his passion for his future, he was older and rooted in something she did not understand. He sat beside her in silence for a few minutes, watching the faraway tide, now on the turn. It was the first time, she thought, she had ever been on a beach for any length of time with anyone other than Darcy.

'I'll do it and not only will it serve the Gaeltacht, it will turn us into a fucking *showpiece* for the rest of Europe.'

He put his arm around her, almost absent-mindedly, and she wondered if she should feel annoyance at the absent-mindedness. Her feelings were at one remove from her, as if she no longer owned them.

In the next few days, she asked him questions. Where did he live? Exactly? What school had he gone to? Where would he learn to be a TV director? He answered the questions with the brief responses he might give to a questionnaire.

He waited for her after classes. He talked about her. When the others made comments to him, he nodded, seriously. When the others made comments to her, she was suffocated into silence by the physical reaction she had to the mention of his name.

They thought she was cool and detached. In reality, she was sucked out of her own identity completely, insubstantial. For the first time in her life, she knew herself to be without control over events.

Because of her lack of sleep, she felt sometimes as if she were floating, slightly at a remove from the classes, although she worked just as hard.

'You don't remember when you first saw me,' he told her. 'But I remember when I first saw you.'

She looked at him questioningly.

'The very first day. You were telling off – Jesus, maybe that was your sister? Big lump of a girl with red hair? You were telling her off very quietly about something.'

Sophia tried to remember it. It was as if it had happened six months previously.

'I noticed you,' he said, and began to recite:

Lá dá bhfaca thú
ag ceann tí an mhargaidh,
thug mo shúil aire dhuit,
thug mo chroí taitneamh duit,
d'éalaíos óm charaid leat
i bhfad ó bhaile leat . . .

'What's that?'

'Never mind what it is,' he replied, laughing. 'Just listen to it.'

He said it again, and the undecorated claims of passion floored her.

'Did you write it?'

'Oh, no. Oh, no. It was written a long, long time ago. So what about Saturday, then?'

Never mind Saturday, she wanted to say. Tell me about after Saturday. Tell me about time and the future. Tell me about us. Why will you not tell me, reassure me, promise me. Something. Anything.

On Saturday, at the beginning of the *céilí*, the teacher made a speech to warn the students against parties on the beach. They were absolutely forbidden to leave the building, he told them, and he was relying on their adulthood and sense of responsibility.

Even as the teacher spoke, around her, she could smell the warm fetid smell of lager. Both boys and girls were slipping out, every now and again, to down the contents of the lukewarm cans secreted under mattresses. When Ruaidhrí kissed her as they danced, she could taste it from him.

'Beer?'

'Don't worry,' he whispered to her. 'I'm not going to get pissed tonight, whatever other night I get pissed.'

When the dancing ended, the students went off in dribs and drabs, some to the dormitories to finish packing, some to dark angles in the building for long frustrating embraces, and some to the beach. On other nights, the noises had been held down. Tonight, there was no concealment. Local teenagers arrived in force. There were even some overseas students, with neon back-packs to be stashed in the sands. The bonfire was built higher and wider than ever before, the potatoes in the ashes underneath. A few of the revellers held barbeque forks to cook sausages in the flames. Ruaidhrí and Sophia, hand in hand, watched the bright white flames, and the sudden spurts as petrol or sugar were thrown on them.

Then he found a dip in the grassy approach to the beach and settled the two of them into it. If they raised their heads and looked over the coarse grass, they could see the sparks flying upwards from the bonfire.

He unbuttoned her blouse, expecting no protest and meeting with none. She lay still, as if to pretend no presence, no participation. His hands curved around her shoulders as they now were used to doing. He held her that way for a long time, looking at the shadow of her below him, silent. Then the tips of his fingers moved under her bra straps and moved them gently back and over the shoulders. With infinite delicacy, he lifted her breasts from the cups, and then his mouth fastened on her, warm invasion in contrast to the quiet cool of the night air. A surge of abandonment brought her hips up to him, to find and know the swelling and to rub it and pull it towards her. Her hands never touched him. Her hands stayed flattened to the grass on either side of her. The rest of her surrounded him in need and demand.

He knelt away from her and undid his own jeans. Then he was on her, in her, his voice saying things she had never heard, did not understand. Her body wondered at the swell and at his rocking ruthlessness. The rhythm of it dragged her, one pace behind him, led her, speeding her, spilled her into an agony of pleasure, him with her, their breathing loud and louder in each other's ears, other sounds distant, themselves more distant, and then a cold-sweated collapse and a weight on her, his relinquishing to her as if he were home.

They lay in the darkness, their breathing slowing and

the night breezes welcome on wet skin. There were whispers between them and the noises from the beach, louder, rolled back into their awareness. 'Stay here,' he said, suddenly standing, dragging the jeans back on, zipping them. Over the grassy hummock he went, into the darkness. In a few minutes he was back, sliding down beside her, finding her hand and pushing a cold wet can into it.

'I'll have you know that that was the very last 7Up and I practically had to fight for it.'

She sat drinking it. He had two other cans. Beer. One opened for drinking. One stuffed into a readiness position in the supportive sand. He drank the first can quickly, gave an appreciative gasp at the end of it and ground it noisily into concertinaed folds before throwing it, overhand, as far as he could.

'Vandal.'

He patted sand into a pillow at the small of her back by way of response to this and then opened the second can. They sat in silence, the happy noises from the beach sounding trivial in comparison to their bruised after-pleasure. Eventually, he crushed and threw the second can in a different direction.

'I'm going for a swim. Come on.'

'*No!*' She was startled by the suggestion, then puzzled because it was so much less a violation of what she was supposed to stand for than what she had already done.

'Oh, come on, nobody can see you.'

'No. Don't even waste your time trying to persuade me. I wouldn't ever.'

'Have you ever swam in the dark?'

'Never.'

'Have you ever swam naked?'

Swum, she thought. Swum.

'Never.'

His face was close to hers, cheek rough against her smoothness.

'What a protected life.'

She waited him out, hoping he would abandon the idea, but he stood.

'Well, I'm going anyway. Time me. I'll be back in ten minutes and you won't know me I'll be so cleaned up.'

'I'd prefer to know you.'

He took her hands and turned them up to kiss the pulse at her wrists. Then he was gone.

For a time, she was quite glad of the solitude. Her own instinct to correct his words upset her. She needed to believe that her love for him was total, leaving no space for selfishness, but as she struggled to be certain of it, another thought flowed in. He had not taken precautions. She was safe and she knew it – the pill, prescribed briefly for period problems, would take care of that – but he had not asked, and maybe he should have asked. Mixed with these thoughts were the thought of going home. Would home be home any more, when the person returning was so changed?. She looked at her watch. More than ten minutes had passed. The group on the beach was now engaged in raucous collective singing.

She could hear him on the grass and then, just as quickly as she had heard him, knew that the pace and pattern of the sounds was wrong, did not belong to him. These were two shapes, stumbling, eyes used to the bonfire-light, judgement softed by alcohol, loose-jointed at the knees.

'Not here,' she said sternly. They fell and fumbled their way off to her left, and she looked at her watch again. Perhaps he had meant he would be in the sea for ten minutes, not away from her for ten minutes. She felt no possessive irritation but a sudden transforming coldness and terror. She stood up. Threw away the can in weak echo of what he had done. Climbed over the bank and down on to the beach. Moving slowly and carefully in the shadows. There was no sign of any problem. Several swimmers were in the water. She stood still, watching the silhouettes around the bonfire. One of them came up towards her, climbed the bank not far from where she was, without seeing her. Going for a pee, she realised, and wondered if the bulky shape was Greg. After a few minutes, he came back over the bank, and she was sure.

'*Greg?*'

'Jesus. Yeah?'

'Over here.'

'Where the frig is "here"?'

'To your left. Yes. Keep walking. Here.'

'Sophia?'

'Yes.'

'Well, wonders will never cease. The virtuous, the law-abiding, the – '

'Greg.'

'Yes?'

'I was with Ruaidhrí.'

'Bully for Ruaidhrí.'

'He went for a swim.'

His hands automatically checked her clothing. Dry.

'When?'

'Twenty-five minutes ago.'

'That's not long.'

'He told me to expect him within ten minutes.'

'Oh, *fuck*.'

'He meant it, too. He was only getting cool, really.'

The two of them stood in silence for a moment, and she could feel decision pulling him together.

'Go back and stay by yourself wherever you were – '

'Just behind us here.'

'There's nothing you can do. Just stay there, OK?'

He ran down the beach. Nearing the bonfire, he yelled for silence, met with counter-yells, shouted them down, conveyed the urgency. The singing stopped.

'Shut up for a minute, then call his name,' Greg shouted.

They were silent. Then called his name. All of them.

A lion roar in the dark over the sea. A silence eventually ended by half-moans of prediction and fear.

'All *right*,' Greg's voice came. 'Any of you with cars, get them, line them up facing the water and give us full headlights. Nicholas, go and ring the police. Aileen, go and tell the people up at the school. Now, I want three swimmers and only three swimmers. Sober. Good strong swimmers.'

She could see silhouettes rising off the beach and lining up in front of him, but could not hear his selection. He seemed to be giving them rules for their swim. They ran for the sea. The headlights of cars were beginning to turn in dumb search of the limitless cold space of the water.

The first police car arrived within minutes and a Guard ordered all swimmers out of the water. Ordered them off the beach, too, but they didn't go. The bonfire was dimming as the police officers went back and forth to their cars, calling up boats and divers and big lights, although the big lights were outpaced by the dawn, which came up bleakly behind the big hulking shape of the *óstán*, confirming the lethal passage of time.

Sophia slid down, her back to the beach, searching the depression in the grass by the gathering light to see if there were possessions of his there. Basketball shoes, one upright, one overthrown.

Then Greg was back. He dropped down beside and her and talked very quietly. They were even talking quietly on the beach. No more shouts.

'Go back to the *óstán*,' he told her. 'There's nothing you can do here except complicate things.'

'I can't just *go* – '

'He's gone.'

The brutality of it winded her and he knew it.

'He's gone, Sophia. No, they haven't found him but he's dead. Now what can you do here? Stay out of it. Go back.'

She stood and reached for the shoes.

'Leave them. I'll find them later.'

'But – '

'How will you know? I'll come and tell you. The minute we know anything. Go on.'

Knowing he was watching her, she walked, gathering speed as she went. There was curiosity in the faces of the teenagers coming the other way in response to the news already reaching into the *óstán* and the village.

Half the beds in her dormitory were unoccupied, and she washed and changed as sleepers awoke and were told the news. Nobody said anything to her, although one girl touched her arm in a gesture of sympathy. Scraps of information reached her. Boats with nets. A helicopter on its way from Shannon.

The bus to take them to the train was due to leave half an hour after noon. Greg found her sitting on a wooden seat in the car park overlooking the beach. He sat down beside her, not touching her.

'They found him?'

'They did.'

Greg quite suddenly wept.

'Oh, *fuck* this,' he said, trying to stop the tears.

She sat, dry-mouthed, looking out over the water, without a question. Then she gathered her belongings about her, stood and thanked him as formally as if they had only just met. He stood, hair greasy and face dirtied by streaks of ashy dried sweat, his clothes reeking from the night's work, and shook his head, baffled to find himself, a confident extrovert, speechless in the face of this event. She walked away from him towards the bus, and Aileen, who had been on the beach the previous night, came and sat beside her, her long black hair smelling of smoke. They sat together on the bus and they sat together on the train, silent for the journey. And it came to Sophia that her silence must be complete and never-ending, a silence to serve as a fire-blanket, snuffing out questions and speculation and the trivialisation of something the scale of which she could not yet judge. Only in that silence could she stay warmed by her belief that he had loved her.

CHAPTER SIX

Sophia walked into her home that night and saw Ruaidhrí's face. As Darcy and her mother rushed to hug her, she could see, over their shoulders, the rough-edged features, eyes half-closed against sunshine, on the television screen.

'Did you know that poor boy?'

'Yes.'

'Well?'

'Not well.'

'What on earth happened?'

'Shh and you'll hear.'

But the newsreader was summing up. It was one of three deaths by drowning that weekend, and someone had issued a statement asking swimmers and boaters to exercise extra caution and to make sure that alcohol was not part of their water sports.

'Would that kid have been drinking?'

She tried to fit 'that kid' to the man she had known.

'A beer. Two, maybe.'

'Drinking,' her father said heavily.

'Two beers do not a drunkard make,' Colette said, and pushed Sophia gently into an armchair. 'Robert, do me a favour. I'm totally out of sugar. Discovered it when you were gone to collect Sophia. Would you ever do the needful?'

As Robert obliged, Sophia looked at her mother in puzzled admiration.

'Tea, coffee or drinking chocolate?'

'Drinking chocolate?'

'Very comforting.'

'Yes, that would be nice.'

Colette went off into the kitchen. Sophia smiled politely at Darcy as if they had just renewed a distant acquaintance, then looked around the room.

'I can tell,' Darcy said after a moment, 'I can just *tell* that you are hungry to know of the triumphs of my month. You had such a dull time down there in *tá tá* land that you need to hear about my achievements. No, don't try to hide it. I know.'

Sophia felt as if she were fading in the onslaught of Darcy's bright colours. Her mother reappeared and she watched the tiny froth bubbles on the top of the drinking chocolate circle, then circle more slowly.

'You can just feel a *madeleine* coming on, can't you?' Darcy said to her mother.

'A what?'

'What's his name and his bloody *madeleine* – Proust?'

Colette shrugged.

'Any moment, Sophia's going to come up with six million exciting memories evoked by drinking chocolate.'

Over the top of the mug, Sophia shook her head and Darcy, like an old trooper called onstage to make the show go on, got launched on a saga of Goggins.

'On Friday last,' Sophia could hear Darcy say, as her father walked back in with the sugar, 'there was a staff party to give the golden handshake and the gold watch to a man who was retiring, and yours truly was there as a full-fledged member of staff. In fact, almost everybody but me got stewed to the gills and I was hard put to it to support all the people who ended up drunkenly weeping on my shoulder.'

'You look thin,' Sophia said, trying to participate.

'Don't be distracting me,' Darcy said loftily. 'Although now you mention it, I am seven pounds thinner since you saw me last, that being exactly half a stone. Don't ask me what my present weight is. I am in Goggins, right? And the man who is retiring begins to see his life pass in front of his eyes, and of what, you ask yourself, does his life consist?'

'I do not know. Of what,' Sophia asked in grateful games-playing, 'of *what* does his life consist?'

'Lino.'

'What?'

'Lino. Linoleum. A floor covering from the distant past.'

'Not that distant a past,' Robert said. 'Vinyl is relatively recent.'

'From the distant past,' Darcy went on, 'when our father was a youth, playing innocently amid the dinosaur droppings. Now, Goggins has sold the last roll of lino in captivity some time ago, probably to that moth-eaten *óstán* in the godforsaken Gaeltacht. But this poor man, Ned Nolan by name, has devoted his life to lino and, on this, his last day at work, he realises that if he doesn't pass on the linoleum holy grail, there will be no human record of its wonders.'

Sophia watched Darcy in gratitude, knowing that her twin was gradually, deliberately, pulling their parents' attention away from Sophia.

'Now, Pater mine, you claim to know about lino. *What* do you know about lino?'

'Oh, it's a kind of thick oil-cloth stuff, rigid and backed by sacking.'

'Anything else?'

'It was nicer to walk on than vinyl,' Colette said unexpectedly.

'And that's all you know?'

They nodded, amused by Darcy the interrogator.

'So my friend Ned is right. Nobody knows that linoleum is made up of barytes or heavy spar, linseed oil and talc. Nobody knows these things.'

'What are barytes?' her father asked, getting into the game and trying to catch her out.

'Barytes are white, blue, red, yellow or colourless barium sulphite minerals,' Darcy announced, closing her eyes to remember the wording correctly, and opening them to gauge her father's response, which was frankly admiring.

'And this mineral is *abundant* worldwide in granular form,' she added enthusiastically.

'Such a relief,' her mother said.

'There is an interesting thing about lino,' Darcy said, picking up Sophia's half-empty cup of now cold drinking chocolate. 'Ned said that because it was natural and organic, unlike vinyl floor coverings, it actually absorbed and killed off germs. He said that if hospitals really cared about patients, they'd have wall-to-wall lino everywhere. So now!'

Robert King suggested mildly that, much as he would like to refloor Angelus Hospital in its entirety to take account of Ned's wisdom, a pathologist was not usually very influential when it came to equipping areas outside his own. As he spoke, the late night news came on. Shorter than the earlier bulletin, it ran without pictures of Ruaidhrí. The reader also called him 'Rory', which Sophia welcomed as a distraction.

'Some of us have to get up at dawn to fulfil our professional engagements,' Darcy announced. 'Idlers like returned sisters can lie abed until noon if they so desire, but us working-class people . . . '

Obediently, Sophia rose and headed for the stairs.

'The hot chocolate was lovely,' she said, and kissed her mother. 'Good to be back.' And she pecked her father on the cheek.

In bed, in the dark, the two of them lay, parallel, in silence. After a while, Darcy stirred. 'If you want me to ask you questions, I will ask you questions. If you don't, I won't.'

'Don't. Please.'

'Is there anything I can do to help?'

'No. Tomorrow I'll be less tired.'

'Tomorrow and tomorrow and tomorrow,' she had said. Or was it he who had said it?

'It's more than tired, isn't it?'

'Yes.'

'But you want me to leave you alone?'

'Yes. I'm sorry.'

'No, if that's what you want, that I can do.'

An hour was what he said was enough, that day they had talked about tomorrow . . .

'Sophia? I'm sad that you're sad. Because when I'm sad you help me. But I know I can't help you except by shutting up, so I'm shutting up right now, OK? And furthermore, you know me, I'll be asleep in five minutes, so I'm sorry in advance.'

'Goodnight.'

'Goodnight.'

The following morning, Sophia woke her sister and, as Darcy got dressed, was determinedly anecdotal about the Gaeltacht.

'There was a guy who said he wanted to meet you some time,' she said.

'Don't tell me. Cross-eyed, spotty and four foot nine.'

'No.'

'Cross-eyed, spotty and four foot ten?'

'No.'

'Thrill me. And thrill me quick or I'll be late for work.'

'Six foot. Big shoulders, thick neck, weighs maybe twelve stone, brown eyes, brownish-blonde hair. Witty. Gentle. Goes to Belvedere.'

'And he wants to meet me?'

'Yep.'

'Sophia, I am *so* glad you came back.'

Darcy plunged down the stairs and grabbed her handbag off the end of the bannister. Sophia stood still in their room.

'Hey, Sophia?'

She looked out the window. Darcy was running backwards down the front path, unaware that the dustbin was lined up behind her.

'What's his name?'

'Mind the bin!'

'What?' Darcy collided backways with the bin, over-turning it in the middle of the path and skidding alongside it on her bottom. 'Oh, shit.'

'Greg,' said Sophia, opening the window. 'Go on, I'll tidy it up.'

'Greg?'

'Greg. You're going to miss the bus.'

'See you tonight.'

Sophia closed the window and went down to gather up the rubbish. When she came back in, her mother was sitting at the kitchen table.

'Mam?'

'Uh huh?'

'You know that quote – "tomorrow and tomorrow and tomorr– "' Sophia stopped in response to her mother's silencing gesture.

'What's wrong?'

'Scottish play,' her mother said. 'I think. May be wrong, but don't say it out loud till you're sure or the roof'll fall in. The dictionary of quotations'll have it. Try under that play.'

Sophia found the dictionary and looked up the index. Yes, there it was. She turned the pages until she found the whole quotation.

Tomorrow, and tomorrow, and tomorrow,
Creeps in this petty pace from day to day,
To the last syllable of recorded time;
And all our yesterdays have lighted fools
The way to dusty death. Out, out, brief candle!
Life's but a walking shadow, a poor player,
That struts and frets his hour upon the stage . . .

His hour, she thought. And not a dusty death, a sodden heaviness of death. They would bury him today, and she didn't even know who the 'they' were, by name. Three older sisters and his parents hastily returned from France. In a graveyard in Spiddal they would bury him, and she would never go there. If she could avoid it, she would never take that left turn out of Galway and travel those eleven miles again.

Just as his ambition and his love had aged Ruaidhrí in the weeks she had known him, so his death and her coping with it aged her in the weeks afterward. She made the decisions of a practised adult. Silence, for one. Routine, for another.

She took the wine-coloured journal out of a drawer and read through some of the entries written before she had gone to the Gaeltacht. Unbidden, images of grinning skulls floated through her head. Images of him slackening away from his bones, puddling in corruption in his coffin. Terror gripped her and for a moment she wanted to run downstairs and ask her mother to hold her. She sat still in the terror, knowing it could not be reached by others. Every time it happened, she would live through it and it would retreat to a point where it could be ignored, but every time, she was on her own with it.

She thought about how she would write about Ruaidhrí, then realised she never would. Words would gather him into a small set of ordered strands, like a plait of hair, and she would never again be able to see him free and uncontained. She closed the diary over on to its own satin bookmark and slid it back in the drawer. She would let a few days intervene, then she would write in it again, using it to discover her future.

CHAPTER SEVEN

17 Glanmire Park
Raheny
Dublin 5
Saturday 27 August 1983

Dear Initials

I was going back through some of the letters you sent and it struck me that you didn't bother your arse answering half the questions I have asked you. That's what professors are supposed to do – answer questions. I am revealing all (not that 'all' amounts to anything, but that's beside the point) to you and not refusing to answer anything, and you can't be bothered to even tell me what the NRA is or why you're interested in twins. You're just going to come back now at the beginning of September with another barrage of questions that *I* have to answer and then sit there with a smart-aleck smirk on you like every teacher I have ever had in my whole life.

I don't even know whether you are a psychologist or a sociologist. Or what you were doing in Seattle. Or what you look like. I know you are very senior and all that, but it would help if I could imagine you, because with nothing but initials and refusal-to-answer-questions, you're like a cement-faced institution.

Hunting and hunters are disgusting, and I find it astonishing that someone who's been in the 'social sciences' (the 'people business') for all their life should go out and get their thrills from killing helpless innocent animals.

I have had quite an interesting summer.
Yours sincerely
Darcy King

Entry in Sophia King's diary

Saturday 27 August 1983

It is a long time since I have made an entry in this diary, but today I see Darcy sitting down and writing a letter to this old American professor she has to send information to, so I should resume writing my journal. I will not refer back to the summer, except to say that there are many lessons for me to learn from it.

The first is that I must not underestimate Darcy. Even though I have been working very hard at being absolutely normal and casual, she knows that there is something different about me, and being Darcy would love to know all about it, but not only does she not ask me any questions, she does not draw attention to the fact that she is not asking any questions. In addition, she quite deliberately sets out to be a distraction when we are with other people – a distraction from my inability to be, I suppose, as young as I used to be.

She has also done very well in her summer job. They ended up getting her to go around the various counties where there are branches of Goggins and teach some of the junior staff in each branch new sales techniques that she had developed. She had a great time and, even though she was working for less than eight weeks, had two raises during that time. Goggins have said that they will take her back next summer or even at Christmas. This is very good, because it has given her something she can talk about to distract from having left the Gaeltacht early. Even saying it that way is not fair. My dad, for example, has nearly forgotten that she left the Gaeltacht early and is very proud of what she has achieved, *not* because she has talked about it, just because he is aware of it. (He is very edgy, though,

100

about the fact that she has been eating almost nothing but hard-boiled eggs for five or six weeks, but knowing Darcy, she will fall off that regime. That last comment is not meant to be unkind, it is probably better for her health if she falls off it, although she is a size fourteen in most things at the moment and looks very well.)

My new word for today is *demotic*. It means: pertaining to the common people. Applied to the popular alphabet of the ancient Egyptians as distinguished from the hieratic.

This autumn is the beginning of preparation for the Leaving Certificate, and also the beginning of preparation for a career. There is not a great deal of career guidance in our school. Nonetheless, I have looked at my own capacities and talents to establish what I should be aiming at.

These are my key strengths.

I am organised.

I am intelligent. (IQ 134)

I can separate out the various elements in a problem and logically approach the development of a solution, rather than plunge* into an instinctive response.

I work hard.

I work intelligently.

People are attracted to me.

I take care about my personal appearance, which is good.

I am interested in the arts, literature and communication.

*Darcy does this, but sometimes she reaches a very good response without being logical about it. She may have better instincts than I have but this is something I am unlikely to develop by watching or imitating her. That sort of thing may be innate.

These are my key weaknesses.

I am too cerebral sometimes.

I am obsessive.

I am judgemental.

I have fine limp baby hair which is difficult to style.

When I say that I am too cerebral sometimes, what I mean is that when I look at a problem that involves people, I tend to look at the issues as if they had no implications for feelings. After this summer, I am more aware that people's fears, feelings and affections should be considered.

I notice girls in our class increasingly like Darcy because she sends herself up and they feel superior to her, or if not actually superior, at least not inferior, although it should be pointed out that I never actively seek to make others feel inferior. It may be that Darcy is more demotic than I am in her style.(!)

Obsessiveness I must combat. The final weakness I have is that I am judgemental. When a problem arises, I often find myself trying to work out who is to blame, rather than looking for a solution. Darcy says that this is because I have not enough experience of disaster, which is ironic, but we will not go into that. It may be, however, that it is a trait that I share with my father. In his case, however, it is more legitimate, because in looking at an emerging illness, it is crucially important that you isolate what is to blame for the illness before you go looking for the solution to it. Otherwise, your solution might be superficially appropriate while not dealing with the underlying realities.

Action: I must go back to praying.

I must talk to Dad about medicine as a career.

I must concentrate on these four weaknesses.

Word for tomorrow is *hieratic*: sacred, pertaining

to the priests. Applied to a kind of hieroglyphics developed by the ancient Egyptian priests.

389 Fairbanks Avenue
Seattle
Washington
WA 48072
Monday 19 September 1983

Dear Darcy

Although I am still in Seattle, your letter was forwarded to me, and I am responding by return.

The NRA is the National Rifle Association.

Twins have been described as a perfect living laboratory for the study of factors such as heritability, intelligence, and the influence of environment on human development. Some of the most interesting work done to date has been on identical, MZ twins, as opposed to non-identical or DZ twins like you and your sister. At the end of the seventies, for example, two identical or MZ twins who had been separated at birth were reunited and studied extensively. They were forty years of age at the time. What surprised researchers was that though they had been separated from birth the two men had remarkably parallel likes and dislikes. They tended to vacation in the same resort, drink the same brand of beer and smoked the same brand of cigarette. They also drove the same kind of automobile. They even had similar migraine headaches.

How much of the current research into MZ twins will be of application to DZ twins is unclear. It may well be that what is learned will have more general application to our understanding of the inheritance of traits and even of problems such as alcoholism. There has been a trend in therapy and in human development in recent years to downplay the impact of genetics on issues such as IQ and on problem behaviors such as alcoholism and family violence, but some of the preliminary findings from the current research on twins suggest that our thinking in such areas will require emendation.

I hope this gives you sufficient information on this topic.

I am both a sociologist and a psychologist.

I was in Seattle in order to contribute to work going on there in relation to the demoralising effects of the loss of traditional employment foci and the development of coping methodology.

Since you appear to have a need for a more self-relevant and intimate level of correspondence, I will now respond to your more personal questions.

My appearance: I am 6'2", 178 lbs, athletic in build.

Hunting: I do not get 'thrills from killing innocent helpless animals', nor, in my experience, does any hunter. Hunting is a sport characterised by profound respect for/knowledge of the environment and for animals, without attributing Disney characteristics ('innocent, helpless') to them.

You make reference to an interesting summer. You might, perhaps, elaborate on this in your next letter, and also address the following questions:

1 Having mentioned the possibility that you might be lesbian, would you examine how you would feel about this if it proved to be the case?

2 What are the opinions of lesbianism and of gay people which have been of most influence on you?

3 How important to your vacation were any relationships developed during the period?

Yours sincerely

A. C. B.

Entry in Sophia's diary

Saturday 24 September 1983

I talked over with my father what I perceive as my weaknesses and strengths. I asked him about medicine as a career. He said that, although it would give him great pride if I became a doctor, he felt I probably could, he used the phrase, 'make a name' for myself if I went into some aspect of communications. I was a little disappointed by this and said to him that medicine was central to the human condition and to the saving of lives and was a profound vocation, whereas communication seemed to me to be somewhat peripheral and superficial.

He thought about this for a long time, and then he said that communication was if anything more central to the human condition and the making of human progress than medicine. He said that sometimes medicine has been unable to make the progress it should have made, and that people have died horrible deaths, as a result of poor communication. My father says that knowledge of itself is not always enough to make people change their behaviour. He gave me examples of this which are too long to write down here. I found this very positive and I would now feel much more hopeful about a career in communications.

Action: Find out about PR companies.

My word for today is *picayune* : inconsequential, insignificant, minor, paltry, petty, trivial.

17 Glanmire Park
Raheny
Dublin 5
Saturday 8 October 1983

Dear Initials
Well, aren't we a touchy little academic, all the same?

Gone all pompous, official and distant, have we?

I did not mean to offend you about the hunting and if you want to tell me how it's so wonderful for the environment, go ahead.

Now, I probably *will* offend you by what I say next, but if you're offended, basically you can shag off, because I have enough people on this side of the Atlantic putting me down and patronising me. The world is full of Older People who think they have learned all the lessons in the whole world and that any of us in our teens are just empty vessels waiting to be filled up with what the Older People decide is relevant which is mostly the greatest load of unadulterated shit.

If you tell them it is shit, they find some lack in *you* that allows them to believe it wasn't shit at all, it's just that you are an inadequate wally who doesn't measure up to the refinement of their wisdom. There's a classic example of that kind of puke in your letter. Where you say that I (Darcy) 'have a need for a more self-relevant and intimate level of correspondence' you are so full of it, it's flowing out your ears.

I am sorry if you are over sixty or something like that, but you haven't told me exactly how old you are so I am not being disrespectful to someone that old, because I don't know you are that old for sure. Anyway, no matter what age you are, don't you define my needs in that demeaning po-faced pseudo-professional way.

Now that I have written it down, I am twice as mad as I thought I was when I began this letter, so I take back all the civil things I've said so far, although I am probably too lazy to go back and write it again and just leave them out. What the *hell* gives you the right to *paste* 'needs' on to me.

Well, you can shove all of that. I am so sick of people deciding that I need one or all of those things. I'm trying to communicate honestly with you, so it would help if I knew what you are and what you look like instead of a grey monolith of uncertain years with nothing but initials, qualifications and the capacity to make quite riveting stuff (the blah about twins) sound ineffably boring by telling it like it was a lesson. I am not your student. I am not your patient. I am not your inferior. Now, it may be that *you* have a *need* to be a teacher or a therapist or whatever, but you can find some other way of meeting that need, because I'm not the solution to your problem. And furthermore, you can shove that description of yourself straight up your arse. With a wire brush. It is quite deliberately meant to put me off, to put me at a disadvantage.

Jesus, are you married? And if so, are you like that with your wife and kids?

I keep rereading your letter and each time I do, another bit of it gets up my nose. It doesn't tell me all I would like to know about twins. I would like to know any nuggety little bits that might help me come to terms with being a twin, which I basically don't like, no reflection on Sophia. No, the stuff about Seattle is not helpful, it is useless. Go back and read it again, why don't you, and tell me honestly if you meant to enlighten me or just make me feel like a ponderous peasant.

I don't know why I am bothering to answer your questions, because I really couldn't care less, but Sophia is still writing in her diary so I will improve the shining hour. (As my father says.)

Lesbianism. I will now do what Sophia calls a stream of consciousness.

I look at men crossing the street or at football

matches, not that I would be seen dead at football matches, but you see into pitches from the top deck of the bus and places like that, and I do not think that there is something intrinsically very arousing, if I know much about arousal, which I don't, about the way men are built. I have never seen a real live man naked. My father has an absolute bee in his bonnet about modesty and won't have Sophia and myself walk around in bra and pants.

In some ways, this is clever of him, because if I walk around in bra and pants, having fallen off my egg diet, it frightens the natives. But I remember this about my father since I was so high. When he used to read to us, he would make us put dressing-gowns on, and he talks a lot about privacy and self-respect. He doesn't quite get to your body as temple, but you can often feel a temple lurking in the background. Bottom line is that I haven't seen a real live naked man, nor indeed a real dead naked man. Women naked, or nearly naked, unless they are very fat and saggy, are attractive. Men naked or nearly naked, particularly *completely* naked, look like someone forgot a bit and tacked it on at the front in a very Superglue way, adding all this dirty-looking coarse hair to conceal the join. The male culture's obsession with the size of a man's penis (in our house we use the real words, it is considered a family *faux pas* to describe penises as your thing, John Thomas or his willy) I do not understand at all.

When you have something like a penis that looks so bockety anyway, the smaller it is the better, I would have thought, and certainly when I have seen illustrations of circumcision this has been confirmed. Circumcised peni are neatly blunt and somewhat minimised. (Quite apart from the health implications for the woman, which my father unexpectedly told me about one day when we were watching a programme about cancer.) Uncircumcised penises, on the other hand, have this sort of hangdog pointed downwards aspect to them like the Concorde coming in to land or a Ku Klux Klan man in full pointy-sheeted regalia, or the face of a Womble. They are bigger than circumcised ones, maybe, but not half as acceptable.

Getting back to the point, which is lesbianism, I was saying that women are intrinsically more attractive than men from my point of view. They have nicer softer places to touch. The whitey bit of a woman's arm (underneath, between elbow and armpit – which reminds me, I don't care if it's chic for Frenchwomen to have hairy armpits; I hate it) is silky to touch – a man's isn't.

Whenever I am up close to a woman who has big boobs (often it's an older woman, maybe as women get older or after they've had children or perhaps along with getting fat in middle age) I always want to put my hand on it/them and gently push in the softness and make it bounce back. This idea does not then move on to having sex with a woman, which is really just a variation on what people can do to themselves. I just think touching someone else's breasts might be good. In books, they always call it fondling, and this makes me uncomfortable, because 'fondle' was a word my mother used to use about babies, and I don't like it sullied.

My sources on all of this. As usual, books. One of the really old books on our shelves is called *The Well of Loneliness*. As a young child I was really intrigued by wells. Wishing wells, you know? Because if you are brought up with taps and showers, there is something very fairytale-ish about a roundy brick well with a little roof up over it and a twirling rod that winds the rope at the end of which is a bucket. So I wanted to read anything to do with wells when I was about seven or eight or nine, and I took down this book one day and there was a picture of the author in the front of it. She was seriously weird-looking. Her hair was cut tight to her head, very dark, sleeked back. What she was dressed in was like men wear, here, to weddings. Very dark formal suit with a bow tie, I think, although I could be wrong about the tie. Very, *very* thin woman with no boobs or had them squashed down in some way, and the man's suit fitted her perfectly.

Although it was weird, it was also quite attractive in the contradictory way that a principal boy in a pantomime is attractive, and I said something along those lines to my father.

He promptly got into an absolute tiz-waz, took the book from me, and made me feel as if I had been out murdering babies on the sly. He said I was not to read it until several years had passed, but the problem was he didn't say how many years. It was like an indeterminate sentence where the prisoner has to keep applying to the parole board to get let out: I had to keep applying to him for permission to read this book about the well, and every time I went to him about it, he got sort of disgusted with me and wanted to know why I was so interested in *that* book. He would gesture at the shelves and tell me that there was reading material there for years, so why was I so homed in on that one, which of course made me feel like a pig, even without knowing what the subject matter of the book was and certainly without being able to explain to him that the reason I was so intrigued was that

110

the effing thing had been put out of bounds. It was like saying to someone don't think of a pink elephant for the next three minutes, for the love of Jasus. When I eventually read it, it was a complete let-down, filled with references to people being inverted. I couldn't make head or tail of it. Long after I had read it, I realised it was about lesbianism.

I had known about male homosexuality earlier, mainly because of Oscar Wilde. My parents used to read us his children's stories. I particularly loved one called 'The Canterville Ghost', because it was the first children's story that kept you interested but sent itself up at the same time. Roald Dahl, later on, did the same.

Because we knew those pieces, and because my mother always used to point out the oval plaque on the wall of the house where he used to live in the middle of Dublin city, they took us to see *The Importance of Being Earnest* when we were about eleven and both of us thought it was very funny. So we got curious about Oscar Wilde and they told us about him and Bosey and going to prison.

I remember we asked our mother precisely what it was that homosexuals did and – she was usually very good at answering our questions – she said that in practical terms we really wouldn't die if we didn't have that information at that point, but that we should never get prejudiced against homosexuals because Oscar Wilde had been one, so we didn't.

So we knew 75 per cent about homosexuals and you pick up bits and pieces. Lesbians we didn't really learn about for a couple of years more. Did you know that there were fierce laws in Victorian England against male homosexuality but not against lesbianism because Queen Victoria baulked when they gave her the law to sign and said what nonsense, women never did things like that?

I am now fifteen and you really know by the time you are fifteen if you are gay or not. I amn't.

The last question you asked me was about relationships during the holidays and how important they were. They weren't. I must be very unattractive because everybody warned me about the dangers I was in and none of them ever materialised.

There is one roundy-faced little man (not even as tall as I am) with a waistcoat and curly brown hair who is a legend within Goggins. He is the accountant in head office, head office being the top storey of the branch I was working in. (Sorry, I haven't explained that Goggins is a sawn-off version of a department store, with branches throughout the country and I was working in the hardware department, flogging doormats to people.) The word was that if you arrived at the lift (elevator?) at the same time as Timmy Quigley – this being the accountant's name – you should take to the stairs or the hills, whichever was handiest, because he was *lethal*. I asked one of the girls to be a bit more specific about *lethal* and she said, oh, come on, hands everywhere. I still wanted her to be precise and she got very red in the face and started to make helpless gestures at the others.

Timmy Quigley was stronger than he looked, and if a girl got into the lift with him, he would press the button for the basement before she noticed. When the lift reached the basement, he would press a button that would keep the lift there for a few minutes. This button was to facilitate loading. The guys in the basement would be loading maybe three pallets of doormats into the lift and someone on the second floor would call for it while the guys were off getting two and three pallets and off would go the lift with pallet one in it, and getting everything mated up together again might take ages. So a special button had been installed which allowed the lift to be kept at the basement stop and every other call on it was overridden. Not only would it stick at the basement but it could be stuck there with its doors open or closed. So Timmy the Teddy would get the girl and the lift to the basement, lock the lift in position, and go to work. One hand down blouse, one hand up skirt. One mouth doing kisses of Olympic slobber all the while.

I said why didn't they knee him in the crotch and the girl who was telling me said that 'knee in the crotch' was just a phrase and she knew no girl who had actually ever done it to a man.

There are classes that teach you how to do it, backways or frontways, she said (I haven't worked that one out yet) but a newcomer to Goggins who is fifteen or sixteen and caught in the lift for the very first time with this mauling marauder isn't going to think or act knee-in-the-crotch.

She said the more experienced girls knew better than to get in the lift with him.

I got absolutely furious and said they should all sue him, but they got so scared of that whole area I left it alone.

I did decide, though, that I was not going to avoid the lift with Mr Quigley and that if he laid a finger on me I was going to go to court, because I knew my parents would support me in this. In fact, I was in the lift with him on my own about eight times and he never moved from his side of the lift, behaved with total courtesy and talked about the weather.

I'd love to hit him. It is no fun to be unattractive enough to be passed over by a known sexual harasser.

That's one half of my summer relationships story. The other half is even more annoying. I am becoming a confidante. The middle Goggin son, for example, is having a tough time with his girlfriend at the moment, and in the canteen every second day, would sit down with me and confide it. He is not the only one. If someone goes out of their way to invite me to coffee or lunch or to find a quiet place in a pub to sit down with me, I know what's coming. It is always some confided details about their marital or extra-marital unhappiness, and my role is not to replace/supplant the one complained about, but to let them talk and convince them that they are sensitive/warm/loving/understanding/fill in the gaps yourself and that the fault is all on the other side and she should be grateful she has such a good mate/boyfriend/husband instead of always whinging.

It is a kind of downmarket Other Woman role. The Other Dustbin. The Other Garbage Disposal. The Other Confessional. Jesus, I hate it.

I have written myself into good humour again and look forward to hearing from you.

Yours confusedly
Darcy

Entry in Sophia's diary

Saturday 15 October 1983
In six years' time, I wish (change to 'plan'; it makes me more responsible for achieving it) to be an executive in a leading public relations consultancy.

Five years after that, or sooner, I plan to run either that agency or my own, and to be branching out into Europe.

I plan to serve on the boards of one major financial institution and one art gallery.

I should be married by my mid-twenties, and have two children before my thirties.

I plan to be the best professional in the world of communications by the time I am thirty-five and to be recognised as such.

Action: start finding out information about PR companies. Procrastination is the thief of time. I have failed to get moving on this.

Word for today: *sophistry*.

Definition: fallacious reasoning.

5345 Tradewinds Ave., #283
Fort Attic
Missouri
MO 33003
2 November 1983

Dear Darcy

When I embarked upon this correspondence project I had some expectation that it might be intriguing. For the most part, it has turned out to be somewhat mundane, with the exception of your letters. Your latest and most abusive to hand.

Having absorbed the abuse, which took me some time, I reread my last letter to you and yes, I have to admit it's a beaut. In protecting the protocols of this study I am being needlessly formal. I can, as I discovered through rereading the letter, be pompous without knowing it.

OK. You mentioned some time ago that I wouldn't know what the Gaeltacht was. I do, you know. I lived in Philadelphia for a time. In the early days of this century, there were Irish speaking areas – Gaeltachts – in Philadelphia.

Which brings me to a recurring question, which is about my age. (The last paragraph could imply that I lived in Philadelphia in the early days of this century.) I am twenty-eight. I married in my final year of college. My wife is an anthropologist. We do not have children.

I genuinely was not trying to be off-putting when I told you my height etc. Women are the group, outside of professions like police officers, most accustomed to describing *people*. I do not think much about my appearance and rarely have to describe myself, so I am unpractised rather than obscurantist. Starting at the top, I have heavy coarse black hair without shine. I have very dark brown eyes and a nose which was broken three times, so takes its own course down my face. My skin, due to adolescent acne, is the texture of one of those fried apple pies in McDonald's. (You have McDonald's in Ireland?)

I was an athlete in college but eventually had to stop playing football because of a bum knee. Since then I ride horses, weight-lift a bit. Swim occasionally.

I also hunt, which, to borrow your own phrase, gets up your nose.

Someone once described prostitution as the oldest profession. Not true. Hunting is the oldest profession and arguably the most skillful, demanding and responsible.

To be the hunter for the family in primeval times (and none of the evidence precludes women from this role) meant that you were close to what was then, literally, 'domestic economy'.

Because you had few satisfactory methods of storing what you killed, you had to pursue food at all times of the year, including those times when most of your prey was hibernating. So it was the hunters, not the gatherers or the home-makers, who first learned the majestic sequences of the seasons and the varied (often seasonal) behaviour of animals, birds and fish.

Before humankind drew on the walls of caves, they hunted. Before they could create and wear decorated clothes, they hunted. If you look at the wall-paintings in Lascaux, they sum up a truth about hunting which carries through to the present day. The figures of the humans in the cave paintings are – proportionally – tiny and insignificant compared to the great animals that they are hunting. It is only by numbers that the little stick figures can hope to force the great animals to their knees. But it is not just that the humans are rendered at small scale. They are rendered without individuality, without differentiating detail, whereas the animals are rendered in their totality, with muscle, flesh, scale, hide, horns and attitude. There is a connotation of speed and massive power, an acknowledgement of the grace and the importance of the animal.

The artists in the prehistoric cave paintings never portray the animals in any but a respectful way. They never cut them up or destroy them, because, as hunter-artists, the animals had a hold on their souls as live objects of terrifying scale and mystic power.

If you think about it, there was very little in the lives of prehistoric man that was not of human scale – if it moved.

Today, we are used to hugeness in man-made moving machines like trains and planes. When we are awed by scale, it may be the scale of something like a 747. In prehistoric times, the only objects of power and movement which were bigger than people were the animals they hunted. The relative awe, therefore, must have been enormous.

The hunter, obviously, had to be physically fit.

But he had to develop a great physical stillness, too, read the wind, get downwind of animals like deer, and stay flexibly still for hours on end. These days, hunters, particularly in movies, are frequently portrayed as gun-totin' violent loudmouthed rednecks, but this misses the collective silences that hunting demands.

Hunters talk about their kill and they admire a shooter who does a clean job. They rarely talk about the beauty of the experience but for many of them, the hunting season and the few weekends when they get into a borrowed pick-up and go someplace where they can lie low in cattails waiting for blue-winged teal amount to their main experience of beauty, year long. The rest of the year is work, baseball on TV, but this is a time when they are together but separate, communicating but silent, waiting to kill but wondering at the beauty of the thing to be killed, surrounded by bird song and insect song, their senses – skin, smell, hearing, everything – overwhelmed, subsumed by nature.

The environmental movement speaks to hunters in a very special way, because without hunters there would be no conservation of certain species. Look at your own country. Ireland is a great fishing country – but it is the need to attract fisherfolk that will keep your rivers and lakes clean and stocked, not the kindly thoughts of the anti-blood-sports people.

The Seattle experience was disturbing. Seattle has been one of the great centers of the aviation industry for perhaps thirty years. Boeing is here and others. However, the demand has dropped, and the involvement of computers and robotics has increased, creating unprecedented wastage within the industry. The job losses affect craftspeople who are highly skilled and whose identity as individuals is often tied up with their skill, their track record and with the culture and public performance of the corporation to which they belong.

The program I was supervising was designed initially to assess the personal damage caused by this wastage and then to develop training programs to enable at least some of the people who have lost their jobs to cope, to pick up and move on. One of the problems we found was a tendency to pick up and move on without new coping skills. This is leading to a pattern of movement whereby a forty-year-old engineer may leave Seattle having spent the previous fifteen years working for Boeing. He has a family and may need to sell up and go someplace else. Where he goes, he finds that his engineering skills may be too precisely aligned with aeronautics to make him readily employable in his new location, and, having undergone no retraining, he is unsure that he can ever rejig his skills to new demands. Instead, he typically will opt for some lower-skilled makeweight job, such as janitorial work. A number of consequences flow from such a decision. His income falls, and this may put the family under pressure. He may do some moon-lighting to supplement a diminished income. This, in turn, will diminish the possibility that he will undergo a retraining program to upgrade and redirect his skills. In effect, what we are witnessing is often the erosion of family identity and control.

So that's what I was doing in Seattle.

There is one last question you raised, I don't know how seriously, about the experience of being eaten by a lion. There is an anecdote on record, but I cannot find the citation for it, which illustrates this point. It concerns Dr Livingstone, the nineteenth-century Scottish explorer in Africa who discovered the Zambezi river. At some point in his explorations, he was attacked by a lion which fastened its jaws on his shoulder, lifted him off the ground, and shook him vigorously before one of his companions managed to shoot the animal dead. (This was untypical behaviour: the lion had been wounded in an earlier encounter.)

Livingstone subsequently wrote that within seconds of the animal's teeth fastening on him, and during the time he was being shaken as a cat might shake a mouse, he had no panic whatever, but a powerful sensation of both passivity and distance, which vanished when the animal was shot and collapsed. Perhaps this sensation of passivity and distance is what generates the lack of fight in some prey when their predator fastens upon them: there may be an hormonal response which readies the animal for destruction.

There is no need for me to make any comment on the personal relationship material you are sending me, other than to say I hope you continue to do so. You combine a high level of self-observation and a capacity to be anecdotal which will be very useful to the final publication.

I look forward to your next letter.

Yours sincerely

Alex

PS Po-faced? Query?

Postcard, 10 November 1983

Po

My father's definition – 'A now obsolete personal portable privy.'

My mother's definition – 'A pot to piss in.'

Darcy

Postcard, 18 November 1983

Thank you re 'po'. I forgot to ask. What's 'Womble'?
A. C. B.

Postcard 26 November 1983

British puppets with faces like uncircumcised penises. Assuming you have a thwarted dirty mind like mine. Twenty-eight?! You are roughly *twice* my age.

Darcy

CHAPTER EIGHT

Sophia's Diary, Wednesday 5 September 1984

This is the beginning of my last year of school. The important year. I am on course, I know, to achieve a good Leaving Certificate and get into university, but I have doubts that Darcy will. She did not do well in the end of term exams but I am trying not to interfere in her life and we are getting along much better than we used to.

I don't know why this is. It's as if the distances between us are what's bringing us closer together. That does not make sense . . . I did not tell Darcy about the Gaeltacht and I know that when someone from the class tried to tell her, she wouldn't listen, and that makes me so grateful. That she would protect something for me that she doesn't know exists. Or existed. Similarly, the fact that I am *not* trying to improve Darcy any more seems to make her more affectionate to me and I don't notice any great disimprovement because of me pulling back, although she is not thin and her exams were not great.

We were in Paris with the school. It was beautiful. The Hall of Mirrors in Versailles was the most beautiful experience. I just wished I was in an eighteenth-century gown. (Darcy said to be surrounded by floor-to-ceiling mirrors was pure hell.)

It happened in Paris, too, something I dread. I will be walking along and I'll catch a side or a back view of someone and for one fleeting second I am so sure it is Ruaidhrí and then the person turns the full way, or just as I start to run to meet him the realisation sets in. Once I raised my hand and Darcy immediately looked to see who I was gesturing towards.

The awful thing is that I cannot recall him except in descriptions. I can't imagine him. The other awful thing is that I can remember what happened but I cannot remember loving him. I know I did, but I cannot imagine again what it was like. I know I am quite different, but all I can remember are the facts. This is a lack in me. But realistically, why am I desperate to remember what he was like? There will never be anybody I can tell it to.

Thursday 6 September 1984

Dear Alex

I thought that once I got familiar with typing I would be drowning you in opinion, sounding off and so on but this summer I hadn't the time.

No, I wasn't in the Gaeltacht.

I was in Paris.

I had hoped to pick up little bits of French to replace the Americanisms I pick up from reading your letters. You should know they get me into trouble in two places.

My English teacher, who is a clueless brain-dead pink person who thinks that creative mapping is how you turn a classful of thicks into a classful of creative writers, picks the Americanisms out of my essays like (that's one of them, I should say 'as if' or 'the way you would') they are dead flies that got baked into a cake in mistake for raisins. The other place where they got me into trouble was when I submitted a feature (does that sound casual or wha'?) to an evening paper here. Newspaper. The editor of the page sent it back with a compliment slip indicating: a) it was peppered with Americanisms (he is an isolationist curly turd and I hope blue-bottles the size of sheep settle on him) and b) he didn't need any more serious stuff. If I felt like doing something funny, I should let him see it. I felt like a fat flop.

I must take that back. I am reading a very feminist book at the moment and it says I must never diet again because fat is a feminist issue and I must not prostitute myself to the perceptions of others by scrunching myself down to a size fourteen.

Enough of this self-absorbed crap. You don't have to look at my spare tyres, so why am I drawing attention to them? And please, don't – not that you ever do – don't get a rush of sympathy to the head and tell me that you really fancy truly huge women. Did you know that there's a book about people like that? They go to fat women's clubs to pick up women and if the women go on diets they have their marriages annulled, assuming they got hitched to them when they were satisfactorily ginormous. Jesus, what kind of creepy thin guy would be turned on by great fat women? Not many, if my personal experience is anything to go by.

A thought occurs to me. I mention annulment all casually in the middle of that last bit, and it may hit you like a kick in the solar plexus. Does it? You mentioned in your Easter letter that you had separated: every time you hear about divorce do you take it personally and feel destroyed? I am sorry if I am invading an area you don't want invaded.

Where the hell was I?

Oh, yes, how busy I have been. I decided that this was the summer that I would get de-virginised or come pretty damn close to it, because it is quite ridiculous to have two nearly-seventeen-year-old virgins in one house in (all together now) this day and age. My entire class, my peers, my compatriots are all hard at it, it seems to me, all the time.

Sophia is pure as the driven slush because Sophia believes in virginity. (Give her her due, she has never said any of this to me. I am projecting like fair hell. Sort of projectile vomiting of attributed saintliness. She is much nicer than I am letting you think – wonder why I do this.)

Sophia comes back from her dates and her swain leave her up the path. The ones that just open the car door for her are never let within a hundred square miles of our house ever again, although half the time they didn't know that was one of her most basic requirements, to be left to the front door and to have her swine civil to my parents. They come to me subsequently, but I'll get to that. Anyway, Sophia will come up the path and will open the front door, before or after a chaste kiss, and the guy will go back down the path on a wave of asexual euphoria.

None of the guys would dare a grope. In fact it is my personal belief that they don't even let themselves *think* of grope because the thought would pollute the wonder of their relationship with Ireland's Teenager of Most Potential.

That, by the way, was the headline of an article that got written about Sophia recently. She went along with some of our class to a television programme and was picked out of the audience to be interviewed. She looked absolutely gorgeous and was very calm and in control. All sorts of people wrote it up. Mainly, I suspect, people like my father, because, if he *wasn't* Sophia's father and therefore used to her, he would be watching this TV programme and saying to himself 'all is not lost, the younger generation still have goals/values/pretty faces/respect for their elders/Biblical references and the capacity to say several paragraphs without dirty language'. The article about Sophia mentioned – because *she* mentioned – that she had a twin, but the tone of it was more or less: 'we have the pretty one here, throw the fat one back.'

If Sophia decides no sex, no sex there will be. No sex will even be thought about. If I decide no sex, no sex there will be, but that's mainly because nobody's lining up to have sex with me. There is a complete and total dearth of aspirant partners. A desert of de-virginisers. A forest of non-ticking cocks. Now, I didn't say all of this in precisely those terms to my mother, but I did register, in a casual, throwaway kind of manner, my teeth deeply sunk in the carpet, that my self-esteem and morale weren't so bubbling that I was standing in the overflow.

Ma, I have no boyfriend, I said. I have no near-boyfriend. Nobody loves me. Nobody fancies me. I do not attract men. I will never attract men. I will go through life a hairy hefty spinsterised heifer, barren as a brick, unloved, unwanted and untouched.

She took her book back up as if I had been an interruption.

'Darcy,' she said, very formally, as if I were several people gathered for a lecture. It was un-nerving. I am used to being vast, but I am not often plural. 'Darcy, any woman can attract any man she wants to.'

She said that men were superficially attracted by looks and that anyway there was nothing wrong with my looks. Go pull the other one, Ma. She then got quite personal and said that if I would ever *decide* what weight I was and dress accordingly and stop making everybody's life a misery, I'd have a hell of a better time.

This, I presume, is provoked by the fact that

when I am truly bulbous, like right now, I feel that I am not fit for human consumption or company and certainly not for expenditure of any money. So I live in shapeless edge-to-edge jackets and elastic-waist trousers and look, she says, like a sack tied in the middle. You're the sociologist. Have you identified the fat woman's edge-to-edge twitch? It's that gesture that happens every minute and a half with fat women, where they twitch their jackets across the rolling pampas of their oversized boobs in the fallacious hope that this will cause the rest of the jacket to fall straight from the legitimate shelf of their womanhood and give viewers the supposition that, due south of the boobs, the jacket-wearer falls away to practically nothing and has a waist like an hour-glass. The edge-to-edge twitch is one of several distinctive body language pieces confined to this species.

Another of these distinctive movements is the bottom tweak. This is the surreptitious use of the hand, preferably when one has one's back to a wall, to pull the vast acreage of cloth in one's slacks out of the crack of one's ass, where these acres have been trapped by the vast encroaching rounded cheeks of said ass.

If the bottom tweak is done on the sly, how about the hem tug? This is done by overweight women wearing jumpers. (Sweaters, to you.) These sweaters have a ribby bit to make them fit snugly around the hips of normal people. However, because the hips of us abnormals are so vast, the ribbing rides up, doesn't it? So whenever we stand up, we do this little circular neatening, pulling down the ribbing in the never-delivered-on hope that the jumper, pulled down, will minimise the expanse of bottom more than slacks alone.

I have nice hands, do you know that? Small, white, pretty hands. Even when I am at my worst, there are these little hands, narrow wrists.

Back to my mother. My mother said that if I bothered myself even a bit, I could *physically* attract any man I wanted, that men are attracted by a coherent, well-planned *look,* meaning sort of overall rig-out and stuff, just as much as they are by conventional beauty. Phrases like conventional beauty really take me to the fair. It's like saying 'conventional millionaire'. She then said that apart from the looks bit, what men really went for was someone who paid them some attention. And they really liked someone funny. She said this in a QED tone, meaning that I am funny, therefore men are lining up in the street outside our house, panting in their need to have me. I must be just short-sighted or something. The final thing she said was that any woman could make any group of men focus on her completely if she just decided to do it. I thought this was so daft I didn't even argue about it, and although I was very tempted to ask questions about her and my father, I didn't.

I decided to try it out over the summer. It was easier than going on another diet. Here, in order, are my results.

Boyfriend 1

Invited me to a party he was giving while his widowed mother was away. The food consisted of meatballs fast-browned in oil and then baked for ever in an oven in a huge pot with sauce and pasta. I helped him to serve it and when everybody was well fed and (bluntly) pissed as newts, I danced with him in his sitting-room with about eight other couples, which was ridiculous, because his sitting-room is so small all we could do was stand in the same positions and move up and down. Which, having a dirty mind, I thought might be efficacious.

After a fair bit of moving up and down, he brought me into his bedroom, which smelled like he was breeding his old socks as a controlled experiment, but who am I to criticise. Sat me on the bed. Sat down opposite me. Told me how much he loved Sophia. I am sitting there, wanting to say, 'You gormless gobshite, you, with your smelly bedroom and your pointless joggling up and down, you have turned me into a waitress for a night for the privilege of hearing yet another hopeless case yatter on about my twin?' But the next thing is he cries. O, God. Not only does he cry, but he puts his head down in my lap to do it. So what do I do? You got it in one. (Another Americanism). I stroke his hair gently. (Well, I couldn't go rake rake rake, could I? I did think of stabbing him through the ear, Mafia fashion, with a pen, only there wasn't a pen handy and although the socks that were present were stiffish, they didn't look like they amounted to stabbing implements.)

When he had cried himself out (that *is* the phrase, isn't it? I'm new to this, remember) I decided I would see how much ham acting this market could take. So I lifted his face up and I palmed the tears from his swollen eyes, I swear to God I did, and I told him that Sophia had nothing against him personally (she will have when I tell her the smell of his bedroom) but that she was resolute that she was not going to have a stable relationship with any one man in this final year of school. Even, I said, gently shaking his shoulder (go on, throw up, it's allowed) someone as sweet and – *sensitive* as him.

At this point, the awful thing was that my mother's law began to come true. Because I was paying attention to the wanker and calling him (pause) 'sensitive' he was swelling before my eyes, although not in any area that could have been of use to me. He was just *thrilled* with himself. Honoured to be cast out of Sophia's sled for reasons of her personal independence. He'd have been happy to talk the night away. Could I have, in the process, converted him to adoring me?

The awful answer is probably yes, if I was prepared to invest enough time mopping, flattering and listening to bilge being pumped. Life is too effing short. He sent me an appreciative little note.

Boyfriend 2

Was a farmer from Cork. He was up for the Horse Show. Now, you don't know Cork, but they talk in up-and-down inflections that give a terrifically light-hearted tone to their conversation. So I was misled, when I met head-the-ball at a party, into thinking he was a sunny, optimistic and even entertaining guy. After three dates, during which he told me the price of everything, including the square footage rental of the restaurant we were in, I told him I wouldn't be seeing him again. Oh, the sheer pleasure of saying 'Don, I've enjoyed being with you (lie) but I won't be seeing you again.' First time I ever got the chance. It was nearly worth all the prices to get to say it.

He was extremely taken aback, having, on this third date, got to the point of kissing me with his hand on my bottom, the better to press my pelvis against his.

I didn't have any particular objection to this pelvis-pressing, in fact rather liked it, but prices followed by pelvis-pressing do not a relationship make. He then got quite shirty and said did I realise how much it had cost him to drive from Cork and stay overnight in a B&B each time he had come to see me. I couldn't figure what this had to do with it, except perhaps that if he had known I was going to can him after three goes, he wouldn't have invested in the petrol. I asked him did he usually get reimbursements on such expenditure and he then got really mad and marched off down to his little Fiesta as if it were a tank and he was going to run over me with it and leave track marks on me.

Boyfriend 3

Was quite old. Very nearly thirty. Had a scattered niceness to him. Wasn't pretending to be anything much, drove a beat-up old Saab and when I said something about it, didn't give me a big long line about how good or safe it was. Just said would I go to the pictures with him some evening. Which I did. Three times. During the third, he got down to it a bit. The arm came over my shoulder and then his head was over near me and a bit of kissing got going.

Hey, I am getting kissed, are you paying attention, Mr Bloodless Academic with the Initials?

Because I have no experience, I do not know whether he is a good kisser or a bad kisser, but I do pay studious attention to his progress, which is slow, him being a gentleman and the film being a distraction.

The progress consists of him getting his hands inside my cardigan. He puts them squarely on my spare tyre, and I have *such* a desire to knee him in the crotch. I may be the only female in cinema audience history who has wanted hands on her boobs simply in order to get them the hell off a roll of fat lower down.

So I squiggle a bit in the seat and he interprets this as passion and gets his hands where they should be. Then I realise that there is no finger involvement in all of this. He is palming his way around my boobs in the semi-darkness the way I palmed my way around Sensitive Man's tears. The association strikes me as very funny and I laugh. Nobody had told me that having given a squiggle which has been understood to mean that one is randy to the point of riot, it is then extremely offensive to whoever it is thinks their palms are arousing you to new heights to give a happy little reminiscent laugh.

The guy got desperately hurt and huffy. Sat looking at the screen as if it held the secrets of life, palms plastered to each other between his thighs.

So there I am, no longer finding the association between his sexual style and Number 1's hysteria as funny as it seemed when I first made the association, and wondering what I should do to put him back in good humour. Revelation. There in the cinema, it came to me: Darcy, you don't *have* to put him in good humour or re-randify him or anything. You have money in your pocket for the bus home, and it's a very short walk to the bus stop. The sense of freedom was wonderful. I leaned across to him and he turned on me one of those wounded-but-willing looks.

'I'm off,' I said, filled with the cheeriness of my own freedom. 'Have a good one.'

I was particularly pleased with that last as an 'out' line, because of its lack of specificity or controlling instincts. I didn't care what he had a good one of, he should just have a good one. Which is what I wish for him, him and his spearminty kisses and pat-a-boob palms. More power to him, he's a nice guy.

I leave you as I shagging left you the last million times I wrote to you. Virginal.

Darcy

CHAPTER NINE

'*OOOK*, then,' the black-jacketed man said, pushing his hands into the back pockets of his jeans and rocking to and fro on the soles of his boots. 'Access broadcasting, first of all. Access broadcasting is community broadcasting. Open door broadcasting. Broadcasting by real people, as opposed to broadcasters.'

I hate you too, you patronising wanker, Darcy thought. You're like those shitty politicians who talk about 'the punters on the doorsteps', meaning the voters.

'What we're interested in,' the TV producer went on, 'is not just giving a voice to people who too often are marginalised by society, disenfranchised and left voiceless – '

Socialist, Sophia thought, disapprovingly. Socialists, in her view, missed the point of the Biblical comment 'The poor always you have with you.' Socialists wanted to abolish the poor, forgetting their usefulness as an object-lesson for the rest of humankind. The twins had recently had a knock-down, drag-out row about this. Darcy told her sister that she was a Bible-belt tub-thumping capitalist. Sophia demanded proof that Darcy had actually read anything by Karl Marx other than the crack about religion being the opiate of the people.

' – we're also interested in seeing what people who have not been schooled in television come up with: what a fresh eye can bring to the television production dynamic.'

Bloody nonsense, Darcy thought. There *are* no people who 'have not been schooled in television'. Everybody in this classroom has been schooled by television just by looking at it. We know the rules and the formulae.

'So what we're doing is a pilot,' the black-garbed man went on. 'What we're doing is a pilot and we've selected eight schools.'

He named them. Good schools, Sophia thought approvingly: four in Dublin, one in Cork, one in Limerick, and two provincial boarding schools.

'The programme produced by this school has its TX date on 3 March,' he said. 'Oh, sorry. TX is transmission.'

And cans are headphones, Darcy thought sourly. Go on, impress us naïve kids to death with a bit more jargon.

It was at this moment that Darina Quinlivan threw up and fainted. Sophia, who was sitting beside her, had a moment's admiration at the timing, neatness and speed of the two actions. Darina threw up in one direction and fainted in the other. The RTE man looked affronted, as if this were a particularly crude form of inattention. Aileen was out of her desk before anybody else moved, and was on the floor beside Darina. She put the unconscious girl's head to one side and wiped her mouth with tissues.

'The room next door is empty at the moment,' Sophia told the producer. Relieved to be removed from the smell and the crisis, he nodded gravely as if moving were the bravest and most conscientious of several options open to him, gathered his leather jacket and went. Half the class followed him immediately. Half dithered.

'Anybody who's staying should clean up that puke,' Aileen said. Most of the stayers became goers. Darcy mopped up the vomit. Aileen instructed another student to get Miss Burke and stayed kneeling beside Darina. Darcy moved closer to them.

'Will she come around?'

Aileen nodded at Darcy. As if on cue, Darina began to move and struggle to sit up. Darcy waited for her to ask where she was. That, in books, was what fainters always did: open their eyes and say, 'Where am I?' Darina, however, seemed to be in no doubt as to where she was.

'Oh, *no*,' she said vehemently. 'Who did you tell?'

'Miss Burke's on her way. She's not one of the mouth-almighty brigade,' Aileen said. 'I figured . . .'

'Oh, *no*,' Darina said again, by way of an affirmative.

'How far are you along?' asked Aileen.

'Two missed. I don't know.'

Darcy sat quietly, only beginning to understand. Darina Quinlivan isn't exactly *Playboy* centrefold material, but she's been Doing It and I never knew. She's never looked any different.

'Darcy, thank you for the clean-up, but you should probably go next door,' Aileen said. 'If there's only one of us around when Burkey gets here, it's probably better, and you can't be put under any pressure to tell secrets.'

Darcy nodded, fascinated by Aileen's authority. She and Sophia left together.

Next door, the RTE man filled the whiteboard with sketches of who did what on a production team. As he talked, Darcy worked out the hierarchy. Producer: Boss. Production Assistant: Producer's gopher. Presenter: star.

'I would suggest that you allocate responsibilities as quickly as possible,' the man in black told them. 'We would need to hear from you in about two to three weeks and get some indication from you as to the shape of the programme you're planning, any training or information that you might need from us in order to achieve your objectives, so on and so forth. We would also need names and phone numbers of your key people.'

Someone started a half-hearted round of applause, which caught him halfway to the door and brought an embarrassed laugh from him. Then he was gone.

It was absolutely clear to Sophia that she, Sophia, had to be the producer. Not for any reasons of personal gratification but because there was nobody else in the class capable of providing the over-arching sense of direction the RTE man had talked about.

In the event, the choice was painlessly made, since those with television ambitions tended to want to be in front of the camera rather than tinkering with the administrative workings behind the camera. Ten minutes after the beginning of the class, Sophia was producer, Meena Holt was production assistant, and a production team of eight had been chosen.

'Now, we need to work out what kind of programme we want to make,' Sophia said, with a slightly theatrical hands-out gesture. From various sides of the room came suggestions. A sports programme. A documentary on how the first world was dumping its toxic waste on the third world. A quiz. A chat show. A documentary on *something*. Sophia sat silent while jeers and disqualifiers were hurled within the group. How the hell could you film in the third world? What about the non-sports addicts? Nobody ever did a once-off quiz? What about teenage pregnancy, someone offered. What *about* it, someone else said. There's more of it about than there used to be and they keep the babies. So?

Darcy worked out when Darina would have her baby and figured it would coincide neatly with the Leaving Certificate. I wonder, she thought, if the Department of Education allows students to sit certain sections of the Leaving in a maternity ward? You get extra points for doing subjects in Irish – maybe you get extra points for producing a baby mid-paper. If the Department of Health cooperated with the Department of Education, there might even be still more points for breastfeeding.

'It mightn't be a bad idea,' Sophia said, 'if we did a programme about our own school – a programme that did some good for the school. Given that this is our final year.'

It was said with the vagueness Darcy knew to be typical of Sophia's opening salvos in a campaign she had no intention of losing. It might take the rest of the production team some time to agree about this idea but eventually they would, and Sophia would make sure that they all believed it to have been their very own idea. Public relations for the school, Darcy thought.

Not only public relations for the school, but a – what

was the phrase the RTE man had used? – a 'demo tape' which would prove to any prospective employer what a good little PR person Sophia would be.

CHAPTER TEN

17 Glanmire Park
Raheny
Dublin 5
Saturday 6 October 1984

Dear Alex

This is by way of fending you off, because at any moment one of your mini-questionnaires is going to surface, so I might as well get in first.

No I haven't. Done It. But one of the girls in my class sure as hell has, though, because she is up the spout. Bun in the oven. Proliferating. Or as one of the ladies with whom I attend school said, 'She's fucked. Been taken for a ride. Literally, both ways.'

So I thought it was time to let you know about vicarious experience. Living dangerously at one remove.

Facts, first. Darina is the girl who is *enceinte*. I say Darina and because Darina is a pretty name, you think pretty girl. Forget it. Forget her. Well, no, don't forget her, because she is the case study to which we are currently giving our joint attention. (Did that last bit grab your academics at all?) But the point is that Darina is just about the most forgettable person you will ever meet. She doesn't even get interesting *spots*. I mean, there's one girl in my class, and she does spots the way other people do flower arranging. She gets them in clusters. She gets them in the parting of her hair. She gets them nestled for shelter behind her ears. She gets them chummily clumped in that little depression above the nostril. She never pops them, either. That, I

138

simply can't understand. The minute I get a spot, which is mostly in the week before my period, I can't wait to get home, get into the bathroom and pop it, clean it off with Dettol.

The thought of going around with little yellow unerupted volcanoes on my face . . .

The fact that Darina never gets many spots does not mean she's attractive. She's not even interestingly unattractive, which is how I'd describe myself. You would at least notice me. You wouldn't notice Darina. She's not ostentatiously silent, not ostentatiously assertive or loud or interesting, just there. *Now*, nobody can take their eyes off her, greatly helped by her being into maternity clothes already, which, given the fact that she's only about ten weeks gone, doesn't really reflect the reality. It's as if she has suddenly become someone as a result of being pregnant and she wants everybody to notice the someone she has become. I'll tell you, *I* notice her. So do all our parents. There may have been pregancies here in the history of our school our school, but they were hushed up. Their owners didn't turn up for class every day the same as the rest of us. I was kidding myself that most of my class were as innocent (in the sense of Not Doing It) as I am, and now I discover that the least sexy, most forgettable of the whole lot was At It.

I feel a complete and utter asswipe. Some fella fancied Darina enough to bonk her several times, because you don't usually get caught the first time. (For this bit of folk wisdom, I am indebted to a girl named Faith Randall, who also says that Cling Film will do instead of a condom. *Cling Film? Oh God*. (You can't get condoms in Ireland.) I have been unable to use Cling Film ever since. Instead, anything I want to preserve gets encased in tinfoil.

Our fridge looks like it's full of obscure weaponry.) The fella involved with Darina is quite presentable, too. Wouldn't set the pulse racing and the heart beating, maybe, but I'm beginning to think that if it's male and can walk upright, sooner or later it's going to set my pulse racing because I am getting so old and so untouched I'm unlikely to be choosy.

The odd thing is that Darina's pregnancy opened up yet more areas of sexuality about which I am dumb as a tree. We were all standing around during the days she was absent, having thrown up on the floor and fainted on my sister and the general thrust (here we go again into double-meanings) of the conversation was that she must have wanted to get preggers because nobody, but *nobody* doesn't know how to prevent it these days.

Even me. I know the theory but I've never met a condom. Nor the need to use one. That's the real problem. Let's assume I was equipped with condoms. Let's assume I was going out with some person of the other sex. Let's assume he plonks a companionable hand on my boob. Or on both boobs. (Different hands, OK?) Is it at that point that I produce condoms and say, 'Get that on your penis'? I can't figure it. I've tried all sorts of phrases in my head. 'D'you think you could?' said smilingly, condom a-dangle from an index finger, doesn't trip off the tongue. Not off mine, anyway. 'Have you thought of — ?' invites the guy to say he hasn't, because he wasn't thinking of sex anyway, this boob-plonking was just friendly. 'Put this on or I won't go one step further,' isn't an approach calculated to improve the erotic atmosphere of the evening. Anyway, he might do his boob-plonking in the cinema or in the dark in a back lane.

There's also the possibility that he might have

brought his own (condoms) and would think me terribly over-involved, not to say a bossy britches, if I produced mine.

Or he might be a shrinking violet who'd be put off his stroke, you should pardon the expression, by my producing the thing. I have this awful feeling that if I ever got near to that stage, which it looks like I'm not going to get near, I might be at the point of no return, like a plane on a runway, before I could stick a windsock on his whatsit.

I listen to all these cool dudes in my class, me trying to look bored as if bonking was something I did in second year and really didn't have that much time for any more, while at the same time, I'm listening out for any hint of answers to the questions nobody ever really answers: like how many times do happy compatible people do it?

You read in one book that they're at it three and four times a night, and then you read about people only doing it maybe once in three weeks. Maybe in the beginning you need to do it a lot to get it right? Or alternatively, you can't get enough of it, but once you get the hang of it, you don't need to do it quite as often.

But what happens if you don't go off it and your partner does? The humiliation of being mad for it when the other half has downed tools. (Oops.)

The fact that I have to write these reports presents you with this picture of a sex-mad, lying, eavesdropping fat flunker, which I am not. When I think about going off sex, for instance, you will think this is utterly silly, since I've never had even a taste of it, so far, but what I am really wondering about is the whole thing of going off people and places and preferences.

I never thought, for example, that I could go off

Mars Bars, but after three weeks on the Mars Bar diet I get shuddery at the thought of another one of them. They have a sweet gloopiness to them now that I cannot bear, and instead I want lemon soufflé. You might not think there was a diet based on lemon soufflé, but I'm reading a book at the moment which says that satiety is the spice of life.

If you're prepared to eat the thing you like best and nothing else at all, for a whole week, this diet book says you will lose weight. So if lemon soufflé was your preference, you would have lemon soufflé for breakfast, lunch and dinner. Snacks, even. You couldn't eat anything else for a week. Similarly if your favourite food was chips (french fries to you). You'd have to eat them all the time. I don't know about that as a prospect. If one Mars Bar a day can turn me off Mars Bars for good, as I suspect it has, but not lose me any weight, then I'm not sure that's the way to go.

I go off people, too. I find them interesting until I really know them and then they bore me. I suppose that's why, although I'm not crazy about being a twin, I still have a regard for Sophia, because I don't really know her. In some senses, she is obvious, limited and predictable, but in others she is mysterious and very skilled at preventing me get near to the privacies at the back of her personality. To say that she is 'obvious, limited and predictable' sounds desperately arrogant, and I am tempted to strike it out but I suppose I can be honest with you, because you're never going to be a real live person I'll have to cope with.

Although I am very unsure of myself and constantly ashamed of the way I look and the disgusting piggy way I gorge food into myself, cramming buns into my mouth and licking the sugariness off my hand, stuffing myself past the point of decency and self-respect but never to the point where greed says 'enough', although I am like that and ashamed of it, nonetheless I have a huge arrogance. Maybe everybody has it secretly and nobody lets on about it.

I am centre-stage in my own life. It is as if my parents were only precursors. I have to almost remind myself that they have a life of their own and that they see themselves as centre-stage in their own lives with me and Sophia as successors.

Here's the really arrogant bit: not only am I centre-stage, but I am convinced that I *deserve* to be centre-stage. I believe I experience setbacks in a uniquely painful way, that I have a level of sensitivity and insight that isn't matched by those around me and that if I am ever to be loved, I need an exceptional love, a love that is magnificent, that is worth waiting for, that will be running through long grass to Mozart, romantic, slow-motioned in pastel muslins, that will be so passionate that my breath will catch in a sob in my throat when he puts his hand on me.

Again, I read the paragraph I have just typed and I think: Jesus *Christ*, this is written by a puddingy nonentity in Leaving Cert year who will probably never be loved by anybody but some frightful freckle-fat-faced baldycoot with piles who will have bitten nails.

If you could just have sex a few times, to know what it was really like, you'd be in a much better position to decide on the men that go with it. If you knew that it didn't amount to anything much, you could get on having friendships, instead of having them complicated by sexual possibilities.

On the face of it, there doesn't seem much

evidence that it is exactly a transforming experience. I mean, Darina may be in maternity clothes and therefore more interesting, but when half the class is married in five years time, she won't be. Even now, she hasn't got any kind of extra glow or visible sensuality. It's like she went to Australia and the only way it shows is she brought back a boomerang. If sex is so all-fired important, why does it seem to make so little difference to people other than pregnancy? People I know who are big in the bonking department don't seem happier than people like me who suffer a complete bonking deficit.

Whenever this gets discussed at home, my parents talk about the pressures on Young People Today to have sex early and often. I smile to myself when I hear them say it, because there have been no pressures on me, except I suppose the pressure that it is unimaginable to have a celibate life these days. Is anybody else examining this area or is it just you and your academic friends?

Yours sincerely
Darcy King

5345 Tradewinds Ave., #283
Fort Attic
Missouri, MO 33003
Saturday 13 October 1984

Dear Darcy
For the past three months, I have been consulting on a small-budget movie about people in a psychiatric halfway house. You may not be aware that our president has developed a system of caring for people who are mentally ill which is called 'care within the community', but which essentially means that the institutionalised and chemical-dependent seriously ill have been released from mental hos-

pitals in huge numbers and are theoretically being taken care of within the community.

However, in the case of schizophrenia and bipolar depression, the sufferers rarely take their medication once free of duress, so what tends to happen is that, once released from the mental hospital, they speedily discontinue their medication, the illness becomes florid, and they then slip through the meshes of society to the lowest level at which they can subsist, and sometimes lower.

That was the theme of the movie, conceived as a suitable project for Robert Redford to direct. As a director, Redford selects projects on issues he finds worth exploring. His movies are not always successful at the box office, but they tend to do respectably and to garner considerable critical praise. However, in this instance, he passed, and a relative newcomer named Bob Malcolm directed. The movie was released about six weeks ago.

You will never see it in any of the mainstream movie theatres, although it has had a sufficient *succès d'estime* to suggest that it will be seen in cinema clubs for some time.

My main function, although I became involved in every aspect of the production, was to ensure the authenticity of the on-screen behaviors of the actors playing the released patients. When I first viewed the rough edit, it struck me that authenticity is the main problem. The anger of the writer is too apparent but does not involve the audience.

Those involved were still ambivalent, caught between the horror visited upon ex-patients and, through those ex-patients, on the community, and, on the other hand, the conviction that the mentally ill have the same civil rights as the rest of us unless they are a real and present danger because of violent tendencies. For the first time I begin to understand Hitchcock's comment about the necessity to treat actors like cattle. He has a point: not only do actors not need to be intellectually engaged in the debate they exemplify; intellectual engagement may inhibit their clarity of performance.

You would have enjoyed the set, however. There was a barnstorming can-do about the team – something of a culture shock for an 'elderly academic'.

Looking forward to hearing from you
Alex

Entry in Sophia's diary

Wednesday 17 October 1984
Making this television programme, I am trying very hard to work as a manager without bossing people. I use a formula, when members of the production team come to me with a problem, of saying 'What do you think, yourself, we should do?' They do not always come up with good ideas but I think it may reduce the perception of me as a know-all.

Darina's pregnancy is something of a distraction, too. All the adults are bending over backwards not to be prejudiced, which I find amusing, because nobody of our generation expects them to be prejudiced or would care that much.

In my vision for my own future, I see myself married in my early twenties and having a baby by perhaps twenty-five or twenty-six. I wonder will my mother be interested in taking care of my baby, because obviously I would not stay at home.

My new word for tomorrow is: *asthenic*.

Definition: Of, relating, to, asthenia: lacking strength: of a slender type, narrow-chested, with slight muscular development (*anthrop.*)

An extra thought: it is now October of our final year in school. I share a large bedroom with Darcy. I am in class most of the day and involved with this project as well.

It is in this context I am learning the difference between being alone and being lonely.

I am almost never alone.

I am almost always lonely.

5345 Tradewinds Ave., #283
Fort Attic
Missouri, MO 33003
Friday 26 October 1984

Dear Darcy

Our letters crossed.

First of all, your question about other people doing this kind of study of sexual habits.

The first researchers in this area were not sociologists or psychologists, such as the team driving this particular study, but biologists (Alfred Kinsey) or medical clinicians (Masters and Johnson). In this country, perhaps ten national surveys of sexual habits and attitudes were conducted in the 1950s, 1960s and 1970s, some of them examining specific segments of the population such as adolescents, or in the case of a researcher named Tanfer, women in their twenties.

Most of the work done has tended to exclude anecdotal or individual evidence.

The study to which you are contributing errs on the other side. It balances the accepted models and paradigms of social and sexual behaviors against the personal ownership of those behaviors, and emphasises the individualistic experience of sexuality.

It can be argued that social factors have profound effects on individual sexual behavior. Your letter gives a good example. Your parents are conscious of the pressures on young people to have sex 'early and often' as you put it. They are no doubt particularly conscious of that since, in their time, the moral pressure within society would have been in the opposite direction; towards eschewing pre- or extra-marital sexual activity.

The pressure on young people to have sex is not felt by you or acted upon by you. However, it is evident that teenage pregnancy within your college is an acknowledged if not routine factor, so the pressures are being responded to otherwise by other students.

Some of my colleagues (even more elderly and academic than myself) believe that a theoretical framework is essential to understand how societal factors determine or influence individual sexual behavior. The group working with me on this study, however, lean to the somewhat contrary view that only through closely monitored anecdotal evidence can a real insight be gained. With luck, by the end of the nineties, contributions from both ends of the continuum will have greatly enhanced our understanding of this area.

In one of your recent letters, you used two words with which I am not familiar: *bodhrán* and *wanker*. Also, what is a Pioneer pin?

With kind regards

Alex

Entry in Sophia's diary

Friday 26 October 1984

Instead of a word, today, I have looked up quotations regarding loneliness. These are what I have found:

> Loneliness is and always has been the central and inevitable fact of human existence.
>
> *Thomas Wolfe*
>
> Man's loneliness is but his fear of life.
>
> *Eugene O'Neill*

Neither of them is very good. I wonder if that is because they are written by men about men, because I suspect men do not suffer the kind of lifelong concealed loneliness some women do.

I mention this not in self-pity, but in observation: the great thing about having a twin like Darcy (as opposed to just having a twin or a sister) is that she is constantly providing distractions. I remember being chilled by loneliness once on the beach when we were children, and being baffled by it, because I did not then know the concept of loneliness.

That day on the beach, when I suppose we were three or four, just as I was chilled by loneliness, Darcy tried to kill a jellyfish with her spade. The noise and excitement completely removed me from the loneliness. She continues to provide that heat and action.

I must learn to provide my own distractions and causes, and to identify what are the activities which fill up my mind today, because otherwise I become overwhelmed by eternity.

I must not cheat by getting quotations. I still have to learn a new word, so today's word will be:

Nescience: want of knowledge.

Postcard from Darcy, airmail, 1 November 1984
Bodhrán: traditional leather-covered musical instrument. Sounds like a soft drum. Hand-held, played with a sort of overgrown wooden Q-tip.

Wanker: masturbator. (Wonder should I apologise

to the US post? On the other hand, they shouldn't be reading postcards sent to elderly academics in the first place.)

Pioneer Pin: badge worn on a lapel to indicate membership of the Pioneer Total Abstinence Association, a reaction against intemperance started about a hundred years ago. Sort of teetotallers for Christ. Badge has a heart on it. Christ's, I think.

Darcy

Postcard, airmail, 10 November 1984

So you could have a bodhrán-playing, Pioneer-pin-wearing wanker?

As you can see, the *mail*man overcame any objections he might have had to your terminology.

Alex

Postcard, airmail, 17 November 1984

You know how kids say to themselves 'I wonder am I adopted?' In much the same way, every now and again I have doubts that you exist. I think, 'There's a shagging computer over there programmed to absorb and respond to what I send.'

Then you prove you do exist by an outbreak of pedantry no computer could match. Furthermore, it's *mailperson*. Being an elderly academic is no excuse for sexism.

Darcy

CHAPTER ELEVEN

'You know this thing about helping any other schools do their TV programme?' Aileen burst in on Sophia and Darcy as they prepared for the programme meeting in the art room. 'Well, d'you know who's asked for help?'

'Who?'

'Belvedere.'

'Oh.' Darcy was unimpressed. 'So?'

'So one of their production team is coming in tomorrow and anybody in our year that sings has to audition for him.'

'*Has* to?'

'Well, not has to. But is asked to. Never mind that. D'you know who it is?'

'Who it is *what*?'

'Who it is that's coming from Belvedere?'

'No. Who?'

'Beethoven.'

'*Who?*'

'Nicholas Watson. You know.'

'How the hell would I know?'

'Well, Sophia knows anyway.'

Darcy looked at her twin, who seemed frozen in position.

'Who the hell is Beethoven and how do you know him and me not?'

Sophia looked queasy. 'Gaeltacht,' she said.

'Oh,' Darcy said, losing interest.

'He's going to be in the music room tomorrow at ten, and anybody with a decent voice is asked to be there.'

'He can shag off,' Darcy said.

Aileen reddened. 'What did he ever do on you?'

'Nothing,' Darcy said, bothered by her twin's silence. 'You going to audition for Beethoven tomorrow?'

'Me? No. Oh no,' Sophia replied.

'Why not?'

'I'm slightly hoarse at the moment. Anyway, it wouldn't be right for someone who's the producer in one school's programme to appear in another school's programme. But Darcy, you should, really you should. He's a very nice guy. You'd like him. I wouldn't want him to think we weren't being helpful.'

'Well, *will* you?' Aileen was insistent.

'I don't know how to sight-read,' Darcy said.

'Neither do I, but at least you have a good voice.'

'Mmm.'

'So you will?'

'OK.'

'All right, we'll go down together tomorrow.'

'You don't know where the music room is, Aileen, is that it? Need guidance and a hand under your elbow?'

'Oh, piss off, Darcy.' And she was gone.

'Now we've established two things,' Darcy said. 'We've established that Aileen fancies this Beethoven guy, and that Sophia King for some reason doesn't want to be in the same room with him, even though she says he's no harm to anybody.'

Sophia gathered her belongings slowly. 'Piece of advice to you, sister mine,' Darcy held the door open for Sophia as if Sophia was a teacher. 'When you make excuses, make them singly. One excuse is a good reason. Two excuses are a lie.'

'I didn't lie. I am hoarse, and I don't think it would be a good idea to – '

'Two excuses *seem* like a lie,' Darcy amended equably.

The following morning, she sat beside Aileen while Beethoven got eleven members of their year to sing, one after another.

'I wish I hadn't offered,' Aileen whispered to Darcy as the third last auditioner sang.

'Why?'

'I'm going to be the worst.'

'That's true.'

'Oh, *Darcy*.'

'You're only here to get re-introduced to him, who're you kidding? If he fancies you as much as you fancy him, it's not demi-quavers that're going to sink the relationship.'

Aileen stood up and sang considerably worse than usual. The young man stopped her halfway through.

'Hi, Aileen,' he said.

'Hi, Nicholas,' she said, and walked back to her seat.

Darcy walked up to the piano, gave her name and sang. He didn't let her finish, either.

'Thank you,' he said, very politely. 'Aileen?'

Aileen leaped to her feet and was back at the piano within seconds.

'Would you do me a favour?' Beethoven asked amusedly. 'Would you ask that last person to stay.'

Aileen, promoted to a speaking if not a singing role, asked Darcy to stay back.

'Do you know *"Sé Fáth Mo Bhuartha"*?' Nicholas asked her.

'No.'

'Do you read Irish?'

'No.'

'Do you read music?'

'No.'

'All right. I'm going to sing a verse of it.'

Darcy listened, her eyes closed.

'Go again,' she said when he went silent.

He sang the verse through again.

'I won't get the words right,' she warned.

'That's OK.'

She sang the verse without any sense of what it meant and without confidence at any point that the next notes sung would be right. In the ensuing silence, Nicholas Watson looked at her with a puzzled expression.

'What's wrong? Did I make nonsense of it?'

'Yes, but that's not the issue. Because you don't know what you're singing, you've actually hit a tone that I want you to hang on to.'

'This is the way *you* sing it,' he explained, playing loudly and bluntly. She nodded.

'Now this is another way to do it,' he explained, and his playing changed. He developed a physical closeness with the keys, his head tilted as if he was listening to his own hands, his hair flopping sideways.

'What's the difference?'

'The second one,' Darcy said slowly, 'the second one was syrupy. Sentimental.'

'Right,' he said, swinging around on the music stool. Darcy began to realise that Beethoven might smile all the time, but his smile had significant variations to it and right now it was demonstrating enthusiasm for whatever she had said.

'When you sing it in the programme, I need you to sing it the first way. You are likely to want to sing it the second way when you understand the words, when you realise that it's a love song.'

'Aah.'

'Exactly.'

'Says who that I'm going to sing it in the programme?'

'Says me.'

'Masterful, aren't you?'

'No. You have a hell of a voice. More mezzo than your sister.'

'How – oh, yeah, Gaeltacht.'

'Tell her I was asking for her, if she remembers me.'

'She remembers you all right. Not perhaps as vividly as Aileen remembers you, but still.'

Beethoven smiled impartially and started to talk about rehearsals.

'What would you like to wear?'

'I'd like to wear an oversized denim jackety waistcoaty thing and a pair of jeans, but that's not exactly going to fit the bill, is it?'

'I think that'd be perfect. I'll describe it to Greg, our producer, and he'll give you a shout if there's a problem.'

'But won't you be in tails and stuff?'

'I won't be near you.'

'Who'll be the accompanist?'

'Won't be one. *Sean nós.*'

'What?'

'*Sean nós* singing. Irish unaccompanied. *A cappella.* You stand up and you sing and that's it.'

'Jesus. How'm I going to learn it?'

'There's a tape in RTE of it being sung by Seán Ó Síocháin or someone like that, and I'll get it sent to you. Plus a rough translation of what it means. Don't learn it word by word, just learn it in phrases and meanings and runs, you know what I mean?'

The tape arrived a few days later and Darcy listened to it. Sophia, meanwhile, had planned their own school's programme along semi-documentary lines, starting with black-and-white photographs of classes of students from one hundred years previously, with a voice-over script outlining the plans the nuns had at that time for the education of girls.

'I want to show that the ambitions and expectations of girls today are just completely different to the expectations they'd have had in the fifties and sixties,' Sophia explained to her parents.

'Yeah,' Colette said sympathetically. 'Dull hoors, those wans from the fifties and sixties. Just wanted to marry doctors and have babies.'

'In twos, if possible,' Robert added, and gestured to the ceiling. From the twins' room, overhead, came Darcy's voice, powerful and unselfconscious. The lack of selfconsciousness was because she was singing along with a tape recording of

Sean Ó Síocháin's voice fed through earphones and had no idea she could be heard. For Sophia, even though the words were muffled by distance, the melody was a kick in the heart. Darcy was singing Ruaidhrí's song. The song he had taught Sophia standing on a scuffed-out beach path halfway between the college and the sea that had swallowed his life.

The song almost dragged her to her knees. She stood in the stillness of revived desolation and tears came unbidden to her. How strange, thought Colette, watching the tears without knowing the reasons. How sweet, thought Robert.

At that moment, Darcy's voice went suddenly off the note and into silence.

'Bugger bugger bugger bugger,' they could hear her saying fervently. 'And furthermore, shite.'

'What do you think are the chances of her saying that on air?' Colette asked, beginning to tidy away the tea things. Sophia shook her head, half-laughing, trying to get rid of the tears and the damp dread that had overtaken her.

In the following three weeks, Sophia made sure she was not around when Darcy was rehearsing her song, partly to avoid hearing it, and partly to avoid running into Beethoven.

It was, on the other hand, quite important to Sophia to have Darcy's contribution to their own school programme. Darcy wanted no part of it.

'You're in charge, you do it,' she said, when asked to look at the script.

'I *have* done it,' Sophia said patiently. 'Now I need you to pick holes in it.'

'I'm not qualified to pick holes.'

'Just read it. OK? Please?'

'Oh, Jesus.'

'Oh, Jesus, what?'

'Oh Jesus, you can't say "The order which was founded on the eighth day of February, eighteen whatever". That's not the way people talk. People never say "which".'

'Of course they say "which".'

'No, they don't. Can you imagine me going down to Da and saying "the script which I am currently reading"? He'd think I'd lost the head altogether.'

Sophia handed her sister a pen.

'Change it. Rewrite it.'

Darcy lay back on her bed, script in hand. 'Why?'

'Because I want it perfect and you can get it perfect.'

'*I* don't know that.'

'No, but I do.'

'You know something? Sometimes you're more like a mother than our mother is.'

'Edit it, would you please, Darcy? I need it for tomorrow.'

Darcy sighed deeply and began to read. Sophia looked out the window, wincing as another deep condemning sigh came from the other side of the room. After a few moments, Darcy sat up. After another few moments, she got off the bed and turned on the electric typewriter. When Sophia went downstairs a few minutes later, Darcy was banging at the keyboard and whistling through her teeth. The end result, an hour and a half later, was a brutally shortened script.

'But you've left out the bit about – '

'Yes, because we're going to be seeing it on screen at the time. Nothing worse than being told what you can see for yourself.'

'But what are we going to hear at that stage?'

'Sounds from the period. Music. Sound effects. Trams. I don't know. Not words, anyway.'

Sophia read through the revised script, beginning to smile.

'You happy?'

'It's certainly going to be easy to read.'

'Yes, but are you happy?'

'I have to get used to it. Since you have made it simpler, it sounds slightly less important, if you know what I mean. But yes, I'm happy. Thank you.'

'Not at all. It distracted me from food for nearly two hours.'

'Are you starving yourself again?'

'Yeah. Until this goddamn TV programme is over. Greg was on the other day and one of his glad tidings was that because TV pictures are delivered in stripes that go this way – '

'Horizontal?'

'Side to side, not up and down.'

'That's horizontal.'

'Well, because TV pictures are delivered in horizontal stripes, they add ten pounds to everybody's face.'

'The make-up people in RTE will probably be very helpful,' Sophia said. 'They probably have all sorts of tricks.'

Darcy met with Nicholas a number of times to go through the song, but was never called to a full-scale run through.

'Greg is a genius for doing only the work that really has to be done,' said Nicholas. 'In geography, for example, he has completely left out tectonic movement in studying for the Leaving Cert, because he figures if he does coastal action and river and glacial action thoroughly, he is sure of a question on them, and won't have to do a question on tectonic plates.'

'How does that apply to television programmes?'

'He came up with a concept that is completely founded on discontinuity,' Nicholas explained. 'So we have a guy from Xavier's who's going to be doing a pop song and then we'll have you doing this unaccompanied Irish song. No commentary, no explanations. That's why you can wear whatever you want to wear, too. Some people's parents are insisting that they get their hair cut and get a good suit, and that's fine because it illustrates another facet of our lives.'

Darcy had never heard Nicholas say quite so much, and realised that behind the cynical smile was an unexpected capacity for enthusiasm which Greg, whom she had not yet met, somehow stimulated.

'Are *you* getting a haircut?'

He laughed.

'Naah. Might wash it on the day, though. But I'll wear a tux.'

'You will?'

'I'm second youngest of nine brothers, eight of them living at home.'

'What's that got to do with it?'

'Don't have to rent a tux. We're all more or less the same size and we all play the piano. As a family, we own a grand piano and a tux. So it'll get an outing.'

'What are you going to be playing?'

'Opus 32 No 1, a Chopin Nocturne in B major. It's a promenade. You stroll through the music. Happy and reflective. It always brings back memories to me of being a small child in the garden. In grass that was as tall as I was.'

Darcy tried to imagine a programme that included her singing unaccompanied traditional Irish songs, Nicholas/ Beethoven playing and – among other elements she couldn't remember – a stand-up comedy trio.

'On the day, you can bring someone along with you to help you,' Nicholas said, closing the lid of the piano.

'To help me what?'

Nicholas's shrug took in two millennia of male wonderment at Things Female. Darcy laughed.

'Someone like Aileen?' she suggested.

'There you go,' Beethoven said, doing his best to be non-committal.

On the day of the recording, Darcy did bring along Aileen, and was quite glad when she discovered that the television station had set aside a dressing room for her use. The Belvedere production assistant, a squirrelly young man named Nigel who was sweating slightly from the excitement and terror of his half-understood job, showed the two of them along a corridor of dressing rooms.

'Look, you've even got your own loo and shower,' Aileen said, running her palms along the counter-top in front of the big mirror in a way that reminded Darcy of the film of Helen Keller as a child.

'Would you like coffee?' Nigel had come back.

'No, thank you,' Darcy said, then instantly regretted it.

The coffee would probably have come with a plate of biscuits, she thought; one Nice, one custard cream, one roundy biscuit with a neon pink icing top, one bourbon cream and two butter cream fingers. Even if she ate the whole lot of them (with the exception of the bourbon cream, which wouldn't be worth spending calories on) it was only six hours away from recording the programme, and you couldn't put on two or three pounds in that time, could you?

Aileen got bored with the dressing room and went down to the studio.

Darcy dialled her home number. Her mother answered.

'Hi, Ma.'

'What have you forgotten and how much time have I got to get in there?'

'Oh, *thanks*, Mother. That the only reason I ever ring you — that I've forgotten something?'

'No, sometimes you ring me because you think talking to me might distract you from eating something, and sometimes because you have a boast that you think I'd enjoy.'

'Sometimes it's just that I like talking to you.'

'I'd say that's true, too,' Colette said in casual acceptance.

'I haven't forgotten anything.'

'Great.'

'But I'm sick with terror.'

'Are you surprised?'

'Well, I haven't *done* a TV programme before.'

'Right.'

'Say something.'

'Something.'

'No, say something designed to make me feel better.'

'Something designed to make me feel better.'

'Ah, *Ma*. That's the sort of thing Dad would do.'

'Gosh. Better watch that. Wouldn't want to have anything in common with that creep.'

'You know I didn't mean that.'

'We could have a fight, if you liked. That would distract you from your nerves.'

'I don't ever fight with you.'

'No.'

'Why is that?' Darcy felt a warm mother-directed glow suffusing her chest.

'Mainly because you're too busy fighting with your father. If you cut back on that, you'd have more time to fight with me,' her mother said. A silence fell between them, comfortable and cooperative.

There was a knock on the dressing room door.

'They're coming for me,' Darcy said.

'Hear the tumbrels, can you?'

'No. There's a knock on the door,' Darcy hissed, terrified of being caught in a star's dressing room talking to her mother.

'You will be superb. Superb. That's all there is to it,' her mother said, and put down the phone. Darcy very quietly cradled her receiver.

In came Nigel. His sweatiness was evenly distributed, Darcy noted. It didn't take the form of drops but of a generalised dampness like condensation on the inside of a window, with occasional runnels.

'We need you on the studio floor,' he announced.

'OK, OK. Lead on M – oh, shit.'

'What's wrong?'

'Nearly quoted from the wrong play.'

'What wrong play?'

'Nigel, just do your job, OK?'

Nigel walked in front of her, his thin back sulking. Suddenly, they were in a vast aircraft hangar with black walls and a black ceiling that seemed about a hundred and forty feet above them, the ceiling gridded to carry heavy lights. A heavy pale curtain ran around the hangar leaving enough room for two people to walk abreast between curtain and wall.

The arm of a man called Rog snugged around Darcy's waist as he steered her to where she was to stand. Beethoven, his hair clean but his body still in denims rather than the promised tuxedo, smiled at her.

'I'm the floor manager,' Rog explained to her. 'I am scum. I just carry messages from up there – ' he pointed up to a gantry that circled the studio. Darcy could dimly make out people behind a darkened window. 'That's the control box,' Rog said. 'Now,' he went on, checking a clipboard, 'Darcy, you directly follow Nicholas here – he says his last note will be the note you pick up on, all right? All right. And when you finish, Pete, you come in. You got that?'

Pete, a carrot-haired but otherwise colourless boy, nodded dully.

'Thirty seconds to go,' Rog called out.

'Fifteen,' he said.

'Ten.' He began to count down.' . . . six, five, four, three, two, one – '

His hand dropped like a guillotine and, like a thump in the lower back, in unison came the sound of about twenty male voices singing a rugby song. Just as they got to the best known profane bit of it, the singers stopped in unison and a single male voice came through, doing a devastating impression of a series of politicians, British and Irish. Darcy was dying to turn and identify who the mimic was.

Suddenly, in mid-joke, he was silenced by a rolling entry of notes from the piano, and Beethoven was in command. In a panic, Darcy wondered if she would recognise when Beethoven came to the end of the piece he was playing. In the event, it caught her somewhat by surprise, so she started her song without a lungful of air. Calm down, her head-commentator said. Calm down. Get a deep one at the end of this phrase. Good. Cool it. She sang directly into the darkness facing her.

The red-haired boy was finishing his poem and a guitar player was taking over. He was followed by a comedy trio

Darcy couldn't quite hear. Almost immediately, the rugby group started to sing, their voices cleverly modulated to imply that they were coming from far away. They picked up just after the obscene bit of the song that had started the programme, and ended it.

There was a long, dissatisfied silence at the end of it. They all stood or sat in position, none of them comfortable.

'We're overrunning by three and a half,' Rog said, having listened to his earpiece. 'So we gotta cut. Tim, Dave and Piers?' Three moans came from the comedy team. 'You're gone.'

'Ah, *fuck*,' said one of the three voices.

'Oh, thank Christ,' said a second.

'I love you too, Greg,' the third called out, and got a laugh.

'Darcy, Greg wants you – '

Rog fell silent, listening.

'Tell him there's a time and a place,' Darcy said, deadpan.

The tension of a poor rehearsal was washed away by the laughter.

'That's enough,' said Roger. 'That's enough. Quiet.'

The laughter died.

'Greg says could you pick some point to sing to,' Rog asked Darcy, who nodded.

'All right, we're going to break now and we're back here at 8.30,' Rog shouted. 'Greg says each and every one of you should know that was a – his words folks, his words – shite rehearsal. Which is a very good predictor, he says, of a great performance tonight.'

Eager to have her face improved upon, Darcy went to Make Up, only to find it empty. She lay sideways on one of the vinyl banquettes and fell asleep. Some time later, the telephone in the Make Up room rang, pulling her back to wakefulness. She sat up slowly, deciding that the phone was someone else's problem. After a moment or two, it stopped ringing. Darcy lay back down.

'My feeling exactly,' a voice said from the other side of the room. 'There's enough trouble around without volunteering for any of it.'

Darcy looked guiltily around, trying to figure how long this unseen person had been there and wondering if she had been snoring. A young man with a leg stuck rigidly out in front of him, a plaster cast showing at the end of his jeans, was sitting in a collapsed scaffolding of crutches.

'You're nothing to do with Make Up, are you?' Darcy asked him.

'No,' he said.

Darcy looked at him. He was as good-looking as a male model. Blonde hair, big build, laughing brown eyes.

The door swung open and three young women came in, clutching half-finished cups of coffee.

'Darcy?' one of them asked, looking from the plaster-casted young man to the girl impartially, as if either of them might own the unisex name.

'Me,' Darcy said.

'Hi!' The girl was putting an apron on. Then she spun a chair in front of the brightly lit mirrors and gestured towards it. 'I'm Lauren.'

Darcy sat in the big chair and had a plastic poncho thrown over her from neck to knee.

'You also for this access programme?' Lauren asked the young man over her shoulder.

'With it but not on it,' he said, collecting the crutches and lumbering forward to take the chair next to Darcy.

'How'd you mean?'

'Theoretically, I'm directing it,' he smiled. 'Which means that a very senior RTE guy sits next to me and translates my instructions into television language when they make any sense, and gives his own instructions instead when they don't.'

'You're Greg?' Darcy asked, trying to hold her face still as foundation went on.

'The very man,' Greg said.

'How do you do?'

'See her trying to be nice to me now,' Greg told Lauren, eyes meeting in the mirror. 'Hoping I'll give her millions of close-ups.'

'On the contrary,' Darcy said, laughing with her voice, but keeping her face still. 'I'd be hoping you'd give me no close-ups at all. Shoot me as a long-distance figure, preferably in soft focus. Lauren, can you take ten pounds off my face?'

'Are you playing some kind of dramatic role?' asked Lauren, unnerved. 'I thought you were just singing?'

'I just want to look thinner,' Darcy said. 'I was told you people up here have all sorts of tricks.'

'We do, too,' Lauren said. 'I could do you a great scar. Right down here,' she said, trailing an index fingernail from Darcy's right eye to her chin. 'Puckered and purple.'

'There's a motif I hadn't thought of,' Greg said admiringly.

'No, I mean tricks to make me look good,' Darcy said.

'I can certainly shape your face to emphasise your very good bone structure,' Lauren said.

'How can you tell I have bone structure?' Darcy asked.

'Close your eyes and look upward,' Lauren instructed Darcy. 'And again?'

A few minutes later, she allowed her subject to sit up and examine herself in the mirror. Darcy was spellbound by the difference make-up made to her.

'You are *wonderful*,' she told Lauren.

Greg beckoned to her, and she assumed he wanted to say something so quietly none of the people around her would hear. Instead, he kissed her on the forehead.

'People will talk about you for weeks,' he predicted.

'I have three people for you, and I can take Darcy down with me.' Nigel was back, all business and all velvety perspiration. Darcy followed him down to the studio.

The other performers appeared, one by one, matted and evened-out with pancake make up. Lauren had obviously made up Beethoven's hands to match his face. Rog was all business, glecking little encouraging winks at Darcy. You're gonna be *great*, the winks said. Trust me. I know. I'm an old hand. No problem. Great bit of stuff. Over before you know it. Handy enough number.

'Going in – forty-five seconds,' he said, and nervous throat-clearing intensified. 'Silence in studio.'

'Thirty seconds.'

'Fifteen.'

Darcy felt as alone as if condemned to death, ice-chilled by the heat, heartbeat raucous in the silence, a tendon flickering at the back of her knee. O please, she prayed. O please.

'Five. Four. Three. Two – '

It began – an avalanche of excitement, stilled to attention when her own voice took over. She sang with a sureness that belonged to someone else, and she sang to a face half-seen, the face of her twin. When she finished, her eyes were wet with tears for a sadness not her own.

The whole programme seemed to take fourteen minutes, she thought, as the final rugby song came up behind her like a big umbrella of noise and colour.

The voices died, and after a few minute's silence, everybody began to talk at once.

'Please stay in position,' Rog said, patting the air in front of him. 'Please stay in position until we check the tape.

There was an uneasy rustling.

'Wonderful. Tape's good. Clear the studio, folks, and thank you very much. Greg says it went superbly, and I think all of us would add our voice to his. Really excellent.'

Rog, all set to be jovial, hugged Darcy. Then Nigel was beside her, handing her a taxi voucher. The three comedians side-to-siding their palms in the air in subdued farewell. Beethoven and Aileen linked in an awkward way, their faces set in kindly separateness: Darcy, you were very good in the show, but now we don't want to share a taxi with you. Good dog, go home, Darcy thought. Button your anticlimax right to the top and go out into the dark.

She stuffed the taxi voucher in her pocket and, make up unremoved, walked through the black-shiny lobby into the chill of the night. I will never work in television, she thought. You don't get to take the excitement home. Even if you've made some of it.

CHAPTER TWELVE

Greg's television programme went out the week before Sophia's and got no critical comment whatever because it coincided with a political crisis.

The following week, when Sophia's programme was broadcast, the political crisis had died down, so the *Irish Times*, the day after, talked about the 'lucid televisual story-telling' that had informed the programme, and credited Sophia by name. This had been predicted by Greg when he telephoned the King household directly after the programme.

'You're very kind,' the Kings could hear Sophia saying, after a long pause. 'I particularly appreciate it coming from you, because your programme was so good. No, seriously. Yes, she was, wasn't she? Sure, I'll get her for you.'

Sophia came back into the sitting room.

'He wants a word with you, Darcy.'

Darcy lumbered out of the couch and headed for the hall.

'Greg?'

'Darcy.'

'Well, this establishes the *dramatis personae*.'

'Sophia's programme was good.'

'This is true.'

'I saw she gave you a script credit.'

'Yeah. I rewrote the script.'

'So you write as well?'

'As well as what?'

'As well as look sexy and sing like – like – '

'Pavarotti?'

'Any chance you'd come in to The Bailey?'

'What's The Bailey?'

'Pub in town.'

'Me?'

'Well, I'm sure your parents are super people, but I didn't ring to invite *them*.'

'I can't.'

'Why not?'

'It's term time.'

'So?'

'It would not be approved of.'

'Darcy, work your butt off the other nights of the week. Work smarter, not harder.'

'Yeah, I know all about you not doing tectonic movement in Geography.'

'*Everybody* knows about me not doing tectonic movement in Geography,' Greg laughed. 'My Geography teacher says he'll give up teaching if I get an A in the Leaving Cert. Which I will. And he won't.'

Darcy couldn't believe the pleasure she was getting from being able to refuse an invitation.

'Anyway, I'm not going out.'

'I knew you were prejudiced against the handicapped.'

'Oh – how's your leg?'

'I'm down to one crutch.'

'Great.'

'You wouldn't be ashamed to be seen with *one* crutch, would you?'

'Greg, I'm not going. But thank you very much.'

'For *nada*. I'll ring you again.'

'You do that.'

'Look after yourself.'

'You too.'

It was not the success of her TV programme that sorted things out for Sophia. It was the all-absorbing activity of it, the sensation of minding everybody. Making the programme while at the same time studying for the Leaving Certificate gave Sophia the first month during which she never thought of Ruaidhrí. Up to that point, people around her always seemed to be using the imagery of the sea. They talked of

169

tidal waves of emotion. Or fighting the undertow. Or drowning your sorrows. Or ebb tide. Or 'not waving but drowning'. Every phrase a drawing-pin impaling her, sticking her back on the notice-board of someone else's brief life.

The TV programme cut across that, filling her mind with other images, her mouth with other terms. Even when she watched the Belvedere programme and saw Darcy singing their song, there were no tears in the back of her throat, and, more significantly, no regret that they were not there. That month taught her that being busy would wipe away almost everything. What had, up to then, been a series of guessed-at possibilities became the unarguable proofs of her life. She no longer felt the need to change Darcy, which Darcy found unnerving, having got used to the gentle nagging of her twin.

So when Darcy announced three weeks before the Leaving Cert that, no matter how good her results might be, she was not going to university, Sophia registered the statement without question. Robert King, on the other hand, absolutely refused to accept it.

'What nonsense,' he said, giving his *Evening Press* a shake as if to punish it.

'Why's it nonsense?' Darcy asked.

'That someone of your intelligence . . . '

'But go on – someone of my intelligence?'

Robert King stood up and rammed the evening paper into the fireplace, where it blazed up and forced him to step back from the sudden scorching heat.

'I don't wish to discuss this,' he said, sitting down at the table.

'But I *do*,' Darcy said.

'I think you two do this deliberately,' Colette said, pouring tea. 'Screw up every mealtime on the rest of us.'

'When else are we all here together?'

Colette looked surprised at the snappishness of Robert's response, but said nothing.

'Where is there a law that says if you have intelligence you have to go to college?' This from Darcy, putting butter on the flat side of Ryvita. When she was not on a diet, she put butter on the dimpled side, which could absorb more.

'Why ask redundant questions? There may not be a *law*, but it is the obvious course of action.'

'That's precisely what I'm saying. I don't want to follow the obvious course of action.'

'Why not?'

''M an individual?' Darcy captured escaping Ryvita crumbs.

'So's Sophia.'

'But Sophia wants to go to college, and I don't.'

'That's entirely debatable. Sophia may believe it is her duty to study and qualify for a good job.'

'I don't *give* a shit what Sophia sees as her duty.'

'Less of that language at the dinner table.'

'I have my own sense of duty.'

'Questionable.'

'No, not questionable.'

'What sense of duty could possibly urge you not to attend university? There are people all over this country who would give their eye teeth for the chance to go to university, and you, who have the chance . . . '

'So start a scholarship, for Christ's sake.'

'Darcy.' In reproof from her mother.

'Well really, Ma. I'm supposed to go to university which I hate the thought of, and be grateful for the torture, because there's some poor nameless hoor in some Godforsaken hole that *can't* go. What the hell kind of way is that to live your life?'

'An unselfish way,' her father said, by way of a clincher.

'It's not unselfish to do something you would hate doing. It's just mad.'

'Huxley said that the most valuable result of all education is the ability to make yourself do the thing you have to do when it ought to be done, whether you like it or not,' Sophia said.

'Oh, for fuck's sake, Sophia, you going to give us your word for the day as well?'

'*Darcy!*'

'I'm sorry, Ma, but I can do without Little Miss Favourite giving me her gleanings for the week.'

'I beg your pardon.'

'Or her pomposities.'

Sophia subsided to consider this exchange, deciding that Darcy was quite right but horrified at the possibility that her sister had been reading her diary.

'Darcy.'

Her father's use of her name as a weapon in itself was interesting, Darcy thought.

'Darcy. Someone of your intelligence cannot feel comfortable about abandoning the process of learning at seventeen years of age.'

Her father presented the thought to her with the calmness of one who has found the ultimate point of persuasion.

'Right.'

'Right?'

'Right. As in "correct".'

'So you will go to university?'

'No, I won't go to university.'

'But you said – '

'I said I didn't plan to abandon learning at seventeen. I don't. It's you that has decided I can only go on learning if I go to university.'

'Let us not waste time on twaddle about learning from nature and the world around us.'

'You're lucky we're not recording this. I'd love to see your face if you could hear what you've just said.'

'I am well aware of what I've just said.'

'So God – who you believe in, I don't – gave us nature and the world around us just as a decoration. Garnish for

172

the main dish, the main dish being university.'

'We don't need you to be blasphemous.'

'Sophia, you want to provide a definition of blasphemous so my beloved father can see I'm not being blasphemous?'

'Darcy, leave me out of this.'

'Me, too,' Colette said, leaving the table.

'I would have thought that as parents – ' Robert protested.

'No, Robert,' Colette replied, 'you *wouldn't* have thought. Because if you had thought, you would know that I do not believe we have to sing an anthem of solidarity, arms linked against the world, in order to raise nice kids. I don't know what your objective is, but mine has always been the same: raise nice kids. Happy kids. I do not see where this unpleasantness is taking us, so count me out of it.'

'Oh, so now I'm the worst in the world because, as a father, I simply – '

'No, Robert, you're not the worst in the world. Don't put feet under what I said. This unpleasantness belongs to you and to Darcy and the two of you are welcome to it.'

The door closed behind her.

'Well, I hope you're very happy.'

'About what?'

'About causing this kind of family tension, when it is utterly unnecessary and undesirable.'

'I didn't cause it.'

'Well, if that's what you choose to believe.'

'Dad, here's the situation. I am not going to university, whether you like it or not. Any tension that comes out of the decision will be caused by you not liking it. Ma doesn't care and Sophia doesn't care.'

'Have you asked them?'

Flummoxed, Darcy looked at Sophia.

'Dad,' said Sophia, 'I think Darcy's life is her own.'

'But *you* want to go to college.'

'Yes, but I'm not Darcy.'

'That's beside the point.'

173

'No, it's not beside the point,' Darcy said. 'It *is* the point, for Chrissake! She isn't me, therefore she is going to college and I'm not. Freedom of choice, you know? What we're supposed to have in this democracy. Or maybe it's not a democracy. Maybe it's dictatorship by parent?'

'That is unfair and untrue. Neither your mother nor I have ever dictated to either you or Sophia.'

'No, but it's never too late to start seems to be the current motto.'

'You have the intelligence, the money is available for – '

'But I don't want to do it.'

'Did it ever strike you that you might have some responsibilities?'

'Yes.'

'And they are?'

'To work hard in order to buy my leisure time. To enjoy the hell out of my leisure time. Yeah, go on, sniff. I suppose I shouldn't admit to even *having* leisure time, just make Calvinist noises and keep my nose to the grindstone.'

'No responsibilities towards your potential or the intelligence God gave you. I beg your pardon – random selection gave you the intelligence, I suppose you would hold.'

'Genetics, actually.'

'Don't give me cheek, young woman.'

'Oh, puhlease.'

'No responsibilities along those lines?'

'Yes, of course. But I'll live up to them in my own way. Learn in my own way. Be an autodidact.'

'So my money is going to support you while you lie around the house reading whatever you choose?'

'Beats your money supporting me while I lie around the loo injecting myself with heroin.'

'As you'd say yourself: *please.*'

'That's ultimately what this boils down to, isn't it? Money. You have it, so you'll use it as a whip to scourge me into doing whatever you want me to do. I do what you want, you pay for it. I don't do what you want, you won't pay for it.'

'I never said that.'

'Father dear, you've talked a lot this evening about my intelligence. Well, let me tell you something about intelligence that you've obviously missed, maybe because you only see it at work when it's dead and on slides. Intelligence allows you to add things together. And what I'm adding together is that my father will do anything – mortgage the house all over again, if necessary – in order to support his two clever daughters through college. But if one of them decides that instead of reading a series of books on a college list, she might read a series of books on nobody's list, to open her mind and enhance her learning without a degree at the end of it to prove it all, then bang goes the second mortgage: money is only to be used for the straight-and-narrow form of personal development.'

'That is a gross over-simplification of what I am saying. I am trying to bring you to a realisation of the wonderful possibilities offered to you by a university education, which can lead you to a worthwhile profession – '

' – like PR?'

'*Darcy.*'

'Yeah, and do you know what's really sad? What's really sad is that I am trying to bring *you* to a realisation of the wonderful possibilities offered to me by a non-university education, and you can't see even for a split second how closed and deafened you are by your own views and your own money. That's where a university education took *you.*'

'Since when am I a rich man?'

'You're not a rich man. In many ways you're a very poor man.'

'I would not go further along that line, if I were you.'

'You going to throw me out of the house?'

'I just would not go further along that line.'

'Well, fire ahead. Throw me out. All my belongings – whoosh. Down on to the driveway from the top window.

175

Boppity boppity bop. Right now this minute, if you want. This minute. Because I can manage fine without being here. I can manage fine on my own. I can manage without someone who assumes that just because I am under their roof I have to obey a whole load of rules and regulations and reflexes better suited to a man of sixty than a man of fifty.'

The door had opened during this last outburst, and Colette stood there in the long silence that followed it.

'Your father isn't fifty that long,' she said.

'Whatever,' said Darcy, with undiminished fury.

'I think we should put off any further discussion of this matter until after the Leaving Cert,' Colette said, and the vibrating electricity of anger in the room was levelled by the upset in her voice.

'I wouldn't agree with you, Mam,' Sophia said, standing up. 'I don't think we should ever discuss it again, because I haven't heard anything from anybody this evening that makes me feel particularly proud of this family. Let's just get on with studying for the Leaving and when that's finished, something else will come up.'

She began to clear the table of the half-eaten meal and Darcy stood to help her, unaware that the large buckle on her leather belt had caught in the crevice between the flat top of the table and her leg, so that her movement toppled the entire table, sending crockery, cutlery, butter, Ryvita packet, teapot, milk-jug and wooden bread plate avalanching across the sudden slope at her father, who, seeing the teapot making straight for his lap, aimed a wild back-stroke at it that put it through the kitchen window, battered cockerel tea-cosy and all.

The shattering window glass was raucous in the back garden.

The family gazed at the destruction for some moments, the only sound a rapid drip-drip-drip of milk progressing from one level to another, although precisely where this was happening nobody could tell.

'There's no answer to that,' Sophia said admiringly.

Robert King stood up, his trousers filthy with butter and milk spatters. Not only had he lost lost his rage, he seemed to have lost his energy too, as if the overturning of the table had weakened him physically. When Darcy began to apologise, he looked at her in the puzzled way shortsighted people who have lost their glasses look at those who are talking to them. Colette walked through the shards of china and took him by the arm, leading him away and out of the room. The two girls tidied the kitchen in perfect silence. It was only when they were standing, surveying the cleanness of the finished job, that Darcy began to laugh.

'You're not going to believe this,' she told her sister, 'but I spend half my life tempted to overturn tables and break windows. One of the fantasies that sustains me in really tough situations is the idea that I will grab the tablecloth and just suddenly yank it from under everything. Or throw jelly at people. Today I did it all by accident. I probably would have enjoyed it more if I'd had a bit of advance knowledge. But I enjoyed it a lot anyway.'

'You couldn't enjoy that wanton destructiveness. Not really, you couldn't.'

Darcy threw a tea towel at the edge of the sink and missed. 'Sophia, sometimes you are an awful pain in the tits. I just feel you need to know this.'

'Thank you.'

'Think nothing of it.'

'Darcy?'

'You don't find me so wonderful either?'

'No, it's not that. How did you know about my quotations?'

'What quotations?'

'That I pick one a day to memorise?'

'I didn't.'

'Even though it's in my diary?'

'Oh, Sophia, give me a break. You don't seriously think I

would read your goddamn diary?'

'Well it was just the thing about the quotations and then you knowing that I learn a new word every day.'

'Oh, that's so invisible.'

'Sorry?'

'Sophia, when I kept *goldfish*, they knew you learned a new word a day. You're not exactly subtle about it. One day every sentence is filled with predicated this and predicated that, and the next day, it's all exiguous this and revenant that. Sometimes I even watch out for them. It's like getting cancer through passive smoking. I figure I pick up about half your words by just paying mild attention to you during an average day.'

'That's a relief.'

'Today's is "ameliorate". Tell me you're ameliorated to death to know I don't read about your wild sex life in your diary.'

'You can't use ameliorate like that.'

'I am eviscerated. That was Tuesday's, wasn't it?'

'Oh, shut up!'

When Robert King heard the laughter from the kitchen, he sat heavily down on the double bed and rested his head in his hands.

'Rodin forgot the Y-fronts,' Colette said, arriving into the room with a clean pair of casual trousers. 'Other than that he got you to the life.'

'What do you think?'

'About Darcy and university?'

'Yes.'

'I think she'd be very unhappy in university, whereas I think Sophia will be very happy.'

'*You* went.'

'And I didn't have a happy minute until I met this medical student who was giving bad thoughts to a whole generation of my girlfriends. After that, everything in my life made sense.'

He pulled her close to him, so that she stood between his knees, hands on his shoulders.

'Was I being unreasonable?'

'Oh, yes.'

'But don't you see that – '

'You were being unreasonable. What does it matter to you?'

'I want the best for her.'

'When I told you I didn't want a fur coat, you didn't force fox on me.'

'It's not the same.'

'It's exactly the same.'

He lowered his head so that his forehead rested on her stomach.

'It's so simple with Sophia. So simple and straight-forward.'

'Why can't Darcy – be more like her twin?' Colette sang, to the tune of the *My Fair Lady* song 'Why can't a Woman be More like a Man?'

'I try to do the best, you know.' He looked up at her.

'Most of the time you succeed.'

He lowered his head again, shaking it.

'But the world is very random. Particularly Darcy's bits of it.'

'Am I as old as she thinks?'

Older, Colette thought. Older in your need to settle into your certainties like an old man settling into his favourite chair. She stood silent, stroking his hair. He heard the kindness of the silence and could not learn its lesson.

'It's very hard,' she said. And meant: it's very hard not to reach for the old rules as a way of staying upright when the external buttresses are being taken away, all in a generation.

'Darcy'll be all right,' she said.

'How, do you think?'

'She's resilient. She's bright. She enjoys life. There's always space for people like that.'

'But she's not disciplined. There's no consistency about her.'

'I don't think consistency matters as much these days as it used to in the days of permanent and pensionable.'

'But everybody needs a degree to get a job these days.'

'Oh, Robert.'

'To get a decent job.'

'Robert.'

She slid her hands over his back inside his shirt.

'She may not meet a medical student with a reputation a mile long, but we can't all be lucky.'

'Tell me about this reputation?' His forehead still against her skirt, he slid his hands up inside it, inside the legs of her panties.

'Legend, he was. Of course, I always thought people were just confusing him with McEnerney the Orthopod Stud, but I was open to being proven wrong . . .'

His head tilted back so he was watching her. 'You still open to being proven wrong?' he asked, his hands moving surely, slowly inside the soft cotton.

'Might be persuaded.'

Afterwards they lay together listening to Darcy telephoning glaziers to come and fix the kitchen window.

'Jesus,' Robert said, suddenly mad again. 'Telling me that for a man of fifty I was like a man of sixty.'

'And you capable of a forty-nine-year-old's performance,' Colette said.

'Thirty-nine-year-old's.'

'Don't push your luck, old timer.'

CHAPTER THIRTEEN

Entry in Sophia's diary

Thursday 4 July 1985

The Leaving Certificate is over and I am satisfied that I have done as well as I should have done.

I will be going to Trinity on my own, because Darcy's resolve to avoid third level education has been hardened by my father's opposition.

I will be going to Paris for a month in a week's time to improve my French.

It has been a good year for me in that first of all, I have largely shaken off the shadow of Ruaidhrí. I have become reconciled to the fact that I will never remember him properly the way he was and that I must therefore remember him in practical ways. So it would be my intention to work on my Irish just as much as I work on my French, and so I will be going to the Gaeltacht in August. Without boasting, the fact is that I can be a role model, and if someone who is young and attractive, who does well in college, who has a good job in an interesting field, is also someone who uses the Irish language, that will make a point and perhaps attract other young people to speak the language too.

I have to admit that proximity to Darcy does not give very positive indicators on this score, since she is very bad at Irish and not that good at French, either, but the other thing I have now come to terms with is that one's family is not a microcosm of the wider public. In many ways, the wider public is easier to manage and to influence than one's own family. Or perhaps I should say 'than my particular family'. Darcy occasionally gets furious with me and blurts insults but at least they tend to be general insults rather than demeaning personal observations. She calls me a pain in the tits (charming) but does not sit around working out ways to make me feel unsure of myself.

The end result is that I am, I would imagine, unusual in my self-confidence and composure. This was certainly reinforced by my production of our school's television programme, which was a very interesting learning experience. I would much rather be in charge of all of the aspects of a project than to be the face in front of a project, which, in the long term is fortunate, because although women are appearing more in the business pages and you read about directors being appointed to the boards of banks and places like that who are women, I do not personally believe that this acceptance for women continues past a certain age.

Men in their late fifties and early sixties are considered to be very handsome, attractive and in their prime, whereas women are really past it, in any area which depends on physical appearance. Actresses like Meryl Streep will not be big stars in their fifties. You never get a female Sean Connery.

So my appearance will be at least as important to my success as my intelligence and my hard work. This is regrettable, because one should not judge a book by its cover, and it is unfair that if one were unfortunate enough to have a birthmark, one would be discriminated against on that basis, or indeed that people would take Darcy less seriously because she is overweight, but one must take it into account.

My hair, which tends to be light and flyaway, I must get styled in a way that is easy to take care of and that always looks smart.

I am going to have to find a new gynaecologist,

because I cannot believe the dragging pain I still experience at periods is normal, and I feel the man I go to, because he has been my mother's gynae man for so long, and also knows my father, regards me as an under-age hypochondriac. I have no hypochondriacal tendencies whatever and neither does Darcy.

When I have that sorted out I will embark on a proper exercise regimen, perhaps asking my parents to give me membership of a good gym as a birthday present. The gym should have all facilities, but should also put me in the way of making contacts that will be good for me in business terms later on.

I will also eat a very balanced diet, and I have decided to only drink wine with meals, and to learn about wine. I do not smoke so my appearance will not suffer in that way. It shocks me to hear Darcy saying that she might smoke because it would help her control her weight. Nothing ages a woman's appearance more than being a smoker, although I am now thinking seriously that I must not get tanned any more, because the sun seems to have the same effect.

Just as I plan to shape my body to an ideal configuration. I should similarly shape my presentation of my personality to the best version of myself that I can achieve.

People always assume that if you have a less successful twin, it is a boost for the more successful twin. (I am using 'success' in a fairly crude simplistic way, here.) In fact, the direct opposite is the case. Darcy is often favoured by people who see her as the more human, more fallible, more *genuine* and more instinctive of the two of us.

It seems to me very unfair that people equate unprepared slap-happiness with being genuine, and assume that having discipline and self-control in some way falsifies one's self. However, that is the reality within which I must live my life.

My new word for today is: *obtund*.

Definition: to blunt or dull, to deaden.

17 Glanmire Park
Raheny
Dublin 5
Thursday 4 July 1985

Dear Alex
Whee!!!!!!!

Don't make pedantic noises at me about exclamation marks, or I will do a whole page of them. Or give you your P45.

Think I wouldn't? Discontinue you? Hey, haven't I discontinued school? Study? Education? WHAP! (That is the sound of my carry-all hitting the wall. Oh, shit, it's brought down Sophia's Dégas of all the little ballet dancers. Hold on till I put it back up.)

Done!

Thanks be to Christ she wasn't under it at the time because – oh, here's a charming little Irish anecdote for you, you desiccated academic you. During the War (WW2, to you) which we, for reasons too obscure to go into, called The Emergency (PR people like wot Sophia is gonna be were obviously hard at work back then), a bloody great German bomber that was planning to disgorge its wares on some hapless British city got blown across the Irish sea and found itself over Dublin, didn't it? And didn't our anti-aircraft lads open up on The Hun, didn't they? And didn't the Hun, thinking on his feet, or his joystick or whatever Huns think on, said to his little self O shit, *Donner und Blitzen*, I better get out of this place pretty damn quick, because they are pricking my undersides, even my fuselage, with their AA bullets, but it is difficult to move this hulking great bomber because what is it fulla? It's fulla bombs, so it is. So what'll I do, Mr Hun asks his Hunnish self? I'll lighten my load by dropping one of these bombs. The heaviest. The land mine.

Off you go, tonnish land mind, says Hunnish pilot (God, you can tell I'm in great humour, it's like drugs) and pulls the switch. Off goes the landmine and lands in a happy little heavily populated bit of working class Dublin called the North Strand. Whoosh! Up, up and away goes half the North Strand. This surprises some of the inhabitants to death. Literally. But some of them survive to hear Mr Hun zipping off, lighter by several tons, and one of them – a butcher by trade, designation or profession – decides to look out his window to survey what damage has been done, not knowing that the glass has been shaken loose from the window on the floor above. Out he puts his head, down comes a sheet of glass, guillotine-fashion, and decapitates him. This, now that I think about it, probably qualifies Mr Hun for a place in the *Guinness Book of Records* as the only German pilot to have decapitated a bystanding butcher in a neutral country in WW2.

Oh, twiddly-dee, an adult's life for me. No more Irish, no more French, no more sittin' on a hard oul' bench. Hump all teachers. (Which reminds me, I found a thing in an American book recently that you might clarify for me. Does 'dry humping' mean what I think it means?)

Did I have moments of regret as I left the school building for the last time? What are you, dumb as well as desiccated? By the way, in case you think I have picked up one of Sophia's words, 'desiccated' is on the front of a little roundy container that I can read through the glass of a kitchen press every day. It's on coconut. Lovely word, isn't it?

No moments of regret. I hated every shagging day of school, 89 per cent of my fellow pupils and 93 per cent of my teachers. Those statistics are put in for the sociologist in you. Meaningless, but obscurely pleasing. The 7 per cent of my teachers that I didn't hate includes Margaret Graham, who put me into your project, because I quite enjoy having to write to you.

There is a great comfort in having a man halfway across the world that I can be completely open with who *has* to find me interesting for professional reasons, who's never going to see me and I'm never going to meet.

Will I go back to school reunions? No bloody way. Will I stay in touch? You out of your tree? Stay in touch with that shower? If I never see any of them again, it will be too soon, with the exception of Aileen, who is much more interesting now she is actively planning to be a nurse. She is also improved by taking care of Beethoven, who is going to be a world-class musician. That is according to Greg, who (she said casually, having worked up this whole letter to give her the excuse to mention it) rang me the day the Leaving Cert exam finished and said '*Now* will you come out for a drink with me on Saturday week,' to which I said, 'Yes, if you've nothing better in mind,' and he laughed and said what did I consider better, and I said I was an eating woman rather than a drinking woman so why didn't he take me somewhere very posh to dinner?

He said the question was could he afford it, and

I said of course he could, wasn't he the son of McEnerney the Orthopod Stud, which put him off his oatflakes for the rest of the day, because – I have now found out – he is self-conscious about sex and his parents.

Not self-conscious about sex anywhere else. Just prefers not to think that his parents ever did it, never mind that his father did it with anything that moved ('Would get up on a cracked plate' was the phrase my father surprisingly used before my mother hit him with the tea cosy) and still does it, according to rumour, with a whole lot more than Greg's glamorous fundraising mother.

He (Greg, not his father) is taking me to dinner at the end of this week and I have warned him that I intend to eat him out of house and home and am three sizes bigger than the last time he saw me. He says he likes a substantial woman. I will wear a black dress with a colourdy jacket and a drop-dead air. I have been practising the latter in front of the mirror, on the basis that for the foreseeable future, I am going to be of a size militating against a fragile, protect-me air, so I'd better go the opposite route.

I have been too busy studying to have much time for sexual or relationship matters. This implies that the front and back door of the house have claw-marks from would-be suitors lusting in a door-clawing way for me, while I lean out the window and say 'get thee hence' or whatever it is one properly says to door-clawing lusters. The nearest I have come to door-clawing have been three phone calls from Greg the Orthopod's son, and I don't figure he's eaten up with lust. I think he just finds me amusing.

One of the things I do notice, however, is that I seem to be developing acute observer skills. I can see who is going to be attracted to who long before they are. I spotted Aileen and Beethoven before either of them were sure of it.

I'm also very good at spotting supposedly illicit or hidden relationships, even though this is relatively recent, since, as you know, I had no inkling about Darina until she fainted in class. A boy, now you ask, seven pounds something, born about two weeks before the Leaving Certificate. I went to see him and her several times until I faced up to the fact that what was attracting me, as a person from a home where there had never been any children younger than me, was the babyness of the baby. I figure babies get made very cute because otherwise their parents would murder them in the first three months through lack of sleep. People are never as delightful again as they are when they're babies.

But, being as honest as I always am at long distance with desiccated (have I spelt that wrong?) academics, I have to admit that I don't hunger, yearn and pine to have a baby myself. When I look to the future, which I don't much, I don't see myself surrounded by little skirt-clingers. I don't *not* see myself as having children, but I seem to be missing this huge appetite others have. (Possibly because I am so well-provided for in other appetites, mainly for food.)

All of this makes me good at analysing other people's relationships, and giving advice to friends on how to attract/retrieve/shaft/survive particular boyfriends or girlfriends. It does not make me good at attracting/retrieving/shafting/surviving boyfriends of my own.

You will ask whether I am anxious and lacking in self-regard as a result of this? Of course I am, you dopey desiccate. Especially when you consider the number of dribblingly pathetic phone calls I have to field on a daily basis for my sister, who is, as you will by now have twigged, perfection itself. Balanced, considerate, clean-mouthed, pure as to the lifestyle. Even her shagging vanities are endearing. Short-sighted she is, but just enough to force her to narrow her eyes to focus. This gives her a slightly helpless air and men's hands instinctively go out to help her. (Me, I have 20/20 vision, which is lucky, because if you were short-sighted and looked like me, not only would men's hands not reach out instinctively to guide you but you could walk into walls and fall down toilets for all they'd care.)

Tomorrow, I am going to go out and get a job. Furthermore, I am going to tell you the job I am going to get. There is an ad in today's evening paper which asks 'Do you have a smile in your voice?' If I do, it says I can make a fortune. Do I have a smile in my voice? I have a smile in my voice that goes ear to shagging ear.

I will write to you again when I am rich and famous from voice-smiling. In the meantime, here's a little reciprocal questionnaire for you:

Are you in Seattle again?

What are you doing that's interesting at the moment?

Have you got married again?

Do you look older? What are you reading about/ thinking about?

Have you murdered any innocent Disney animals recently?

Yours in delirious freedom

Darcy

5345 Tradewinds Ave., #283
Fort Attic
Missouri, MO 33003
Thursday 11 July 1985

Dear Darcy

Query: what is a P45?

Yes, dry humping is what you think it is.

No, I haven't been to Seattle again. My time has been taken up, over the past nine months, with two movies. One of them should be released in Europe fairly soon. It's entitled *Zip Code* and concerns a mail fraud which occurred here in the United States. Kiefer Sutherland, Tom Cruise and an Irish actor named Stephen Rea. Nice guy. Sort of guy you never expect to be an actor.

The other movie is called *Fire Without Smoke* and deals with an accusation of sexual abuse against a clergyman. It centres mostly on the court case and to that extent is risky. Based on a Broadway play, the script makes it obvious why it would work very well in the theater: it's intense, wordy, very Chayefsky scripting. Whether that will transfer to the screen, who knows?

The director is the guy I worked with a couple of years back, and he's using an almost unknown cast. We wrapped it about a week ago, and it moves now into post-production.

I am hoping to go to Canada in a few weeks to do some fish-murdering. I could do with a dearth of people for a while. ' . . . just uninterrupted grass, and a hare sitting up.'

I have not married again, nor am I involved with anyone in any serious way. My hairline is receding.

Alex

17 Glanmire Park
Raheny
Dublin 5
Thursday 19 July 1985

Dear Alex

A P45 is the bit of official paper you get the day you lose your job or get made redundant. I presume your mention of not being married again means you're divorced. Thanks for telling me.

Saying your hairline is receding is like when they put sales labels on things saying '30 per cent off'. 30 per cent off *what*, is the key question. Receding from where to where? Are we talking marginal erosion, here, or are you seriously bald? Have you started to comb your hair downwards in front like a gloomy old centurion? Will you buy a sliding roof? Aren't you lucky that you're in a business where it doesn't matter?

I mean, you can wander around film sets with no hair anywhere on you and as long as you can advise on how many times the psycho should drool and out of which side (of his mouth) they won't mind how un-hirsute you are.

Sophia says you can spot quite early who's going to be bald. She says Beethoven is (Beethoven is the musician I mentioned to you in one of my letters – doing a serious line with Aileen, the girl I used to share a desk with, back in the bad old days of desks) but that it'll probably suit him. The key thing, she says, is to look at a guy's father. I must look at Greg's father. Jesus, I haven't even had one single date with this guy and I'm already foreclosing on his hair.

Is Tom Cruise as small as they say?
Darcy

Telegram to Darcy 26 July 1985
  Smaller.
  Alex

Telegram to Alex 26 July 1985
  But *deadly* attractive, right?
  Darcy

Telegram to Darcy 26 July 1985
  I must have another look at him and report back to
  you.
  Alex

CHAPTER FOURTEEN

For Sophia, there was a rightness about university she had never expected. She mapped out her year's course as soon as she received timetable and booklists, and combined study with social life without effort. Three days a week she went to the gym for a forty-five-minute workout. She joined the Historical Society and spoke at several debates. She joined Players. So happy was she with her first months in college that she managed to irritate Darcy with her sympathy over Darcy not being in college.

'I didn't want to be in college,' Darcy said.

'Yes, but you didn't know how much fun it would be.'

Darcy, meanwhile, had landed the job with the company which wanted a smile in her voice. It turned out that they were a newly arrived telephone services company.

'In the Derramore Industrial Estate, they have this section of a building, laid out in pods,' Darcy told her parents.

'Pods?'

'Lines of workstations, four this side, four opposite, then a partition, and another eight. At the moment, there are only four pods, but they say that if they get underway, really, there could be hundreds and hundreds.'

'Doing what?'

'Taking telephone reservations for hotels. You might have people wanting to book hotels in the United States, and let's say they're in Germany, they'll ring a number there and get transferred at no cost to them, to Derramore Industrial Estate, where the call will go to the German pod and a German speaker will deal with them, find out what kind of accommodation they need and organise it for them. The caller doesn't know that he's talking to someone in Ireland and he doesn't care, either. But just over the partition in the next pod there might be eight guys dealing with service calls about a particular kind of computer – again, calls coming from all over Europe.'

Darcy was in a pod of operators handling queries for a major utilities company in Britain which was about to be privatised.

'What do people want to know?' Sophia asked.

'Details about the price of the shares, when the offering is going to happen, commission to brokers, how they can get information about the procedure.'

'But you don't know anything about stocks and shares.'

'They give you a chunk of data in the beginning, and nine times out of ten, the questions the caller asks will lead you to one of the bits of data you already have. The tenth caller you refer on to your supervisor, but you go over and listen in to what he tells them, and next time someone comes along asking that particular question, you're ready with that answer, too.'

'Don't they notice the Irish accent?'

'People who think they're on the way to make loads of money don't pay much attention to the accent of the person giving them the information they need.'

'D'you get to know them?'

'You don't try to get to know them. I'm paid a basic amount and a bonus depending on how many calls above a minimum I deal with. They've worked out that their really superb people can absolutely satisfy the average caller and get them off the line in sixty seconds or less. That's one of the reasons they wanted someone with a smile in their voice: people at the other end of the phone must have the feeling that they're getting ages of your time and absolute commitment.'

'But that's phoney,' Robert King said.

At this point, the front doorbell rang, and Darcy ushered Greg McEnerney into the kitchen. As always, Greg arrived in mid-anecdote and had everybody laughing as he turned a kitchen chair around the wrong way and sat astride, his hands joined on the top of the back of it.

'You have to admit it,' Darcy said, patting him on the back. 'For an accountancy student, he's not dull.'

'But he may *get* dull,' Colette said, handing Greg a cup of tea.

'Receivers are never dull,' Greg said.

'Is that what you're planning to be?' Robert King crumpled his napkin and put it on the table.

Greg nodded.

'Tax guys are dull,' he told Colette. 'Insolvency guys are dull. The guys that specialise in contract of information stuff are duller than dull. But receivers? Look at John Donnelly.'

'I've never heard of John Donnelly,' Sophia said.

'Well, if you were doing PR for a company that was going down the tubes, you'd know him. King of the Receivers. For this generation. Gimme five years, and I'll be King of the receivers.'

'No attraction to medicine at all?'

Greg looked at Robert. 'I think if my father wasn't who he is, I might be very attracted to medicine. But I don't want to be Son Of.'

'You wouldn't have to be an orthopod.'

'I'd *certainly* not be an orthopod. I'd be a paediatrician.'

Sophia looked at Greg as if she had never seen him before. 'A paediatrician?'

Darcy smiled to herself. One of the things she knew about Greg was that he loved children and was very good with them. He was the favourite adopted uncle in many families.

'Yeah. Keeping kids well would be a great thing.'

'But instead of that, you're going to condemn companies to death?'

'Mrs King, I'm going to be a human wrecking ball.'

Delighted with his own outrageousness, Greg stood and twirled the chair back into its normal position.

'Listen, Hulk, we gonna hit the road?'

'*What* did you call my sister?'

'Hulk. As in Incredible.'

'Darcy, do you let him – ?'

'Sure what can I do, Sophia. You know yourself. The offspring of doctors never have any sensitivity.'

Darcy and Greg got into Greg's eight-year-old Alfasud, which had never come to terms with Irish weather. On damp days it refused to respond in any way to the turn of the ignition key. Now, however, it sprang into life.

'That's my girl,' Greg said, patting the dashboard.

'Sexist.'

'That's me.'

'Derek Cullen isn't sexist.'

Greg instantly did a drawling South Dublin imitation of Sophia's current boyfriend.

'Stop it. He's very romantic.'

'Bullshit.'

'He is, though. Sometimes when she comes out in the morning, there's a single red rose tied to the front gate with red ribbon.'

Greg rolled down the window and made a spirited mimicry of throwing up through it.

'He leaves her home and walks around the corner and rings her from a call box to tell her he's missing her already.'

'Oh, Jesus, there should be a law.'

'My father doesn't like him.'

'Your father goes up in my estimation.'

'Says he has no sense of humour.'

'I wouldn't have thought your father had a cast-iron future, himself, as a stand-up comedian.'

'No, but he does at least have a sense of humour. He can be very funny. And he sees the odd sides of things. He is not mordant.'

'Sophia's word for the day, is it?'

'Yeah. Harsh, piercing, sharp, stinging, biting.'

'Mordant?'

'Right. My professor uses it, now and again.'

'Your professor?'

'This old guy I correspond with in the United States.'

'Love letters from academics?'

Darcy laughed so much at this that tears squeezed out the sides of her eyes.

'Couldn't be less like love letters, this correspondence.'

'Think you can fool me, you wanton hoor? I know a love letter when I hear about it.'

'In that case, I started getting them when I was about ten. Well, maybe thirteen.'

'Jesus, underage sex by post.'

'Greg!'

'Well?'

'By the way, my father wants to know if you'll ever get back to rugby or did that injury last year finish you off?'

'Never mind your effing father, tell me about this sex by post.'

'Don't call him my effing father.'

'Why not? You do.'

'Only in a rage. Look, these questionnaires come from the States about – about relationships and stuff like that. It's a big university study and this academic over there has a number of respondents he has to circulate with questions and then collate their answers.'

'Relationships?'

'Mmm.'

'Like this, you mean?'

'Greg, not when you're driving a car!'

'I'm not driving a car. I'm stopped at traffic lights.'

'Yes, and there's a bloody great double-decker bus also stopped at traffic lights, and every passenger on this side is dying to know what you're going to do next.'

'Will I show them?'

'Try and I'll break your arm.'

'So some old fart professor sends you questionnaires?'

An old fart professor with a receding hairline, Darcy thought.

'That all?'

'That's it.'

'*Bor*ing.'

'Well, we can't all have Derek Cullen leaving flowers on our gate.'

The Alfasud coughed several times before agreeing to move away from the traffic lights.

'Thank your father for his concern,' Greg said, remembering the query about his rugby. 'My father's orthopod pals say that I should not go back to playing rugby. In fact, they more or less said that if I was a few notches better they could prop me up and I might get a cap for Ireland but that in the process I'd end up half-crippled for life. I'm just that little bit below international talent. So I'm going to concentrate on my upper body for the moment.'

'Me, too.'

'Me too what?'

'I'm going to concentrate on your upper body for the moment. Safer that way.'

Greg lifted her hand and put it firmly on the front of his trousers. He drove, as he always drove, with his legs wide apart at the knee. Darcy left her hand where he had put it for a moment, then took it back.

'But if you concentrate on upper body development, everything due south of your belt will probably atrophy, so I should vamoose while the going's good,' Darcy said.

'*Atrophy?*'

Greg took his hands off the steering wheel and made the cross-index-finger sign against a vampire.

'Well, do you not remember what your leg looked like when it came out of the plaster that time? All shrunk and pale and wrinkly.'

'Listen, kid, I can get better conversation from women I give lifts to than predictions about the atrophying of my private parts.'

'Don't worry about it. You're not going to be giving me lifts much longer. I'm going to buy a car.'

She told the family the same thing a couple of evenings later.

'What kind of car?' Robert King asked.

'Don't know yet. I've been advised to pick a few second-hand ones in my price range and get a good garage guy to check them out for me. Even if it costs a bit of money, they say it saves money in the long run. I'm not in any hurry, anyway.'

Later that evening, Sophia asked her about the car. 'I know what you told Dad, but what are you *really* going to get?'

Darcy laughed.

'Something as odd as I can afford. A bright yellow convertible Morris Minor, maybe. That's as near as I could possibly get to my dream car, which is the one Noddy had in the Noddy in Toyland books. Remember? Little yellow convertible with a front door that opened the wrong way and a running board. I'd love Noddy's car.'

Sophia tried to remember Noddy's car and failed.

'I notice you're fighting less often with Dad,' she said.

'Yep. I have this new system.'

'Oh?'

'I do the fights inside my own head first, then I don't have to do them for real.'

'How do you mean?'

'The car's a good example,' said Darcy. 'Decision: buy a car. Possible fight with Da? First issue: don't buy a second-hand car, the dealer will always tell you it was owned by an elderly spinster who drove it once a year to a meeting in the Royal Dublin Society, but in fact it was owned by a drug-taking drag-racer who turned the milometer back so it has done seven million six thousand and twenty-three miles, most of them over broken glass and with no oil or water in the engine. Where does this viewpoint take my father? This viewpoint takes my father to the point where he says I should borrow from the credit union or the bank and he will guarantee the loan. When I say 'Da, the insurance on a new car would be through the roof,' he says 'Darcy, your mother and I would be very happy, in the interest of your safety, to give you the insurance premium as a birthday gift.' What I can't say is 'Da, get your well-meaning micro-managing little mawlers out of my life, I don't want to start on the conveyor belt of debt-servicing or establishing a good credit rating.' So I just talk about good garages and how they'll check out my Noddy car to make sure it hasn't a crack in its suspension or worse.'

'Have you the cash?' asked Sophia.

'I have two thousand seven hundred and twenty pounds, as of this morning's count. After tax. In the top drawer under the computer, if you want to check it out.'

'Oh God, Darcy, why don't you put it in the bank?'

'Because I don't want to. I want to be able to count it and check it and tell myself that this is the twenty-pound note I got when I did up that document for Greg's father, and that bundle of single pound notes is what I got when I took books to the second-hand shop.'

'If the car you like costs anything up to three thousand seven hundred, you can count me in for a thousand, if you're prepared to lend the car to me,' said Sophia.

'Sophia, this is kindness.'

Darcy spat the word 'kindness' as if it was slimy.

'No, it's not. It's advance rental.'

'You wouldn't be seen dead in a Noddy car.'

'You're right. But you won't succeed in getting a Noddy car, so I figure I'm safe enough.'

Sophia was correct, both about Darcy not getting a Noddy car and about her need for an extra thousand pounds.

'The car I've found costs just under four thousand,' Darcy told her. 'The garage people say it's sound as a pound. So I'd be grateful if I could borrow the thousand from you.'

'Not borrow – rental.'

'Not rental – it's a Volkswagen Beetle,' said Darcy.

Sophia laughed out loud.

'And you think I wouldn't drive around in a Volkswagen Beetle?'

'Right.'

'Darcy, you make very strong judgements about me.'

'Right.'

'I'll have the money for you tomorrow. Unlike you, I *do* believe in banks.'

'How have you got any money, anyway? You're not working.'

'I save birthday presents and Christmas presents and I get interest.'

'You buying a pension yet?'

'Oh, shut up.'

'Thanks, anyway.'

'No problem.'

'And it's a loan, Sophia, are we agreed on that?'

'Of course we are. You think I'd be caught dead in a Volkswagen Beetle?'

'No. Particularly not when you see the colours.'

'Colours? Plural?'

'Somebody did a magic mushroom psychedelic number on it. Neon pink, luminous glow in the dark green and yellow spots.'

'You're joking.'

Darcy wasn't joking. When Robert King arrived home from work on Tuesday of the following week, the Beetle was at the kerb outside.

'Pulsating, I swear to God,' he said to Colette.

'Yeah. You can sort of see it through two walls, can't you?'

'It's like something *diseased*,' Robert said.

'Motorised septicaemia?' Colette suggested.

Robert nodded, dumbly.

'At least she didn't put it in the driveway,' Colette said consolingly.

'Why didn't she?'

'She thought you'd be upset.'

'It's a bloody sight more noticeable out there on the roadway.'

'But it doesn't provably belong to one of your family.'

'Oh, I see. We're hoping that the neighbours believe someone abandons this suppurating wreck outside our front door on a nightly basis?'

'D'you want it in your driveway or d'you want it at the kerb?'

'I don't want it either way. She could have had a brand new Honda Civic.'

'The little car for women professionals,' Colette said knowingly. 'I don't think it would quite match Darcy's image.'

'What does Greg think?'

'Greg thinks that like everything else about Darcy, it's great gas.'

'Greg thinks life is all fun and games.'

'Sophia has a lot of time for Greg,' Colette said. 'Thinks he's the best thing that could have happened to Darcy. Says he's gentle.'

Discreet too, Colette remembered Sophia saying. Discreet. She had tried to fit the description to Greg ever since Sophia had used it, but was still perplexed by it and by Sophia's saying it.

CHAPTER FIFTEEN

Entry in Sophia's diary, Sunday 11 May 1986
Whatever garage Darcy had look at her car must have done a good job, because it's going strong. It still sounds like a cross between a lawn mower and a helicopter, and whenever I sit in it I am acutely uncomfortable. It makes me feel undersized because its dashboard is so high.

Owning a car makes more difference to Darcy than having a boyfriend. She loves the freedom of it and sometimes gets up after she has gone to bed and goes out driving.

If I had picked someone for Darcy, I couldn't have picked better than Greg. He makes her feel great. Because he's a big man, he is not bothered by the fact that she's big, too, even when she wears her highest heels and the top of her head is even with his. (Whenever Darcy puts on an awful lot of weight, she wears very high heels and very large jewellery. At first I thought this made her look like an ice-cream cone with speckles on top, unsteady, but as she gets more confident, she has developed A Look.)

She has already insisted on paying me back the money I lent her. Plus she gave me a gift token for Brown Thomas in lieu of interest, because she knew I would not have accepted interest. She is doing very well in her job and is very happy at it.

The thing that bothers me at the moment is that I get the feeling that Darcy doesn't like my boyfriend Derek very much. She often praises how generous and solicitous he is to me, and when Greg completely forgot our birthday but Derek didn't, she hit Greg with a folded-up newspaper and said he was to take lessons in being a proper boyfriend from Derek.

I suppose if I were madly in love with Derek I would reject these little subliminal vibes, but I must confess that I am not madly in love with him. Perhaps I had only once in my life the capacity to be totally in love. I find myself patting myself on the back for being nice to Derek, which is ludicrous.

Today's word is: *adventitious*.

Definition: accidental, additional, appearing casually, developed out of the usual order or place. As in 'This is a description, not an adventitious comment.'

17 Glanmire Park
Raheny
Dublin 5
12 May 1986

Dear Alex

I have shared with you before the fact that my sister never lets her weight vary by more than three pounds, learns a new word every day, writes down a quote at least once a week and learns it off. This evening she told me she writes five letters a week, because they will make someone else feel better or remind someone of her existence. She cuts little bits out of newspapers and sends them to people she thinks will find them useful.

I bet she was neatening up my goddamn umbilical cord for me while we were in the womb.

It is also kind of awkward because she was asking me about how polite Greg and I are (am?) to Derek, the boyfriend I told you about. I could not tell her it is the careful politeness you reserve for the touchy old or for a Rottweiler you have been told is really very tame. I just don't believe in Derek. I find him improbable.

Suppurating Septicaemia, my car, is in wonderful shape. My father is very grateful that we're having a mild winter, because he says Beetles have a reputation for rolling over when there's ice. I find this endearing, the idea of a car rolling over like a cat wanting its tummy scratched.

The only awful thing about having the car is it gives you freedom to be a complete shit if you want to be. Twice in the last month I have actually got out of bed after midnight, got (sort of) dressed and driven to the twenty-four hour shop to get sweets. I'm currently into Mintolas and Tiffin bars. Sophia woke but said nothing. Maybe she thinks I am having complicated times with Greg and needed some time to think about them.

There are no complications with Greg. He is just about the best thing that has ever happened to me. It strikes me as extraordinary that I should meet this man, develop this uncomplicated friendship with him and have it get more affectionate all the time. I never thought that would happen. Go on, tell me I fit into some statistic somewhere.

Greg is also very clever. Clever enough not to need to *be* clever all the time.

One of the things that makes me like Greg so much is his attitude to my weight. There was a discussion the other evening in a pub about property prices. Greg said that when he and I bought our house, we might kid ourselves we were buying a three-bedroom house but it would really be a two-bedroomer: the third bedroom would be for my fat wardrobe or my thin wardrobe, whichever I wasn't wearing at the time. I didn't know he knew I have two sets of clothes. The smallest is a size twelve jacket and I think the label is a mistake on that one. The largest is a size 18 pair of trousers that looks like it's waiting its chance to star in one of those newspaper pictures where the slimmer stands inside her old trousers and holds the waistband out a mile to show how thin she's got.

Darcy

Postcard 25 May 1986
Darcy

It's not a statistic you fit into. It's a concept called *homiphily*, which refers to the likelihood of recruiting your sex partners from among people with similar characteristics. Just as we tend to pick our friends from our own social background so we also tend to recruit our sexual partners from within similar networks.

One of the points of commonality is looks. If Greg is as handsome as you suggest, then the odds are in favour of you being equally handsome.

Alex

Postcard 31 May 1986
Alex

You've lost your marbles. How could Greg being handsome make me handsome?

Darcy

5345 Tradewinds Ave., #283
Fort Attic
Missouri, MO 33003
Tuesday 3 June 1986

Dear Darcy

One of the findings that crops up again and again in studies of mating among humans is that the physical attractiveness of the partners tends to be pretty evenly matched. Some theorists hold that this means people actively, if unconsciously, seek out people of an attractiveness to match with their own. Some researchers, notably Kalick and Hamilton, indicate that the reason may be simpler: the most attractive potential partners of either sex are picked off quickly and so the less attractive have less choice. (This is a crude version of the theory, but let it stand.) Thus, your sister, whom you would rate as extremely attractive, was, if I remember your letters at the time, in a relationship within a month of going to university – and with someone of equal (perhaps?) attractiveness.

Bottom line: if Greg is handsome, you're probably handsome too.

Alex

Postcard 10 June 1986
Attention Alex

1 This is the first time I have received a conditional compliment based on statistical probabilities.
2 Never forget this: there are exceptions to every rule.
Darcy

5345 Tradewinds Ave., #283
Fort Attic
Missouri, MO 33003
Wednesday 18 June 1986

Dear Darcy

You will appreciate that although this correspondence takes in issues other than those central to the study from which it started, I must occasionally resort to formality and request some specific information. As I understand it, you have now had a stable relationship with GM* for almost one year. You have dealt with various aspects of that relationship, so I have some understanding of the young man's appearance, habits of speech, attitudes, etc. However, you have not dealt with the physical aspects of the relationship at all, and this, I suspect, has two causative factors.

The first is that because this relationship is the first which has seriously engaged your feelings, you are experiencing a need for privacy and so are reluctant to write about the more personal aspects of the relationship. In that context, I would ask you to remember that GM is unknown on this side of the Atlantic, and the details you provide are not attached to *any* known or identified individual.

The second is that because you have been writing to me for some time in an informal and friendly way, you may now be inhibited by that 'relationship'. It is most important that no such inhibition would impinge upon your contribution to this study which, thus far, has been immeasurably valuable. I will consult – given your permission – with my colleagues to examine the advisability of assigning you another contact within the study.

Please advise

Alex

*The use of initials might defuse anxieties around this issue.

17 Glanmire Park
Raheny
Dublin 5
25 June 1986

Dear Alex

Wonderful, your capacity to turn into Professor Stoneface. (I must introduce you to my sister

Sophia. Her 'shalls' and 'cognisants' could have a ball with your 'please advises'.)

The use of initials would *cause* anxieties rather than diminish them. I never think of people except as first names. Somebody rang in to my company about a week ago and asked to speak to Mr Dunwoody. (I'm a supervisor, I'll have you know. I could nearly buy a BMW, but Suppurating Septicaemia owns a part of my heart.)

Wrong number, I said, and put the phone down. Phone rings again. Same voice. May he speak to Mr Dunwoody? I'm still sorry, but this is a wrong number. We ain't got no Mr Dunwoody. You don't? No. But aren't you Tele-Prompt? Yep, that's us. Davey Dunwoody? Oh, *Davey*! Hold on, I'm putting you through . . . I had never thought of Davey as Davey anything. I never think of you as Alex anything. (Well, sometimes, when I get one of your more formal fits like today's, I think of you as Alex the Elderly Academic with the Receding Hairline. But this may be out of date. Your hairline may have passed receding and be terminal.)

I will think about your request and come back with details. For the moment, suffice it to say (this is a free sample of Sophia) that we have been Doing A Lot but not It.

Don't even suggest transferring me to some remedial teacher. Took me long enough to get used to you.

Yours, resolved to try harder
Darcy

17 Glanmire Park
Raheny
Dublin 5
2 July 1986

Dear Alex

Stream of consciousness coming up. Greg and me. Stages. Phases. Starting with will he ring, won't he ring, pretend you're cool, fall over yourself answering the phone, be barely civil when you get one of the millions of what my father calls Sophia's swains. The Gadarene swain. Days of swain and roses – such are all of Sophia's days. I bring up the rear, ever hopeful, but I keep the cynicism flag flying because hope is shameful and naïveté merits the death penalty.

Astonishment when he does ring, unease with the ease of him. The sense of being set up for a bad joke. Thought you were getting a date with Greg the Gorgeous, didnya? Didnya, didnya? Looka the face of her – gotcha. There always is laughter at fat girls. Meant, unmeant, it's all the same. Like a heat-seeking missile, the laughter. A fat-seeking missile. Everywhere you go, just waiting for the fuse to be lit. Try on something in a shop, bring it out of the dressing room, lie about not quite liking the way the collar sits when the truth is it rode up at hip or gaped at bust or mutinied at thigh and you had to stay there, four mirrors multiplying you a million gross times, until the fat redness of your struggle with it seeped down out of your face below your collar.

Trying to justify his attention by getting thinner, then in a one-sided war with him, dammit we'll check him out, damn him he says he doesn't care, we can test *that* one, let's see how much he doesn't care when you add a stone and a half to already overweight and have to live in cover-all jackets and drapery. Looking with contempt at all other fat women, no sympathy.

Pretending every day, waiting for the comment 'I don't know how you're not fading away, sure you eat nothing', right, I eat nothing all day when normal people eat. Like my sisters in suet, I eat nothing except at night in gorging when no one can see and judge.

Then beginning to hear him when he talks about great hair, thick glossy red auburn, light with gold in sunshine, manageable and splendid like a Jim Fitzpatrick Celtic cartoon queen. To look at them when he talks of the little white hands and circles the small wrists with his big strong hands. Uncrouching to match the confident scale of him walking hand-in-hand with a man proud to belong with you.

Then, trying out his name in conversation not casual but dressed up as casual. 'I notice the same with Greg.' 'Greg was telling me.' 'Did you ever notice, with Greg.' Facile with the certain pessimism of one who has aquaplaned into a million stone walls.

Then kissing and being kissed and the pure affectionateness of him so pleasing. Not a toucher, he nevertheless kisses his grandmother, hugs his father, lifts his mother in laughter. Cats and dogs seek him to rub against him and his big hands go down to them absent-minded, homing in on the behind-the-ear place.

Kissing becoming more than affection, the knowledge in his face, see what I can do to you, see how I can rearrange your breathing and make the floor fall away beneath you, and see how I can stop when you half don't want me to and see how I can make you laugh and *pant* in a welter of desire and denial and laughter. The big hands on neck and slithering inside collar. On shoulder and sliding down upper arm.

Through cardigans and blouse and bra. Touch-fondling, finish, pat leg, let's go home. Inside cardigan through wafer-cotton top, soft sports bra, palm bringing nipple up through fabric, pleasuring, promising, postponing. Unbuttoning, watched in fascination, big hand slowly, harsh-skinned palm curved inside bra. Smaller hand seeking hardness . . .

Dot dot dot.

In fact, I like that so much I'll do it again.

Dot dot dot.

End of story. End of story to this point. Still haven't got to the stage where I hang a condom on the gate before Greg arrives. Have not discussed any of this with Sophia, because I know I would get the priceless virginity line. Of course, there is a truth to this. Virginity is so damn rare these days, it practically *is* priceless, but I'm not gonna die wondering. (I hope.)

By the way (she said, skittering wildly out of an area which is liable to cause her to go into a decline from embarrassment), remember you read it here first: my sister Sophia is going to be offered a job in *Positionings* the very minute she gets her degree, and will probably be running the place a year later. To say she has impressed the knickers off them during her summer stints is the understatement of a lifetime.

Reverting to bodice-ripping stuff, let me remind you that I did ask you some considerable time ago for data on happiness as related to bonking and you gave me damn all information. Are you still advising actors on how to play weirdos?

Darcy

Dear Darcy

Thank you very much for the material which is now in the proper file. No questions arising.

I am still working on films, yes. Currently a mini-series for TV about a serial killer on Long Island who from his very earliest years was marked out as a victim at kindergarten and school.

It would, to my mind, be both accurate and interesting to show two things; the genetic component of his social dyslexia (how did children spot so early that this child was different, to be avoided and/or brutalised?) and, at the same time, the environmental component – in other words, the damage to his development done by the bullying of his peers while at school. However, the writer and director have chosen instead to revive the old Bettelheim paradigm. Cold mother turns out nutcase son. It is highly satisfactory in dramatic terms, and from an actor's point of view gives a lot of scope.

On happiness and sexual satisfaction, it would not be true to say that the jury is still out, but it's not all the way back in. Starting with the negative, with *un*happiness, the early studies tended to find that unmarried men were much more unhappy than unmarried women.

In fact, the indicators were that (this is the crudest of generalities) women tended to be happier if they stayed single, whereas men tended to be happier if they married. When we look at the factors common to people who describe themselves as 'very happy', those factors include age, with happiness centering, although not exclusively, on the twenties, education, health and affluence.

Young, well-educated, healthy and affluent people have a statistically better chance of being sexually active and of deriving satisfaction and physical pleasure from the activity, but whether this is a cause or result of happiness has been difficult to establish.

Warm regards

Alex

18 July 1986

Dear Alex

I don't think I often say thank you for all this long distance education. Thank you.

My sister says: 'Happiness is a decision you make, like courage.' Her theory seems to be that repeated brave acts add up to a trait you could call courage and that repeated chirpiness in the face of life's depressingness adds up to happiness.

I can't get my mind around this at all. To me, happiness is like the day of the high wind, when the plastic bag came flying around the front of the church and pasted itself to Mrs Corcoran's face as though it had been waiting all its life to meet her. Happiness comes around the corner some days and pastes itself to my face, and other days what gets pasted to my face are misery, resentment, guilt, depression or blind rage. Sophia's happiness is sort of virtuous and I should admire her for it. Curious thing, though, the more you *should* admire someone for a particular thing, the less you actually admire them for it. Not that Sophia wants to be admired. She spends her whole life fending off people who think she is bright, beautiful, talented and great to be with.

Darcy

PS Thank you for the cheque for my expenses.

CHAPTER SIXTEEN

In the autumn of the following year, 1987, Darcy and Greg were separated for ten weeks when Greg and several of his fellow accountancy students did project work in the Chicago head office of his partnership. He came back in November.

'You are a swine, you know, for not writing to me,' Darcy said, settling into his car. 'You will not change, but I'm still going to state it as a way of putting it on the record. Sophia has swains. I get swines.'

'Would you seriously prefer Derek the Dutiful, dorking around and looking like a candidate for the Samaritans all the time?'

'No, but that's because I have pathological sadomasochistic tendencies. I prefer fun to fetid faithfulness.'

'*Fetid* faithfulness. That Sophia's phrase of the week?'

'Listen, fart-face, I can think up my own phrases. You have no permission to use fetid faithfulness without paying a royalty.'

'Enough. Enough. Beethoven's going to get married.'

'What? He's only a kid. What is he, barely twenty?'

'Aileen wants a full white wedding, with you as bridesmaid,' Greg said. 'Beethoven doesn't want a wedding, white, red or blue. But he's going along. Beethoven is really good at going along.'

'Why does he?'

Greg shrugged.

'Keeps Aileen happy, and when Aileen's happy she lets him alone to compose.'

'So really he's marrying her in order to get married to music.'

Greg wrinkled his nose, the way he always did when Darcy over-analysed what seemed easy and obvious.

'I hate the idea of being a bridesmaid.'

'Don't tell me,' Greg said. 'You'll feel you have to go on a diet.'

'Yeah. Bridesmaids' dresses are always shagging shiny shagging satin with bloody bows bloody everywhere. I'd look like a brillo-polished piggybank.'

Having decided that the parking space he had found was as near as he was going to get to the restaurant, Greg pulled in the car and turned off the engine, then leaned over to Darcy, tucking her long hair behind her ears.

'Ever strike you that Aileen and Nicholas are inviting you in the knowledge of whatever weight you are now and that they're not asking you to get thinner?'

'Oh, I know *that*,' Darcy snapped.

'Ever strike you that on the day, Aileen is going to be much more concerned about how she looks than about how you look?'

'So?'

'Ever strike you that the best man is going to have a hard time keeping his hands off the shiny satin curves?'

'*You're* going to be the best man?'

'Who did you think was?'

'It never struck me.'

Greg removed his hands from the sides of her face and pretended to be ratty.

'Charming. You were going to go up the aisle, linking arms with a total stranger. A nameless total stranger . . . '

'All the more reason for losing weight.'

'A total stranger?'

'No. The fact that it's you. The whole church would be saying, "Would you look at Mr Perfect, hormones on the hoof, and him going out with that blob, Sophia King's sister." The ugly sister.'

Greg pulled her over to him.

'They're much more likely to be saying, "God, aren't they good looking, that pair – they fit together."'

'You're very kind,' Darcy began.

'Darcy, it may take me a long time, because you're a slow learner, but some day I'll get it through to you. I don't love you in spite of the way you look. I love you because of the way you look. I'll never forget seeing you that afternoon of the camera rehearsal in RTE. God, you were the sexiest woman I'd ever seen.'

'What'll you be wearing?'

'I await Aileen's instructions on that.'

Aileen's instructions included wing collars for her husband-to-be and his best man, and grey tail-coats with top hats. Nicholas smiled silently and went along with it. Greg was delighted with his fitting. Darcy, in the three months leading up to the wedding, lost twenty pounds and looked very well in the peacock-blue satin Aileen had chosen for the bridesmaid's dress, with peacock-blue satin ribbons threaded through her auburn hair.

'*Told* you we'd look fantastic,' Greg muttered to her at the altar.

At the wedding reception, he made a speech that was witty, observant of bride, groom and their families in a way that was pointed but just a notch short of cruelty, and delivered with a deceptive ease.

'You have to do television,' Darcy told him afterwards, as they danced.

'Mmm?'

'I was looking at the audience while you were doing your speech. They were in love with you. I mean, they *yearned* towards you.'

Sophia, who was there with a desperately dapper Derek Cullen, said much the same thing.

'That speech was no accident,' she told Greg. 'A lot of work went into it.'

Greg winked, over her head, at Derek. 'Derek, you know Sophia, but let me tell you one thing about her. When she pays you a compliment in that deadly serious tone, there's a moral lesson hanging on to the end of it.'

Sophia laughed. 'I just think someone with your talent

should be doing television,' she said.

'You'll be glad to find yourself in agreement with your sister on this,' Greg replied.

Just then, the band stopped playing. Nicholas stood at the microphone and gestured for silence. His limp hair damp with sweat, he looked like a derelict who had borrowed a bridegroom's clothes for a few hours and wrecked them in that period.

' . . . for Aileen,' they could hear him saying. 'Darcy?'

Darcy, on the other side of the room, gave Greg that expressionless look which substitutes for rolling-eyes-to-heaven in situations where eye-rolling is inappropriate.

'Darcy hates this,' Greg muttered to Sophia. Sophia sat down behind Derek and waited.

Darcy stood at the microphone for a moment in complete stillness, then began to sing. The wedding guests unfamiliar with the song looked politely bored at first, then were pulled by the powerful voice and almost angry passion of the singing. *This* is love, the song said. This is the definition. Everything else is second-rate. Derek, startled by the voice and the type of song, looked at Sophia as if for explanation, and found her in a sort of reverence, her eyes focused somewhere further away than Darcy's peacock-blue figure.

As Darcy finished, Greg put one big hand on Sophia's shoulder, rubbed it gently, then went walking forward through the applause, lifted Darcy off her feet, swung her around, and demanded that the band play 'The Most Beautiful Girl in the World'.

'For the bride – and dammit, for the bridesmaid, too!' he called out, reviving Darcy's round of applause.

'Neither of them are half as beautiful as you,' Derek whispered to Sophia, as she had known he would.

'Derek, could you get me a glass of orange juice and something for yourself as well. I want to talk to you,' she said, so gravely that Derek rushed to find a drink of orange, livid with terrified anticipation. Darcy and Greg, on the other hand, were on the dance floor in high good humour with each other.

'D'you want to be paid now or later?' Darcy asked, laughing as they danced.

'I just want to get out of here reasonably soon and do unspeakable things to you,' Greg said, moving hard against the sheen of her satin skirt.

'Can't leave before the bride and groom,' Darcy said, her voice husky from wanting him.

'If Beethoven doesn't get a move on, I'll drop-kick him into the limo myself,' Greg muttered.

The band moved to a slower number, and someone turned down some of the lights in the room. Sophia and Derek went out a side door into the hotel grounds, Derek's arm around Sophia's slender waist.

They came to a garden chair and Sophia sat down. Derek ended up separated from her without knowing how it had happened. It was colder than Sophia had expected. Better make this quick, one part of her mind suggested. No, another part corrected. This must be done with care and concern.

'Derek, I want us not to live in each other's pockets as much as we have been.'

To her surprise, Derek tilted forward on the chair like a child learning to dive from a sitting position, smacking his hands against his forehead as if they were all that was preventing him falling face down on the gravel in front of him. 'I knew it I knew it I knew it,' he said. He hammered his face and words fell out of it, slime-slopped with tears and spit. She sat silent. Eventually he checked to see if she was still there, finding her looking at him not with sympathy or guilt but with the mildly caring curiosity of a mother checking the duration of a coughing fit in a child.

'You are *cold*,' he suddenly shrilled, leaping to his feet and almost dancing in front of her.

Your grief does not entitle you to abuse me, she thought, standing and brushing her linen skirt. As she watched him, he folded down like the legs of an ironing board, kneeling on the gravel, canting forward, thin neck extended.

Sophia left him there and walked back into the hotel just as Beethoven and his bride were leaving. Aileen threw her bouquet so determinedly that Darcy could not have failed to catch it unless her arms had been pinned to her sides.

'We're *outa* here,' Greg said in Darcy's ear.

'Has to be in my car,' Darcy reminded him.

'Oh, shit.'

'Oh, shhh.'

'I'll get the coats.'

Within minutes, they were in the car, Darcy driving, Greg, now in casual clothes, sprawled – in so far as it was possible to sprawl in the Volkswagen – in the passenger seat.

'Where we going?'

'Bull Wall.'

The causeway to the Bull Island, with its seven miles of beach, was brighter than usual.

'Moonlight an' all,' Greg said.

'You laid it on?'

'That's not all I plan to lay on.'

Darcy parked the car about a hundred yards from the causeway.

'Are you not going to lock the car?'

'Nothing in it to steal,' Darcy said, stuffing the keys into her pocket.

'And not worth stealing itself.'

'Shut up about my car. I love that car.'

'A supervisor should be driving a better car.'

'A supervisor may be driving an Oldsmobile or something like that very soon. They want to send me to America.'

'Oh, come *on*.'

'Greg, you went to Chicago.'

'For three months.'

'My time in the States might be only three months.'

'I'd miss you, Darcy, a lot. But you have to do whatever

is right for your career.'

'You been paying attention to your few feminist friends?'

The softly breaking waves at the water's edge were luminous in moonlight. Other couples loomed out of darkness, some corduroyed and booted for businesslike walking, some in velvets and dress-shirts from a deb's ball.

Darcy's high heels sank in the sand as they kissed, pressed close against each other, their unbuttoned heavy coats opening to allow bodies to touch closer and in warmth. His hands, inside her coat, pressed her against him, stroking the shiny fabric at her back, tilting back from the waist to watch her as he brought his hands around her to her breasts. Her eyes closed at the pleasure, her hips moving against him. His hand pushed the shoulder of the satin dress away and down, freeing her breast to his mouth and the cold night air. She moaned and reached between them, unzipping, hand inside through cotton, then on throbbing hardness.

His hand pushed, sliding on the satin, then on the equal satin of the inside of her thighs, opening to the hand, hand higher over pants waistband, then into warm moistness and the two of them heartpounding pain-moaning with near-pleasure, gasping at how far and how near they were.

'Oh, Jesus, let's go back to the car.'

He let the long heavy skirt fall and pushed the fabric of the dress back up over the firm softness of her shoulder, turning her so that they half-stumbled, stopping every few steps to kiss again, her hand still fondling him, the pleasure of it pushing her past wonder at her own abandon. At the car, as if to frustrate and prolong the aching swollen desire, they kissed more, touched more.

Then the door of the car was open, and he was shoving the two seats back as far as they would go and she was sliding half across them and he was slithering on the satin of her dress, then teeth-tearing a condom from its pouch and fiddling with plastic folds and she was trying to get her back between the seats, her hands finding naked hips, him stripping the pants off her and playing with her and then elbows and knees for pivoting, impossibility in such a squared-off metal and vinyl unfriendly space. He swore at the space and it aroused her more and she was under him and right and *there* and he was in her . . .

17 Glanmire Park
Raheny
Dublin 5
9 March 1988

Dear Alex

I'm going to write this. I may never send it. Question: can one die of embarrassment or shame? Question: is it worth my while dieting or am I always going to be a gross gorb? Question: am I trying to avoid getting to the point by asking questions?

But then, what is the point? (What is the stars, Joxer, what is the stars?)

The point is the de-virginising of Darcy. Mark it in your calendar. 4 March 1988.

Furthermore, imagine this. Take one rust-eaten Volkswagen Beetle and put it on a beach at Dublin Bay. Acres of hard sand on which to walk, waves lapping on the shore, lovers lapping in the dunes.

So you have imagined one VW Beetle. Add to the picture one weight-lifting chunk of manliness of six foot three or four, built like a truck. Add further to the picture one large woman, five foot nine or thereabouts, somewhere between twelve and thirteen stone. Favouring thigh and ass somewhat at the expense of boob, but built as to boob, too.

Insert both these big people, plus coats x2 plus condom x1 into the VW. The backs of seats in the old VWs do not go down, so there is roughly half the space in the car that would be required for anything.

222

Add enough randiness to fill a double-decker bus. Fog up the windows with heavy breathing.

Now, we are ready for It. Well, actually, no, we're ostentatiously *not* ready for It, but since we've got ourselves into this situation and since It is only dying to happen, we get on with It. I (the big female) am so far-gone I cannot think straight. Something like a tampon was what I was expecting. What I got was a two by four.

Splintered and squared off, it felt like, and when he stopped dead, two by four impacted, there was this temptation to say, 'If you're gonna stop, stop outside, and close the door behind you.'

But he wasn't going to stop, was he? No. Just need a better purchase, here. Like whosit who said if someone got him a good position, he could move the earth. Greg is like whosit. Without a good position, he can't move the earth. Suddenly there is this crushing, splintering, rending roar. He's falling on me and pushing me even further down between the two seats and my ribs cannot move and I imagine my mother's face as she reads the headlines of my shameful death.

He is moaning in a concentrated way and I am doing two things. Suffocating. And trying to figure out is that it. Wasn't there supposed to be a climax or something? I don't mean for me – I just want removal of two by four and unsuffocation, my needs are simple and pure. I mean for *him*.

'Oh, shit,' he says after a while.

Oh *shit*? Thanks a lot, Greg.

'Oh, Darcy, I'm sorry.'

For which of many? The two by four? Don't mention it. The suffocation?

'Could you get up a bit off me, I can't breathe.'

'I don't know if I can, that's the problem.'

'What's the problem?'

'I'm stuck.'

All sorts of possible rejoinders suggest themselves, including 'stuck in what?'

He managed to get enough purchase with his elbows to bend himself back off me and I pulled myself up out of the gap between the seats and sideways, pushed the door handle, fell arse-first on to the hard sand. I swore and he laughed and then swore at me for making him laugh because at the angle he was at, it hurt him to laugh.

'You might as well laugh it as cry it,' I heard my mother saying. Not now, Ma. Some other time. But that's the thing about our mothers' sayings. They are lined up ready to fall through any crack in the unconscious. I reached past his head and got the overhead light on. He now had one shoulder on each of the backs of the front seats, his head hanging into the back of the car. The dashboard looked like it had eaten him, Jaws-fashion. Or got a great bite out of one leg, anyway. Sitting on the wet sand, I worked it out. In the effort to get at a better angle, he had brought his feet up to the dashboard. In one movement, he had activated the mechanism that opened the door of the glove compartment. In another, his foot had driven into the glove compartment and splintered through the old brittle plastic at the back and was entangled with coloured wires and flexes. Tarzan of the glove compartment. Rambo of the Dashboard. I sniggered. He got shirty.

'We laugh that we may not weep,' I said helpfully, wondering what that was a quote from. (Do you know?)

'Don't make me feel worse, Darcy,' he said in a suddenly virtuous tone as if he was on a pilgrimage to Knock or maybe Lough Derg. Gimme any lip, you glove-compartment wrecker, I thought, and not only will I leave you here on your own, but I'll turn on the lights to attract people so they can look at you.

'Well, come on, get me free.'

I sat in beside him.

'Greg, let me tell you something. This is not the most pleasing night of my life.'

'Oh Jesus, Darcy.'

'It may not be the most pleasing night of *your* life, either, but – how can I put this so it's not crude? Getting me to where you got me and leaving me there and making ribbons of my dress and my car and possibly my spine does not *ipso facto* entitle you to order me to disentangle your oversized awful foot from the place I would remind you that *you* put it without any assistance from me.'

'Darcy, shut up and help me.'

'Greg?'

'Oh what, what *what*?'

'Don't ever tell me to shut up.'

'I was joking, all right?'

'No you weren't. Now, if you're nice to me, I might get you loose. And if you're not nice to me, well, I walk home and you're fucked.'

There was a small silence.

'Half-fucked,' he said plaintively and we both laughed, which was probably the worst thing we could have done, because he lost his grip on the backs of the seats and did a 180 degree turn. His leg went halfway into the bonnet and there was more splintering and more roaring with pain. Plus the overhead light got turned off, perhaps because he shorted a connection. I went groping in the dark around his leg, trying to find what was catching where, and he alternately giggled as I tickled him and swore with impatience.

'Greg, I can't get you loose.'

'Oh Darcy, I said I was sorry.'

'You didn't, actually, but that's not why I can't get you loose. I can't get you loose – your father would understand this – because you've smashed a series of triangular rents into the plastic, and only someone of your leg power could do it. That's the good news. The bad news is that I don't have the strength to break away all the triangular bits. Nor a way to get at them.'

'What's that got to do with my father?'

'It's like the way valves in veins work. They open one way, but if you try to push them back the other way they don't go.'

'Bugger my father. I'm getting out of this.'

He braced himself and delivered a full-force kick of the trapped leg, which of course drove most of the points straight into his ankle and hurt like hell.

'*Darcy!*'

'I did tell you.'

A very long silence fell.

'What are you thinking?' he asked me.

Like a fool I told him. 'I was just wondering would you like the radio on.'

He told me what I was to do with myself and sounded truly desperate.

'I don't see I have much choice,' I said, eventually. 'I have to walk to the causeway, I have to walk the length of the causeway, I have to find a phone box and I have to ring the fire brigade.'

'Jesus Christ,' he said, ignoring the length of the walk facing me, 'don't ring the fire brigade. Ring bloody Beethoven.'

'On his wedding night?'

'He won't mind.'

226

'Aileen will. And I will.'

He considered this for a moment and made another attempt to get free.

'All right,' he said, as if allowing me a great treat at his expense. 'Go on.'

'Thank you,' I said, and started to walk.

By the time I am on the causeway, never mind across the causeway, I am exhausted, which is not surprising, since it's now one in the morning and I have been bridesmaiding and dancing in high heels, then attempting congress in an undersized car with an oversized ineptitude who has left me short on orgasms, workable cars and – now that I think of it – small change for phone calls. As I am trying to work out how I will make a phone call without any money, lights come on to the causeway at the other end, and I can make out three people in the car. Murder, Rape and Pillage, I think, like they were the names of the three Stooges or the Marx brothers.

Murder, Rape and Pillage are travelling in a white car with a blue light slightly cock-eyed on its forehead and therefore they are the police, the cops, the fuzz, the Garda Síochána, The Man. I debate leaping into the path of the squad car and bleating 'Help', but I don't have to, because as they draw nearly level with me, the car slows and the window rolls down and they look at me.

'Have you a problem, Miss?' they ask.

'Have I got a problem?' I trill laughingly and Murder, Rape and Pillage look at each other with the 'got a right one 'ere' expression on their faces.

'Well, *have* you got a problem?' Pillage asks from the passenger seat.

'My boyfriend has a problem,' I tell him. 'In fact, my boyfriend is about a hundred yards in that direction, in a Volkswagen Beetle, upside down –

himself, not the car – with his foot jammed in the glove compartment and no way can he get it loose.'

Murder, Rape and Pillage exchanged confirmatory glances. Murder, who is an ill-lit presence in the back seat, speaks after a moment.

'That'd be a problem, all right,' he says. We have superintendent mettle here, I think. This judicious analysis of problems is the stuff of which promotion is made. The back door opens and I get in alongside him.

'Are you all right yourself?' he asks, in a casual verbal pat-down that for some reason makes me want to cry.

'Oh, I'm fine. I just need to get the fire brigade.'

'We'll see about that,' Pillage said authoritatively.

The squad car pulled up at a T-angle to the Volkswagen, flooding it and its occupant with light. I swear to God, he smiled and freed a hand to wave. He waved at the oncoming forces of the law, did Greg, and when Murder, Rape and Pillage got up close, he made jokes to them. They patted their hands on the rounded roof of the car in consideration of the seriousness of it and they did not laugh. Rape duplicated what I had already done and said right enough, we'd need the fire brigade. An ambulance, too, he said, as Pillage started making car phone calls. Greg denied the need for the ambulance. Rape told him he was very swollen In Behind There.

Within minutes, we could hear the siren. Greg woofled resentfully and Pillage stuck his head in to hear him better.

'The hell do they need their siren on at one in the morning. They're hardly going to meet with much obstruction?'

'You have a point,' Rape said, patting the roof of the car. 'You have a point.'

Then the fire brigade was lined up in huge shiny redness beside the blue and white of the squad car, shining pipes, shining wheels, lights bathing us again and again and again in a swinging, swinging red. Big lads with short hair cuts and great free-standing jackety coats shining with a plasticky coating and boots vast with good intent from children's books, they climbed lumpily down and clump clumped to let the Guards tell them. But didn't quite believe the Guards either, holding on to the 'let us make the decisions here' tone of special expertise and checking the state of Greg. Then another light, blue this time, turning with head-lamps onto the causeway. White ambulance pulling in beside the red brigade unit. Bystanders coming out of dunes, cars sneaking up out of darkness, can we help, no move right along there, everything under control, nobody hurt, move right along.

The door of the Volkswagen filled with red-jacketed backs, big stiff fabric sections rubbing against each other as they struggle. Then one with an iron lung and a probe plus his own transparent mask like a high-tech crusader. Sparks. Silence. You OK, Sir? Yeah. Sparks, silence. Got to let the heat dispel. Oh, right. Sparks. Silence. That's it, I think. Yeah. Hold it just a second sir. Mikey, can you pull that? Hold the panel back and I'll – great. Great. Very good. You OK, Sir?

The ambulance men moved in and surrounded the leg with splints. It put him back to where I had first known him, in the Make Up Room in RTE, with his injured leg splint-stiff out at an angle. He was protesting about going to the hospital, but they were taking no shit, and the three sets of them knew they had him. They stood there in groups, the brigade men the biggest, but the ambulance men the most important – now. The Guards in overview mode. You OK, Miss? No I wouldn't try starting the car, if I was you. The electrics wouldn't be the best, now, after that. Wouldn't be the best. Safest thing lock it up and come back tomorrow. Things'll look a lot better tomorrow. We'll drop you home.

They minded me as if I were untouched by the scene and all I could think of was what had he done with the condom and that I couldn't ask him. The questions were owned by the ambulance men.

'What's your name, Sir?'

The questioner stood, board in hand, ready to fill the letters of the name into those little ruled stalls.

'Nicholas Watson,' he said. Clear as a bell, I thought. Clear as the coppery bell on the fire brigade unit. Nicholas Watson. Beethoven. He has stolen his friend's name on his friend's wedding night to cover his nakedness. I thought it and wanted to say it. But the fire-brigade guys were all in the business of gear-checking and departure, the ambulance guys were loading the stretcher into the vehicle and promising me he'd be released in the morning. Murder, Rape and Pillage were looking as if they wanted me to get on with getting into the squad car.

So I did.

'See you tomorrow, Darcy,' Greg said before the two back doors banged him into silence.

Wrong, I thought. *Not*, I thought. Thank you, gentlemen, I said, old-world style, gathering my skirts about me. I had locked the car, my pants startlingly white on the floor in the front, but could I pick them up and put them on in front of three big Guards? No knickers, but a lot of dignity. I gave them directions and told them they had rescued me from a very difficult situation and I was very grateful to them. They revved at the curb outside my house, window rolled down. Then I was in the front door, waving to them as the squad car purred away. Maidens in distress a dime a dozen. Stuck studs ditto.

Two days later, Greg rang.

'Anything broken?' This from me.

'No. Just bruised and pulled and bashed about.'

'How bad is the car?' This from him.

'Very bad. A write-off, probably.'

'Oh, Jesus, Darcy, I'm so sorry.'

'Not the problem.'

'*Not* the problem.'

'No.'

'What's the problem, then?'

'You know.'

'I wouldn't be asking if I knew.'

'That's another lie.'

'Oh, now I know.'

'Yeah, now you know.'

'I knew I was only going to be in Casualty. What business was it of theirs?'

'None.'

'Well, then.'

'Well then nothing.'

'Oh, Darcy, what harm did I do?'

'On a scale of one to ten? Thirteen and a half, probably. On the Richter Scale? Irreparable harm.'

'I could have made up any name.'

'So why didn't you?'

'Darcy, when I see you we can discuss this – '

'You won't.'

'Sorry?'

'See me. You won't see me. Ever. For all eternity. This is it. Good night, sweet prince.'

'Oh, spare me the melodramatics.'

I did. I put down the phone and I did it quite gently. Now, you will say, being an old academic who knows how everybody bonks and how little it means and how relationships form, shatter and reform stronger at the glued joins, you will say that I will forgive and forget in a couple of months, because this is a good guy and one does not cut off one's nose to spite one's face and all those useful axioms. When I have had a chance to think about all of this, I may explain why you are wrong, but for the moment, this is all there is. This is all she wrote: I will not see Greg any more, ever again.

Darcy

PS This may be completely irrelevant but my father has just had a fax machine installed in our house because people from overseas need to send him clinical details and stuff, so if it made more sense to you to fax me your instructions and questionnaires, here is the number from where you're situated: 001 353 732417.

CHAPTER SEVENTEEN

A. C. B./Fort Attic
813 276 0716 23 March 1988 9.17

Attention Darcy

Darcy

At the beginning of your last letter, you asked whether or not you are likely to stay thin as a result of this latest or some other diet. Most dieters regain all their lost weight.

What happened your car?

Whenever you feel like expanding on the thoughts you flagged at the end of the last communication, please do so.

Yours sincerely
Alex

Dr Robert King/Dublin
353 1 732417 24 March 1988 21.47

Attention Alex

Alex

Thank you. So I might as well throw all this bloody cauliflower out and decide I'm meant by nature/God/The Force to be thirteen stone?

My car turned into little more than a hundred quid's worth of scrap metal. I have not replaced it because I am thinking of going to America.

Yours
The blob, Darcy

That Easter their parents surprised the twins with the gift of a holiday together in the Canary Islands.

They lay on a gravelly beach in Tenerife and held sporadic conversations.

'Do you miss Derek, Sophia?'

'No.'

'Have you seen him since you got rid of him?'

'I didn't get rid of him.'

'Whatever. Have you seen him?'

'Too much.'

'How do you mean?'

'He's been hanging around me in college and leaving notes for me everywhere.'

'Gosh, he's seriously in love.'

'I don't think so. I think what he's doing is very abnormal. I don't like it and if he keeps it up after I get back I'll do something about it.'

'Sophia?'

'Mmm?'

'Did I miss much, not going to college?'

'Oh, Darcy, you know I can't answer that. I love it, you'd hate it. I love the lectures, I love the tutorials, I love the work, I love discovering what you would call the obvious and I love the social life.'

'Sometimes I hate that I didn't go.'

'You're not exactly Methuselah. You can go to college whenever you want to.'

'Yeah, right.'

'Darcy?'

'That's me.'

'D'you miss Greg?'

'Yep.'

'Why?'

'Oh, Sophia.'

'No, tell me. Why?'

'Because he was funny, because he was affectionate, because he was generous, because he was a big handsome easygoing chunk of sunshine.'

'What Mam would call a cod liver oil and orange juice kid?'

'Absolutely.'

'Would you take him back?'

'No.'

'Why not?'

'Because.'

'But seriously, if you miss him?'

'Sophia, because because because.'

'That makes sense.'

'Thought it would. To a bright woman like you.'

'Attending college.'

'Shaddup.'

'But if he came begging?'

'He won't.'

'But if he did?'

'He's had six weeks, and he hasn't.'

'But say if he did?'

'I would never take him back.'

'You mean that, don't you?'

'You know something? For someone going to college, you're awful slow at picking up quite simple truths.'

'But you don't hate him.'

'No.'

'Will you work with me?'

'What?'

'Will you work with me?'

'What's that got to do with Greg?'

'Nothing.'

'On what?'

'On what what?'

'On what do you want me to work with you?'

'In our own company.'

'Like when you qualify and get years of experience under your belt?'

'Yes.'

'Sure, sure, sure.'

'You don't mean that.'

235

'Oh, sweet Jesus. Ma? Da? You know you had this idea for a holiday? Well, I want to tell you it would have been fine if I hadn't had this interrogator with me. Sophia King: yap yap yap question question question.'

'I won't say another thing for an hour.'

'Sophia?'

'My hour is not up.'

'I'll give you a dispensation. Parole.'

'OK.'

'Why would you want me to work with you?'

'Because I think we're a great combination.'

'Of what?'

'Talents. Complementary capabilities.'

'Like Jack Sprat and his wife?'

'Not exactly. I just think if you put the two of us together, we'd be unbeatable.'

'Sophia, I think on your own you've a hell of a bigger chance of unbeatability.'

'So you don't want to work with me?'

'What are you going to pay me?'

'Darcy?'

'Yeah?'

'Turn over. Your chest is going to be blistered.'

'If I lie face down, I'll go to sleep.'

'Don't worry. I'll time you.'

'Sophia, people here don't know we're twins, you know.'

'Yes?'

'They don't even know we're sisters.'

'And?'

'And they can't figure why we keep waving away hand-some holidaymakers who want to jump our bones.'

'Want to – Oh, *Darcy*!'

'So they think we're dykes.'

'They *don't*.'

'Yeah, they do. I think I will put my hand in yours.'

'Darcy, I am not joking you, I will throw a drink over you.'

'Nice and cool.'

'Would you like another?'

'Yes I would, please.'

'Another reason I'd like to work with you?'

'Mmm?'

'I like you.'

'Always thought you were crap in the judgement department.'

'Darcy, listen to me.'

'Now they *really* think we're dykes.'

'I like you, I trust you and when I'm feeling down, you pull me back up again.'

'I never thought you felt down.'

'Sometimes, I feel so down if I didn't have you as kind of the other side of things, I would be overcome with sadness.'

'Come on, Sophia, you have all these systems for making yourself productive and happy.'

'I think they only work because you laugh at them and make me laugh, too.'

'Did you ever wish you weren't a twin, Sophia?'

'Oh, no.'

'Never?'

'Never for a moment.'

'Oh.'

'Did you ever wish *you* weren't a twin?'

'Yes.'

'Oh.'

'Not often.'

'Oh.'

'Sophia, it wasn't because *you* were my twin, it was just the being joined to someone, being compared, being less pretty, less lovable, less bloody everything.'

'The thought of not being joined used to give me a shiver when I was younger. I used to think that the loneliness would take over completely.'

'What loneliness?'

'Just. Loneliness.'

'And being a twin prevented that?'

'I used to say like a mantra the thing about magpies.'

'What thing?'

'One for sorrow. Two for joy. It was as if I learned it about us two long before I knew it applied to magpies.'

'One for sorrow. Two for joy. I could live with that.'

'Darcy, will you work with me?'

'Listen, you domineering dyke – '

' – sweet God, Darcy, keep your voice down – '

' – I've just *had* your constant demands for sex – '

' – *Darcy!*'

' – and your sadistic mind-games. I'm outa here.'

'Darcy?'

'Yo, Sophia. I need you to put aloe vera on my back. You didn't time me right.'

'How could you *do* that to me in the restaurant?'

'Had a tough time walking out clothed in dignity, did you?'

'It was dreadful. And it wasn't helped by the fact that I got slightly hysterical and laughed. Some of them wanted to hit me for giving you such a hard time.'

'Damn right, too. Brutal bitch. And you the thin one, as well.'

'Darcy, are you OK?'

'Shh. Go back to sleep. Just getting painkillers – the sunburn is bloody awful, I'll have skin cancer by morning.'

'God between us and all harm.'

'If I get desperate, I'm going to have a hot shower. Someone told me it takes the sting out of it. Sophia?'

'Mmm?'

'You looked very funny in the bistro.'

'Darcy?'

'Mmm?'

'Will you work with me?'

'Cost you a convertible Merc.'

'Done.'

'C'n I go back to sleep now?'

'Sleep tight.'

'More baby-talk.'

'How do you mean?'

'Sleep tight. One for sorrow.'

'Two for joy. That's the important bit.'

By autumn of 1988, Sophia was in her final year, Darcy was packing to go to America, Derek was passionately in love with another girl in Sophia's class, and Greg had put his fourth year of accountancy on hold in order to take up a job presenting an RTE quiz programme.

Robert King was impressed by his daughter's coolness about emigration.

'Well, it's not really emigration,' she said cheerily. 'They fly me home for two weeks in six months' time.'

'You'll be based in New York?'

'Manhattan. Insofar as I'll be based anywhere. They want to shunt me from plant to plant.'

'Don't you love the casual way she says Manhattan?' Colette asked her husband.

'I suspect she has it wrong,' her husband said. 'I can't figure they mean Manhattan. They probably have digs in Long Island or Brooklyn or the Bronx.'

'Manhattan,' Darcy said firmly, getting out her dossier. 'Madison Avenue and 49th, to be precise. You want the zip code?'

Sophia was sleepless for the last few nights before Darcy left.

'You will write to me?'

'Soon as I get near a fax.'

239

'You could do old-fashioned stuff like posting letters.'

'Oh, frig that for a haircut.'

'What did Greg want?'

'To wish me luck. Stateside. As he put it.'

'That all?'

'What did you want, a slashed wrist bleeding into the receiver?'

'His programme is very popular.'

'So I told him.'

'He's still big buddies with Aileen and Beethoven.'

'Good.'

'Why do you sound so grim?'

'Sophia, I have more to do with my thoughts than contemplate the depth of feeling between Beethoven and Greg. It's deep, it's meaningful, it's male bonding at its purest and at any moment Nicholas may put it to music.'

'You're not lonely at all, are you?'

'Sophia, that's like asking someone who's just had a meal are they hungry. I haven't gone yet, so no, I am not lonely. Scared shitless yes, lonely no.'

Three days later, Darcy was shaking hands with the president of the corporation which employed her.

'Would you care for coffee?' he asked.

'What's the right corporate answer to that?'

The president looked at her searchingly for a moment. 'There is no right answer.'

'In that case I'd love a cup of tea, please. Hot, with milk.'

'Why did you ask me about the correct corporate response, Darcy?'

'Because this corporation is like a medieval court in Europe. It has a special language. The progress of an individual within the corporation is linked to that much more closely than it is to performance.'

The tea and coffee arrived. Clive Brautigan poured tea for Darcy and left it to her to sort out milk and sugar.

'I get the feeling I may be going home on the next plane,' Darcy said.

'Tell me more.'

'Well, first of all, you have to quote the Major all the time.'

The founder of the Borchgrave Corporation, back in the twenties, had been an army major.

'What's wrong with quoting the founder?'

'Point one, your major market is Europe. The EEC doesn't give a rat's knackers about some turn-of-the-century unknown American. Point two, it's symbolic of the kind of ritual crawling that goes on in this organisation.'

'I pride myself on operating an open-door management policy.'

'Yeah. So you said in the corporate video. Gather round, you Irish peasants, you're gonna be educated in the sophisticated thinking of our new president, the man who is going to take us into the twenty-first century, the man who will revitalise our great corporation to make us lean and mean. Look at him – he's a human. He wears shirtsleeves when he talks to the lower orders through the video. He's telling us we're in a changing world. Never have known that, would we? He's telling us we have to change to get along in that changing world, well, who'd have thunk? In other words – work harder, work cheaper, ignore the old lines of demarcation and don't ask questions.'

Brautigan looked at Darcy, who felt a chill of fear run up her spine. Sophia? Having a wonderful time up to about a minute ago. Wish you were here, now. You might smooth over whatever crack I have managed to fissure into this possible relationship.

Brautigan went to his desk and pushed a button.

'Bring me the second quarter story, please.'

After a moment, his secretary appeared with a Xeroxed cutting from a newspaper. Brautigan gestured to her to hand it to Darcy. *Wall Street Journal* had been typed at the top.

The story said that the second quarter figures from Borch-grave showed the same flaccid pattern of the previous two quarters, thus posing a time-limited problem for Clive Brautigan, poached as president from the highly successful Pelz Group just six months before. If Brautigan didn't get the figures to improve quickly, shareholders would get antsy, the paper predicted, and the corporation would become a target for an unfriendly takeover bid.

It went on to mention that the greenfield operation in Coolock, Ireland, was doing very well.

'I want to know if the figures coming out of Coolock are trends or just a blip on the radar,' Brautigan said. 'At the same time, I want the communication within this corporation addressed in an innovative way. Hence your presence here.'

'What do you want me to do?'

'Read a steamer-trunkful of material and come up with a corporation-wide training plan.'

> Darcy King/Manhattan
> 212 8645312 21 October 1988 20.55
> Friday

Attention Sophia

Sophia, fingers crossed for me. If he agrees to even half of what I'm going to propose, I'll bring you home a Gucci handbag.

Darcy

PS Ask me how I know about a Gucci handbag.

> Darcy King/Manhattan
> 212 8645312 21 October 1988 21.13
> Friday

Attention Alex

Alex

I have just impressed the knickers off my new boss in his office overlooking Central Park. Before you get pompous, I know I am way overdue with the considered thoughts I said I would get to you post-Greg, but I have to draw up a huge training plan, so I'll be later still. Sorry.

How's your life?

Darcy

Dr Robert King/Dublin
353 1 7324172 22 October 1988 8.34
Saturday

Attention Darcy

Darcy?

Aren't you worried, in an apartment in New York on your own? Do you carry pepper in your pocket? Tell me how you know about Gucci handbags. I'm thrilled to bits it went well for you.

Sophia

A. C. B./Fort Attic
813 2760716 22 October 1988 11.07
Saturday

Attention Darcy

Darcy

Short answer: Good.

The movie I was working on in the spring has its première next week. The advance word is good. Do you ever go to movies? You never mention movie stars or favourite soundtracks. Will you go to this one, because I would like your opinion on it?

Welcome to America!

Alex

Attention Sophia

I know about Gucci handbags because when I
arrived, the apartment had six books. Three of them
were by Danielle Steele and one of them was *about*
Danielle Steele. (Very rich, into having loads of
babies and marrying prisoners, if you want to know.)

The book was full of brand names like Gucci
and Armani, plus details about which grain of
leather should be in your briefcase if you don't want
to look a complete *arriviste*.

Then on my way to work, I passed a Gucci shop.
Plus a whole Yves St Laurent shop and Tiffany's.
Do you like Gucci handbags?

Darcy

PS What the hell would I want pepper for?

Dr Robert King/Dublin
353 1 7324172 22 October 1988 17.08
Saturday

Attention Darcy

I do like Gucci handbags and unless he gives you a
quite improbable budget, you won't be able to afford
one. Pepper to throw in the eyes of assailants.
Sophia

Darcy King/Manhattan
212 8645312 25 October 1988 23.09
Tuesday

Attention Sophia

Sophia

You are in bed and I hope this doesn't wake you.
He agreed everything. I have a beautiful black
assistant named Sharletta, a portable computer and
a new contract. Sophia, he is paying me twice what

they said they'd pay me, and *that* was much more than I wanted.

Sophia, I am so far out. Frightened, frightened, frightened. Shrunk and shrivelled by terror.

Love
Darcy

CHAPTER EIGHTEEN

Entry in Sophia's diary, Tuesday 3 January 1989
This was probably the best Christmas ever, partly
because of Darcy coming home. I heard Dad saying
to Mam that he should mention to her that she
could lose some weight, because she has put on
perhaps a stone. But Mam told him Darcy wasn't
stupid and probably knew to the last ounce what
she weighed. I am glad he took her advice, because
it meant we had no unpleasantness. Dad is genuinely very proud of what Darcy has achieved. I am
getting copies of as much of it as I can from her
while she's here, because I think it will be very
relevant to public relations in the future and I am
more than ever convinced we should work together.
Greg came over on Christmas Eve with flowers for
us both.

Good lad, that,' Robert King said, as the front door closed
behind Greg. 'Good lad.'

Darcy smiled at her father. Sophia, who had left Greg to
the door, came back into the room. 'He's such a nice person.'

'C'mon, Ma, you better get on this bandwagon while it's
rolling,' Darcy said.

Colette laughed. 'Greg's a wonderful example of what
you can achieve by dolloping loads of self-esteem on top of
good genetics.'

'I wouldn't have thought the McEnerney genes were
anything special,' Robert King said.

'The McEnerney genes are coded for looks, intelligence,
size,' said Colette.

'Sexual continence and marital happiness being non-
genetic matters?' her husband replied.

Alex

Hi, Happy Christmas, Happy New Year, Seasons' Greetings, Happy Holidays, Hanukkah, Cool Yule, Joyous New Year and whatever you're having yourself.

I know it is quite ridiculous that I have been promising you a major report (see, now I am a corporate animal, I think in terms of reports, not letters) since March but not getting around to it, but you have to remember I've changed continents, lifestyles and functions. Also, it's been time-consuming having to make judgements on carrot cake, brownies, key lime pie, mud pie, Fettucini Alfredo, linguini with clams and sun-dried tomatoes, Ben and Jerry's ice cream, burritos, tacos, french toast, bagels and lox (not worth a toss), macadamia nuts, Crackerjacks (NWAT), corn chips, fried butterfly shrimp, tortillas and black beans on saffron rice.

However, I did say I would come back to you when I had put a little time between me and the Greg incident, so here goes, in two sections.

The first may not fit into your study, but has that consideration ever stopped me from communicating before? No. Is it going to stop me now? No.

I am giving up diets and talking/thinking/writing about diets.

I have read some of the material you sent me, and it is not cheery material, particularly the stuff that says you might help yourself to get breast cancer by putting on weight in your twenties. However, here's what I have decided. For at least eighteen years, fat, diet, weight, shape and shame have been my daily companions.

I have thought more about being fat or trying to be thin, more even than I thought about Greg when I was half-daft about him. This is a sinful waste of time likely to make me, if, from your point of view, it hasn't already made me, into the fat bore of the century. So I am going to gather together some thoughts, spew them at you right now (you can skip the next page and a half if you've already had more than you can take on this topic) and hope not to refer again to it in correspondence.

(This reminds me. You haven't referred to hunting for years. Have you given it up?)

First of all, I despise all fat people, mostly me. Fat women always sympathise with other fat women. Then when they go home they're sorry and they despise the other fat person worse than they despise themselves, because they secretly believe they're only temporarily a fat person.

Secondly, I especially despise communal fat-shedding and excuses about metabolism. Fat people, me included, are just pigs. Trying to extend the whole alcoholics thing to fat people is bullshit. 'My name is Darcy King. I am a chocoholic.' Poor helpless victim of bad upbringing. Here's the truth of it. My name is Darcy King. I just eat everything that's not nailed down.

Thirdly, I think the medical profession are so full of shit on this one they deserve annihilation. They keep recommending things after they have fifty years of proof that these things do not work. It mystifies me that they continue to get away with it.

They have all these rubbish theories about anorexia and bulimia as if you needed theories, for the love of Jasus. If you know that everybody thinks you're a big lazy incompetent thick-skinned elephant when you get fat, then you're going to do everything to stay thin. When you eat everything in a wild binge, of course you're going to make yourself throw up. (No, as a matter of fact, I don't. Nor laxatives either. But that's for reasons of personal comfort and fastidiousness rather than morals, decency or a serious concern for health.)

Give you an example. I can starve, no problem. Line me up there with the anorexics with their wasted shoulders and their bony chests and the saggy skin on the inside of their thighs and I can starve for as long as any of them.

I can get through a whole day, knowing that I can eat stuff at night. During that day, I will not even be very hungry, and any hunger I have can be damped down by hot coffee and skim milk. Total deprivation? No problem.

Moderation, on the other hand, is a huge problem. If you give me a bit of bread in the morning, or an apple at coffee-break time, then by three o'clock I'm going to be stuffed with food, because something happens to me when I eat even a small item. Within about half an hour, I am consumed by a raging hunger and I would eat anything, even things I don't like. It's as if the small item eaten earlier triggers a reflex that stays untriggered if I haven't eaten anything. The medical profession says: 'Eat a little, so you don't get fiercely hungry and break your diet.' The exact opposite is what happens to me.

That's one thing.

The other thing is slightly closer to your study. (So if you've skipped these two pages as I suggested you might, look what you're missing.)

249

It's this. About three times during the last few years, I have lost a great deal of weight and kept it off for as long as six months. I have three or four wonderful out-of-date outfits in size twelve, and I have stretch marks *below my knees* for Chrissake. But the more important point is this.

When I am fat, I am not only into food, I am into sex, too. (This is only theoretically. Since parting with Greg I have been living a nun-like life, but we'll come to that.)

When I am fat, I am so strongly sexed I'm almost a danger to the male populace, ignorant as they are of my raging appetites. Mad for it, I am. I think about it. I imagine it. Bits of books stick with me so that out of nowhere, I begin to recall the stories that the Kennedy brothers groped Marilyn Monroe over and under the table when they were having dinners with her. I would like that. Or rather, when I am fat, I *imagine* I would like that a lot. I would like that, and almost every other kind of sex too.

If I'm on a plane, I imagine sex in an unlit back row of seats during the movie, or in one of the loos standing up – the mile-high club. If I am on a train, every rhythmic undulation over joins in the tracks sings sex to me. If I am in a car, I imagine a man's hands massaging my knee and up under my skirt. Half the time I'm in trousers, but my imagination is not stopped. There's something about transport that, in combination with being fat, is very arousing. No wonder truckers have the reputation they have.

When I am thin, I feel wonderful, I look wonderful, I fit into everything, including jeans sold as 'tight and sexy'. But my sexual instinct/drive/appetite drops in direct ratio to the lost weight.

Is there any research on that, or am I just a bizarre exception? (Don't answer this question.)

Thinks: maybe that's why there are these men who always go for very fat women. Maybe it has less to do with the weight and more to do with the fact that they know very fat women will always be on for a bit of the other.

If you are reeling back in amazement at this onslaught, let me remind you it is my last communication on anything to do with weight, so I'd better get it all said in this one go, since the rest is going to be silence.

There can be no doubt that people make negative judgements about you if you are fat and female, but I am not going to play into that any more. End of story. Closed book. Finito. Forget it. The End.

Now, let us address relationships.

I told you I would never take Greg back, I haven't and I won't. It's all very civilised, though. He arrived at Christmas with flowers for me and flowers for Sophia.

What grace. What charm. What shite.

Men always assume a bouquet has this almost supernatural effect on a woman. Cellophane-wrapped murdered flowers. You might as well send someone decapitated sheep. I hate cut flowers. I have always hated cut flowers. I give them away to other people and get kudos for generosity and I am always astonished that the other people are willing to take these dead bodies from me.

Greg was always big into bouquet-giving. Once he even brought me an orchid. Now, I think God had his off-moments, but when He invented orchids, He was really having a bad day. Amputated vulvae. They usually come with their stem, their stalk, their *stoma* stuck in a little bottle as of plasma and you think you should do some kind of medical experimentation with them. Teach clitoridectomies, maybe, like women used to teach each other to examine their own private parts as a gesture of feminist empowerment. (Can you imagine looking through a scope into one's intestinal tract as a gesture of culinary empowerment?) Anyway, piss on cut flowers, particularly piss on orchids, and thank God Sophia got rid of that creep who used to hang a floral corpse on our front gate.

I need more than a big pleasant guy coasting on genetics and self-esteem (as my mother defines Greg). Greg is a smashing guy, let's be clear on that. I am not now going to find him guilty of a range of things I didn't find him guilty of when I was going out with him. He's a smashing guy. He's probably the best I'll ever come upon.

And he's not good enough for me.

How's that for whistle-in-the-dark drummed-up arrogance? Bit like Quasimodo saying he'll pass on Esmeralda, thanks all the same, and wait for Miss America in a couple of centuries' time.

I mean it, though.

Because Greg was so near it, I know what the ideal is, and I will not settle for anything less, although something less is all that will ever be offered me.

I want a man who is independent of me and linked inextricably with me. Who will fight for me, who will wait for me, who will toil in the wilderness for love of me, like Jacob did for Rachel. In case you are a Godless Protestant and don't know Bible stories, Jacob worked seven years to win Rachel ' . . . and it seemed as but a day because of the greatness of his love.'

I want a man generous in plan, in thought, in possessions and in time, not simply generous in reflex or reaction. A man gritty with his sureness of himself and where he stands, bulwarked against my inundating inevitable attempts to modify, improve and change him. A man of ideas and silences, of speculations, reflections and earned unstated certainties.

A man not needy of audience or approval. A man whisper-hoarse in spoken voice, that roughness lost in the singing of his songs. A man of steel and silk strengths, of clean soap smells and spice-sweated sleepfulness.

I want a man who walks and stands in the unselfconscious ease of the athlete, whose hands have the control and discipline of sport, a man gentle in the control of mechanical things. Who does not weep to prove sensitivity, and who scrapes, sandpaper-raw, to remove adherent sentimentality. Who can be part of a team, arms-linked, minds at one with other equals, then walk away into his own individuality. A man so self-defined as to be without need to change others.

I want a man of quiet developing beliefs, not all of them shared with me. Of trusts and unequivocal relish. A man of wisdom, of reading. A steadfast man. Steadfast. A man whose temperament is like the great movements of the deep ocean, not the shoreline fussiness of the shallow sea: no tetchy volatility.

I want a man who never bores me, is never predictable, except in his casual presence in my life. A man who has only to look at me, head glecked a-tilt, eyebrow raised, to send the breathing ragged in me and the curling weakness between my legs, who puts his hands on me in demand that meets demand and is unfazed by the vivid recklessness of the response he gets, a man who will take me like a train thundering unstoppable and nestle me afterwards like a cat with kittens.

I want a man who is superb at whatever he does,

be it carpentry or high art, of whom I can be proud, who is proud of me, of what I do.

I imagine him to be a big broad bludgeon of a man with an unhandsome face of angles chiselled and textures punished, eyes dark and filled with secrets, no ready sunshine smile but a slow-shared humour curling the edges of the mouth.

That is him. That is my man. After that, could I settle down with someone who might be decent/goodlooking/kind/warm/successful? Someone to be measured against the dream every day and found wanting, so that my attention went to his annoying little habits and I changed into a marauding virago henpecking the poor little bastard to bloodied shreds? Well of course I could, but it doesn't add up to living happily ever after.

There's the rub. There is no happily-ever-after any more. There are 'stable relationships'. Emotional compromises. Career-driven people with sex on the side. There is co-habitation. But if happily-ever-after is thin on the ground, I'm still not settling for some discount yellow-pack version which won't lift my heart in gladness at a name, a melody, a voice, a touch. Nor am I likely to have a series of one-night stands.

I do not even have an *ambition* for a love on the scale I'm talking about. If it happened, it would be splendid, but I'm not holding my breath, nor am I setting out to have a great career as a substitute. I would have a great career with or without this wonderman. But I think one of the reasons these last few months have been so good, in career terms, is because 100 per cent of my brain has been concentrated. Post-Greg.

Darcy

Dear Darcy

Thank you for relevant and interesting material about which I should make no comment.

I would not wish to lecture you on comparative religions, but – particularly in the last hundred years – the Protestant churches have had a much greater affinity with the Bible than the Catholic Church, with Protestants much more likely than Catholics to cite Biblical references.

You mentioned Ben and Jerry's ice-cream. Here are two under-achieving guys who just about finish high school, mess around, luck into the ice-cream business, and are very successful, not only at producing a premium product but at marketing it in an off-beat way which includes naming one of their flavours Cherry Garcia.

However, these two young men are filled with self-righteous change-the-worldisms. It is im-possible to go into one of their emporia without having to submit to lectures, whether these are printed on the front of T-shirts or on leaflets at one of the fountain tables, about the rain forest, child abuse or the jolly community-involving activities of the Ben and Jerry staff at Christmas and other holiday periods. Your sister would prob-ably be very interested in this kind of 'doing good and getting credit for it'.

However, I am not. And because Ben and Jerry based their plant in Vermont and their industry on Vermont milk – there would be a temptation for me to shoot Vermont cows.

Doesn't Sophia graduate in a couple months?

Alex.

Alex

God, wouldn't you think after a hundred million years in academia you'd know basic grammar. A couple *of* months. Answer: yes. Already has an offer from *Postponements*, oops, *Positionings*. Account Executive.

By the way, I don't understand what's clever about calling ice cream Cherry Garcia?

I am now in Atlanta, Georgia, and if I see one more picture of Vivian Leigh, I'm going to run through the streets naked and screaming. However, this photograph has reminded me that the movie you consulted on most recently was premièred a few weeks ago. I am beginning to see daylight and could find the time to go to a cinema, of which there is no shortage around here. Please fax me quickly with the title of the movie.

Darcy

A. C. B./Fort Attic
813 2760716 25 January 1989 9.27

Darcy

Movie is called *Tear on Dotted Line*.
Cherry Garcia as in Jerry Garcia?
Alex

Darcy King/Atlanta
903 7146849 27 January 1989 23.02
Friday

Alex

That was brill! The script, first of all, was witty, the pace was just so fast, cut to the chase, no boring bits. and it made me look at the whole issue in a new way. I could have done without the leaking membranes bit – turns me giddy to even think about it. Plus the acting was fantastic. Hadn't seen the Brookes guy playing the revenge-seeker before: wonderful concentrated impersonal venom. You couldn't take your eyes off him. (Well, maybe you could, but I couldn't.) By the way, either the credits went too fast or you weren't there. All I spotted was a fast-moving thank you to the U of Mis.

I'm moving to Greenville, North Carolina tonight and I will be there for a few weeks, looking at the way they train the Borchgrave people. I am only beginning to come to terms with the way American business thinks in quarters of the year.

Talk to y'all from Nawth Carolina, y'hear? (Thanks be to Christ to get away from peaches.)

Who's Jerry Garcia?

Darcy

A. C. B./Fort Attic
813 2760716 29 January 1989 8.17

Darcy

I did figure in the credits. You may be poor at reading movie credits.

You will have to make it to North Carolina without fax support. I'm headed for the Sun Bark Hunting Lodge, Custer, South Dakota.

Alex.

Darcy King/Atlanta
903 7146849 29 January 1989 19.02

Murdering Bambi's mother again? I hope a wolf eats your legs.

Darcy

Darcy

Deer hunting is in November. I gave up deer and elk hunting some time back. The bigger the kill, supposedly, in the mind of the hunter, the bigger the thrill, but I don't shoot deer any more. Many of my friends who have hunted big animals quit after some years. You get that you just like to watch. The thrill of seeing a big animal drop is maybe a young man's hunger. I got a lot out of it, though, that phase. I particularly liked elk hunting. Elk are at higher elevation and in rougher terrain than deer. Plus you get a lot of meat. Not as much meat as a moose, but then a moose you cannot drag out when you've brought it down. You have to bring chain saws with you and quarter it where it fell. You can drag out an elk, and elk meat is very good. Much better than venison.

Back when I did shoot deer, Bambi's mother was safe. I shot bucks only. Most of the licences are bucks only. At any rate, the real trophy of a deer is not the size of the deer but the size of the antlers. You don't full-mount a deer. You mount the antlers. So a doe is of little value.

The only wolf which might do me damage would be a wolf reintroduced to the environment because of pressure brought by conservation-minded hunters.

Alex

Alex

Did I need to know all that?

Darcy

A. C. B./Fort Attic
813 2760716 1 February 1989 10.12

Darcy

Strange, the gaps you have. Jerry Garcia is the lead singer of a band called The Grateful Dead, who have been around for so long they make *me* look young. The Grateful Dead were around when tie-dye was new. An accretion known as the Dead Heads has built up around them. Loyal fans among the baby boomers who attend their concerts and ingest whatever chemicals will make the experience unmemorable.

My hunting, you will be delighted to hear, was unusually successful. One of the guys had his fourteen-year-old son with him. Wonderful to see the great traditions passing through the generations . . .

Alex

Darcy King/Manhattan
212 8645312 6 February 1989 20.22
Monday

Alex

Great traditions my arse. The poor pimply gobshite of a terrified adolescent, dragged out to the jungle by some macho-maladjusted father with a frayed phallus proving to himself that he can still at least get a gun up, and the kid thinking this is love as experienced by manly men.

Darcy

A. C. B./Fort Attic
813 2760716 6 February 1989 20.00

Darcy?

I don't know if a phrase common in sexual parlance in the US has reached Ireland, but we

Americans, when talking about oral sex, say: 'She gives great head.'

You give great abuse.

Alex

Darcy King/Manhattan
212 8645312 25 May 1989 21.56
Thursday

Attention Sophia

Sophia

Thursday I'm back at the number in Greenville. Every move I make seems OK and Brautigan is in all the business magazines as a big success.

Hope the studying is going well.

Darcy

Darcy King/Manhattan
212 8645312 15 June 1989 22.06
Thursday

Alex?

You're probably halfway down a volcano in Peru advising actors how to play people whose loved ones have got swept away by lava.

Say something. You haven't said anything for ages. Just because I am eschewing certain subjects doesn't mean you have to totally eschew, goddammit.

I'm going for six months to Greenville, North Carolina, with time out for good behaviour in New York.

As an elderly academic, do not be intimidated by the following: I am doing things that are having a life-changing, life-improving effect on people. Giving some of them the opportunity to be fulfilled, to achieve their full potential, maybe even be happy. To be young *is* very heaven . . .

Darcy

A. C. B./Fort Attic
813 2760716 15 June 1989 21.37

Darcy

Hope the heaven continues. I'm heading for Washington. Talk to you when I get there.

Alex

Darcy King/North Carolina
519 5558632 20 June 1989 19.54
Tuesday

Attention Sophia

Sophia?

I must have got the dates wrong. I thought your exams finished two days ago, and was kind of sort of possibly expecting to hear from you. (Sob, sob, no I'm not hurt, think nothing of it.)

If you felt a sisterly urge to communicate with me over the next three days, you might remember I'm in New York. Leaving right now, in fact.

Darcy

As Darcy came out of the last meeting on the second day in New York, Sharletta was waiting for her.

'Someone to see you,' she said sombrely.

'To see *me?*'

'Uh huh.'

'Name?'

'Said you knew her.'

'Is this someone from HR?'

'No, not from the corporation at all.'

Darcy realised that she was being pulled forward on the corridor by the need to stay within earshot of Sharletta, who was moving right along.

'Now, wait a minute, Sharletta. You've never done this to me before. Jesus, I don't want to meet some anonymous hardly-able who walks in the front door from God knows where and – *Sophia!*

The two sisters were locked in each other's arms, circling, half-dancing, laughing and crying.

'Oh, Sharletta, you *wanker*,' Darcy said affectionately, pulling her into a three-cornered embrace.

'How long has this plot been cooking?'

'Months,' Sophia told her. 'I needed to get the cheapest student flight I could, which meant booking ages in advance. Then I had to make sure you didn't know about me coming. Then I had to figure out did I have to go to Greenville or could I meet up with you here in New York? If it hadn't been for Sharletta, it couldn't have happened. I've driven her bananas in the last few weeks, haven't I, Sharletta?'

'No,' Sharletta said. 'No, you haven't. It was quite interesting to liaise with a King sister who didn't lose keys, luggage, computers, tickets, credit cards, shoes, the documentation for the meeting or anything much at all.'

Out in the open air Darcy walked, jamming her hands deep into the patch pockets of her long jacket and looking up at the oblongs of glass on the high-sided buildings that narrowed the street into a canyon.

'God, I love this city.'

'Do you?'

'Wouldn't you? Even after a day, wouldn't you?'

'Why do you?'

'The buzz. The speed. The smells. The – the – anonymity.'

'I would never want to be anonymous,' Sophia said, disapprovingly. 'I plan to be quite well known by the end of my first year in PR. Not famous in the sense that people in the street would be looking for my autograph. I have no time for that at all. But famous in the sense that the Irish business community knows my name, sees me as a force to be reckoned with, views me as on the leading edge of public relations and image-making.'

'All aiming at what?'

'At 1994.'

'Why?'

'That's one of the reasons I'm here.'

'Mmmm?'

'I want your advice on how to do it. And, eventually, be part of it.'

'Say if I don't want to be in this company? Ever?'

'You will.'

CHAPTER NINETEEN

Over lunch, Sophia's plans continued. She would start to collect paintings, she told Darcy. Probably Stephen Cullen's work. It would help to build her image as a fully rounded career woman.

You are, Darcy thought in wonder, prepared to define your life by what will make you publicly interesting. You *don't* have an interest in collecting paintings. You think you *should* have an interest, but that's not the same thing. On the other hand, once you have committed yourself to being A Collector of Stephen Cullen's *oeuvre*, you will develop an interest that will be as genuine as the natural version.

'Do you ever think of Margaret Graham?' Sophia asked, out of the blue. 'I still get the shudders when I think of her. Did that report thing she wished on you die away or do you still write to that old professor in Seattle?'

'He was only in Seattle briefly. Yes, I do.'

'Like an annual report?'

'Oh, no. Much shorter and more frequent and less formal than that.'

'Less formal?'

'But still distant. I don't know how to describe it. I enjoy it, though, it's stopped being a task. In fact, once I got the hang of it, it was never really a task. I'm quite grateful to Margaret Graham for roping me into the whole thing.'

'I've always been jealous of the professor.' Sophia sat back with an air of having confessed an unspeakable crime.

'Jealous?'

'I used to watch you pounding away on your typewriter to him, and sometimes you'd be smiling to yourself, sometimes you'd look as if you were giving out about something, sometimes it was as if you were trying to understand something. It completely excluded me.'

'You had your diary.'

'But there's no *person* at the other end of a diary. You might as well be writing on water.'

'Anyway, there was no point in being jealous of my old professor with his receding hair. You wouldn't have wanted to know about the sort of stuff I was reporting on to him. Trust me. You wouldn't.'

'How do you know he has receding hair? Does he send you pictures?'

'Oh, no. The protocols of this study say we shouldn't have any person-to-person contact. No pictures or phone calls or visits. The whole thing stops if we ever meet. It's just correspondence. A while back he mentioned that his hair was receding. He's probably bald as a coot by now. Greg isn't, is he?'

'Bald as a coot? No. Why?'

'I've done away with several videos out of the year, but there's one annual video that's a given. I want to change. I need to make a current affairs type video with Brautigan. Him and an interviewer he doesn't know. I've been looking at interviewers here, but frankly, American current affairs interviewers aren't a patch on Irish ones. I'm thinking of bringing over an Irish interviewer to do a half-hour grilling of Clive. It would be much more real, exciting and involving than the usual diatribe. I don't need any of the front-rankers like Gaybo or Olivia or Brian Farrell. Just someone pleasing and competent who can take a brief and get on with it. Greg's doing current affairs programmes, isn't he?'

Sophia nodded.

'Would you like me to mention it to him?'

'If you see him, yeah. Tell him I'd bring him over, Business Class, put him up for two nights in the Plaza and pay him two thousand dollars plus expenses. All he'd need to do in advance would be read a few pages I'd fax him.'

Darcy King/Manhattan
212 8645312 26 June 1989 19.37
Monday

Dear Alex

Sophia and I talked a bit about you in Tavern on the Green. I didn't tell her about your film advice work. In fact, to be brutally honest, all I told her was about your receding hairline . . .

Darcy

A. C. B./Washington
202 6613198 26 June 1989 20.12

Darcy

I'm in Washington working on a political thriller, full of psychological twists and physical action. Several good actors – *USA Today* has a story about the movie today. Have a look.

The actor playing the lead is not doing well. The guy wants to be liked. He wants to invest every character he plays with what he calls 'the human touches'. So he subverts a good script with long empathetic looks. In five years time he will be forgotten. The need to be generally liked is such a fool contradiction. Invariably, it leads to dislike, because you adapt yourself to what you think other people would wish you to be and in the process become spurious.

Because the filming is not going well, there's a lot of drinking. I am taking long lone walks.

Alex

Darcy King/Manhattan
212 8645312 26 June 1989 21.05

Attention Alex

When *you* drink, what do you drink?

Darcy

A. C. B./Washington
202 6613198 26 June 1989 21.17

Attention Darcy

Beer, mostly. I don't like the drunk I become on spirits.
Alex

Darcy King/Manhattan
212 8645312 27 June 1989 19.06
Tuesday

Attention Alex

What kind of drunk do you become?
Darcy

A. C. B./Washington
202 6613198 27 June 1989 19.47

Attention Darcy

Caustic.
Alex

Dr Robert King/Dublin
353 1 7324172 5 July 1989 17.39
Wednesday

Attention Darcy

Darcy

I had a word with Greg and he would be delighted to do the job for you. I gave him your number – is that OK? I am settling down nicely in *Positionings*.

Malachy has given me three of his existing clients: Boarding Pass Travel, Pete's Pet Emporium and a knitting wool company in the Donegal Gaeltacht. This would bring me to less than half the billable hours I should have, so say prayers for me that I get new business fairly quickly.

Sophia

Attention Alex
   Caustic? Oh jay.
      Darcy

Attention Sophia
   Sophia, dear
   I would not for a moment let an unworthy
thought pass through my mind to the effect that
was it for Pete's Pet Emporium Dr King sent his
beautiful blonde daughter to University . . .
   So what are you doing? Selling seals? Flogging
fleas? Purveying Pekinese?
      Darcy

On Sophia's first visit to Pete's Pet Emporium, the noise
and smell of the place knocked her sideways, although Pete
(the Emporium had a real Pete) said that compared to other
pet shops, the smell was minimal and he had insulation in
the walls to absorb the sound of yelping.

'Ah, fuck off, fuck off, fuck off, why don't you?' a voice
yelled in the coarsest of Dublin accents. Fearful of drawing
a knife-wielding member of the underclass on herself, Sophia
did not turn around, widening her eyes at Pete in scandalised
fear.

'The mynah bird,' he said. 'The kids from the local school
come in on their lunchtime, and even though I run them,
it's difficult if we have a lot of customers.'

'Give us a ride, give us a ride, give us a ride,' the mynah
bird said to Sophia when she looked at it. It put its head on
one side quite winningly as it made the request.

'They teach it dreadful things,' Pete said.

'McGill plays with himself,' the mynah bird offered, by

way of confirmation.

'Who's McGill?' Sophia asked Pete.

'A twisted creep fulla shit,' the mynah bird announced.

'Their teacher,' Pete amended.

'McGill plays with himself,' the mynah bird said again.

In the room at the back, Pete told Sophia his plans. He was in the process of setting up emporia in every major city in Ireland, and if it all worked out, would expand into Britain and Europe shortly thereafter.

'Think about it,' he requested. 'There's no such thing as a chain of pet shops, like there are chains of fast food restaurants, where you could be sure of the same standards of service. That's what I'm going to create. A chain where if you have a pet or want a pet, you just wouldn't think of going anywhere but to the branded emporium, because you know the animal you buy will be certified, tested, inoculated, everything, and that there will be an advice service.'

He needed lots of coverage for the emporium, he told her, so that the phrase and the concept stuck in people's minds. If it suited her to stitch him into the emerging image of the emporium, that was fine. He didn't mind how household name status was achieved, as long as it *was* achieved.

Sophia looked at him. He was completely bald on top, with wrinkly reddish hair streaming back over both ears as if he had recently been swimming in permanent wave liquid. His tie was hanging, knotted, about an inch below where it should be. His navy cardigan had white feathers on it and a narrow strip of the cut paper the puppies nested in was coming up over one shoulder as if it meant to undulate, caterpillar-fashion, down his front. He looked, she decided, as if he had been slept in, which might explain why Malachy had not, in the first year of the contract, set out to make Pete a star.

'Tell me why the things you sell, like goldfish, aren't dull,' she invited.

Pete looked outraged. '*Dull?*' he repeated, as if goldfish had been proven to be the most exciting companions available. 'Dull? Let me tell you, there's a television programme in America with nothing but goldfish. *Nothing but goldfish,*' he repeated.

'My sister had goldfish, once,' Sophia remembered. 'One day they just bent over and died. It was awful.'

'If she'd stirred the bowl, it might have helped. Get oxygen into them.'

'Stirred it? Like a cup of tea?'

Pete nodded.

'The puppies outside are just lovely,' Sophia said.

'There should be a law that required you to do a training course before you bought a puppy,' Pete said sourly. 'Bloody eejits come in here, fall in love with a little yoke eight inches long that's going to grow into a huge demanding animal, and they don't think past the lick on their face.'

Writing as fast as she could, Sophia began to learn about *toxocara canis*; how children could be blinded by a virus transmitted from a pet dog if the child wasn't taught to wash its hands directly – and always – after petting the animal. She learned about training and its importance. About the food stupid pet owners fed their dogs and cats as treats, and the damage it did. She learned how personalities should be matched to pet types – there was a certain kind of person, Pete opined, who was best suited by a lizard as a pet.

'There should be a delay, too,' Pete said. 'A delay between deciding to buy and actually walking out of here with the animal. They have a delay in America about guns and that's a good thing. I'd have no problems if someone had second thoughts and didn't buy. That'd be so much better than if they bought a good animal and gave it a bad home. It's awful when you put a lovely dog like a Labrador into the hands of someone that'll mistreat it, and the poor bloody beast still loves the bastard owner.'

'Listen, I have wonderful stuff here. I'll be back to you

within a week with some suggestions,' Sophia said.

'No hurry. Whenever.'

Sophia couldn't avoid looking at the mynah bird on the way out, and her glance provoked the bird into a spectacular dam-burst.

In handing over existing clients to Sophia, Malachy had picked the least controversial. He pointed out that of all the clients served by *Positionings*, Pete's Pet Emporium was not likely to erupt in a sudden crisis. He was proved wrong in the first week.

'There's a controversy about Pete's Pet Emporium,' Sophia's secretary Genna said, reading from her notes when Sophia came back after meeting another client. 'And it may be on the nine o'clock television news.'

Sophia stopped dead, rapidly running through in her mind the possibilities of the spread of a doggy virus to humans or some other health disaster.

'The Emporium sold a gross of white mice,' Genna said.

'What's a gross?'

'One hundred and forty-four.'

'Thank you. Go on.'

'They sold this gross of white mice, it is alleged, to a senior student at St Barnabas College, at a cost of one hundred and twenty pounds. It was a reduction because there were so many white mice involved.'

'And?'

'They didn't check what they were going to be used for.'

Sophia considered the possibilities. Maybe St Barnabas were into some kind of animal testing. Live dissection or something equally cruel.

'The student, whose real name has yet to be ascertained,' Genna went on, quite pleased with her own police-report style of delivery, 'collected the mice at lunchtime.'

'And?'

'And released them on the three floors of St Barnabas at around 2.30 in the afternoon.'

'Oh, no.'

'Oh, yes.'

The pandemonium which ensued, according to Genna, was of epic proportions. St Barnabas was co-ed, and if the release of the mice had been by way of a gender experiment, it had certainly proven a central male prejudice about women and their fear of mice. Middle-aged male teachers were amused or irritated by the mice. Middle-aged female teachers climbed on chairs. The entire school was evacuated and students sent home early while the prefects, male and female, captured most of the mice.

Sophia sat down at her desk to think about this.

'Now the bad news is that the television cameras were there.'

'How?'

'Someone telephoned the newsroom at the station this morning with a steer that St Barnabas's most famous alumnus, Daragh Kinsella the sports star, would be arriving to announce his funding of a complete new wing for training gifted students who would be given scholarships. And that although the school authorities would deny this if telephoned, the informant could tell them that Kinsella's Bentley would be pulling through the gates at 2.40 precisely and they could doorstep him if they wanted.

'At 2.40, students and teachers came flying out of every exit. People climbed out windows as if the black plague had broken out inside. So they apparently got great footage and also grabbed numbers of the students and interviewed them about what happened.'

'Get me Pete, please.'

Within seconds, he was on the line.

'Ah, fuck off, fuck off, fuck off, why don't you?' the raucous Dublin accent of the mynah bird roared behind him.

'Oh, for Christ sake,' Pete muttered and the mynah bird was suddenly silent.

'What did you do to him?'

'Threw my cardigan over his cage.'

'Pete, did the emporium do anything it shouldn't have done?'

'We did everything right. The guy who bought the mice wasn't a kid: big tall adult eighteen-year-old, full uniform, well spoken.'

'And it never struck you?'

'When little old ladies come in here to buy Alsatians, it doesn't strike me they need them for sex,' Pete said furiously. 'The odds on this happening are kind of small, Sophia.'

'Relapse, relapse.'

'This could be very bad.'

'Or very good.'

'*What?*'

'I can try to hold back the sea, or I can get you up on top of the wave. I can try to stop the TV station running the story tonight, or I can ask them to put you in the story.'

'Why the hell would I want to be in a story that makes me look a complete buck eejit?'

'Doesn't. You can make the points you were making to me about the law needing tightening up.'

'That was off the top of my head.'

'Listen, I'll have Genna ring you in twenty minutes and read a suggested press release to you. If it makes sense, then I'll talk to the TV station and the papers and get them on to you.'

In less than twenty minutes, Genna was reading aloud into the telephone the heading on the press release: 'Pete's Pet Emporium calls for Tightening of Laws on Animal Purchase.' The press release called for a 24-hour mandatory delay between agreement to purchase and actual delivery of a pet. This, the pet shop owner said, would allow 'thinking time' during pressured seasons such as the pre-Christmas weeks when pets were purchased which might later be abandoned, and would also allow for checking with parents or schools in the case of under-age pet purchases. '*We're talking about live animals,'* Pete Muldoon said today, *'and it should not be forgotten that as a result of this dangerous and irresponsible prank seven of the little mice were dead and three were still missing.'*

'Sophia wants to know are you happy with that?' Genna asked Peter.

'Tell her yes. Tell her I'll do the interview with the TV people if she wants. Do I go out there? Have I time to get into my best suit?'

Sophia, meanwhile, was on to the TV station, meeting with some resistance from the editor in charge.

'C'mon, Sophia,' he said. 'It's a light story. It's a visual story. We don't need it weighed down with platitudes from a pet-shop owner.'

'Brian, you'll close this man's business,' Sophia said, her voice shrill with shock. 'Overnight. You'll be putting eleven people on the street. Closing a Dublin landmark.'

'No, we won't.'

'Oh, you will, Brian, you will, be in no doubt about it. Your story will make it look as if the pet shop was irres-ponsible, and that's just the opposite of the case. This is a man who's been fighting for *years* – ' Sophia crossed her fingers under the desk by way of an apology to God for the exaggeration, not to say actual falsehood '– to get proper standards into the buying and selling and keeping of pets.'

'It's not news, what he'd be saying.'

'Brian!' Sophia sounded astonished. 'It's the *real* news in your story. He's calling for changes in legislation, he's talking about the way you buy guns in America – I'm telling you, Brian, this transforms a light funny accidental story into real reporting.'

Brian considered this, damping down his instinct to tell her that as a brand-new PR hack, she shouldn't be lecturing him, a serious journalist, on reporting, real or otherwise.

'Wait'll you see him,' Sophia went on. 'He's so genuine, Brian. None of your mohair suits stuff. This is an animals man, big old cardigan, straw in his hair kind of person.'

Brian sighed and said he'd have a crew in the emporium by five, and this Pete had better be good. Sophia assured him that 'good' was an inadequate word for how marvellous Pete would be. Genna had Pete on the other line as she put down the phone.

'Don't change your clothes,' instructed Sophia.

'*Don't* change my clothes? My wife is on her way here with my good suit.'

'Ring and tell her not to bother. Trust me. Wear your cardigan.'

'The mynah bird's bitten it a bit.'

'Wear it. I'll be there before the crew arrive.'

When she reached Pete's Pet Emporium, there was a towel over the mynah bird.

'I've been thinking,' she told Pete, noting that the mynah bird had indeed bitten lumps out of his cardigan. 'Leave the cover off the mynah bird until they start filming. They'll love it and we might use it as a hook for a later story.'

Pete shrugged and took the towel off the mynah bird, which immediately told Sophia that McGill played with himself.

'What are you going to say to them?'

Pete looked baffled.

'It depends what they're going to ask me, doesn't it?'

'No, it *doesn't*. They're going to ask some general question like how could this happen or should it have happened. Just a hook for you to hang an interesting point on.'

Pete told her the two things he most wanted to say.

'Tell them to me again and be more interested in them yourself – believe in them.'

Pete told her the same thing again in half the length and with twice the energy.

'Great,' she said, and the TV crew arrived.

'Hi, I'm Sophia, and this is Pete – '

'A twisted creep fulla shit,' the mynah bird finished.

Sophia pretended not to notice.

'Brian, will you want the cages in the background or – '

'Give us a ride, give us a ride, give us a ride.'

Brian stood irresolute.

'Because if you don't like any of the options here – '

'Fuck off, fuck off, fuck off, why don't you?'

The television crew gathered around the mynah bird, which became nearly hysterical with the attention it was getting. Pete put the towel over it and the bright lights were put on. Brian asked him a question and Pete delivered an impassioned forty seconds, a feather on his cardigan trembling as he spoke.

'Cut!' Brian said. 'Fair dues to you, Sophia. He's just what you said.'

'If we have a problem with the tape, you can lend us your parrot,' the sound operator said, spooling cables and moving towards the door. Neither Sophia nor Pete corrected him.

'You're a star,' Sophia told Pete. 'You're a star, too,' she told the mynah bird, which invited her, head seductively on one side, to fuck off.

'Where are the mice?'

Pete gestured at what looked like a portable cage.

'They even brought back the dead ones,' he said grimly.

'Oh, *great*,' said Sophia.

Pete looked at her with the patient silence of someone who does not understand what is happening to him but is prepared to leave his fate in the hands of experts.

'I've been trying to think up angles for tomorrow morning's papers, and that's one,' she said. 'I want a picture of you holding three tiny dead mice in your hands.'

'Lucky you only want three,' he said sourly.

'Why?'

'Because all the other poor little bastards got mangled to mush, that's why.'

Within minutes, a photographer was there, taking pictures of Pete as fast as he could, convinced that the only reason Sophia King was letting pictures be taken of this bedraggled pet shop owner was because she was so new to the job she didn't know she should be dolling him up in a respectable shirt and tie.

The following morning, two of the national papers had Pete on their front page. One showed him holding the little dead mice. The other showed him looking into the cage of live retrieved mice. Was he going to resell the mice? the story enquired. No, he was going to give them away to the first hundred and thirty children who arrived at Pete's Emporium in the company of their parents and who gave a handwritten promise to take good care of their free mouse.

Sophia sat at her desk at 7.30 am, hugging herself with delight. The phone rang.

'May I speak to Sophia King?'

'Speaking, Pete.'

'Why are you answering the phone?'

'Secretaries don't come in at 7.30.'

'Have you seen the papers?'

'Of course I have. Are you thrilled?'

Pete told her how thrilled he was. She then told him how profoundly thrilled he should be, in view of the fact that he had been turned into a brand name and a figure of influence overnight. It had been careful and inspired management of what might have been a disaster, she told him, praising him for all she had done. He basked in a confused way.

'My wife didn't like me in the cardigan on the telly,' he said after a moment.

'Your wife will have to understand that anybody can wear a suit and look respectable, but that our objective is to have you looking instantly identifiable. Like Colonel Sanders. Or Tony O'Reilly.'

Pete accepted this equity membership of the globally famous without demur.

'There's only one disadvantage,' he said.

'What's that?'

'The minute the primary schools let them out today, I'm going to have a queue around the corner of little feckers and their parents. It's a schools half-day.'

'Gosh.'

'Yes,' he said grimly.

'But that's *wonderful*,' shrieked Sophia. 'We can get the evenings, too!'

The evening papers duly arrived on the streets that afternoon with front-page pictures of the queue outside Pete's Pet Emporium. One of them had an additional picture inside of a particularly cute six-year-old with a white mouse on her shoulder, peeping around her blonde pigtail. The six-year-old was the daughter of one of the *Positionings* executives, and the picture took a hired photographer three hours but the effort was worth it, since the shot created what Sophia described as the 'Aaah' factor. One of the city radio stations did vox pop interviews with the people who were queuing and topped the item off with a reprise of Pete's strong comments about the responsibilities facing pet-buyers.

Positionings/Dublin
353 1 6740767 14 July 1989 21.03

Attention Darcy King

Darcy

Have a look at the enclosed. Isn't it great? I would say it only to you, but my main reaction is one of relief. I was quite worried that I was doing the wrong thing about the TV news report.

At first, I thought I would get the head of the school to ring the TV station and talk to someone very important there, perhaps even the Director General, and put it to him that this kind of report was questionable for two reasons:

1 The TV station colluding with a practical joker who did cause mayhem and could have caused injury

2 The likelihood of stimulating copycat pranks

The latter has already happened but on a much smaller scale than St Barnabas' gross of mice. Of course, there has been no media coverage bar a token half-inch buried on the inside pages: 'Copycat Mice Attack'.

The reason I didn't go that road was that I suddenly realised where my professional loyalties lay. I am not being paid by schools to prevent practical jokes. I have no moral obligation to them. Pete, on the other hand, does pay us a retainer. So my job was to get the best possible publicity for him that I could manage.

I must finish this – I've invited the editor from RTE, Brian, to lunch, so that I can get to know him and understand how their system of selecting stories works.

The company is going to put wheels under me but I may have to put some money towards it myself, I need your advice on this.

Love
Sophia

Darcy King/Manhattan
212 8645312 17 July 1989 13.17

Attention Sophia King
Sophia

Sharletta has the cuttings pinned to the notice board in the New York office where people met you. She thinks the whole thing is both wild and cool.

I have to meet this mynah bird. We were mates in a former life, definitely. (Might as well be mates in this life, too, for all the good I'm doing in the human mating game.)

You need advice from me on wheels? You gotta be kidding. Me, the former owner of Suppurating Septicaemia?

Darcy ⌐

Dr Robert King/Dublin
353 1 7324172 18 July 1989 19.32
Attention Darcy King

Darcy

The car I could get from the company would be a Toyota Starlet. But if I put a couple of thousand more to it myself, I could get a Honda Civic or a Golf or something in that kind of range. Or I could borrow a bit more and get a BMW. From an image point of view, I think the best option is to borrow and get the BMW.

By the way, would you ask your professor if any studies have ever been done on 'therapeutic calming by goldfish': have any psychiatrists used goldfish as therapy for mentally ill people?

Sophia

Darcy King/Manhattan
212 8645312 19 July 198918.58
Attention Sophia King

From an image point of view, indubitably a Beemer.

Darcy

Dr Robert King/Dublin
353 1 7324172 19 July 1989 18.45
Attention Darcy King

Are you being cynical?

Sophia

Attention Sophia King

Indubitably. But I know you won't let that stop you.

Darcy

Alex

Under the heading of Weird but True, file this. My sister wants me to ask you if you know of any 'therapeutic calming by goldfish;' have any psychiatrists used goldfish as therapy for mentally ill people? I would not ask you such a damnfool question except I had goldfish once as a kid and Sophia was very good to me when the poor little farts died.

I probably *shouldn't* ask you anyway, you being a trout/salmon and pike killer. You probably keep an aquarium in your sitting-room so you can go spear fishing in moments of boredom.

Darcy

Darcy

I would hope to come back to you within forty-eight hours regarding studies on therapeutic use of goldfish.

Not only do I not do in-house spear-fishing but I had tropical fish when I was growing up and for the most part, they lived to be very, very old. People at one with nature tend to create longevity in the flora and fauna around them.

The only time any of my tropical fish came to an unexpectedly early demise was due to my father.

When you mentioned, some time ago, your fascination with the way corporations here think in (yearly) quarters, it recalled my father to me, because he did binge-drinking on a quarterly basis. Five days, once a quarter, you could bank on his being speechlessly drunk. He was not a caustic drunk, just physically uncoordinated when inebriated. When I was twelve, he came in one night, very drunk, and lurched so heavily up against my aquarium that he put his elbow through the glass. I came running from the next door at the sound of the crash, and found him standing in front of this glass box with water and fish fountaining out through a jagged hole, trying to catch the fish in his hands to rescue them . . .
Alex.

Darcy King/Manhattan
212 8645312 27 July 1989 21.20
Thursday

Alex

Did you save any of them?
Darcy

A. C. B./Washington
202 6613198 27 July 1989 22.16

Darcy

No. I gave it up as a pastime and went elk-hunting instead.

My search of the data on goldfish has not yielded much. (If, on the other hand, I could interest you in poodles, there is quite an amount of data on record about their efficacy. Particularly in relation to isolated elderly homosexuals.)

There is a book written by one Alan Beck who's Professor of Ecology at Purdue University School of Veterinary Medicine. It's called *Between Pets and People*. He claims that whenever people touch their pets there's an immediate, if small, drop in blood pressure. Now touching is not usually how people interact with their goldfish but he maintains that just looking at fish in an aquarium has similar effects.

Much study has been made of the influence of an animal on social interactions of nursing home residents in a group setting. Findings indicate that animals can be an effective medium for increasing socialization among residents.

Animal Assisted Therapy (AAT) programs have been studied. In one study of elderly psychiatric patients, dog intervention was found to be the most effective method of increasing interaction.

In general, the use of companion animals or pets is gaining popularity as a therapeutic approach, especially to isolated older patients and patients in institutions. The benefits of animal-human bonding would include positive physiological effects on the heart, reduction in the requirement for some medication, and raised morale/self-esteem.

Dolphins and other mammals have been used with children who are nonverbal, autistic or schizophrenic.

Dogs and other animals have been used in experimental therapy with Alzheimers' sufferers with no very significant difference in behaviors observed on the part of the patients.

It may or may not be of note to your sister that the first therapeutic use of animals was in 1792 at a Quaker facility for the insane. Since then, animal therapy has been widely used to relieve loneliness, provide emotional support, decrease inner turmoil and improve tactile stimulation. However, goldfish have not figured in most of the databases I have accessed. With the exception of one mention: Aaron Katcher, a psychiatrist at the University of Pennsylvania, found that the blood pressure of people watching fish in an aquarium dropped measurably: more than if they had sat down and watched a blank wall. This effect was stronger in hypertensive subjects and those who had normal blood pressure.

Other than that, what follows is somewhat random.

There are at least 250 million pet fish in the United States. I do not have figures for Europe, but the best work on collating this kind of information has been done by James Serpell, a research associate in animal behavior at the University of Cambridge. I quote from his *In the Company of Animals* (Basil Blackwell, 1986, Oxford): 'At one time pet turbot were all the rage in Rome. The daughter of Drusus adorned one with gold rings, while the orator Hortensius actually wept when his favourite flatfish expired.'

The Samoans kept eels as pets. Does this count?
Alex

CHAPTER TWENTY

When Greg travelled to New York to interview Clive Brautigan on videotape, he brought a portfolio of cuttings about Sophia.

'She said you'd want to see them all,' he said, handing them over with an air of don't-blame-me. 'Or rather, she said you *should* see them all. You know Sophia's sense of duty.'

Darcy nodded, leafing through the cuttings.

'Oh, look, the two of you – '

He looked over her shoulder at the picture.

'Yeah. She asked me to escort her to the People of the Year awards.'

'Oh, and it was *such* a bother?'

Darcy continued to turn the pages. One of the most recent cuttings was a feature from one of the Sunday papers, profiling three businesswomen in their early twenties. Atop Sophia's picture was the heading: The Hype Priestess. Darcy patted the page lovingly.

'God, that's not bad for a kid who only started in business eight months ago,' she said admiringly.

'She's already known around Dublin, she's already a name in the business. I would say Malachy is feeling very pleased with himself that he took her on.'

The interview with Brautigan worked. Greg was an easy but probing questioner, and being pushed brought out an energy and conviction in Brautigan that had been missing in earlier videotapes. He took Greg to lunch after the recording and talked about Darcy's impact on the corporation.

'How is her sister doing? I met her when she took a vacation with Darcy last year.'

'Extraordinarily well. And it's not easy. Ireland is a difficult country to do public relations in. Everybody knows everybody else. We start checking each other out immediately.'

'Checking each other out?'

'Let's say someone is introduced to me in Ireland,' Greg said. 'Even if they don't know me from television they'll know my accent is Dublin. My build suggests rugby. So they go by school. Belvedere? Oh, was I there when X was there? No, he was a year ahead of me. Oh, then I must have been there same year as Y, yes, how do you know Y, oh, my sister's married to his cousin. Or they go by surname. 'McEnerney? Nothing to Charles McEnerney, are you?' Charles McEnerney being well known in medical circles. 'Yeah, I'm Charlie McEnerney's son, do you know my dad?' 'Not directly but my aunt was his secretary for three months when his normal secretary was on maternity leave.' That's what I mean.'

Sipping coffee, Clive Brautigan wondered aloud why this made public relations more difficult.

'Because you can't just create an image out of nothing for a man or an organisation. Here, you can issue advertising material or press statements and that's how people hear about an individual or an organisation. In Ireland, you can advertise, you can issue press statements, but everybody knows the real story, everybody has a pal in the company who'll feed them the unofficial line of information.'

'You say Darcy's sister is particularly good at this business?'

'The best. She's very young, of course, and she's new to it, but in ten years' time she'll have branches of her own company here in the States, you mark my words.'

'In ten years' time, where would you predict Darcy might be?'

'Much more difficult to work out,' Greg told him. 'Sophia has a game plan. A two-year, five-year, ten-year strategy within which she'll employ different tactics, she'll tack with the wind. But Darcy never has a plan. Darcy only knows when she's finished with something and it's time to move on.'

Driving to the airport with Darcy later, Greg told her what he had said. She smiled but made no comment as she pulled up to the kerb outside the Aer Lingus terminal. Greg gathered his overnight bag and leaned in the open window of the car to kiss her.

'Brautigan thinks you're the best thing that ever happened to him,' he said, very seriously.

'And isn't he right?' she said, gunning the engine so that he pulled back, mimicking terror.

Before Greg was airborne on his journey home, Darcy sent a fax to her twin.

Darcy King/Manhattan
212 8645312 21 August 1989 8.09
Monday

Attention Sophia King
Personal and Confidential

Sister mine

Not nice. Not nice to kid your twin. Not nice to conceal relevant info from your twin.

Clear as the proverbial ding dong that you and Greg are an Item. Doing a Line. Seeing each other (as you'd say yourself). Dating. Keeping company.

Do I have a problem with this?

No.

Why should I have a problem with it?

So why spend the last few months making artificially casual throwaway references as if you had just run into Greg once in the middle of O'Connell Street in a fleeting encounter on a manhole cover when in fact you are wining and dining, getting your pitcher took and generally being seen as a couple.

If you want to know what I think about this, I

think it is shitty beyond belief. Only because I am a good listener did I not look a complete fool when he was talking about you. At any stage in my letters home to Mam and Dad or phone calls I could have looked a prize charlie.

You are not often a straight-up, no messing, no excuses shit, but on this occasion, that's what you are.

In continuing affection
Darcy

Dr Robert King/Dublin
353 1 7324172 23 August 1989 18.18
Attention Darcy King
Darcy

I'm sorry. I really couldn't bring myself to say it in the beginning. Then I felt that by postponing saying it I had made it worse. I can only apologise.
Sophia

Darcy King/Manhattan
212 8645312 23 August 1989 18.03
Attention Sophia King
Sophia

What in the hell is wrong with you? You knew that it was me that ended the relationship with Greg. Did you think I wanted him marked off like a leper (excuse me, in PR terms you'd call that 'a sufferer from Hansen's Disease') so that nobody else would touch him? He is a ray of sunshine, a very good TV interviewer and looks deadly handsome in pictures along with you.

But may your arse wither and fester for being such a secretive shite.

Love
Darcy

Alex

See enclosures. Why is she sending me crap from her sister, I hear you ask.

Why I'm sending it to you is because although you may have (given encroaching years and receding hair) forgotten the original thrust of our communication, the fact is that you and I are supposed to be examining sex, lies and relationship development on my part, and since there is damn all happening in the way of sex and relationship development, I thought it might be helpful to do a little work vicariously. As in my former boyfriend Greg and my beloved twin, Sophia. GregandSophia, as the tabloids would put it. Closerthanthis.

The simplest way to tell the story is through a recent spate of correspondence between me and my sibling. Spate follows.

Darcy

Sophia never mentioned Darcy's letter to Greg except to comment that Darcy seemed pleased with his performance.

'Listen, you have no idea how hard I worked at it,' he said. 'Frankly, I was more scared about that job than I've been about any job since I started presenting. I seriously did not want to let Darcy down. I sweated bricks, all the time being casual and throwaway.'

'I rang you for a particular reason, Greg.'

'Oh, I thought it was just for the cheap thrill of hearing my voice.'

'That, too. But I thought you might hear about the flights to the Canaries.'

'How soon? Have I time to pack?'

'That's what I was afraid of.'

'Sorry?'

'I knew you'd want to go. Well, you can't. Boarding Pass Travel have a plane going to Tenerife on Saturday, and because of a computer failure, they have about sixty empty seats. By pushing like hell, they'll fill maybe forty of them, but they have at least twenty they know they can't fill, and Owen Keating was on to me to ask me to give them as special favours to a number of key journalists. Fortnight in Tenerife. The only thing to be paid for would be food and entertainment.'

'*Sophia?*'

'Greg, I'm not giving you one of them.'

'*Sophia?*'

'You're well able to pay for your own tickets to Tenerife.'

'So is any goddamn journalist.'

'But that's not the point. How would it look?'

'Look to who? Mother Teresa? The Pope? God?'

'You could not claim to be writing a feature or doing research for a feature. If your programme ever did a hard-hitting item about international travel, you'd have to rule yourself out of presenting it. You'd be tainted.'

'You know something, Sophia, my uncle the bishop talks about women of a certain age becoming "over-scrupulous". Don't look now, but I think you might have reached the age.'

'I'm not doing it, anyway.'

'OK.'

'You don't mind, really, do you?'

'Naah. A fortnight in bracing sunshine, great food, wonderful bird-watching on the beach. I wouldn't want that. Which of the hacks get lucky this time, then?'

'I've drawn up a list of about forty.'

'I thought you only had twenty seats?'

'But I've worked out that at least twenty journalists on the list aren't going to be able to take up the offer for one reason or another, so I'm offering it to them first. That way, they feel very grateful for the possibility, and they feel regretful because they weren't able to take it up. Then I can move on and offer it to the journalists that probably *can* take it, and that way I get double value out of each ticket.'

'Sophia, my mother has an expression for a girl like you.'

'It is?'

'"She will meet herself coming back, that girl." Anyway, get off the line. I have television programmes to make. Love you.'

'Ditto.'

'Oh, Genna of the elephantine floppy ears is right in the room with you?'

'Greg.'

'Even as we speak, she is sucking up the syllables, is she?'

'That specific detail we might discuss at a later stage.'

'Tongue hanging out for a hint of her boss's love life, right?'

'OK, Greg, I'll talk to you later.'

Genna looked disapprovingly at Sophia as Sophia grabbed mobile phone, bag and Filofax and headed to the door. Sophia prided herself on her punctuality, but Genna had noticed that as the day wore on, her boss tended to run anything from twenty to forty minutes late for every meeting. A BMW might look impressive in the guest slot of the client's car park, thought Genna, who was stretched by the payments on her own Ford Fiesta, but it didn't get you any quicker through congested traffic. As Sophia pulled out into such traffic around Harcourt Street, her phone rang.

'Hi, this is Sophia King.'

'Hi, sweetheart.'

'Oh *Dad*. Where are you?'

'At the hospital. Sophia, I don't think you ever met our Head of Internal Medicine, Lawrence Deevy?'

'I don't think so.'

'Well, I want you to take a phone call from him about a . . . media issue.'

'Dad, I don't want to sound disobliging, but I don't handle the Angelus account, and there are good reasons for that.'

'I know that, honey, I know. Are you in very busy traffic? I can hear beeping?'

'I pulled out in front of a guy who's going through a grieving process over it. Don't worry about it.'

'It's just a very awkward situation, and I'd like Lawrence to explain it to you himself. I don't know what he's going to ask you to do about it, if anything. He may just want to talk it out with you.'

'All right. I'm heading into a meeting now and I'll have the phone switched off for about an hour. Tell him to ring me after that.'

'You're very good, Sophia, thank you.'

'Oh, *Dad*. Don't be silly. Talk to you.'

Lawrence Deevy was obviously anxious because, when Sophia's meeting under-ran and she turned on the phone earlier than she had told her father she would, he came through almost immediately. It was the ensuing phone call, transcribed, which was published in a major Sunday newspaper five days later.

'Miss King?'

'Dr Deevy?'

'Well, now, I'm technically *Mr* Deevy, but we won't worry about that.'

(Silence).

'Are you there, Miss King?'

'Yes.'

'Oh, well. Right. Now, I asked your father if you would mind taking a call from me and he assured me that you would have no objection.'

'Yes.'

'I know that you do not handle the Angelus hospital account for your company, but I thought I might impose upon your good offices for perhaps a little advice . . . ?'

'Yes.'

'Well, you might not be aware that your company has been dealing with a journalist from that Sunday newspaper with the magazine – I forget its name – you must forgive me, this is not an area with which – '

'I know the name.'

'Oh, you do. Oh very good. Very good. Now, this young woman came from the paper a couple of days ago to interview me and to see some of the work we do in the department.'

'Her name?'

'Her name? Oh, quite so. Her name was Amanda Nelligan. Good medical name, what? No connection, though, I did check.'

'So Amanda came and spent time in the department?'

'Indeed, yes, and I impressed upon her some of the most important implications of our work and how we are regarded internationally. I even gave her printouts of a paper I gave at the Stockholm Conference. That was very well received.'

'Yes?'

'Purely out of courtesy, I should tell you, at the end of the interview, I elected to show her to the door myself. To the front door of the hospital.'

'That's a *long* way from your department.'

'Quite so, quite so. But I would not grudge the time because I do hold that we must communicate and develop the image . . . '

'Mr Deevy?'

' . . . oh, I'm here, I'm here.'

'You were saying?'

'In essence, then, I suppose you could say that I accompanied the young woman to the front door of the hospital and during the walk we conversed in a casual way about this and that.'

'Yes?'

'Of course, the young woman was not making any notes of any kind.'

'No, that would be difficult.'

'I beg your pardon?'

'Difficult. Difficult to make notes as you walk.'

'Oh, indeed, Ha Ha.'

'So she wasn't making notes?'

'No, indeed. Quite so. Very definitely not.'

'So?'

'I beg your pardon?'

'So she wasn't making notes, and in some way her not taking notes . . . ?'

'It would be fair to say that she put me off guard.'

'She put you off guard?'

'By not taking notes.'

'I don't understand.'

'I suppose it might not have been deliberate, although you know journalists – how silly of me, *you* know journalists so much better than those of us who toil in other fields.'

'Mr Deevy, I'm getting lost. Do I assume that you told her something you shouldn't have told her?'

'What an extraordinarily pejorative assumption to make.'

'I do beg your pardon, Sir. Would it be fairer to say that you told her something you're no longer comfortable that you told her?'

(Silence)

'Would it be – '

'I suppose if – '

' – I'm so sorry. Go ahead, Mr Deevy.'

'The best approach may be if I outline for you the topic areas.'

'That would be excellent.'

'Good. Good. She made some comment about cutbacks possible in the next Budget, and I said something jocose about having positive expectations of the Minister for Health in that regard.'

'Precisely what did you say, Sir?'

'I said something like "Oh, old Dots won't let the Rottweilers be used on Angelus . . ." or something like that.

Maybe I might have – '

'Sir, try to recall it precisely. What exactly did you say?'

(Silence)

'Sir?'

'I'm trying.'

'I beg your pardon.'

'I said, "Old Dots won't let the Rottweilers be used on Angelus. She owes us too much for that."'

'What does she owe you?'

'That's what the journalist asked, too.'

'I figured she might.'

'Oh? Oh. Well, you know, I talked generally.'

'What did you say?'

'I said that when she had her bout of gall bladder trouble, I had personally come in from the golf course to deal with it, and complicated it had been, too and I mentioned the complications. Well no, I mentioned *some* of the complications.'

'Of this specific case?'

'Pardon?'

'You talked to this journalist about the specific complications of this particular case, not about the possible complications of this condition in a general sense?'

'No, it was about Dots.'

'Oh, Sacred Heart.'

(Silence)

'Go on, Mr Deevy, go on.'

'And I told her how we had put out a false statement about why the Minister was in the hospital.'

'What?'

'We probably did that on the advice of your company, Miss King.'

'I doubt it, Mr Deevy. I have yet to see inaccuracies put out on the *Positionings* letterhead.'

(Incomprehensible noise.)

'You told her a false statement was put out by the hospital?'

'To protect the Minister. To protect the Minister.'

'With the Minister's connivance?'

' . . . with the Minister's – I suppose, yes, although I would not use that term.'

'Finish it off, Mr Deevy. Tell me the rest.'

'I made some jocose comment about the need for privacy in such circumstances, we shook hands, and the journalist took her departure.'

'Back-track there for me. You made a joke about the need for privacy in such circumstances? In what circumstances?'

(Silence)

'Mr Deevy?'

'Please.'

'Yes?'

'I said something like, "Old Dots wouldn't have wanted it bruited abroad that she had the problem of females fat, fair and forty, when she's very fat, artificially fair and considerably on the wrong side of forty."'

(Silence)

'Now, Miss King, you have the whole story, perhaps you would pass judgement on it and tell me what you think.'

'Mr Deevy, you don't want me to pass judgement on what you said?'

'No, no, Miss King, I wouldn't feel the need for that.'

'I see. So what *do* you want judgement passed on?'

'How malicious is this journalist?'

'Malicious? I would never think of Amanda as malicious but then I wouldn't think of many journalists as malicious. That doesn't mean that they won't go in and eat your liver if your liver looks good to eat. You have, in effect, handed Amanda Nelligan a wonderful story which sideswipes you, the hospital and the Minister all in one go. With great quotations. I would be amazed if she passes it up and I would be even more amazed if they don't run it under a headline that calls the Minister Old Dots and refers to her as fat, fair and forty-plus.'

'But surely, Miss King, there are ethical considerations here?'

'Oh, there are, Mr Deevy. That's why I wondered if you wanted me to make judgement on the comments you made to the journalist.'

'That is not what I am talking about.'

'I know that. You are suggesting that there is some abstruse ethical consideration which would constrain Amanda Nelligan from running the story that'll get her this year's A. T. Cross award and an extra five K into her back pocket. If there is such an ethical consideration, I don't know about it.'

'But she wasn't taking notes.'

'She has a mind like a steel trap.'

'But it was clearly off-the-record stuff.'

'Did you agree that with her in advance?'

'No.'

'Then don't comfort yourself with that idea. It won't fly.'

'Miss King, perhaps you could outline for me the various options to be considered?'

'Options?'

'Indeed.'

'Whose options do you want me to look at?'

'The options for the hospital. For me.'

'There *are* no options. You just hope for a major disaster, local rather than national, national rather than international, that will take up media space and make this less interesting to the editor. Amanda Nelligan's editor has three hot buttons: public funding, ethics and secrets. This links all three, so the odds are he will go with it.'

'But presumably not without giving the hospital a chance to – to ensure legitimate balance in the story.'

'Balance?'

'Balance. In the story.'

'What balance?'

'The excellence of the work we do, the hinterland we

serve, the national service we offer in some disciplines.'

(Silence)

'But you are acquainted with this journalist, anyway?'

'Me? Oh, I know Amanda, yes.'

'Would you be friends with her, now?'

'Mr Deevy?'

(Silence)

'It would appear to me, as something of an outsider, of course, I do grant you that, but it would appear to me possible for you to – to – take the requisite action. For the sake of the hospital.'

'What requisite action?'

'Oh, come, come.'

'I *beg* your pardon?'

'I think you know what I mean.'

'I don't know what you mean.'

'I believe the expression is "calling in favours".'

(Silence)

'It would be helpful to the hospital if you ensured that this story did not appear, and I'm sure you could talk to this girl and indicate that I wouldn't want to have to deny it and call her a liar.'

'It wouldn't work if you did call her a liar. Mr Deevy, I don't think there's a lot I can do for you. You have an account executive, who also happens to be the CEO of my company, with years more experience in such matters – '

'But not related to someone working in the hospital.'

'No. Malachy doesn't have the good fortune to be my father's son.'

'Well then.'

'Mr Deevy. You don't want my judgement. You want me to kill off a story by misusing a friendship I don't have with a journalist who, if she has the brains or the independence I believe she has, would tell me to go take a running jump for myself.'

'Oh, now, now, now. Of *course* I want your judgement.'

'Then here it is. I think you committed a disgraceful and unethical act in hawking confidential patient data to a journalist as gossip. If the journalist uses the story, you will have done yourself, your hospital and your profession profound damage and, in the process, you will have done at least equal damage to a politician you would claim is a friend of yours, was certainly a patient of yours and deserved better from you. I do not believe, myself, that my company can or should do anything, other than possibly issuing a statement regretting what I hope could be described as untypical behaviour on the part of a senior consultant at the hospital.'

'Perhaps we will leave it there. Thank you, Miss King.'

'Not at all, Mr Deevy.'

Sophia rang her father and told him what she had said. Robert King, who had not known the reason for Deevy's distress, told her he was proud of her. She then went back to the office to tell Malachy, who listened somewhat doubtfully.

'Was I wrong?'

'I am wary of shouting at clients from the high moral ground,' Malachy said mildly. 'There's usually a way of getting out of doing what you don't want to do for a client without tattooing the refusal on his forehead.'

Sophia was still deflated by this at the weekend, although she dressed dutifully to go out to dinner with Greg, who arrived at about 9.30 on Saturday night, waving the early editions of the Sunday papers. 'Kid, you're famous,' he told her. 'Or infamous,' he added fairmindedly. 'I'm not dead sure which it is, yet.'

Robert King gestured Greg into the sitting room ahead of him. Colette pulled cushions out of the way to let the two of them sit on the couch.

'How have you tomorrow's papers on Saturday night?' she asked. Greg explained there was always a special edition out in Dublin the previous evening.

'I just want to make it clear to you, Dr and Mrs King,

that I fancied Sophia before she was ever splattered across the pages of the Sunday newspapers. Before her confidential taped telephone conversations were – '

Sophia snatched the newspaper from him. The story took up a full page. The main top-of-the-fold section was about the wonders of internal medicine at Angelus Hospital. In a box on the right, under the heading 'No Budget Fears – Minister well-disposed' was a single column, quoting the surgeon's comments about the Minister. Below the fold ran the transcript of Sophia's conversation with Deevy.

'But how did they get it?' Sophia asked, transfixed by seeing her own words thus in print.

'It says it on the front page,' Greg pointed at a box, which said that the newspaper had been offered a tape of a conversation and while the taping of such mobile phone conversations was not a desirable practice, nonetheless, it would be remiss not to allow the general public to make its own judgement on the comments made.

'They shouldn't have published this, should they?' Colette asked Greg.

'No. Stolen goods. Private communication between Sophia and Deevy. They were paying for the connection and for the privacy. Some guy with one of these scanners twiddled the knobs – '

'Scanners?'

' – yeah, gadgets you buy that range over the whole cellular phone frequency and tap in where you hear something going on. There are even black-market directories to some of the more interesting people who have mobile phones. Politicians who are having affairs, that sort of thing. So one of these guys tunes in to Sophia, has his recording machine going and realises he has something he can sell, possibly for a lot of money.'

'The newspaper would have paid?'

'I assume so. Effectively they were buying stolen goods, which for a self-righteous posturing prick like – I'm so sorry,

Mrs King – but he really gets on my wick, the editor of this thing, and for a guy like him to buy that kind of material and run it, I just think is very hypocritical.'

'Particularly when the story itself is about a failure in ethics and discretion.'

'Absolutely, Dr King. There's a phrase in Amanda Thingummy's copy there somewhere – "the entitlement to privacy". She's dead right. Patients in hospitals have that entitlement. So do people making telephone calls. Not that this entitlement is going to do Deevy any good.'

'Mr Deevy,' said Sophia and her father simultaneously.

'Mr Deevy,' Greg conceded.

'What is this going to do to Lawrence Deevy?' Colette asked.

'Dreadful damage. There will be various committees that will have to take this on board, and his reputation is shot. He was always known as a man who talked too much, but . . .'

There was a long silence while Greg read through the report, pen in hand as if to parse it.

'From Sophia's point of view, there's no downside to this,' he eventually said. 'Effectively, she says "You're a big mouth, you got caught, I'm not going to rescue you, sod off."'

'Will it do irrevocable damage to her prospects in *Positionings*, do you think, to have her sympathising in public with her boss over his misfortune in not being Robert King's son?' Colette asked Greg, deadpan.

'Given the relative ages, I think Malachy should be flattered by the suggestion that he physically *could* be Robert King's son,' Greg said. 'Anyway, let's go eat dead fish, Kid. While you still have an income.'

Before she went to bed that night, Sophia faxed her sister.

Dr Robert King/Dublin
001 353 1 7324172 30 September 1989 22.09

Attention Darcy King

Darcy

You don't usually hear from me on a Saturday afternoon (your time) and for all I know you have gone white-water rafting on the Caloosahatchie river, but if you're there I need your help. In this transmission you will find, cut up a bit awkwardly, a full page from the Sunday paper, involving me. This will not go away and I'm in an ambiguous (ambivalent?) position. Tell me what you think.

Thank you

Sophia

Darcy King/Manhattan
212 8645312 1 October 1989 17.36

Attention Sophia King

Sophia – my Hero! Pure defender of the virtue of all PR prostitutes! Straight-talking kicker in the goolies of blithering old fart colleagues of my father! Un-swearing, clean-talking communicator of the shining monosyllables! Christ, she talks *prose*. No 'eh' anywhere. No spitting over her shoulder.

If I were you, I would do one of two things:

1 Go on a week's holiday and let *Positionings* indicate that you're studying something somewhere. The red tides in Marbella, maybe.

2 Shut up.

The second is cheapest. I mean total. Not a word. Not to Malachy. Not to Angelus. Not to a newspaper. Not to a radio interviewer. Not on the record. Not off the record. Not nuthin'. Button your lip, raise your two hands in the air, smile as sweetly as only you know how, shake a sadder-but-wiser ash-blonde head. They can write the issue or broadcast the issue, but you're not feeding any flames. Oh, and one other thing, I'd postpone every other plan you have because for the next few months, every other story is going to U-turn back into this one.

It is neat to have a sister who, caught completely unawares, still comes out as clean and principled.

It is also a pain in the twin's tits (or even the twin tits) but what's new?

Your fan

Darcy

A. C. B./Washington
202 6613198 1 October 1989 20.19

Darcy

If you happen to want to fax me after tomorrow I'll be in the Blue Haven in Kinsale for a spell. 001-353-21-774268, Room 306.

Alex

Darcy King/Manhattan
212 8645312 2 October 1989 17.55

Attention Alex, Room 306

Jesus Christ you're in Ireland?

Darcy

Blue Haven/Kinsale
001 353 21 774268 3 October 1989 15.18

There a law against it?

Alex

Darcy King/Manhattan
212 8645312 4 October 1989 19.56

Attention Alex, Room 306

What are you doing?

Darcy

Blue Haven/Kinsale
001 353 21 774268 5 October 1989 6.04

Filming. Kinsale is a very cute village, you know that?

Alex

Darcy King/Manhattan
212 8645312 5 October 1989 19.21

Attention Alex, Room 306

Filming *what?* I was only ever in Kinsale for a day on the way to somewhere else and I suppose 'cute' would do as a description.

I prefer big raw mountains like Kerry or rough wind-scoured stone like Connemara. Scale and harshness, grandeur and no desire to please. As in my taste in men. (Men? Remember them? Two legs, no boobs and a hanging whatsit? They all went someplace else. Maybe Kinsale.)

Darcy

Blue Haven/Kinsale
001 353 21 774268 5 October 1989 16.14

Filming a small-cast period movie. Female director – very good. Wrap next week, go home.

There was a big story in one of Sunday's papers about a PR executive named Sophia King. Is this your sister and are you aware of it?

Alex

Darcy King/Manhattan
212 8645312 5 October 1989 19.21

Attention Alex, Room 306

Yes and yes. I am just so proud of her, I wanted you to read it. This is a great girl, you have to admit it.

Darcy

Blue Haven Hotel/Kinsale
001 353 21 774268 6 October 1989 15.39

Darcy

Questionable judgement, though, in some areas. I thought you mentioned, *en passant*, that she is dating the sex maniac of the glove compartment?

Alex

Darcy King/Manhattan
212 8645312 6 October 1989 17.58

Attention Alex, Room 306

Listen, you. Go back to your college for a while and learn how to be a proper formal elderly academic. You're losing the run of yourself. He is very good to her and with her and she will improve him no end. Over and out.

Darcy

Blue Haven Hotel/Kinsale
001 353 21 774268 6 October 1989 23.09

Slán agus beannacht.

Alex

Darcy King/Manhattan
212 8645312 6 October 1989 18.36

Attention Alex, Room 306

Jasus

Darcy

Dr Robert King/Dublin
001 353 1 7324172 6 October 1989 23.39

Attention Darcy

I can't afford the time to go to Marbella, but I will take your advice other than that. When are you going to come home and work with me?

Sophia

CHAPTER TWENTY-ONE

Little more than a year after the mobile phone incident, Sophia was a Senior Account Executive carrying much more clout in the Dublin PR scene than a relative newcomer might have expected to carry. She was also sitting well above target in billable hours – which was why she was slightly late for a lunch date with Dale Proctor.

She came through the irregularly spaced dining tables, smiling, stopping briefly with people she knew very well but nodding all the time towards where Proctor was sitting.

'I *do* beg your pardon,' Sophia said, extending a tiny hand across the table. Her gesture, as she sat, indicated a graceful helplessness in the face of circumstances. I'm *never* late, the gesture said, just very occasionally when something *so* important comes up, something so confidential I couldn't even mention it to you.

The waiter brought the menu and Sophia read it carefully before selecting grilled sole off the bone with spinach. No starter. Ballygowan would be fine. Unless they had de Braam? Oh, they did have it? Oh, splendid. Proctor examined Sophia quietly while she ordered. Examined her and noted the covert responses from other tables as people identified her to each other. She had the slightly larger-than-life glow to her that an actor has on stage.

Menu gone, she turned to him and complimented him on his firm's handling of a recent government controversy.

'*Positionings* doesn't have any government or political clients,' she told him. 'Malachy believes that the consultancy would be besmirched by association with politicians, because it's not as big as Proctors.'

'What's size got to do with it?'

'Well, you know, Proctors has its own building, three floors, and it has so many clients in so many other areas of life that the political issue doesn't sully the company's image. But *Positionings* is so much smaller, relatively speaking, that it would be easy to be swamped by political involvement.'

'Malachy and I went to college together, did you know that?'

'He mentioned it at some stage.'

Briefly. The brevity in deference to the fact that Proctor ran the leading PR agency, with an annual turnover in excess of four million pounds, whereas Malachy ran what he inevitably called 'a tight ship', employing eleven people and turning over perhaps £1.5 million annually.

'Good guy,' Proctor said perfunctorily. 'What was Malachy's reaction to that mobile phone incident last year?' He tilted the soup bowl and scooped up the last of the contents.

'Dale, you're Malachy's friend. I'm sure he would be delighted to hear from you.'

Swwit, Proctor thought, making in his mind the wind-hiss of a sword in play. He pushed away his soup bowl.

'Sophia, our business is changing direction. I plan to break this company up into a series of functional units in the broader communications field.'

Sophia nodded at him with a reverence which implied that her arriving fish was an unconscionable intrusion on an educational discourse by a figure only a notch south of Einstein. Proctor knew he was watching a performance. It created two responses in him. The first was confirmation: I am talking to the right woman, here. The second was a self-mocking: I know what this woman is doing to me and why, but it is nonetheless pleasurable.

'Longer-term, I plan a constellation of potentially inter-relating services.'

'A constellation of potentially inter-relating services,' Sophia repeated, memorising the phrase for future ownership and personal use.

'Lobbying, for example. Lobbying didn't matter a few

years ago. Now it matters at three levels. It matters locally, where, if you cannot influence local county councillors or city councillors, then you will not get a development through. It matters nationally. It matters in Europe.'

Proctor finished his steak, wiped his mouth again and sat back. He was telling her all this, he said, because he knew she was a bright, discreet woman and that, although he had no problem if she told Malachy they had once had lunch together, he knew he could trust her not to reveal his plans to Malachy.

'That would be absolutely inappropriate,' Sophia agreed, pouring more of her de Braams mineral water.

Proctor had been looking around, he told her. Nationally and internationally. For someone to head this up. Under his supervision, of course. Of course, Sophia nodded. Ultimately, he thought he was willing to take a risk on a very young person, if that young person showed unusual capability. As Sophia King had.

'And of course, the person would be working under your supervision,' Sophia said affirmatively, tying a little bow in the ribbon supplied.

'Are you interested?'

'Wouldn't you expect me to be?'

Proctor nodded heavily.

'We'd be talking £30K in the first year and a carried interest.'

'Let's not talk money until we have other ducks in a row,' she said. 'Because money is not the central issue.'

Proctor seemed to have no problem moving away from money. Sophia looked at her watch. 'I don't even know the right questions to ask you yet,' she smiled at him. 'Let me go away for a week and meet you again, not for lunch but for a working session, I can book a room in the Berkeley Court where we can thrash out all the issues.'

Proctor nodded and she left him at the table. She reached Greg on her mobile phone in the taxi taking her back to the office.

When Greg arrived at the King house that evening, Colette was out at the library and Robert had not arrived home. Greg and Sophia had the dining-room table to spread out their paperwork.

Briefed about the lunch, Greg thought hard for a long time, then began to talk.

'This will require enormous amounts of money. Repositioning costs more than initially establishing a position. He'll have to move premises, recruit heads for each of the separate units, probably do publicity to establish a completely different name.'

Sophia made extensive notes before her next meeting with Proctor, who was both impressed and threatened by the questioning she put him through. Recapitalise? Yes, this was part of the plan. Three million minimum. He had guarantees from various investors. Private investors who took the long view. The long view being that the new company, after a few years of steadily growing profits, would be floated on the stock market. The individual units would not be separate companies but divisions within the overall organisation, all their managers reporting directly to the chief executive.

'Managing director?' Sophia asked innocently.

Proctor said it might be better, at least in the short term, to have a chief operating officer, so to speak, and an executive chairman. Especially since Sophia, although very successful, was in the business, full-time, for not quite two years.

'Oh, *right*,' said Sophia agreeably.

The negotiations stretched over months. By the third meeting with Proctor, Sophia understood the corporate structure, marketing plans, business plans, strategy and tactics of his concept. Greg was almost as knowledgeable, and, at long distance, Darcy was used to getting ten- and twelve-page faxes and responding briefly but quickly. After the third meeting, Sophia rang her sister.

'Darcy?'

'Sophia? Have you beaten another ten thousand out of Prostate?'

'Darcy, you're in New York, aren't you?'

'Seems like it.'

'For the next two days?'

'For the next two weeks.'

'I'd like to come over and see you.'

'When?'

'I could fly out on Thursday morning.'

'OK. Walk across to New York Helicopter. Get the chopper into the city. I'll pick you up at the Heliport on East 34th.'

When Sophia arrived into Darcy's car, she was still exhilarated and scared by the experience.

'To fly so close to the Statue of Liberty. We could see Ellis Island, too, where all the immigrants used to be processed. A helicopter never feels as safe as a plane, somehow, does it? With all these tall buildings around, you feel sure a rotor is going to hit off someone's roof.'

'Welcome to New York,' Darcy said, pulling up in front of the Waldorf Astoria and giving her car keys to the doorman. 'Everybody should stay once in the Waldorf. It gives you a different perspective on downtown Manhattan.'

In the hotel coffee shop Sophia outlined the Proctor venture.

'So what did he say when you told him you wanted to have training in it?' Darcy asked.

'I didn't tell him.'

'You *didn't* tell him?'

'Why would I tell him?'

'If you're going to work for him, it would help if you weren't springing surprises on him from day one. Or are you saying you'll let him set it up whatever way he wants to in the beginning and only later change it to what you want?'

'I'm not going to work for him.'

'So what was the purpose of all these meetings?'

'To get information for our own business,' Sophia said, going back into her briefcase and taking laminated sheets out of it to put on the table between them.

'See,' she said, pointing to an organisational structure grid, 'These would be the core units in the first five-year span, although we might decide to add other units or even to sub-divide the existing units sooner than that if it suited us.'

Darcy's hands flapped in smoke-dispelling movements.

'You mean you had three meetings with a man –'

' – four, if you count the initial lunch.'

' – got him to tell you all his plans. Now you're stealing them.'

Sophia went very quiet. 'I have stolen nothing,' she said. 'The plans I'm laying out before you are my own plans. They differ quite considerably from what Proctor is envisaging.'

'You worked them out in talking to him.'

'True, and he gained a lot of insight through talking with me. The traffic was two-way.'

'But you got him to tell you all the funding requirements he had worked out.'

'Darcy, Dale Proctor is fifty-three years of age. He has been in business for thirty years, at the top of his own business for twenty years. He is a clever, opinionated and self-interested man. He was not offering me charity. In fact, the going rate for the kind of job he needs done is much higher than he *was* offering me. He was trading, quite cynically and quite properly, on my relative innocence of the world of business. At no stage did he show me spread-sheets of the figures. At no stage did he leave me in possession of as much as a sheet of paper that could be useful to anybody in setting up a rival operation. He picked my brains as ruthlessly as he knew how, and asked me several things about *Positionings* it was quite unethical to ask me.'

'In other words, he's a big boy.'

'He's a very big boy.'

'He can look after himself.'

'He does look after himself.'

'I shouldn't be wasting my sympathy on him?'

'Frankly, no.'

'Frankly, I wasn't. Frankly, I was just thinking, I really hate that my sister would tic-tac with this old hack in order to bullet-proof her own plans.'

'So you don't believe in market research?'

'Of course I believe in market research. Nobody in their right minds goes out selling something without sussing the marketplace first.'

'But if it isn't somebody clutching a clipboard, it's not market research. Is that it?'

'Market research takes all sorts of forms.'

'Including one-to-one in-depth interviewing.'

Darcy thought about this for a moment.

'I don't like it, still,' she said.

In that case, thought Sophia, I will not tell her that I indicated to Malachy I had received an offer of 30K from a major competitor and if he couldn't match it, I'd have to give it serious consideration. This has effectively doubled my salary this year, but tax will take a chunk of it.

Darcy sighed. 'You're right, Proctor's a big boy. I just wish I didn't know about all this because it takes away some of the pleasure.'

'The pleasure?'

'Yes. I think this – ' she gestured at the company chart on the table between them ' – could be wonderful. It feels right.'

'I want you to come home and do it with me. No, Darcy, don't give any of your reflex negatives for a minute. Listen to me. Just listen to me, OK?'

Darcy nodded.

'First thing is that you're getting bored within Borchgrave. You don't know it yet but I do. I suspect your old professor does, too, because I imagine you're writing to him a lot more than you used to and a lot more generally than you used to.'

'What's amazing is that he's answering me in much the

same kind of way – there are evenings I can't wait to get to the apartment to find out where we've got to on a particular idea. I'm buying books along particular themes.'

'I honestly think you've reached the end of the Borchgrave story, and that your priority should be negotiating some kind of ongoing relationship so that you're on a retainer to them, but you come back to Europe,' Sophia said.

'Back to Ireland, you mean.'

'Europe, really. One of the key differences between Proctor and myself is that I see Europe in the next ten years as *the* prime market for our wares. I figure a lot of time will have to be spent in Brussels. Let's just say back home.'

'But not back *home*, back home.'

Sophia carefully kept her facial expression open and enquiring, despite her internal glee that Darcy had become sucked into the discussion of the details. She had her, she figured, but it was vital that it did not show. Just for badness and spite, Darcy could dig her heels in and absolutely refuse to do something which was obviously for her own good.

'No, you'd need an apartment. Possibly still on the northside, though. Maybe one of those new ones down at the Customs House thing – '

'The Financial Services Centre?'

'Yes, they have beautiful apartments there with tiled balconies so huge you could hold a dinner party out on the balcony on a warm summer evening.'

'*I remember that summer in Dublin,/And the Liffey as it stank like hell,*' Darcy sang softly.

The hairs at the back of Sophia's neck prickled. 'Do you remember Mam used to sing us that old Noel Purcell song?' As she spoke, she was getting cash out of her briefcase to leave on the bill. The two of them walked out into the New York evening.

'*Dublin can be heaven/With coffee at eleven . . .* '

A few blocks up from the Waldorf was a municipal building with an open courtyard. As the twins reached it,

Darcy, glancing behind to make sure they were impeding nobody, stopped her sister and half-conducted her through the rest of the song:

> *So if you don't believe me,*
> *Why not meet me there*
> *In Dublin on a sunny summer morning . . .*

Impromptu, Sophia did a soft-shoe music hall shuffle, and passers-by smiled. Darcy grabbed Sophia by the shoulders and turned her around to see the traffic – the single-decker buses with their big Broadway signs – *The Best Little Whorehouse in Texas*, said the one in front of them – the traffic lights with their staccato strictures *Walk* and *Don't Walk*, the Hispanic street sellers who could fold up their elaborate displays of tin jewellery as fast as a grand prix race track team changing a tire if a cop hoved to, the big boaty yellow taxis bucking and bypassing, screeching in diaphone.

'Sophia, come on. How could I leave this?'

'Very easily. This is an old city, not a new city. Look – '

Sophia gestured with her hand at the frontage on some of the buildings.

'Last time I was here, I was struck by how much it's like walking back into the fifties. New York was push, push, push, the leader, the buzz place, during the sixties and seventies, but since then – look to your left.'

Darcy did, to see three huddled figures sleeping over a big grating.

'It's a cliché of New York life now.'

It's a cliché of American city life, Darcy corrected inside her head. Dublin isn't immune, either.

'Been here. Done this,' Sophia said.

Darcy walked along, listening to Sophia's voice against the background of noise she was so used to.

'Been here, done this – *end of story*.'

'It doesn't have to be immediate,' Sophia continued after

a few moments of silence.

'Oh, thank you,' Darcy said with heavy irony.

'I figure in a bit more than two years from now we should be ready to go. But that would mean you'd need to be home in a year from now. That wouldn't be difficult, now, would it?'

'When would that be? April? May?'

'April. You'd be home anyway, around then.'

'Why would I be home in April?'

'For my wedding.'

'*Won*derful!'

'Oh Darcy, isn't it?'

'Sophia, I'm thrilled. The two of you are just so perfect together.'

'He's always been very kind to me.'

'Oh, kind your arse. Jesus, the pictures from this wedding will be so gorgeous. Dad, all tall, ascetic and wry, then you, all – hey, what kind of dress are you going to wear?'

'Very simple. Line and cut rather than decoration. Long, long train. I can't figure whether I should wear a veil or a rose in my hair – '

'Doesn't matter. Either way, you'll be gorgeous.'

'I want to have children,' Sophia said, in so low a voice that Darcy had to tilt her head to hear her.

'Well, that's good, because Greg's certainly into kids. He's really really good with children, and it's not put on. He's just unaffectedly a dad waiting to happen.'

Sophia nodded and Darcy suddenly realised that her sister's eyes were glassy with tears. Darcy put a gloved hand to Sophia's face, then tore off the glove and put a warm palm to her cold cheek.

'What's wrong, love?'

'No, it's nothing wrong.'

Sophia sat on the edge of one of the shrub holders and Darcy sat beside her.

'It's just over the past two to three years I yearn to have

315

children. No, that's not true. A baby. Babies. I don't know. I dream about babies.'

How noble of you, Darcy almost said. You dream about babies. I dream about pizza. She stayed silent.

'I have such a need to hold and cherish a baby.'

'So what's your problem?' Darcy asked, puzzled.

'I never expected this,' Sophia said primly, as if describing a recent incident where she had flashed at a group of nuns. Darcy sat silent, torn between asking more questions and expressing her own position, which was that if you wanted children, fire ahead and have them and don't make such a bloody Federal Court case out of them, because she, Darcy, for one, wasn't that pushed about babies. Take them or leave them. Mostly leave them.

Sophia sat, miserable in the face of an aching need which ran so contrary to all of her conscious plans for her life.

'It's the one crime I could understand,' she said.

'What is?'

'Stealing a baby out of a pram or a hospital.'

'Really?' Darcy regarded her with something akin to new respect. She was not prepared to encourage baby-snatching tendencies, but the new slant they lent to her sister was not unwelcome.

'I look at babies asleep and the urge to put my hands in around their back, where they're warm against the mattress, and hold their soft velvety head in my hand – ' Sophia regarded her own slightly cupped right hand in a mesmerised way.

'I get it,' Darcy said suddenly, needing to defuse an emotional tension she could not quite understand. 'You just want me to come home so the minute you go barefoot and pregnant I can take over.'

'It's not a factor that any businesswoman can afford to ignore,' Sophia pointed out.

'Sophia, I love you dearly and I am delira you are getting hitched to Gorgeous Greg, but I will *never* come home and work with you if you give me pompous mini-fucking lectures in the middle of an otherwise delightful discussion.'

'Sorry.'

'Anyway, I might want to get barefoot and pregnant at the same time.'

'Well, we could discuss that.'

'No, we shagging well couldn't. What's the wedding date?'

'4 April 1992. And you'll be the bridesmaid.'

'Oh, no I won't.'

'Of course you will.'

'Sophia, not after what happened the last time.'

'What happened the last time?'

'Never *mind* what happened the last time.'

'You couldn't refuse me.'

'Oh, sweet living – '

'I mean, Mam and Dad will be there, and Beethoven will be Greg's best man, and – '

'Oh, all right, all right. But if you put me in peacock-blue satin, so help me God I'll haunt your honeymoon.'

'You can decide to wear whatever you want to wear.'

'Oh, Sophia, don't cave in as easily as all that.'

'Darcy.'

'Yes?'

'This is like a dream come true for me. Dad and Mam to be in good health . . . '

'Never mind good personal health, they're in good marital health,' Darcy said. 'One of the great indoor sports at your wedding will be seeing if McEnerney the Orthopod Stud and his estranged wife can keep smiling through their mutual loathing.'

'Detestation.'

'Abomination.'

'Abhorrence.'

'Revulsion.'

'There's a consideration, now. Prenuptial agreements are the thing these days. You'll have to work out who gets to keep your list of words in the event of a split. Jesus, it must be the length of the Empire State Building by now.'

'Don't say such awful things.'

'Is Dad thrilled?'

'Dad and Mam are very pleased, yes.'

'Have you warned them that only the barest decent interval will elapse before you force them into grandparenthood?'

'You couldn't mention things like that at home.'

'No, but you've imagined Dad as a grandfather, haven't you?'

Sophia nodded dumbly.

'This is all very exciting,' Darcy said. 'But my arse is freezing from this marble. Let's head back to the Waldorf, drink champagne and talk about the details. OK?'

Arms linked, they walked back to the hotel.

CHAPTER TWENTY-TWO

Darcy King/Manhattan
212 8645312 16 April 1991 15.26

Alex

My sister says I am using my communication with the venerable professor to alleviate boredom with my job. I am *not* bored with my job, I don't do anything other than send brief notes to you, and you are much more involved in film-making these days than in legitimate day-jobbing professorship. However, there may be a certain truth to her comment. (An instant denial would be acceptable here.)

The certain truth is this. You do interesting things and have interesting ideas (some of which I continue to disagree with and every time I see a squirrel I hate you) plus you don't precisely give me advice, but you point me at understandings. Also, occasionally you make me laugh.

Here goes with some factual input. (No, not about sex or romance, although I will be honest on this one later on. Stick up an asterisk here, Darcy, so's you won't forget it.*)

My sister has been wooed by an alternative employer.

Said alternative employer is wishful to have her set up a new kind of company, completely different to the traditional PR consultancy.

This fits in with what she was thinking about anyway.

In negotiating with this guy, she got costs, structures, names of investors, everything, and now she's going to do it without him. *I think this is shitty.*

I don't care how naïve this makes me sound. So I suffer from ingrown naïveté? So what.

She wants me to come home and do it with her.

She's going to marry Greg next April and start being prolific.

Dear Abby

What should I do?

Worried, Wyoming

A. C. B./Fort Attic
813 2760716 16 April 1991 19.14

Dear Worried Wyoming

Wyoming?

Alex

Darcy King/Manhattan
212 8645312 16 April 1991 20.33

Dear Unworried Uninvolved Ancient Academic,

You got something against Wyoming? Unearthed a prejudice, have I? Or is it just not a great place for murdering harmless little creatures?

Answer my serious questions, goddammit.

Still Effing Worried, Wyoming

A. C. B./Fort Attic
813 2760716 17 April 1991 9.17

Dear WW

I am very glad your sister is marrying Greg.

Until you fill in your asterisk, I will go no further.

Alex

Darcy King/Manhattan
212 8645312 17 April 1991 11.06

Alex!

Sorry, I completely forgot the bloody asterisk.

Here's the story. You will recall Clive Brautigan, our Pres.? Good egg. Decent skin. Man of vision. Also married with semi-grown-up kids to a red-headed pre-school teacher of some charm.

In the last year, I see a yearn in Mr B. I don't think he even notices it himself, but he is attracted to the blunt one from Ireland and it is giving the blunt one a pain in the tits, not only because she is not attracted back, but because she knows if she hangs around it will screw up the really neat non-sexy thing they have going.

So there's my asterisk.

Why are you glad Greg is marrying Sophia?

Darcy (Still worried, but tiring of Wyoming.)

A. C. B./Fort Attic
813 2760716 17 April 1991 13.19

Darcy

I have always been afraid you would go back to Greg. Remember Wolfe: you cannot go home again.

On the other hand, you can go back to a location, but it won't be home any more – until you make it a different home.

You said Sophia would be prolific. In what?

Alex

Darcy King/Manhattan
212 8645312 17 April 1991 15.35

Alex

Don't you go cryptic on me.

Answer to your question: babies. She yearns, hungers, aches. Jesus, her biological clock hasn't practically got *wound* yet, but she's up to ninety and thinking about snatching snivelling neonates from buggies. She did suggest that if I wanted to get prolific in the same way, we should consult on

optimum mutual timing.
    Darcy

A. C. B./Fort Attic
813 276 0716 17 April 1991 16.59

Darcy
    'You have one now, and I'll have one in a year's time'?
    Alex

Darcy King/Manhattan
212 8645312 17 April 1991 18.04

Alex
    Right
    Darcy

A. C. B./Fort Attic
813 2760716 17 April 1991 19.13

Darcy
    Your sister is a v. strange bundle of molecules.
    Alex

Darcy King/Manhattan
212 8645312 17 April 1991 21.22

Alex
    No, she shagging isn't. She just sounds odd when taken out of context. She is like a fairy princess that just slipped into real life and is doing her level best to act within real life as it demands, whereas fairyland made much more sense.
    Darcy

A. C. B./Fort Attic
813 2760716 17 April 1991 22.03

Darcy
    She don't sound to me like no fairy princess. She

sounds to me like Snow White's Stepmother.

Alex

Darcy King/Manhattan
212 8645312 17 April 1991 23.07

Listen, you wall-eyed wanker, you can shove your scholastic observations straight up the nearest asshole, yours or anybody else's that offers. I didn't ask you for criticisms of my sister and you should know bloody better, as someone supposedly trained in relationships and stuff like that, than to make judgements based on bits and pieces you've heard from someone, half the time you're only hearing the stuff because I'm mad, but that's only a fleeting thing. (This may not be proper grammar, but I'm not one of your dozy little under-age students to be intimidated, so may your willy fray.)

Darcy

A. C. B./Fort Attic
813 2760716 17 April 1991 23.52

Darcy

In the King family, it is considered very low class to refer to the genitals as 'John Thomas', 'Peter' or 'Willy'.

Alex

Darcy King/Manhattan
212 8645312 18 April 1991 19.16

Alex

You are very clever and you have a good memory. Apologise.

Darcy

Darcy
　No.
Alex

Alex

You're a pisser and I'll make my own decision without your help. You may be more at home dealing with concepts than with the contradictions and complexities that make human beings so interesting.

I'll probably go home because I'd like to be near my parents again. Not with them, near them. Absence doesn't make the heart grow fonder, it just puts a wider frame around the same picture so the details that, up close, make one obsessive in one's irritation become pleasing idiosyncrasies.

Oh, shit, I can't think straight. I don't know whether I'm defending my sister against you because you're completely wrong about her, or because I am afraid your negative comments on her mean that by comparison (comparison inevitable as putre-faction and as smelly, I know) you approve of me more and it is incumbent on me to reject this, or because of some primeval blood imperative. There is something very special about Sophia, underneath the dogged detail, hidden behind the looks, the designer labels and the all's-fair-in-business ruth-lessness. I don't know the hell what it is. Every now and again I get glimpses of it, and I find myself summing it up inadequately, almost in slogan-exemplars. Like the definition of a friend as someone you can ring at two in the morning and tell that you have a body to bury and he/she's around twenty minutes later with a shovel, no questions asked. If things were ever tough enough for me, I figure Sophia could be called on for shovel duty. But there's more to it than that. It's as if she's marked out in some way. Not for suffering, because she's had damn-all suffering.

This is bloody silly and if you hadn't been so gratuitously rude I wouldn't have got into it. Let this be a lesson to you.

Darcy

Having sent the letter, Darcy found herself thinking, not of Sophia but of their father, and of how comfortable she was at the prospect of being closer to him – a comfort she would not, she knew, have felt a year or so before this point. Back then, she always felt fore-defeated in any encounter with her father, as if life were an endless mutually defeating contest out of which neither could choose to climb.

Darcy's move to America and the necessarily truncated visits she paid home had shown her that when she, Darcy, was taken out of the equation, Robert King was not diminished but rather ennobled by the lack of someone to fight with and seek to control. She imagined that without her as irritant, he would be a stirring stick with nothing to stir, a spoilsport without a sport to spoil, a fly with no ointment to be in. Instead, he settled into his certainties quietly. Unquestioned in his beliefs, he lost the constant need to assert them.

In the time donated to Darcy by no longer fighting with him, and in learning about him through his elegantly humorous letters. Darcy began to see her father as the definition of his kind: the doctors who remembered the miracle sulpha could achieve, who saw antibiotics defeat the horrors one after another. Antibiotics stuffed those terrors back into some bag belonging to the dark ages. Then the black bag into which the horrors had been stuffed came bump-bubblingly alive again, disgorging ghastly new diseases their drugs could not touch.

A generation, theirs, with catechism answers and eternal rules that would be torn from them by the bouncing round-faced Pope who called a council that changed the fount of their beliefs. Robert King's was really the lost generation, the generation that had children like Darcy who would not go the right way, nor even acknowledge that the ends to be reached were the right, the eternal verities.

In many ways, Darcy thought, her mother seemed less scarified by the gravel-bearing speedy wind of time. Curious and half-amused, she watched most of her certainties float away. The ones that stayed with her stayed in good humour. Once, trying to explain her father's views on pre- and extra-marital sex to Darcy, Colette had suddenly laughed, side-tracked off the main theme. 'Anyway, let's be honest,' she said. 'Sex without the covert is not worth a damn.'

It had made no sense to Darcy at the time, but it had stayed with her. As had another comment of her mother about her father, offered when Darcy, spitting vitriol after a fight, demanded to know what her mother loved in a man so self-evidently intolerable.

'But you don't love people for what they are,' Colette had said. 'When you're young, you love them for what they're going to be. When you're old, you love them for what they were. Or for what you thought they were.'

She would go home, Darcy thought now, and she would keep a loving distance between herself and her father. A distance that would allow her to focus on the unexpected slants of him – like the time he had told her that his best memory of his childhood had been racing the moon on his bicycle: pedalling fast to beat the moon as it travelled behind a cloud.

She would go home. She would work with her sister. She would work at loving her sister, rather than admiring and being infuriated by her.

Darcy was able to go home a week before the wedding, fit into the bridesmaid's dress and witness the calm organised way Sophia planned everything.

'There will probably be loads of pictures in the newspapers,' she told Darcy, 'Because of Greg being famous.'

'Isn't it funny, because I haven't been in Ireland over the last couple of years, I don't think of Greg as famous at all.'

'Well, he's much more famous than I am.'

'Tsk, tsk.'

'But the one thing I do want to achieve is that Malachy and *Positionings* get any benefit that's going from those pictures – I owe him that.'

'In other words, "Darcy, don't cuddle up to some gossip columnist and tell her you and your sister are going to set up a completely new business and knock hell out of Malachy."'

Sophia ignored this.

'I presume you've arranged great weather for Saturday?' Darcy prodded Sophia.

'Well, I'm praying for sunshine,' Sophia said seriously, and Darcy smiled at her.

'If He does nothing else for you in your life, I'm quite sure He'll see you right for sunshine on the Big Day.'

'Yes,' said Sophia, half-listening. 'Darcy?'

'Yes, Sophia?'

'You'll probably be asked to sing. Would you be very offended if I asked you not to sing *"Sé Fáth Mo Bhuartha"* even if people ask you for it?'

'No problem,' Darcy said quietly, backing away from the issue as if it were surrounded by an electric blue aura.

The day before the wedding, unexpectedly, Greg dropped in to see the new apartment picked for Darcy by Colette and Sophia.

'You are really the returned Yank, aren't you,' he laughed,

looking into the luxury from the balcony with its views of the river.

As Darcy made coffee, she watched Greg wander around the room, hands clasped behind him.

'Greg?'

He turned to receive the coffee.

'Spit it out.'

For a moment, he was so obviously confused by being handed coffee and told to spit it out that the two of them laughed.

'Spit what out?'

'Whatever you have come to say. Because, Greg, you're a great guy, I think you are perfect for Sophia, and I wish the two of you forever and a day of happiness, but you were never big on subtlety, and you might as well have a message printed there – ' she ran her index finger gently along his forehead ' – saying "I have to get something off my chest." Well, do so.'

'No, it's such a small thing, really,' Greg said, apologetically, and downed half the coffee. 'It's just tomorrow, after the ceremony and so on, when we're all together – '

'Please, Darcy, don't sing "*Sé Fáth Mo Bhuartha*".'

His mouth opened and laughter took the tension out of his face. 'Right. How'd you know?'

'Your bride-to-be already made the same request. I didn't ask *her*, any more than I'm going to ask you, why my pet song is suddenly covered in toxic waste. Ours not to reason why, ours to sing some other shagging song.'

'Darcy, you're a star.'

'Absolutely.'

'Now, I must fly – million and one tasks Sophia has entrusted to me.'

'Foolish move, I would have thought myself, but maybe you have improved in the task department.'

For just a second, she could see the debate in his face about getting into look-back-in-banter. She shook her head, and like a baby imitating an adult, he solemnly shook his at her. She walked to the door and showed him out.

'Be a good little groom tomorrow,' she called down to him from the balcony.

'You be a good little bridesmaid.'

'Big bridesmaid.'

'Big groom.'

'Always boasting.'

'Mind yourself, Darcy.'

'You too, Greg.'

The following day was not only filled with sunshine, it was filled with happiness. Nothing went wrong. But more important, there was so relaxed a buoyancy about the day that even if something had gone awry, it would have been accommodated, enveloped by the luminous quality of light, happiness and peace to which the priest on the altar referred.

Sophia had tried every bridal shop in Dublin and quite a few in London before reading of a designer in Marseilles whose wedding dresses echoed specific periods in history and who made for her a twelfth-century-inspired gown of panelled ivory silk. Its unadorned lines were so starkly elegant they turned her regal, tight cuffs around tiny wrists contrasted with long outer sleeves falling to points at mid-skirt, so that a small gesture was made gracefully significant. Her hair was pulled into a pearl chignon, tendrils feathering the severe style into softness.

In slipper-shoes covered in matching ivory silk, she walked at measured pace beside her tall father to meet her husband at the altar, the scale and muscled bulk of Greg emphasised by the formality of the morning suit he wore. Fragile beside him, she was nonetheless a more impelling presence.

Darcy, in bronze raw silk, hair pulled back into a matching chignon, wore high heels that put her on eye-level with Nicholas Watson.

It was one of the largest weddings Darcy had ever been

at. She met journalists, TV personalities, medical friends of both her father and Greg's father, old schoolfriends, some solidified and matroned by maternity, some predator-eyed and prowling, and several of Sophia's favourite clients, including Pete, owner of the now tripartite pet emporia. When Darcy was introduced to him, her first priority was to get a date with his mynah bird.

'I'll give it to you,' he said, strangling on enthusiasm and a very white tight collar.

'No thank you,' Darcy said. 'I live in an apartment block, and the other residents already have a problem with my language when I drop something or lock myself out. I don't need a bird imitating me in my absence.'

Greg's parents managed to stay casually civil to each other the whole day, although for some reason Greg's accomplished speech reduced his mother to near-hysterical tears. Dancing with Darcy later, Greg identified this as the one dodgy moment of the day.

'I still haven't worked out how I caused Niagara Falls,' he murmured. 'Jeez, I thought I did a very light easygoing speech.'

'So you did,' Darcy told him. 'Presume empty nest and that sort of stuff.'

Greg agreed to make presumptions about his mother's tears as long as they got him off a guilt trip, and laughed with Darcy about Beethoven's best man speech, which, typical of Beethoven in his student debate days, consisted of him walking up and down behind the guests at the main table, cracking jokes, only about 40 per cent of which worked, and then making half-heard comments about the failure of the jokes which had died. Beethoven, by mid-evening, had abandoned his jacket and was at the piano, calling on guests by name to come up and sing, as the name struck him or was proposed to him by Aileen.

Greg's father sang, and a *frisson* of fear went around the big room as people wondered if Greg's mother would be reduced to tears again. However, she sustained her ex-husband's singing much better than she had sustained her son's speech, and the wedding ended in a lengthy sing-song involving the happiest and most bizarre assortment of people Darcy had met in a long time.

Darcy King/Dublin
001 353 1 378212 5 April 1992 03.31

Dear Alex

It is three in the morning and my beloved sister is in Paris (where else?) married to Greg.

Because I have been away for a while, I was rediscovering people I had once known but who have changed a lot (or, although rarely, stayed the same) and meeting people I had heard of but never encountered before. I looked wonderful. Sophia was so ethereal you felt if you spoke too loudly to her she might shatter.

The food was great, too.

Darcy

331

CHAPTER TWENTY-THREE

It was a busy, unplanned, unbalanced place unfit for any gardening magazine, the King parents' garden. The only logical element was the final bank, rising to where the railway line ran past. That apart, the garden was an accretion of needs, impulses and old habits, piled together with a rockery here, strands of raspberries there, a pergola, potted shrubs and hanging baskets, with geometric intrusions of hedge asserting an order that the rest of the garden rejected. Colette had a small kitchen garden where spiky chives and aromatic mint overwhelmed the less assertive herbs.

'Mint,' she would say sadly, encountering the distinctive leaves marauding in the middle of a rose bed ten feet away from where they had been planted. 'Why did nobody tell me about mint?'

She would pull it up and Darcy would come to crush the leaves between her fingers as Colette would lift the knee-pad Robert had bought her and move to another spot for weeding. Darcy was banned from weeding because of her indiscriminate enthusiasm for the job. Sophia never weeded because she could not bear to get dirt under her fingernails.

During their growing years, Darcy had seen her father going to war against the garden each weekend. He would arrive home in his Citroën, and – like all Citroëns – it would settle down on its wheels after he got out of it, as if relieved to see him go. On Saturday morning, he would get up, listen to John Bowman on the radio, dress in old trousers and start attacking growing plants. The hedge-clippers went sideways across the front of the hedge, snipping off those random shoots that got out of the line with the rest of the infantry. Then across the top. He would get back down off the kitchen chair and walk across the garden to have a look at how even he had the top, and if it had a slant, he would go at it again.

'Some day it's going to be uneven on this side and then uneven on that side and he's going to keep at it until it's an inch off the ground,' Colette predicted. She preferred Robert to be in the garden at weekends. If he wasn't in the garden, he was in the house. In the house, he was always coming up with alternative systems for storage or cleaning and it tired her out.

What Robert loved was a hedge where the sides met the top in a perfect right angle. He had no patience with curved hedges and even less with topiary. Carving hedges into the shape of crinolined ladies or turkey cocks seemed to him a vile contradiction in terms. Hedges were hedges: barricades against the barbarians. They should be tall, uniform, angular and thick.

Once Robert had attacked the hedges, he would gather up the clippings and put them into a plastic bag, forcing them down into one another. Clean as you go, he would say aloud, approving of his own actions. Clean as you go. Then he would have a cup of tea and read the paper. Next step was to drive the small manual mower through the grass with a mathematical venom, the shorn blades of grass spurting in a contained arc into the tin container at the front of the mower.

Because the grassy areas of the garden were on so many different levels, much of the grass cutting had to be done by hand. On his birthday one year, Sophia presented him with tools for this purpose: a clippers bent at an angle at the end of long handles, so the user could stand upright, not have to go down on one knee to make progress. Another year, she gave him a petrol-powered strimmer, which made Colette very uneasy. No matter how Sophia and Robert explained to her that the moment the strimmer came in contact with anything solid, the power was short-circuited, she still saw the machine as likely to remove feet in one stroke. Sophia went to some trouble to explain the scientific principle involved in the strimmer. Colette listened with the passive resistance of one who knows themselves to be privy to a greater truth.

'Famous last words,' she summed up when Sophia was finished. Sophia looked at Darcy and Darcy looked at Sophia. I would kill her, in your place, Darcy thought. I would kill her. But Sophia controlled her response to a slight sigh and left it at that. Nor did she criticise her mother to Darcy. She never did. Neither twin could remember when this unspoken compact had been made between them: you don't criticise her to me and I won't criticise him to you.

Sections of the garden had particular meaning for each one of them. There were begonia and hostas and anemone growing in shady corners from slips Robert had begged from neighbours when Colette had admired them. Around the base of the rockery were bluebells, because Sophia loved the graceful clumped delicacy of them and Colette had planted them for her. Against a wire fence climbed sweet pea, because Darcy loved the winding tendrils, curled ready to clutch on the next bit of wire that offered, and was helpless in her addiction to the overwhelming sweetness of their scent.

It was a garden where wasps were caught in jam-jars half-filled with water in late August, where snails made statements of themselves, stuck bulbous and black to white walls. A garden of niches and nooks, favourite places and hidden pleasures.

On an evening visit in June, the year she married, Sophia stood in the dining-room window and watched her mother straighten slowly, with evident difficulty, from a bent-over position in the garden. Colette stood crouched for a moment or two, the knuckles of her right hand pushed into the hollow of her back above her belt.

'I asked Thornley to have a look at that, you know,' Robert King said, his hand dropping on his daughter's shoulder.

'And?'

'And he said to consider spinal fusion.'

'And?'

'Naah.' Robert King went back to mending the telephone, the pieces neatly laid out on an opened newspaper in the order in which they had come out of the phone. Some years previously, Darcy had mended the upstairs phone, but had ended up, when the job was complete, with three component parts for which she failed to find a home. The phone worked perfectly without the three, but every time Robert opened the sundries drawer where she had put them, it bothered him.

'Why not?'

'Spinal fusion is iffy. The odds aren't good enough.'

Sophia watched as Colette, hand still clapped to the small of her back, half-bent at the knees to retrieve the knee-cushion and skim it sideways about a yard before kneeling on it again.

'She's not going to be able to keep up this amount of gardening.'

'Well, we're coming to the end of the summer,' Robert said philosophically. 'Less to do in the winter.'

'No, I mean generally. In the coming years.'

Sophia turned and looked at him very directly.

'Or you, either.'

'I wouldn't have thought either of us was decrepit.'

'Neither of you are.'

Robert went back to the telephone.

'But why wait until you are decrepit? Surely a garden is something to give you pleasure at every stage of your life?'

He hefted the main body of the phone in his left hand, lowering the cream plastic frame on to it with his right. Gently. Surely. Carefully. Deriving satisfaction from the meeting of the two parts, the spaces for short metal screws lining up perfectly.

'If you just let it continue, then in three years' time, you'll have to get Suttles or one of those other gardening companies to come in and do most of it.'

Robert folded up the newspaper and put it in the bin. As he washed his hands, out of old habit, scrubbing as thoroughly as a surgeon preparing for the sterility of the theatre, he murmured that they could afford Suttles.

'You can afford cleaners for the house, too.'

Sophia was developing quite a knack, thought her father. A knack for simple statements that attracted other truths to them. Yes, they could afford cleaners. But what had happened when they engaged Mini Maids twice a week? Colette ran herself ragged getting the place in good shape for Mini Maids and then stood over the cleaners, making them nervous by pointing out flaws. Even though she thought the cleaners were very good, her approval sounded like a reproach. Their hours were gradually cut; they came once a week, rather than twice, and then three times a month. Three times a month, Darcy yelled, was like a bi-monthly magazine. It was the shagging kiss of shagging death. Betcha, Darcy fumed (since the cleaners had been her idea in the first place) *betcha* within three months the cleaners won't be coming regularly at all and Ma will be as bloodywell exhausted as ever. Nobody had taken up Darcy's bet. It was, her father mildly pointed out, somewhat unethical to bet on certainties.

Towelling his wet hands, Robert went back to where Sophia stood at the window.

'I can't amputate half the garden,' he observed.

'No, but you could let Darcy and me redesign it.'

'How do you mean, redesign it?'

'Take out all the different levels. Put in a big beautiful pond ringed with Howth stone and a waterfall. Places to sit where you'll always hear the sound of running water. Maybe goldfish.'

Running water, Robert thought, would please Colette. She had an affinity with water, an ease and a fascinated absorption with it.

On their honeymoon in Rome, they had walked on an evening to the Trevi fountain, her hand folded into his, brought under his warm arm. He had looked at the statues and the family groups around them, talking with that loudness he had begun to realise was symptomatic, in Italy, of happy agreement rather than strident dissent. Colette had taken his arm and used his support to get standing on the rounded wall of the pool, looking down through the darkened water at the thousands of coins, copper-shine and silver sparkle against sombre duller circles of metal, some greened with age, all given that extra silence and symbolism of water-depth. She let go of his arm and he was momentarily disappointed. She dived without warning into the pool in front of the fountains, and he could see her lime-green-and-white longish skirt under the water. They cheered her, the Romans and the tourists, and smiled across at him as if sharing a sudden revelation. She walked back to him through the water and many hands willingly lifted her into his arms. And he held her, she tall as a statue on the wall of the fountain, the chill of her wet summer dress welcome in the warm night.

She kicked off her sandals and he carried them as she walked through the little streets leading away from the fountain.

'Ah, Trevi,' would come the laughing comment of people heading the other way. As if she'd made a gesture inter-nationally understood. Halfway up one of the little streets was a dress shop with a deep porched entry between two big display windows, darkened because business hours were over. A loudspeaker played music in the ceiling of the porched entryway, and she took her sandals back and danced with him on the tiles between the glass with the shadowed mannequins. They never talked about it again.

He became aware that his daughter's face was turned to him, concerned. Now, he smiled at her.

'Your mother likes water,' he said, and it sounded as footling as if he had announced that his wife approved of air. 'It would be very expensive, though, that kind of thing.'

'That's my problem and Darcy's,' she said crisply.

When Colette was asked about it, she stood, sweet-faced, and hummed a considering wordless hum which they took for consent. She would get catalogues and measurements, Sophia promised. Consult at every point. Because this was something for them, not for her.

I don't want you to be spying on me from the window, thought Colette behind her vague expression. Spying, spying. Watching my limitations. Deciding my future limitations. You and he together, plotting with kindness against me. Stealing my garden and giving me an old person's garden twenty years before I will be old. With your Deanna Durban good Samaritan puss on you and your money so available to hem me, contain me, handcuff me. With your father so besotted with your goodness and generosity that if I fought it, I would be painted into a corner, left labelled miserable and begrudging.

'I wouldn't want the raspberries to go,' Colette said, in a non sequitur later that same evening, as she dotted the last few stragglers of that year's crop on top of ice cream.

'Nothing has to go that you're really fond of,' Sophia reassured her.

Thank you, Colette thought. I kow-tow to your bene-ficence, you hostile takeover merchant with your father standing there like a sap in an American sitcom, one arm tight around you, hand clasped around the ball of your shoulder to send a message to me, haven't we got a great girl here, though, didn't we raise a good one. Nothing has to go that I'm really fond of, but it is *all* of it that I'm really fond of, the intricacies and the inter-relationships and the contradictions and the pleasured weariness of the tasks. There is no one thing that you can allow me to keep, like a souvenir of the Big House. If you pull it apart, there is no value in the things I get to keep, because it's all unravelled.

None of it said, so none of it registered but all of it stored in corrosive bile. None of it said. When Darcy asked if her mother approved of the idea, her father mentioned the need to keep the raspberries, and the idea rolled on. During the winter there were catalogues and plans. Bright brochures of pools as falsely royal-blue as a postcard. Laughter about gnomes and sculptures of leaping fish. A growing understanding of the costs, the quietness of the pumping machinery, the small amount of water recycled *ad infinitum*.

Colette glanced over shoulders when asked to, never sat at the table. Shrugged and smiled. Told Sophia that she relied on her good taste. Sophia took it for a compliment whereas it was the silken shiv of the dispossessed and disenfranchised. Colette developed a craving to arm-sweep their sales literature into the fire and watch the flames spill into each brochure from the corners like black water. She was filled with hatred for each of them. Robert, because he tail-wagged in joyous support of Sophia's plans. Sophia, because the idea was hers. Darcy, because she hadn't the wit to fight it.

When the frosts softened and the snowdrops began to poke through, she welcomed them with a grieved rage. She and Robert went to London for a week, knowing the earthmovers, the rotovators would go in while they were away. Colette sat through *A Chorus Line* wondering if she would have hated the show quite as much had she not been so preoccupied with the garden at home. *'One – singular sensation –'* seemed to be the only number the musical had. The long-legged dancers looked like tulips.

When they came home, everything was flat and smooth, apart from the bank up to the railway line at the back of the garden. The rocks from the rockery were gone, the three steps leading up a little hill were gone. The grass was gone. Smoothly raked dry soil stretched on all sides, the plane of it uninterrupted except for a great green hose snaking in a figure of eight.

'There's your pond,' Sophia said, delightedly.

My pond, don't call it my pond, it is your pond and where is it anyway?

'The hose,' Sophia explained. 'That's the way you pick the shape you want. You can design any shape at all.'

I am to be grateful, Colette thought. Grateful for this green-snaked children's toy I may cast this way and that. I may choose my weapons of self-destruction.

Darcy stepped onto the raked soil in her sneakers, making footprints across it, and took hold of the hose, trying to make it into wavy shapes.

'I thought you could do a pool with a mad bendy outline,' she said, deflated, coming back to them, the hose abandoned, its two ends not joined. No, her mother thought. They are clever, these people who give you the illusion of choice. Design your own pond. Within the limits of a plastic hose's flexibility. You can have a car any colour as long as it's black.

She was unsurprised when the finished pond was figure-of-eight-shaped, a little waterfall over stones between the two sections. The stones, she thought, had the unevenness of a Foxrock fireplace. Shrubs were put into place so that the garden came suddenly, unnaturally, into being. Everything had a wearisome explanation. Sophia and Robert took turns as explainers so that Colette felt, for days, as if she were watching a news bulletin with two presenters. See these shrubs here? They trail over the pond so that the fish will have safe places, cool places to go into. Did you notice how cleverly they've concealed the mechanism – they can get at it in a minute if it malfunctions, but you'd never be aware of it. Did you see the garden seat? It's Victorian, from an old, old house in Ballsbridge. Someone painted it white, but we had it stripped so that the real wood shows through.

She sat on the ribbing of the seat and Darcy took a picture of her on it. Rushed to have it developed. Viewed it first as all photographers do: to appreciate the balance and composition of the shot. Viewed it again to see if her mother would like it. Saw the lifted mouth and the uninvolved eyes. Didn't bring the picture with her when she dropped in to see her mother a few days later.

It was an evening when her mother should have been in the garden but she was in the kitchen with her back to it. Darcy, at the kitchen window, looked out at the moving water.

'You don't like it, do you, Mam?'

Colette smiled without looking out at it. Did the 'It's fine, it's fine' expression generations of mothers have done when faced with a Christmas present badly chosen by a loved one.

'But you really don't like it, do you?'

Colette looked puzzled. 'No, I'll get used to it. It was very generous of the two of you – '

'Oh Mam,' Darcy snapped. She tipped the button on the kettle to make it come back to the boil. Colette watched her as she made a cup of tea. Darcy was very vigorous, she thought, particularly when she felt guilty about something. Even the milk made a *blurp* noise as it bootled into the mug.

'It's OK, really it is,' Colette said. Meaning it is not OK, but surrender in defeat is a necessary skill too.

Darcy ate the chocolate biscuits off the plate, leaving the bourbon creams and the custard creams. If she was ever left in a house where there were no chocolate biscuits, only cream, she would take a knife and scrape off the brown or yellow filling and eat these biscuits without it. Colette watched in quiet delight as her daughter's right hand picked up biscuit after biscuit, her left hand cupped around her calorie-free sweetener box.

'When the fish go in, it'll be better,' Darcy said.

'That's true.' Easy acquiescence without consolation.

'But it *is*,' Darcy said. 'Goldfish don't expect anything. You don't have relationships with fish.'

'You did. Remember Finn and Haddie?'

A round bowl and two goldfish, one with brown stripe. Always moving, owned, fed and talked to by a six-year-old. They would come to her side of the bowl and mouth lippily at her and she would do it back to them. Then, one morning, Finn lay bent in two on the gravel at the bottom, the other fish nudging him. Robert took action. Get the sick one out of there and the other one might survive, he explained, spooning the sick one out with a plastic spatula and turfing him into the sani-can in the kitchen on top of the old cornflake boxes, last night's newspaper, sodden spent teabags. Darcy screamed the place down. Sophia got an old pencil box and took Finn back out of the sani-can on the spatula, Darcy's screams reduced to smothered roaring by a sharp smack from her father. Sophia gently ran the lid of the pencilbox into place and took Darcy by the hand as if her twin were a generation younger than herself.

'There has to be a proper burial,' Sophia told her father reprovingly. The twins went out into the garden and picked a place under the apple tree.

Sophia did the digging while Darcy stood, racked with sobs, holding the pencil case with its cargo until there was a neat deep hole ready to receive it. They prayed for the soul of the goldfish, then covered the place over. The other fish died the following day. But this time, Robert had learned his lesson. He came up with a fish-coffin of his own: an imitation-leather box which had housed a fat fountain pen in black velvet. So Haddie, nestling, bent by whatever ailment had done him in, along the depression designed for the fountain pen, was buried alongside the pencil-cased Finn. Darcy felt very close to her sister that week, and horrified by her father. Twenty years later, whenever her father failed in the sensitivities stakes, she remembered her dead goldfish tossed into kitchen rubbish. ('As if,' she had explained frantically to her mother at the time, 'as if Finn wasn't a person.')

Colette smiled at her daughter. 'I never threw out that goldfish bowl, you know. It's still up in the attic. I was always afraid you'd ask for it.'

Darcy smiled back.

'One of the nice things about the garden,' Colette said, 'is the sound. You can hear the water in here but it doesn't stop you hearing the birds. And the birds seem to like it, too.'

All the little palliative phrases designed to comfort losers, Darcy thought. Like: 'Remember, it's not winning that matters, it's taking part'. She had a confusion about who to comfort, because the only one totally happy with the new garden was her father. Sophia, she sensed, was experiencing defeat for the first time, a sense made stronger by her father's lavish praise. And you so busy, he kept saying, yet you found the time to get every detail right, to pick guys who wouldn't leave the place looking like a bomb hit it because you knew your mother would be vexed by that. It was a piling of enthusiastic emptinesses one atop the other to reassure her, undercut at every point by her mother's acquiescent dissent. Darcy felt surprised pity for her sister. Close on the heels of that feeling came a desire to send a letter to her American professor, to make him understand how Sophia was definitely not Snow White's Stepmother, but sometimes victimised by circumstances into looking like her.

The weekend the goldfish went into the pond was the culmination of the enterprise. Robert suggested asking the neighbours in. Colette hated the idea. Robert, who felt that funerals were the main occasions on which people his age now seemed to meet each other, agreed that it might seem ostentatious. He had just, he shrugged, wanted to make something of an occasion of it. Their wonderful daughters had given himself and his wife a new lease of life, something they were going to enjoy for a long, long time without having to slave over it. He just thought the occasion should be marked in some way.

In the event, he marked the completion of the garden in the most memorable way he could have imagined, if he was a man given to imaginings, which he was not. He died in it.

On the Friday afternoon, he went back into the hospital

to finish off a report and attend a meeting. During his absence the fish arrived. Forty of them, the delivery man told Colette, getting her to sign for them. You'd never think, now, that there was forty there, would you, ma'am? Not when they're exploring their new place and hiding under rocks and plants. But there are. Forty of them. You'll be putting names on them in no time, he told her, and she let him think he was right.

The goldfish delivery man was leaving when Robert came back from the hospital. Both were delighted with the encounter. The delivery man promised Robert that Robert wouldn't know himself now he had all these fish. Colette started to make a cup of tea. Robert told her he was going first to pull up some of the lamia from around the roots of the plants which had been allowed to live on the bank rising up towards the railway line.

Thus it was that two trainloads of people witnessed his dying, although none of them realised it. The earlier of the trains ran past the end of the garden as Robert rose from kneeling and put the back of his hand to the spine-cramp caused by bending over.

So he was standing, watching the passing train, when the heart attack took him and pitched him up against the strong wire fence, both hands clenching it, scrabbling for purchase against the pain.

Colette had been watching him from the kitchen window. The meaning was clear to her instantaneously. She ran, wiping her hands on a tea towel, and followed the outside edge of the pond, knowing the extra seconds the journey took because of its curve would not count for anything. He was dead and she knew it, was so certain of it that it delayed her touching of him, because he was no longer him. Alive, he would never have fallen in such a helpless way. Alive, he fought to save things, to minimise breakages, to pick where he came down and what bit of him hit first. There had been none of that. He had sunk, poleaxed.

Yet she talked gently to him when she reached him. I'll get you down, she promised him, struggling with the silent weight that was hanging from the wire fence by cardigan buttons. The weight brought her to her knees and she sat among his flowers and pulled him to her and patted down the cardigan, rucked by the fence into indignity. I'll mind you, she promised him, faces touching as she rocked him in the warmth of the July sun. The second train passed, its passengers seeing a stiffened *pietà*, a cradled body in a holey cardigan with suede inserts.

When Colette's eyes were closed, she was in her own garden. When her eyes opened, she was in a strange garden with a piddling parody of waterfall and waterflow, but she never remembered his death as having happened in the new garden.

CHAPTER TWENTY-FOUR

It was Sophia whom her mother, flat-voiced and careful, reached first, at her office in *Positionings*. Sophia, who was gentle and who got the facts. Who promised she would be at home within a half an hour, who took the responsibility of reaching Darcy.

'Oh, bloody hell,' said Darcy on her mobile phone, her inflection suggesting to Sophia that it was the timing of the death, rather than the death itself, that was the worst thing.

'I'm about ten minutes away from you – I'll pick you up and do the driving,' Darcy said.

When they arrived at the house, neighbours were already there, ready to back away in sensitivity as the daughters held their mother, who seemed possessed by a resolute, untearful devotion to the middle distance. When spoken to, it took her moments to pull herself back to focus on the speaker. While conversations eddied around her, she looked past them as if listening for a distant word that would quiet the helpfulness. Quiescent in the face of suggestions, she reminded Darcy of a picture Greg had once shown her, of a rugby player who didn't manage to scrum down with the rest, and who got left, looking bothered, while all the other players were locked at his knee level, head-ramming each other with righteous energy.

Sophia made lists and harkened to neighbours' words about her father, heedful always of where her mother was and what she might need, a running reproach in her mind blaming her mother for her father's death, despite the denials that the same mind so quickly produced. Coming, as she did, from a generation that fights off death with bolts of electricity and racing, howling journeys to casualty wards, she could not but think that her father might have been saved if her mother had cried out. The neighbours would have heard her voice, Sophia thought, looking at her father's carve-cornered hedge. An ambulance might have made the difference.

Sophia said none of this and the neighbours went, as neighbours do, to make casseroles and sandwiches with crusts amputated. Sophia said none of it, Darcy never thought of it, yet her mother knew Sophia's thoughts as if they had been written in the sky at which she looked more and more fixedly as the funeral days went on.

On the details of Robert's burial, and on those only, Colette had focus. It was she, dark-coated and purposeful, who went to choose a casket and to discuss the readings with the priest. Greg met her on the driveway and held her, his face close to hers, filled with a gentleness that brought her own face down on to his shoulder before he handed her his big clean white handkerchief and made her laugh with the almost theatrical suitability of it.

He saw her to the car and then came in. The house was empty apart from the two sisters. He hugged Darcy in silent commiseration, then sat, knee to knee on the couch with his wife, foreheads touching, big hands gathering small hands. Darcy left him and Sophia in the sitting room and went to make coffee. As she came back into the sitting room, she could hear the whisper of his voice, its volume lowered by compassion.

Whatever he said released the tight-wound wires of Sophia's control and Darcy was stalled, tray at chest level, by the sight and the sound of her sister possessed by a great haemorrhaging of clotted grief.

Darcy put down the tray and walked out, hearing the noises half-stifled in Greg's hug. Isn't it strange, Darcy thought, leaning up against a bright white surface in the clean kitchen, all the time I knew Sophia, I had no idea. The more I know the less I understand.

In the days of the funeral and immediately afterwards, the twins hit turbulent patches of grief and disbelief. Their

347

tall, sinewy father with his instinct for moderation: there was no justice, they told each other, in his dying that way.

Colette, on the other hand, talked about 'your father's death' as if the essential relationship, in the context of his demise, was with his daughters, his wife there purely as an extra. He had been her husband in life. In death, he became their father. She seemed unsurprised by a death nobody had expected, but took it as a certainty whose time had come.

She tried to explain this to Darcy and Sophia. 'The insistent song of middle age is death,' she said.

They didn't understand. She couldn't explain. It enraged her, and this was new to them. When their father, as she called him, had been alive, their mother had been a reflective, absorbent, ameliorative presence, turning contention into laughter, tilting intolerance into diversion. Robert King had owned the rules, tending them as he tended his garden. Robert King owned the rages and the condemnations, defining issues aloud in monologue. Without this verbal buffer, his widow found herself defenceless and deafened by public opinion. Within days of the funeral, the girls noticed that she had stopped listening to the radio or looking at television.

Sophia rang her every day and dropped in to see her at least three times a week. Greg, because his hours at the television station were irregular, often arrived in the middle of the day, demanded lunch from Colette and made her laugh. Once, he brought her a goldfish in a plastic bag, holding it at shoulder level as he walked up the driveway.

'There are millions of them in the pond,' Colette said impatiently, as if being forced to re-engage in a battle she had conceded a long time before.

'Ah, but you haven't looked at Hannibal, here,' Greg told her, as if she were missing the point. He unplugged the kettle, one-handed, still holding up the plastic bag, and dragged her after him into the garden. She shivered and he rubbed her back to warm her.

'What's special about Hannibal?' his mother-in-law asked, humouring him.

'He's a reverse albino, I think. Look at him.'

Hannibal gawped at Colette. He had great black patches thrown, paint-blob-fashion, over his burnished bronzy gold.

'He's like a Freisian cow,' Colette said.

Greg turned the bag so Hannibal was facing him. Hannibal immediately swam back to face Colette and gawp his mouth open at her.

'See, he likes you already,' Greg said. 'That's the thing about Freisian goldfish. They have a special extra strand in their DNA. The relationship strand, it's called. First goldfish in history to do serious bonding with humans.'

For a moment, Colette believed him, then gently punched him with a half-closed fist. Greg dropped to his hunkers on the edge of the pond and looked at the other goldfish, quick-flicking in metallic orange slices of moving light. He turned Hannibal's bag towards him again. Hannibal immediately swam to where he could see Colette.

'Are you listening to me, you thick fish?'

Hannibal turned.

'He is, you know,' Greg told Colette. 'Look at him: he's saying wha'? wha'?'

Hannibal lost interest.

'Come back here, you haven't finished your lesson, you under-achieving thick fish,' Greg remonstrated through the thick soft plastic. 'Don't lose your individuality, that's all I want to tell you. None of this peer pressure crap from those dumb-ass lookalikes in there, OK? I come back in a week and find any of your black bits faded, I'll have you on toast for tea that night. Are we clear?'

Hannibal said wha'? wha'? at this point to both Colette and Greg, and Greg dumped him into the pond, scattering his future cell-mates.

When Darcy noticed Hannibal later on, his colours led her to assume that he was sick and should be removed before he sickened the rest of them.

'No, no,' Colette said confidently. 'That's Hannibal, he's fine. He was like that when he came.'

'Oh. Was he always bigger than the rest of them?'

'No, he was smaller.'

'Must be a happy little frigger, then,' Darcy said and forgot Hannibal. Her mother sat silent, contemplating, with pleasure, the possibility that Hannibal was thriving by eating some of his companions.

Two months after her father died, Sophia told Malachy that she would be leaving in three months' time to set up her own company. Once he was sure that she was really going and that no incentive would dissuade her, his response surprised her.

'Don't take the three months,' he said coolly. 'Go as soon as you like.'

'But I'll need,' Sophia pointed out, 'to ensure an orderly transition for clients – '

'Sophia, this is PR, not world diplomacy,' Malachy said. 'I'll take over your clients in the short term.'

'But my contract stipulates three months' notice?'

'We'll pay you the three months.'

Frozen by the intended insult, Sophia was silent for a long moment.

'You will certainly pay me for the three months,' she told him. 'And for any holiday time which would have accrued to the end of that three months. If there is any dispute about the monies involved in transferring my car to my personal ownership, I will seek to have an independent mediator appointed to adjudicate – '

'Oh, we won't need any of that – ' Malachy said, aghast at the clinical wrath he had brought down upon himself.

'Malachy, my desk will be cleared on Friday,' Sophia said, and left his office.

On Friday morning, at about ten, Malachy rang Sophia's

secretary to ask her to come to his office, where he was striding about, bouncing with bogus bonhomie.

'Now, Genna, I want you to arrange something very special for me,' he told her. 'As you know, Sophia is leaving us today. Not many of the staff know this, and what I'd like to arrange is a really splendid surprise party. I know it's short notice and you don't often hear me say this, but money is no object. Get on to one of our catering people and tell them to be over here about three, four at the latest, with a good spread and lots of champagne. My own secretary is out at the moment buying Sophia a lizard-skin briefcase, and I'll do a little presentation at some point in the party.'

Genna wrote down all his requirements.

'So there you have it,' he said in a generous and good-humoured way. 'There you have it. Let's make her final afternoon here a very special afternoon, right, Gen?'

Genna, who hated being called Gen, nodded dumbly at him, a hot ball of apprehension lumping her throat. He nodded to her; she stood. She turned at the door in coward's resolution.

'It's just,' she said, and he smiled encouragingly to her, ' – the only thing is, really – '

'Yes, Genna?'

'Sophia's not going to be back.'

'Back when? How do you mean?'

'Back this afternoon. She has final meetings with a whole lot of clients and she's going from one to the other.'

'She's not coming back?'

'No, she's said goodbye to everybody already and she left me a letter for you.'

'Oh dear,' Malachy said, trying to do PR for a one-woman audience. 'She never thought that we'd be doing a party. Isn't that typically Sophia? Delivering her professional best right up to the last minute.'

Figuring the safest response to this was a silent nod, Genna silently nodded.

'But do you know what we might do?' Malachy said, schoolboyish in his delight at his own acuity. 'We could ring her on her mobile and ask her to come back in the afternoon for an important meeting, couldn't we?'

'Her mobile phone is on my desk. She told me to give it to you.'

'Genna,' he said, hands out in good-humoured helplessness, 'what can we do? What. Can. We. Do. Not a lot, I think. Not a lot.'

It's all 'I' when you have big plans and boasts, isn't it, Genna thought maliciously, but it's all 'we' when there's blame to be shared. As she trudged back to her now quiet room, Genna thought about ringing Sophia at home that night to tell her of Malachy's disorganised dismay, but decided against it. It would give Sophia pleasure, she surmised, but Sophia would regard the expression of that pleasure as unprofessional so she would not react at all.

Worse, Genna conjectured, Sophia would probably think the worse of Genna for passing it on, because Sophia was always talking about the moral dimension to work. Anyway, Genna thought, what was there to gain? She didn't want to work for Sophia any more and it was perfectly clear that Sophia wouldn't want her as PA in this new joint venture with her big fat red-headed sister.

From Darcy's point of view, the news that Sophia was jobless, as of that weekend, but not salary-less, was wonderful.

'Why on earth did he take it like that?' she asked. 'You were even promising not to take any of his clients with you?'

'He knows some of them will come to me in a year anyway,' Sophia said. 'But he's incapable of emotional compromise, Malachy. It's very unusual in a man. He either loves you or hates you. Not to mention the fact that he is convinced, and always has been convinced, that people who are working out their notice deliberately knock cups of coffee into their machines.'

'What machines, for God's sake?' Greg asked in unexpected annoyance. 'Bloody *Positionings* is in the dark bloody ages as far as technology is concerned. They wouldn't know a modem if it bit them in the arse.'

Darcy got bored, instantly, at the mention of technology, and asked Greg why the black-spotted goldfish was named Hannibal.

Greg blinked slowly, accommodating the change of subject.

'I've always been a big fan of the real Hannibal. Great showman. Could have gone across the Alps on something dull like donkeys, but did it with elephants. I thought a black-and-gold goldfish was a showy animal that needed a showy name.'

'I think he may be a cannibal, as well as a showman.'

'Comes up out of the pond and eats a few of your mother's neighbours?'

'No. Eats his pals.'

Sophia looked horrified.

'How *could* he?'

'Don't worry about it,' Greg said, patting his wife on the knee. 'He probably only does it to fishes he's gone off – '

' – Malachy-type fishes,' Darcy said.

' – or fishes he never had a meaningful relationship with.'

'I may be imagining things,' Darcy said. 'I just thought he looked very voluptuous and there didn't seem to be such a crowd in the pond as there was at the beginning. Seagulls may be having their share, too, of course.'

Sophia, refusing to be distracted, said that she would deal with the computer people and would also make decisions on the interior design. Plus she would talk to the insurance companies. Darcy would do the recruitment interviews.

So the following week, Darcy spent a day asking questions of eight people selected from the thousands who applied, pulled by the glamour already growing around *The Image Makers*.

By lunchtime on the day of the interviews, Darcy's desk was covered in notes and her mind was addled.

'Why do teachers become teachers when they all want to get the hell out of teaching as soon as another job is advertised?' she asked her new secretary, Neasa, who had come into her office with coffee and sandwiches.

'All teachers?'

'Three of them. Wonderful academic qualifications and damn-all experience of running anything.'

Neasa sat at the edge of the desk, rifling through Darcy's notes. 'This is very impressive. Loads of data for you to go through afterwards.'

'No. Loads of make-work to keep me from falling asleep as one of them after another tells me I should give them the job because they really want it. They'd like an "interesting job meeting people". Me, I'd like an interesting job *not* meeting people. Don't you think it a beautiful thought, a world empty of people, just uninterrupted grass and a hare sitting up?'

Had Alex once said that in a letter, she wondered? And if so, why? He wasn't a great man for quotations.

Neasa got off the desk, all business. 'So, other than the teachers, was there anything?'

'Well, the third this morning,' Darcy said, 'was a bright young thing from one of the PR companies, says she's sick of buying journalists drinks and doing their work for them and being patronised by them.'

'*There's* a strong sales pitch.'

'She also said nine out of ten journalists are pompous self-serving shits looking for freebies while pretending that they're high-minded investigative scoop-getters.'

'Did she name any of her favourites?'

'Yes.'

'She going to get the job?'

'No.'

Darcy, having eaten all the sandwiches, was now tackling

the crinkly potato crisp garnish.

'This afternoon you have an ex-nun, another teacher, an early retirer who doesn't like retirement and a former PA to an MD in England.'

'What did the ex-nun do?'

'Ran a hospice.'

Darcy began to look interested, as she ate the cheesecake.

'Why would running a hospice make you enthusiastic?' Neasa asked.

'A hospice would be an interesting thing to run. Practical considerations and moral decisions. The atmosphere. Keeping the staff from becoming burned out.'

'I wouldn't have thought that putting little cooking women into supermarkets to fry up sausages would require much in the way of moral decision-making and that's what we're looking for – someone who'll do that.'

In fact, the ex-nun came so close to what Darcy was looking for that she had to restrain herself from showing how positively she felt towards her. By the time she had reached the last interviewee of the day, Darcy had decided that unless Shari Burke was exceptionally promising, the nun had the job.

Shari Burke, when she arrived, turned out to have completely white hair, although she was twenty-eight. The dyed hair was shorter than a GI's crew cut. She had perfect bone structure and beautiful make-up.

'Tell me about yourself,' Darcy invited, and sat through the usual recital of what was in the CV. Went to school here, went to secretarial college there, started in such a company. Darcy got bored.

'You ambitious?'

'Very.'

'For what?'

'For being the one at the top. Soon.'

'Money?'

'No. Fun.'

'*Fun?*'

'Your job shouldn't be something you drag yourself to every day. You spend most of your life at it. So it should be fun.'

'Have all your other jobs been fun?'

Shari claimed that they had, and Darcy, not believing her, asked for an example, then stopped listening. She opened the CV and began to go through it. This was a device she often used when interviewing. It put people under pressure and you got to see what they did under pressure. Shari finished her story and sat quietly waiting for the next question. Darcy read the CV in silence and eventually found what she was looking for. The discrepancy. The missing bit. The dropped stitch.

'You haven't been in the workforce for fifteen months?'

'I was taking care of my father, who was dying.'

'I'm sorry,' Darcy said gently.

Shari looked enraged. 'I've had eight interviews in the last three weeks, and this has been the stumbling block each and every time. Isn't she a nice girl, she went home and minded her oul fella when he was dying but she'll be completely out of touch so we'll take somebody else.'

'I don't know about the other jobs you've been going for,' Darcy said, 'but I'll tell you what I need in the person to whom I give this job. I need a self-starter. I need someone with cop-on and judgement. I need someone who doesn't need a secretary running around mopping up after her every three seconds. Must know how to get stuff into a computer, get stuff out of a computer, use her car as a mobile office, keep track. I want this person to be a "virtual" company: I want clients to think she's backed up by about eighty people whereas in fact she'll be on her own. I want someone who can cope with disaster on a daily basis and who's good to have around, because – yes, we do think you should have fun at work. I have interviewed seven other people today, and I spent a lot of time with each one of them talking about their most recent experience. Your most recent experience is unusual, but it's highly relevant. So why don't you tell me about it.'

'Tell you about it?'

'It was your most recent job, wasn't it?'

The girl ran her hands over the soft fuzz of her tight haircut. She took a deep breath through her nose, mouth pursed.

'First thing is that I'm from a big family. Six children and I'm second youngest. My mother died a couple of years ago and my father was there on his own.'

'Where's "there"?'

'Just north of Navan.'

'Go on.'

'He was doing OK but then he had a stroke, September two years ago.'

She went to the window and began to talk without looking at Darcy.

'I'll never forget going into the hospital to see him. My father was a words man. Great talker, great man with the off-the-top-of-the-head witticism. But there he was, lying with his face tilted all to one side, like a candle melting. The awful thing was he kept thinking things were funny. I kept expecting him to be frustrated because he couldn't make sense and speak to us. He thought it was all very funny. That was the worst thing.'

She grasped her upper arms, standing there in the window and came up on the balls of her feet as if she was exercising. Darcy asked her where she had been working at the time. Lancashire, she said. The CV confirmed it. Personal assistant to the MD of a computer manufacturing plant. She had taken a fortnight's leave, assuming that two weeks was all she would need.

'Ten days after the stroke the hospital can't wait to get rid of him. I'm not joking you. He's lying there, incontinent, his face all collapsed to one side, he's speechless and he's laughing and they're saying "get him out of here" and my big brother the priest is nodding. I said why would we want to take him out of the hospital, wasn't he in the right place, and they said recovering from a stroke took a long time and so forth. What they *didn't* say was that he was old.'

Darcy sat still as a rock. The girl began to pace the office, talking as she went. A driven monologue.

'My big brother kept putting words into their mouths. I mean, *he* was telling *them* that they couldn't afford to have their beds taken up by old people! He said this in front of my father as if because my father can't talk, he can't hear either. But he *could* hear. He heard that, all right. He went awful quiet and he sure as hell stopped laughing. Public health warning: you lose your right to a hospital bed after sixty. They shunted him off to a nursing home and he was there for three months. I came home at Christmas to see him. He was beginning to communicate. A bit. But he was desperately uncomfortable and eventually a nurse came, *eventually*, after he'd rung for ages and ages and he indicated that he needed to go to the loo. You know what she told him?'

Darcy shook her head.

'She told him that he had a protective thing on and that they were very busy and to go ahead. I'm saying that she told this dignified old man that he had a nappy on so he could go ahead and pee in the bed. She said that in front of his own daughter!'

'What did you do?'

'I told her I didn't know how the hell she ever got to be where she was but that she missed out on the basic qualification of humanity and I just took him home. I wrapped him up and took him back to his own home. I rang my boss and told him he'd have to give me six weeks to get things sorted out, then I called the family together to tell them what had happened. I met with total horror. Shock horror. The whole bit. They said he'd have to go back to the nursing home, it was the only place that could give him all the proper care and that none of them were in a position to look after him, because they had *commitments*. Married, with children. That's what that means. I'm sorry if you are.'

Darcy denied that she was married. The girl talked on in a monotone powered by hatred and despair.

'I didn't have commitments, of course. I didn't have kids. Like they had their kids for the good of the world. Kids: the ultimate cop-out. "I can't put out your fire, I have my kids to look after." "I can't visit you in hospital, my kid has hives." "I can't take responsibility for our father, my youngest is making her First Communion." So the priest was gonna save souls and the rest of them were busy rearing children. Wasn't going to stop them having holidays or bridge nights, but it'd stop them taking on any responsibilities. Me, I'm living with a guy in Britain and I had planned on spending the rest of my life with that person, but to hell with that. I was single. I could do it. Or I could put Daddy back in the nursing home.'

'Hobson's choice,' Darcy suggested.

'So I come home. I lose my job. I lose my lover. I have very little money. I'm left nursing an old man whom I love dearly but who half the time I'd love to poison because I know what he was and I know what he is. He's just the dregs of himself. He's a sad parody of who he used to be, and I have to guard against developing this awful British nanny optimism and addressing him in the plural, like, "How *are* we today, Daddy?"

'The family thought I was *mah*vellous. Full of praise for me. Redeemed myself after a flighty life, I had. Now and again, they'd actually come over for a few hours to be nice to him and let me off to Dublin on the skite. You know what happened the last time I did that? My sister came over and she couldn't bring herself to clean him up, because she'd be too "sensitive" and she knew that he'd be sensitive too, so she left him for eight hours sitting in his own shit. She left him like that for eight hours and when I came home and cleaned him up, he couldn't look at me. He started to die. That day.'

Shari went to the window and stood in it, head tilted so far back her neck contorted as she swallowed and swallowed again to prevent tears coming. Stood, dry-eyed in the window. Swallowed again. Came back to the chair in front of Darcy's desk. Sat. Hands palm-flattened to each other between her knees for warmth.

'You know that saying "he turned his face to the wall"?' Darcy nodded.

'He did that. He turned his face to the wall. Not a look. Not a look. He couldn't bring himself to be in contact with a world that would treat him like that. I could hear his chest getting congested and I climbed up on the bed and slid up between him and the wall and – Oh, Jesus, he closed his eyes. He closed his eyes. The only thing he had left to do to keep the world out. He closed his eyes. I just said, "I'm only going to be here for a minute, I'm not going to torment you, you've been tormented enough. You don't have to look at me, you can listen to me and just tell me if I'm going wrong. I can hear your chest getting bad. If I call the doctor, he'll put you back in the hospital. I think what you would want me to do is keep you as comfortable as I can and let you sleep as much as you can and just mind you here. But if I'm wrong, oh, Dad, please tell me. Show me, because I do love you and respect you. You're all I have in the whole world and I'm all you have."'

There was a long silence in the room.

'I just lay there then for a minute and he never opened his eyes and I didn't know what to do. But then he nodded. Just once. With his eyes closed. So I kissed his forehead and I got off the bed and I minded him for ten days. I washed him and I slept on the floor beside the bed and I turned him and suctioned him and gave him oxygen. But mostly, I gave him sleeping pills. It doesn't take many sleeping pills to put an old thin man out of discomfort. But of course, it – what's the phrase – "depresses the breathing centre" in the brain, so ultimately, I was helping him to die. Which he did.'

Darcy watched her and Shari watched Darcy. The beautifully made-up twenty-eight-year-old face suddenly took on a slightly frightening version of an intense social smile. Shari rose, took her briefcase off the floor and made ready to depart.

'So there you have it. Not only have I not been customer-friendly in the last year or so, but I probably helped an old man to opt out of life, the universe and everything. A nice bright company called *Image Makers* couldn't have *that* on its books, could it?'

Darcy stayed behind the desk and held out a hand. The girl shook it in a businesslike way.

'What you've said is in confidence and will not be shared with anybody, including my sister, who will help make the decision on this job,' Darcy said, glad of the officious formulae of the recruitment routine. 'We'll contact you within the next few days.'

'You not going to thank me for my time?' Shari asked, suddenly mischievous.

'I *beg* your pardon,' Darcy said, sketching a bow. 'I thank you for your time. Of course.'

The girl walked briskly to the door and started through it. At the last moment, she turned and flapped the briefcase at Darcy to demonstrate its weightlessness.

'Empty. But a good prop, right?'

Darcy nodded, speechlessly.

Two days later, she met Sophia to give her the name of the manager she had chosen for the promotions division. It was the ex-nun. Sophia raised an eyebrow.

'It'll work,' Darcy said. 'It'll work.'

'Any progress on getting a PA for me?' Sophia asked. 'I think Neasa's double-jobbing is cutting years off her life.'

'I have an odd candidate for you,' Darcy said.

'No, you mean you have an odd selection for me.'

'No, a candidate. You have to see her and make up your own mind. It's too close for me to call.'

'Too close to the other candidates?'

'No, I haven't found anybody within miles of what you need, other than this dame.'

'So why may she be wrong?'

'She didn't apply for the job, she applied for the promotions job, and she's not qualified for that one at all. She's been out of the workforce for the last year-and-a-half, looking after her dying father – and *don't* ask about that if you see her, because I promised I'd give you no details, all right? She's twenty-eight, looks thirty-eight, bleached blonde Paula Yates crewcut and has a – a ferocity to her. I believe you need someone with a lot of toughness in them, because you're a very demanding boss. You also need someone who can learn fast and who is highly motivated. She seems to me to be all those things. She may be a whole lot of other things as well, I don't know. If you decide to see her, tell me and Neasa will set it up. If you don't, tell me and I'll write her a kind letter.'

'Could I have her CV to take home and discuss with Greg?'

'Sure,' said Darcy, handing it over.

Next day, Sophia said that she wanted to meet Shari. Fleetingly, Darcy wondered how Greg had influenced the decision. Had he told Sophia not to worry about the possibility that she might favour a woman who had taken care of a dying father? Darcy didn't know and didn't care. It was now at least 50 per cent Sophia's decision. At least 50 per cent.

A. C. B. /Fort Attic
813 2760716 29 November 1993

Darcy

Please clarify for me one of your terms. Is it 'Wall-eyed wankler?'

Alex

Darcy King/Dublin
353 1 3784212 30 November 1993 14.40
Alex

The blonde storm-trooper I mentioned to you made it on to our staff. She was able – for the reasons I gave you – to start work immediately, and bendy waves of electric air are now coming out around the door of Sophia's office whenever it's closed, which is pretty rarely, given that one or other of them is always leaping out to kill a problem. (You, me and the rest of the world solve problems. Shari and Sophia *kill* problems.)

Thanks re reference source on ' . . . just a hare sitting up.' Were you flattered that I remembered? Do not answer this. I know you cannot – unlike the actors whose egos you constantly bolster – be flattered. Or insulted. I think I've notched up more than ten years of trying to dent your impregnable self-esteem re your advanced age, retreated hair, general pomposity and disloyalty to academia, as evidenced by your willingness to bullshit actors for money into the theory behind their role. It's been about as effective as throwing marshmallows at a cliff.

I do think, however, that you may be getting a little touched. As in not the full shilling. As in a slight screw loose. Asking me to clarify my terms of abuse. Well, whatever turns you on . . .

It's 'wall-eyed *wanker*', not 'wall-eyed wankLer.' You happy now?

PS You mentioned Internet a while back; could you now educate me about it, fast.

A. C. B./Fort Attic
813 2760716 3 January 1994 7.08
Darcy

The Internet.

The Internet, like all good things, came out of academia. More than twenty years ago, a bunch of researchers in the defense industry needed computer networks to tap into. A network was established then known as ARPANET. By 1984, only a thousand computers were linked to it. Then, like an epidemic of understanding, researchers in a range of academic fields realised that computer networking was crucial to their needs, and in 1986 the US National Science Foundation got involved to provide more network connections to more research institutions and thereby improve international network cooperation. Internet was born. Millions of computers are now linked into it. Someone has used the phrase 'The Information Superhighway'; in my view, the Internet is the actuality behind that phrase.

When you're on the Internet you could send me something and I would acknowledge immediately, and then you'd be able to E-mail me anywhere, E-mail material directly into your secretary's computer, ready for her to work on and feed out and, because you'll have your own mailbox, any of your regular correspondents could dump mail into the box for you to access whenever you felt like reading your letters, even if that's in the middle of the night.

Alex

Darcy King/Dublin
353 1 3784212 6 January 1994 7.17

Alex

Thanks. Heading for the States for 10 days, Borchgrave work. Will be arriving back in Dublin the Monday we officially open.

Darcy

CHAPTER TWENTY-FIVE

It was ten-thirty before Darcy arrived at the *Image Makers* building on that first Monday morning. Double-parked outside was a van with *Pete's Pet Emporium* on its side.

'I thought you weren't going to steal any of Malachy's clients until a year was out?' Darcy asked, barging into Sophia's office. 'I see a van from Pete's Pet Emporium outside.'

'Yeah,' said Shari. 'Just dropped in a big box for you.'

'For me?' Darcy asked.

Sophia opened her hands wide and looked genuinely puzzled.

'Can we all have a gawk?' This was from Neasa.

'Sure, follow me,' Darcy said, and led the way to her section of the building.

On the coffee table in a corner of Darcy's office was a big, giftwrapped box, perhaps two feet square. Darcy examined the big cube, quickly realising that the giftwrapping was not secured but had simply been lowered loosely over the box-shaped thing underneath. She took hold of the bow centred on the top of the wrapping and pulled.

'Ah fuck off, fuck off, fuck off, why don't you?' inquired the resident of the cage.

There was a stunned silence from the group. Darcy gaped at the mynah bird, which tilted its head, sure of its own capacity to endear, and crooned at her.

'Who's a wall-eyed wanker, then?' it said.

'*What?*' Darcy found herself asking it. Obligingly, it repeated itself.

'Who's a wall-eyed wanker, then?'

'Hey, I know him – ' This was Sophia, amazing her staff by her apparent affection for a filthy-mouthed old caged bird, who immediately suggested she might give him a ride. Sophia laughed at him.

'I've missed you, you know,' she told him. He told her to fuck off and went back to asking Darcy about wall-eyed wankers.

'Hey, that's one of your phrases,' Sophia said.

'Have you met this bird before?' asked Shari.

'No, never,' Darcy said. 'Someone must have taught it my phrase.'

Shari and Neasa began to wander off. Sophia however, stayed, poking her finger into the cage and laughing when the mynah bird chewed on it.

'What a lovely idea,' she said, to Darcy's surprise.

'You don't mind it being here?'

'Oh no, I think it's great. I'll visit it whenever I need a lift.'

'But say if your clients down the hall hear it shrieking swear words – like that?' Darcy gestured.

'People love to be let in on the underside of a business, and the bird can be our underside. It'll be a funny detail, unorthodox in the middle of all of our professionalism.'

'Sort of like Streisand's nose?'

'More or less.'

Shari handed her a single sheet of paper, which gave instructions about taking care of mynah birds. Darcy read it and then turned it over. The back of the page was blank.

'Where did you get this?'

'I rang Pete's Pet Emporium, and the minute I said I was ringing to get some information about a gift that had been sent to Darcy King, they put me right through to Pete himself. He must have been expecting a call. Anyway, I asked him who sent the mynah bird, and he said he wasn't at liberty to tell me but that it had been an overseas credit card purchase. Is that any help?'

Darcy nodded.

'Anyway, when I was on to Pete, he seemed very anxious to know did the bird say the right thing. Here is where it gets confusing,' Shari continued, 'because I asked him what the right thing was, and he said he couldn't say. I said had the bird been trained to say a particular thing, and he eventually admitted that much, and I told him all the things I could remember that the bird said, which was quite difficult –'

' – to remember?'

' – no, mostly to say. I'm not used to saying fuck off three times to total strangers on the phone. I usually get more friendly with people before I tell them to fuck off.'

'But you rhymed off whatever you could remember of the bird's sayings?'

'And at some point he gave a sigh of relief and said, grand, grand, the bloody bird had done what he was supposed to do. Perfectly obvious he had taught the bird to say Willy the wicked Wanker –'

At this point the mynah bird had something of a seizure, correcting Shari three times with, 'Who's a wall-eyed wanker?'

'Well, whatever kind of wanker is relevant,' Shari said resignedly. 'So then Pete got all bossy and businesslike about what you were to do for the mynah bird, which, by the way, does not seem to have a name.'

'Oh, for perversity, let's call him the Real Macaw,' said Darcy, writing it on the back of the list of instructions and showing it to them.

'McCaw,' Shari said. 'Do you feel like McCaw?'

'I feel like a ride and a rasher,' Mc Caw replied.

'I haven't heard him say that before,' Sophia observed. 'But then, he seems to have given up on McGill. Maybe he forgets things.'

'McGill plays with himself,' McCaw said, proving her wrong.

'How will you manage important phone calls?' Shari looked worried.

Sophia turned on her way to the door. 'That's not a problem,' she said to Darcy. 'You just keep a heavy cloth to throw over the cage. Once he's in darkness, he doesn't talk.'

Boss and PA exited. Darcy and the mynah bird looked at

each other in perfect amity.

'You'll have to excuse me,' she told it after a moment. 'I have to do a letter.'

'Who's a wall-eyed wanker?' the bird asked, playing its trump card.

Darcy King/Dublin
353 1 3782412 17 January 1994 11.23

Dear Alex

I got into the office about three-quarters of an hour ago, and your gift was waiting for me. You'll be pleased to know it said its party piece almost immediately and about a million times since.

Thank you very much. I'm so grateful I'll even go and see the Kinsale movie you told me about. It's opening in one of the smaller cinemas here next week. Kind of a cautious launch, I would have thought, given that it has that guy Brooke Stone in it. From what I've seen of him he has the same kind of get-the-hell-out-of-my-way appeal onscreen as Tommy Lee Jones. But maybe that won't work in a period piece. I'll give you an honest verdict and you can rely on my mynah bird to tell me what to do with same.

Today is a big day. I get weak in the knees when I realise we have twenty staff here. By instinct, I think I'm a loner always looking for a windmill to tilt at . . .

Oh – I've given him a name, by the way. McCaw.

He has an expressed preference for 'a ride and a rasher'. Which – getting back to the almost-forgotten purpose of this correspondence – is a raunchy description of bed and breakfast. 'Ride' in Ireland means sex. It also means other things, but it means sex to everybody with a dirty mind, and so one of the much cherished bootleg tapes in a local radio station here is one where, after a government lost a vote of confidence and was turfed out of office, an interviewer (male and pure) asked a minister (female and ditto) about the personal implications of the parliamentary set-back.

'Minister,' he asked, 'is this your last ride in a state car?'

Now, Stateside, they talk about riding all the time, and I am always on the verge of trouble. One time when I was training a group in Greenville, one of the men asked very politely and quietly if I could avoid saying 'Jesus' as much as I do because he was a Baptist lay preacher and he found it disturbing. I did my best, and this obviously impressed him, because at the end of the training session, he came up to me and asked me if I'd like a ride. Keeping a straight face was v. difficult.

I've just asked this bird to contribute to your study, as a gesture of gratitude for you sending him to such a glamorous and exciting place, and he said McGill plays with himself. I told him McGill must be frayed to flitters by now, and McCaw is silently giving this some thought. By the way, I'll be sending you in the next few days, by real airmail (even overnight courier if Sophia doesn't see me and reprove me for being extravagant) the King Report or at least a proof copy thereof. It is a research-based book we plan to bring out once a year, examining trends in public communication.

Your comments should be appreciative and affirming.

I will leave McCaw with the final statement.

(He said 'Who's a wall-eyed wanker?' right on cue.)

Thanks again,
Darcy

The launch of the King Report established Darcy King as Sophia King's equal. This was partly design and partly accident. Darcy was dismayed, when reading the bound proofs, to find herself credited as joint author.

'The hell are you at?' she yelled at Sophia. 'When we invented this concept, it was quite clearly part of your persona. I had no part in it.'

'But that was a long time ago,' Sophia pointed out. 'That was when I was working for *Positionings*. The objective isn't quite the same any more. Anyway, you came up with the idea and you wrote at least half of it.'

'But this means I will have to be part of a goddamn launch, filled with precisely the kind of wankers I spend my life trying to avoid, being all sweety-sweety to journalistic jades that are going to say I'm trying to climb on Sophia King's bandwagon.'

'Darcy, you never lost it,' Greg's voice said admiringly behind her. 'Journalistic jades.'

'And that's off the top of her head,' Shari said, coming in behind him with a tray of coffee.

'Shari, would you ever make another mug for yourself and join us. There's something I need to *meitheal* about,' Sophia said. Shari nodded and left.

'What the hell is *meitheal*?' Darcy asked suspiciously.

'Brainstorm,' Greg said, handing coffee to Sophia.

'It's a wonderful tradition from the old farming days in Ireland,' Sophia said. 'When your crop was ready, you sent out the word, and all the neighbours would come, bringing their machinery and their animals. They would pitch in, giving time, expertise, energy. Then they would go away. No money changed hands. But when it was time for their crop to be brought in, you did the same for them. A *meitheal*. Lovely word, isn't it?'

'Hump lovely words,' Darcy said. 'Get back to the point. I'm not Sophia King.'

'You're not? Hell, it's a relief to get that confusion sorted out,' Greg said.

'You know what I mean,' Darcy snapped.

'Darcy, I'm probably in a unique position to know what you mean,' Greg admitted good-humouredly, as Shari returned with her own mug of coffee. 'You are not Sophia King. And furthermore, Sophia King is not you. Other than absolving me of bigamy, I'm not sure where that takes us.'

'I can't do a launch,' Darcy said desperately. 'I can't pretend to be disciplined and happy. I can't say things without bad language. I just work. I just do things. But I don't pretend things.'

'What the hell is wrong with you, Darcy?' Greg looked impatient. 'You prepare people for media appearances. You knock the pretences and the artifice out of them and get them to be real. Real, to the point, vivid. That's all Sophia wants you to be.'

'But say if they ask me tough questions about public relations?'

'Like what?'

'*I* don't know. You're the bloody television interviewer. You think up some tough questions.'

'Darcy King, don't you have reservations about the kind of image-making your sister does for politicians?'

'I probably would have if we did, but we haven't any politicians on our books yet. Come back to me in a year. By then we might have a politician and I can be embarrassed in more detail for you.'

'See?'

'Anyway,' Sophia said, cutting across the impromptu rehearsal, 'that's several weeks away. More urgent is a problem. We have taken on this client that makes knitting wool.'

'Can I go now, teacher?' Darcy asked.

'Why do you want to go?'

'Jesus, Sophia, I don't get orgasms from knitting wool.'

'Nobody does,' Sophia said.

'D'you think we're heading for another of those "I'm not Sophia King" conversations?' Greg asked Shari. 'Because that's what it sounds like to me.'

Sophia became very businesslike. The problem was that knitting was not a skill much practised by people under thirty.

'Women,' Greg said in happy sexism.

'People,' Sophia corrected. 'That's one of the problems. It's an activity defined by age and sex.'

'Female old farts,' Darcy clarified.

Sophia had a number of thematic approaches she was planning to take to this issue, she told them, but she needed some event, some prize, some picture which made people look afresh at the whole concept of knitting. Greg facetiously suggested a picture of fencing champions duelling using knitting needles. Sophia withered him with a look and Shari swiped at him with a notepad. Darcy was silent, pleased with the realisation that the brutal woundedness of Shari was being softened, although Darcy was not sure what precisely the solvent was.

'Come on, Darcy, you're the creative one,' Sophia said anxiously.

'That's one of those self-contradictory statements,' Darcy said resentfully. 'The minute you're told you're creative, you turn to soap.'

'You want something totally unexpected, yet involving knitting in some way?' Greg asked.

'Knitting something huge for the *Guinness Book of Records*?' Darcy thought aloud, then shook her head. 'No. Remind people of the AIDS quilt.'

'Totally unexpected people,' Greg said, implying by his emphasis that he was halfway to a solution. Darcy was filled with a rush of affection for him, and an equal rush of gladness that it was not she who was married to him. His unswervingly sanguine cast of mind would have driven her berserk, she thought. Or even, as her mother used to say, beresk. Sad, Darcy thought. Her mother didn't tend to use those family-formulated terms any more. Maybe, Darcy thought, they were life terms. The terms of a shared life, no longer valid when one of the sharers died.

' – looks as if she's come up with something.' Sophia's voice washed into her consciousness, and Darcy shook her head.

'Sorry. Nothing that would work,' she said.

'I have it,' Shari said, then lost confidence, laughing at herself.

'Go on, Shari,' Greg said, leaning forward.

'Knitting and unlikely people, right?' Shari got them to nod. 'OK. Imagine the front page of the *Irish Times*, six columns across, top of the fold. Picture. Four people. Totally absorbed in their knitting. All well advanced in the making of – oh, very delicate stuff, like baby bootees. You with me? Each one of them a man. Each one of them as near starkers as we can get away with. Each one of them a weight-lifter. Like *huge* muscles and tendons on them, and no body hair: skin shined up with Vaseline. Big, *big* guys.'

'With tiny thin knitting needles,' Greg said, bringing his own big hands near to each other in a fussy fastidious gesture.

'This is quite mad,' Sophia said approvingly.

'My professor might be able to turn up some studies on knitting as a tension-reducing hobby,' Darcy said. 'Look how well he did on the goldfish.'

'Excellent. Offer him a fee to do it quickly,' Sophia said crisply. 'Shari, great idea. Now, in the next three weeks, I need you to find the guys and get them taught to knit.'

'It's only a picture,' Darcy pointed out. 'All they have to do is pose.'

'We can get much more out of this than just a picture,' Sophia said. 'But I need them to be genuinely knitting and able to talk about it. So Shari, find them for me, get them to agree, you know the budget, and get them up to speed with the knitting.'

Darcy headed off to her own office. In the background, she could hear Greg talking.

'Shari?' he was saying. 'On the day of the picture, you'll need the guys to actually weight-lift, so that they're really pumped for the camera.'

'D'you know what I was thinking?' Shari's voice floated after Darcy. 'I was thinking one of them might be a sumo wrestler.'

Darcy went into her own office, laughing. Neasa looked up, puzzled.

'Neasa, be very grateful you work over here in the sane side of the business,' she told her. 'Sophia's secretary has to find four half-naked sumo wrestlers and teach them to knit. All you have to do is teach McCaw to talk clean.'

'Forget *that*,' said Neasa fervently.

'Shut up, now,' Darcy said to the mynah bird as she sat down at her computer. 'I have to compose a letter to the professor who gave you to me to ask him if he's broke enough to come up with data to justify teaching mud-wrestlers to knit. At least I can tell him the Kinsale film was a class job.'

On the day the King Report was launched, even Sophia seemed taken aback by the media response to the book. She briefed Neasa and Shari on who the priority names and outlets were, emphasising that a local radio reporter was not to take up as much time as a national TV camera team. Sophia also briefed Darcy, making no bones about her determination that Darcy would take whatever interviews were allocated to her without argument. Darcy headed into the reception on a deep breath and a prayer. After the third interview she began to be reckless in her truthfulness, and, as a consequence, to hate the experience slightly less.

'Frig it,' she muttered to Neasa at one point, 'at least I'm telling them the truth. I'm not going to like it when I read it, but if they quote me right, I told it like it is. Hump them.'

By the fifth interview, a different worry was taking hold.

'Neasa, could I have a word with you?' she asked, before Neasa could get to the next journalist who wanted to 'have a quick word'. Neasa, looking worried, followed her into the smaller interview room.

'Neasa, where's Sophia?'

'Over in the other room being interviewed, isn't she?'

'Neasa, what's going on?'

'Darcy, what do you mean?'

'I mean that I'm getting to do too goddamn many interviews, of the level Sophia should be doing, that's what I mean. I mean that I'm out there wandering about socialising like a bloody eejit in between interviews, and I've only encountered Sophia once. Now where is she and what's going on?'

'She *is* doing interviews, she's keeping going, mostly – '

'Keeping *going*?'

Darcy was on her feet and halfway through the drink-holding guests at the reception within seconds. Beaming, exchanging one-liners, promising longer chats, be right back, no seriously, I will be back, hang on there, keep me a drink, but moving. When she got into the break-out room, there was Sophia, half-standing, knees bent, hands clawed on the surface of the table.

'Jesus Christ, Sophia, what is it?'

Sophia staggered. Darcy's hands held her at her sides, and Sophia, spasmed by unspeakable pain, clutched her sister's arms so hard, so tight, that answering pain ran up Darcy's shoulders and into her neck.

'Shhh,' Darcy hushed her, as if she had been screaming. But it had been a silent scream, shut off by a throat gripped like a vice, her features in a rictus of clenched agony.

'It's easing,' Sophia said through teeth fenced to keep louder noise in. It came out as one word. Over her sister's bowed head, Darcy looked at Shari. Got a scared shrug as an answer.

'Why's it easing?' Darcy said, trying to get low enough to see into Sophia's face.

'I had a couple of morphine tablets in my bag from my father's prescription,' Shari said.

'Morphine?'

'What else could I do?' Shari said desperately.

'Stop her. Get her to hospital. Anything.'

Sophia's head went back. She began to straighten up.

'Sophia, you have to go to hospital.'

' – hour's all.' Aware that the words were distorted, Sophia pulled her head up and faced Darcy. 'Another hour, that's all,' she said.

'You have no idea what's wrong with you?'

Sophia shook her head.

'It could be anything,' Darcy said. 'It could be a heart attack. You can't stay here. Jesus, what are your priorities?'

'Another hour. Just an hour. Just an hour.'

For the first time, Sophia seemed to realise how tightly she had been holding on to Darcy, and as she released her sister, the blood came back into Darcy's arms.

'Darcy. Go back out. Please go back out.'

'Sophia!'

'I promise I'll be in a taxi in an hour from now.'

'Do you? Really?'

'Shari'll make sure I am. As long as you do any interviews that are left.'

'Listen, I'll dance naked in front of every camera out there if you'll really go to the hospital.'

Sophia linked her arm into Darcy's and walked her to the door with a – to Darcy – dreadful burlesque of camaraderie, laughing at some pretended joke as the two of them were surrounded by friends, by staff and by guests, then sliding her arm out of Darcy's and gently pushing her towards the other side of the big room.

Long afterwards, Darcy met interviewers who complimented her on the material she had given them that night and was embarrassed, not by the compliment but by the fact that she could not remember ever having met them before.

Two and a half hours later, she was in a taxi headed for the Mater Hospital. Oh, yes, a sister said. Miss King. In theatre at the moment. Yes, theatre. Perhaps the best person to fill you in would be her husband? Oh, yes indeed, he came with her, carried her in, in fact, because she was in a bad way, as you probably know – there you are, Mr McEnerney – Miss King's sister. I'll leave you here, would you like tea? Coffee? We'll let you know as soon as . . .

Greg put his strong arms around her and she knew it was to comfort his own grief, and she knew it was grief before she knew what grief it was. After a few minutes, he consciously controlled his breathing, pulled loose from her and, facing away from her, wiped his face with a fierce self-dismissiveness. Don't apologise, Greg, she thought. Please. He walked away from her and leaned his forehead against the cold of the window, dark against the night outside.

When he spoke, his breath misted the window in surges.

'Sophia was pregnant,' he said, and the past tense choked him. 'Ectopic,' he added after several minutes of silence.

'That's in the tubes, isn't it? The baby's not in the womb?'

He straightened up and in straightening up, saw the spot his forehead had misted, now breaking into runnels. Like a child, he brought his jacketed forearm up to it to wipe it away.

'She was in pain last night but thought it was just a bad period coming on. It was bad enough this morning, but she felt she had to get through today.'

'What do they do in situations like this?'

'I don't know.'

'Yeah, you do.'

'They go in and they take it out.'

'But Sophia'll be all right?'

'That's what they say.'

The two of them sat in silence.

'That's what they say,' he said again.

CHAPTER TWENTY-SIX

Darcy King/Dublin
353 1 3782412 20 February 1994 14.40

Alex

Thank you for your gentle comment.

Sophia is back at work. She really is convinced – still – that if you work hard and do good, you can control the world and make it behave. But the bastarding thing *never* behaves. Not only that, but it behaves *least* for the people who try hardest. I mean, the worst outcomes for me from the launch of the *King Report* were:

1 A picture that made me look like one of those inflated figures – Santa Claus or King Kong – you see as advertisements outside shops.
2 A profile that described me as 'the Junoesque twin'.

Yet Sophia, who works like a dog at getting every detail right, is stricken with this horrific pain, keeps working through it, loses a baby and ends up convinced that she is to blame for the baby dying. They tell her no ectopic foetus has ever survived, or could survive, but at some level below intellect, there's a deep-seated conviction that if she had behaved differently, she'd be two months pregnant now. The terrible position I'm in is that I truly feel she should have behaved differently, but I know it had no impact on the final outcome.

What can I tell you that is not depressing and that is of some relevance to you? Me and Greg are still wobbly, Shari still hasn't got over the whole episode. I am looking at my own upper arms as I type, and several weeks later, I have fading yellowed bruises where she held on to me. But Sophia is back in the line of duty.

She's an approach to us all, as my mother used to say of a neighbour.

Darcy

When Darcy and Sophia had planned Sophia's persona in New York years before, they agreed it was important that Sophia should be a good cook, even a gourmet cook, although up to that point, not having much of a personal interest in food, she had made no gestures at learning to cook. Having identified it as an integral part of her persona, however, she had gone to several *cordon bleu* courses and was now a superb cook. This was increasingly useful as Greg and she maintained a brisk social life and also tended to feature in newspaper articles, where Sophia appeared, slim-waisted and ravishing, in colour pictures of her kitchen. Darcy was deeply suspicious of Sophia's kitchen, which always seemed to have a wooden platter of ostentatious authenticity casually in view, containing red and green peppers and aubergines.

'Plus she always has a fruit bowl, and we're not talking common or garden apples and oranges here,' Darcy told Shari, who was slightly curious about Sophia's home scene. 'She always has frigging *star* fruit, for the lova Jasus. I think she polishes her shoes and her peppers each morning.'

Darcy's own kitchen, except after one of her shame-driven fortnightly clean-ups, looked like the aftermath of a visit by a psychopath. Her dishwasher had both dirty and clean dishes in it, mute illustration of her unjustified claim to be able to tell which was which. Her freezer overflowed with Marks & Spencer Danish pastries, Haagen Dazs ice cream and *pain du jour* part-baked French bread. Her fridge was filled with yogurt, leftover Grand Marnier gateaux slices (again from Marks & Spencer) diet 7UP, plastic containers of pasta salad, three-bean salad and coleslaw, paté ranging from the recent to the rancid, the third sandwich out of three-sandwich sets, skim milk, diet jelly, leftover spaghetti floating in cold water, half-tins of tuna, water chestnuts and soup, containers of mayonnaise running the gamut from Trista's full egg-yolk to Heinz no fat, bunches of broccoli, half lemons and – occasionally – money.

Whenever Greg visited Darcy, as he did several times that spring to talk to her about Sophia's unexpressed misery over the loss of the pregnancy, he would always start the encounter by visiting Darcy's fridge, to put himself in good humour.

'Hey, you have five hundred quid in your freezer. Look, it's stiff,' he said during one of his visits.

'Burglars don't look in freezers,' Darcy told him, as if she were intimate with several burglars.

'Like hell they don't. On the other hand, no self-respecting burglar in his right mind would rob this place. Once he saw it, he'd know the best he could do would be get out before cholera and mange struck. Why do you keep biscuits in the fridge?' Greg helped himself, discovering in the process that refrigerating an opened packet hardens them into fossilised dog biscuits. He fought with the biscuit, gnawing it sideways with his molars.

'You're obviously dentally better endowed than I am,' Darcy said, handing him a mug of cappuccino from her recently acquired espresso/cappuccino machine. 'I'm having to have a complete re-boring of my teeth with a very expensive guy in Merrion Square at the moment.'

'Sophia has very good teeth,' Greg said, surprised.

'Sophia didn't spend her youth eating sugar-covered shite,' Darcy said. 'Sophia takes care of her foundations, internal engineering and external appearance like a management company takes care of a good building. She could probably tell you how many grams of calcium she swallows every day to keep her teeth and prevent osteo whatever that thing is.'

'But why do you keep biscuits in the fridge?'

'Mice.'

'Do you have mice?'

'No. But I figure I'm so filthy, I might get mice quite easily.'

'Five storeys up?'

'Mice have no problems with steps. Buns of steel, mice have these days. But the fridge is the one thing they can't get into.'

'You could put them in a tin.'

'That's if I caught them.'

'No, I mean the biscuits.'

'Oh, Greg, don't be so tediously domestic. That's housekeeping. I don't do windows and I don't do housekeeping.'

Greg drank the cappuccino and praised it.

'I'm ashamed of myself for buying that machine,' Darcy told him. 'It's too puke yuppie for words. Also it's not worth the trouble. You have to clean spits of steamed milk off everything within a hundred yard range. Hardened steamed milk has the same texture as refrigerated biscuits. I'm avoiding the main issue, amn't I? Greg, I'm being no use to Sophia. I know she's working away as if she weren't bothered, but I know bloody well she is bothered, yet I can't help her. I've never had this craving, this pining for a baby that she has – that both of you have. So I find myself on the verge of saying that you can both try again, but I know the baby she lost was very real to her.'

'Even though she hadn't known she was pregnant,' Greg said.

'Mmm.'

'Don't worry about it. She's keeping busy and getting on with things.'

'Like what?'

'Well, for example, when I left this morning, there were lined up on the kitchen surface – ' Greg made chopping gestures with his left hand to indicate serried ranks ' – about thirty little Tupperware containers, all ready for single servings of various dishes she knows your mother likes, because she's afraid your mother, without your father to cook for, will live on Fig Rolls and cups of tea.'

The two of them sat in Darcy's buttermilk-papered sitting room and thought of this possibility.

By nightfall that Saturday Sophia duly had the single-servings lined up, labelled and cling-wrapped, brick by frozen brick, in her mother's freezer. They were received gracefully and with genuine gratitude. Greg, who carried the carton in from his new blue Volvo, threw an anorak at Colette and demanded she walk with him in the garden. Colette stepped out into the chill. They stood by the pond while Sophia made cocoa.

'I'm beginning to think you're right about Hannibal,' Colette said. 'He's getting very large.'

'And his companions are getting very scarce,' Greg said, delighted. 'I'll bring him a dozen or so more. Don't want him to end up eating rubbish. Nothing like the nourishment provided by a natty neighbour. Don't go hungry: feed yourself a friend.'

'Consume a companion,' Colette offered.

'Munch a mate.'

'Swallow a sidekick.'

'Chow down a chum.'

'Ingest an ally.'

'Feast on a familiar.'

'Oh, come on, that's reaching a bit.'

'Bet you can't come up with another.'

'Banquet on a buddy?'

A few weeks later, because Greg was filming in Britain, Sophia went on her own to her mother's house with another consignment of frozen food, and found herself, ice-cold Tupperware brick in each hand, looking at a freezer full of stacked bricks from the first set. She wondered aloud why her mother hadn't eaten the meals. Suddenly, a blowtorch of rage spurted from her quiet mother.

'What are you, a yellow-pack meals-on-wheels?' her mother snarled. 'A discount Florence Nightingale? Why'n't you bring calves' foot jelly, while you were at it? You want me to fill in a form for what I eat and don't eat, or do you prefer to keep count personally?'

The second consignment of little meals was taken away, Sophia fighting tears at this sudden onslaught, and sympathised with by Darcy during a puzzled phone call. Darcy felt that the attack was unfair and unlike their mother. Then was shamed by her own post-phone call thought that perhaps her mother might have some right on her side. Sophia did tend to do good deeds in a very conscious way. Darcy fancied that she herself was more instinctive in her generosities.

She was more instinctive in her speech, too, and it was this that brought the blowtorch of Colette's rage to bear on her. Darcy arrived at the house one evening to find her mother tucking a black and white photograph of their father as a very young man into the frame of a more recent colour portrait of him. Encroaching on the sixty year-old-tanned face from all sides of the frame, these days, were little black-and-white pictures of him when he was fifty, when he was forty, and – in this most recently added snapshot – when he was thirty.

'When was that taken?' Darcy asked.

'Ballybunion. A lovely holiday,' her mother said, standing to make tea as if she had provided the time detail asked for. Isn't it funny, Darcy thought, how often we answer the question we're not asked, don't ask the question we should ask, or ask precisely the wrong question. She watched her mother moving around the kitchen, noting that she looked heavier than usual, and, knowing that she was not eating Sophia's bricked-up offerings, looking at her again to see why she seemed bulkier. Colette had two skirts on, the top one shorter than the other. An inch of purplish tweed poked down below the hem of the outer garment.

'What gives with the two skirts?' the daughter asked.

'What are you talking about?'

'The two skirts. You have two skirts on.'

The older woman's hands patted the fabric, identifying the odd double-whispering of linings. 'I was gardening,' she snapped.

'But,' Darcy ventured incautiously, 'I still don't see why – '

Like a hose filling and uncurling to spew, her mother's face was suddenly whipping words out at her. 'You don't *have* to see why. I'll thank you not to come here with your questions and your queries and your interrogation face on you like a Black-and-Tan invading my privacy. If I want to wear twenty skirts, I'll do it and I don't have to justify myself or explain myself to you, you busy, busy, *busy*body.'

Darcy was more mystified than hurt by this attack. She rang Sophia that evening to tell her about it.

'You're not going to believe this,' she said. 'She called me a Black-and-*Tan*, for God's sake. *Mam* . . . Called me a Black-and-Tan. I'm beginning to think the first sign of madness isn't talking to yourself, it's getting blind with rage over sweet damn all.'

The twins then went on to other things, and their mother never mentioned either the Black-and-Tans or the frozen food again. But then, as another summer came around, she mentioned very little, content, when they visited, to have them tell her stories about the phenomenal success of *Image Makers*, about the individuals who were emerging as shining stars on the staff, about contracts won and trips made. It was a great year for the company, and she was glad for them.

The squalls of spiteful rage they knew to be not in keeping with the essence of her, so they re-interpreted them as a final uncharted phase in her mourning for their father. The squalls passed, as did her half-humorous warnings to them. She no longer warned them about the weather, rampant viruses or about the possibility of apparent friends turning treacherous. Because they had grown up with the belief that it is a parent's job to surround their children with an invisible fence of repeated warnings, that it is a mother's job to fulfil the little duties of praise and blame, they found themselves with an unwelcome chilly freedom.

The issue surfaced one day at the office, after each of the divisional heads had reported their quarterly figures. Darcy was particularly happy after this meeting. Her American-inspired emphasis on quarterly reports had, the meeting revealed, saved them from a significant bad debt. In addition, the ex-nun was doing amazingly well with the promotions division. Darcy was ready to go to her own room and feed McCaw a celebratory lump of banana when Sophia, almost formally, called her back. Sophia had formatted the phrase in order to remove all threat from it, so the moment she used it, Darcy felt threatened.

'Could I have a few words with you some time,' she began casually, 'just about non-work things.'

The 'some time' and the 'just' were like hand-strokes on a nervous horse, Sophia believed. Strokes against the grain of the horse's hide was how Darcy experienced them.

'Sure. When? Where?'

Sophia went vague.

'Oh, whenever.'

They met that evening in Sophia's house. Greg was out. Darcy felt he was so proud of his new car that he was probably inventing reasons to be off driving it.

'I wanted your opinion,' Sophia said, drinking her eighth mug of hot water for the day. This regimen she had begun when they were in school and had never given up, believing it contributed to the health of her skin.

'Of what?'

'A granny flat.'

'Where?'

'Here,' Sophia said, nodding to the acre of land that surrounded the big house.

'For Mam?'

'Yes.'

Darcy's mind took off at a tangent.

'Have you told Greg that he might have his mother-in-law living in his back pocket?'

'Greg adores Mam.'

'True. And familiarity breeds contempt. You're not that long married.'

'What's that got to do with it?'

'Oh, come *on*, Sophia. These are the years when you're supposed to be having sex on the kitchen table, halfway down the stairs, standing at the sink, bent over the bookcase and on top of the CD player. You can't do that if your mother-in-law is a real and present witness. Or your mother. Or both in one.'

'Honestly, Darcy,' Sophia said. The knowingness of the dismissal floored Darcy momentarily. Either, she thought, Sophia had already done it in all those places and preferred bed, or didn't do it much at all. She favoured the second possibility, and the instant backwash of guilt at the thought propelled her into positive mode.

'I think it's very generous of you. I think Greg is very tolerant so you don't even have to worry about his reaction. I think you're great to take it on as if it were your sole responsibility. You know, of course, that I'd pay my share. But why?'

'It would put Mam nearer us. More in contact.'

It would also provide the best live-in baby-minder God ever invented, Darcy thought, and felt even guiltier, wondering if she was the only person in the world who supplied a running hostile commentary to every harmless observation made to her.

'The loss of Dad has caused her much more than grief. She's very lost.'

'How d'you mean?'

'All the normal things she's always done – the shopping,

listen to the radio or buy a paper – seem not to matter any more. I was looking in the kitchen presses the other day and it was as if she had just bought *anything*. Three different kinds of jam, yellow-pack tea-bags. Even coffee.'

Diminution of brand loyalty hadn't struck Darcy before as a symptom of loss of enthusiasm for life, but it made perverse sense. If you didn't care which coffee you bought, having always bought one particular brand, then something of the savour of your life must be missing.

'I'm not sure it's Dad's loss, though,' Darcy said.

Sophia looked instantly reproachful, as if Darcy had desecrated their father's grave.

'I know she misses him something fierce, and she's going through all the layers of grief, but I think Mam actually lost her identity when Mandela became President of South Africa. That and the Berlin Wall. Up to then, she had a series of little gestures that made even shopping significant. Like avoiding South African fruit.'

Sophia thought about this.

'Do you remember, whenever we'd be buying books she'd always check where they were printed, and if they were printed somewhere like Czechoslovakia, she wouldn't buy them because it was slave labour.'

'Those enamel bowls and mugs from Poland you should buy once Solidarity won,' Sophia nodded.

'And not buying Heinz tuna until Tony O'Reilly promised they'd stop using those nets that trap the dolphins.'

'She even used to buy yogurts from over the border because maybe buying it would contribute to peace in the North.'

'Do you remember when she paid three quid more for a Moulinex liquidiser than a Krupps one because Krupps had made equipment for Hitler? And never allowing fly sprays because they were made of the gasses they tried out in Auschwitz and if they leaked out the window they'd kill every passing butterfly?'

'Buying soaps and shampoos from the Body Shop because they were into the Third World. And sometimes going to the health food shop because, although the coffee was three times as expensive and tasted like twice-stewed shite, it was bought from some commune of peasants on the side of some Columbian hill and this way, you could be sure they weren't being exploited by some Third Party,' said Darcy.

The two of them sat in joint consideration of this pattern. Neither mentioned that their mother had been an assiduous hunter-out of fats and salts, too, and that the sudden loss of their slender unsalted father from a heart attack was undoubtedly the poorest payoff informed activism had ever had.

'Let me think about it,' Darcy said, trying to inject approval into her voice. Sophia looked unsatisfied, mouth pursed.

Listen, the last time you pulled me into a Good Deed, Dad died in it shortly after it was finished, remember? Darcy thought, and wondered if she loved her sister more when her sister was in trouble. Maybe it was impossible to be an efficiently good person without provoking in others the desire to snap your neck.

The sisters tended to drop in on their mother on different days of the week. Without planning, it just worked out that way. It was unusual that they should both be there the day the final picture went into the frame, joining all the other snapshots around the big, more recent shot of Robert King. The newest picture showed their father as they had never known him, at twenty-four, a reckless rogue of uncomplicated laughter, head thrown back in bright sunlight.

'The way he was when she met him,' Sophia murmured, so as not to be heard by their mother, who was brewing tea.

Darcy looked at the laughing face, the face of a man you'd think might die while axing down a great tree. Not a man to be defeated by a plant bought for ground cover, creeping invasively around the roots of all the other plants. In half-whispers, the twins began to feed the truth to each other.

'Did you notice,' Sophia asked, 'She's stopped calling him

"your father" the way she always used to?'

'That's the reason for the snapshots,' said Darcy. 'She doesn't remember him the way he was recently – the old pictures are the way she remembers him. Knows him, rather.'

She brought them tea and they told her about opening the office in Brussels. How they would soon need to look at the US as more than a market to be occasionally visited by Darcy. How Shari had bought an MG with a spiteful roar to it. They asked her no questions, knowing now that questions harried her.

Darcy and Sophia slowly built an understanding. Colette's memory was going backward, they told each other. Nothing recent was sticking. She was talking of the music and the people of her twenties as if – as if they were not memories but contemporary realities.

'The granny flat idea won't fly, will it?' Darcy asked Sophia one day as they stood in Darcy's office, watched and shouted at by McCaw.

Sophia shook her head silently. Just as well, Darcy thought. Sooner or later, you and Greg will have kids.

'The frozen meals are still there, do you know that?' Sophia asked.

Darcy shook her head, wondering why the sums had not added up sooner. Their mother knew only the past, not the present. It was the abrasive rubbing of the present day that caused her rages. That day they said the name of the disease with dread and certitude. Medical confirmation was almost redundant.

Not only did they know for sure, but their very sureness seemed to speed the dissolution. Colette King's competences fell away suddenly, trivially, like a river going over, not a waterfall, but a weir. What they had once seen as bizarre behaviour options perversely chosen by her, they now knew to be unwilled, unchosen and irreversible. The burbling waters washed away passion and fun, knowledge, belief and essence. Impartially. Promiscuously.

When she began to get lost coming back from the shops with an evening paper bought out of habit but never read, they tried a companion for her. Greg was given the job of selling the idea to her. She knew Greg, now, in the same way that she knew the twins: none of them seemed directly related to her, but they were pleasant familiar people she was glad to see arrive into her home.

Greg and Colette stood at the edge of the pond, looking at Hannibal, who was now eight inches long and the lone occupier of the artificial pool. He had eaten all his relatives. A word game involving 'incest' and 'ingest' suggested itself to Greg, and he was saddened to realise how recently Colette had been able for word games. Now the shadings in an ironic comment either eluded her or bothered her. He talked to her of a companion, and she watched the fish. He could not tell what she was thinking, so talked aloud about her positive response, and she did not contradict him. Within a week, Sophia had a highly recommended woman. Within a month, that woman was gone, Colette unhelped by constant helpfulness, but cabined, cribbed, confined like a rabid dog.

They got her into a specialist home. There were three storeys in it, with patients being moved progressively higher as their condition worsened. Darcy and Sophia, like parents of an honours student, were ludicrously pleased that their mother, for the first year, was on the first floor, the rages now gone and replaced by the innocent joyous charm of a six-year-old. The great sadness of the first year there was that she ceased to know Greg, and, when he visited, was terrified by him, his vividness and size seeming to suck the oxygen out of her. Sophia was concerned that Greg would be hurt.

'Honey, there's bugger-all personal in it,' Greg said. 'Instead of going in there and making her think Attila the Hun has come to terrify her, I'll go once a week to her house and keep it unmusty. Better than leaving

Hannibal in total charge, anyway.'

Neither twin could face the possibility of renting out their parents' house or selling it. Not yet. Not as long as they had enough money to keep their mother in the home. Since *Image Makers* was turning in profits in excess of what even Sophia had projected, money was not their problem.

'I think we'll have to move your mother up a floor,' the matron said one evening as the two arrived together.

It was like a condemnation. But why, they asked. Isn't she grand where she is? What radical disimprovement do you see? The matron sent them mild but astute glances and assured them that no decision needed to be taken *immediately*. Nothing needed to be *rushed*, she said tranquilly, and watched them go to their mother's room.

'I brought you one of your favourites,' Sophia told Colette. 'It struck me that you haven't had bananas for a long time and they were always something you liked. So.'

Darcy kissed her mother's smiling face and her mother, as she now always did, took her daughter's face in both hands and kissed it with a child's ardour. That done, she beamed at the bananas, the bunch bright as a still life on the teak coffee table.

'Go on, have one,' Sophia said, breaking one off and handing it to her. With a smile, half of obedience, half of anticipated pleasure, Colette bit into the skin of the banana.

'Oh, no, no, no, no, *no*,' her daughters said together, and Colette flinched, caught out doing something wrong without knowing why it was wrong. Sophia comforted her. Darcy took the fruit, peeled it, pulling away the long threads that stick, longways, to peeled bananas, and handed it back, nodding. Bite it again, the nod said. It's all right. You're allowed. We'll let you.

Darcy, holding the empty fruit skin, looked at Sophia as if they were colluding in sacrilege and began to weep, her head hanging heavily, until their mother pulled insistently at her long auburn hair to make her admire the half-eaten banana.

'This is the best,' Colette told them, delighted with the taste of it and eager to reassure them and make them happy again. 'This is just the best. Ever. So it is.'

CHAPTER TWENTY-SEVEN

To: alex@antro.missuni.com
From: darcy@imagmak.iol.ie
Tuesday 9 January 1996

Alex

Happy New Year!

Thank you for the wonderful books. You are quite simply the best book chooser in the world. Two of the rooms in my apartment are now completely shelved, and one of my great pleasures is to walk around of an evening, cup of coffee in hand, touching the spines of particular favourites, shifting any that are out of place, and noting just how many of those favourites are gifts from you. I would never have believed that I would spend almost two full days reading a book about viruses, disease and the horrific non-future that seems to face us all, but *The Coming Plague* was just stunning. The weight of it alone must have cost you a ton to ship airmail (is that a contradiction in terms?) but my mother always said one should make no comments on the price of a gift – bad taste – so I won't.

My mother – thank you for asking – is much the same. This thing with her seems to progress, then hold still for a time. She is still mobile and, if not happy, at least not actively unhappy, and they take good care of her.

Sophia – ditto – is playing a blinder. All the year-end newspaper stories mention her and the opening of the branch in Brussels. There's a lot of coverage, too, about the opening of a lobbying division. She's seen in the business community as a very clever, very innovative but very cautious businesswoman, and there has been speculation about floating *Image Makers* on the stock market. I don't even ask her, I trust her that much, and one of her great things is that she trusts me equally. No sign of babies, and I don't ask about that either, since you sent me that information about reduced chances after an ectopic. Greg has put on about two stone (sorry: twenty-eight pounds), but, as often happens with former athletes, has put it on in an even, non-paunchy kind of way, so that he looks, if anything, better than he did ten years ago.

Me? Hold your breath, you might get a whole paragraph for your study in the following. I'm successful, fulfilled and fat. Not flow-over-the-edges-of-seats fat, but fat. Not prolapsed rolls of sinking sludge fat, but fat. I am a great big well-dressed woman on the right side of thirty, 5'11" in high heels, and I walk like I own the world. Magnificent is how you would describe me if you saw me on a good day. (Like a swelling, sagging bloat you'd say if you saw me on a bad day.) Tomorrow morning I have to have root canal work done but, other than that, I'm sound in wind and limb.

I am, however, and this is continuing bad news for your study, single and celibate. I suppose the difference between now and when I decided to pull the plug on Greg is that now being single and celibate is not so easy, because I am well known from TV appearances, mentions in papers and so on. Hostesses making up guest lists think, 'Wouldn't it be smart to match up X with Darcy King?' X is always some willy-wobbling little wimp recently and wisely discarded by a wife, or some guy who's been living with a woman for about ten years and has suddenly decided he looks young, she looks old, therefore he has moved intellectually beyond her. Now and again it's a closet gay, which is a problem, because I cannot say to them in advance 'Relax, I'm not going to start unzipping you before the soup is finished'. I am generally perceived as being ripe, randy and practised.

I learned one thing from Greg. If you tell the truth about sex, nobody believes you. Greg told everybody, including Sophia, that he wrecked the glove compartment of my Volkswagen making mad passionate love to me and that the relationship was never the same after that night. Which is absolutely true, and nobody has ever taken it seriously. Similarly, when I'm asked, whether in profiles or in TV programmes, about my love life, I widen my eyes, hold out my hands and tell the truth. 'I live a life of nun-like purity,' I say. 'No man in a decade, nearly. Sex? What's that? Where do I find it?' They think I'm a riot. One late-night radio guy even had the goddamn cheap nerve to tell his listeners that you only had to look at me to know I was getting it regular.

The fact is that I have all the facilities for a relationship, but no relationship. Hell, I even have a balcony for bonking and no bonkee. Am I *distrait*? Frankly, no. About a month ago, Aileen (remember her that married Beethoven?) rang to invite me to dinner. Much as I would have enjoyed playing with their two kids, who are good gas, I realised I had been through this performance with Aileen before.

'Don't tell me, Mrs Watson,' I said. 'There's a man coming, and you personally think he's one of the nicest people you've met in a long time and you *know* I'm going to love him?'

She was so taken aback it was patently the truth. I told her please not to be offended but I was getting reclusive and liked staying at home. I thought it was pretty civil of me not to add, 'Since you're always whingeing to me that this, that and the other is wrong with Beethoven, why're you so eager to get me into a mated situation?'

This civility availed me nought, because she gave me a little lecture about compromise as a necessity of adult living. It was time, she told me, to realise that Mr Right had been discontinued.

'Mr Right may well have been discontinued, Aileen,' I said before putting down the phone, 'But I'm not settling for Mr Half-Arsed.'

That may not rank with the best of Ben Hecht or Paddy Chayevsky (thanks for the biog of him, too) but it summed up the situation. I get the shudders when I think of what it must have been like in times when women *had* to find a man by a certain age or be regarded as muck. Me, I have so good a life that if I didn't have to think about this every now and again for your purposes, I wouldn't think about it much at all. Certainly, there's the cyclical hunger for sex, but you don't die without it or get warts.

I need to belong but not to be owned. I need to confide but not to be interrogated. I already have most of the things I hear women talking about as important in a relationship with a husband or boyfriend. The missing things are sex (I miss it), babies (although I have yet to have an overwhelming urge or even a medium-whelming urge) and odd conveniences, like tomorrow morning when I come home from the dentist all wibbly from being torn apart, I'd love to have a man who'd help me get clothes off, tuck me into bed and bring me weak tea . . .

I did a computer search recently on all your E-mail letters, which are taking up more and more disk space. I was surprised how much I knew about you, or perhaps I should say, more truthfully, how much information I had available to me about you. What you eat. (Too much protein, probably. You're very carnivorous.) What you wear. (Denim and boots and flannel shirts. You must own a suit, though, for pilgrimages to academia.) What you drink. (Beer, mostly.) What you read. (Too much to cover here.) The music you like. (A very strange mixture of obscure classics, particularly baroque, Gregorian chant – and bluegrass.) I think you're still single although I haven't asked you recently and I suspect you're Republican because you're into guns and hunting. Also, I know your views on some things. Like my sister (Snow White's Stepmother, you wall-eyed wanker) and the kindness of strangers – infinitely preferable, you hold, to the kindness of loved ones, which always comes with strings attached.

I have difficulty adding you up, because of never having had a picture of you (did you appreciate how punctilious I was, sending a copy of the *King Report* with the back cover cut off because my picture was on it?) and also because, having started to report to you when you were very old from my standpoint, I cannot give you an age nowadays without giving you false teeth and a wheelchair. Question: do you have either? Be honest. Are you now totally white/ bald?

I wish I believed in God. Then I could pray before the dentist. Question: do you believe in anything?

Darcy

To: darcy@imagmak.iol.ie
From: alex@antro.missuni.com
10 January 1996

Darcy

Wash yo' mouf out with soap. I am a Democrat. Go do a computer search on my views on Reagan (mental health lack of provision).

I am still single. Bald? No. (You see, you don't ask the right questions. Sometimes, even with a computer search at your fingertips, you don't notice the right answers.)

False teeth? No. However, I do have implants at the front of my mouth where an actor rehearsing a brawl knocked four of my teeth out with the butt end of a rifle. The insurance paid . . .

I believe in lots of things. God? Not much. On the other hand, remember I sent you Paul Monette's book about AIDS? He has a book of essays out now, and one of the statements he makes is to the effect that even if God doesn't exist, we still need 'the people of God'. Lest the questions be one way, think on this: if you could look like/be someone other than yourself, would you?

I should also add that I anticipate terminating my involvement with this study in the near future. Accordingly, I will be coming through to you with a formal disengagement questionnaire in the next week or so.

I will think about you, rather than pray for you, when you're at the dentist.

Alex

To: alex@antro.missuni.com
From: darcy@imagmak.iol.ie
13 January 1996

Alex

Just heading out the door. What the hell are you talking about right questions and wrong answers? I don't have the time to think it out. What the hell are you talking about, terminating your involvement? Like that's it? Stick a sock in it, Darcy, nice knowing you, go be an unbonking blob on someone else's time? Thanks a whole hell of a lot. If this is thoughtful scholastics, I'm glad to belong over here among the autodidacts. You can shove your formal disengagement questionnaire on the highest rafter of the roof of your arse and your poxy parrot with it.

And another thing, aren't you the vain little oul' fella, all the same, with your implants? I'd say implants are rare among tenured academics, maybe as rare as civilisation and courtesy and old-fashioned stuff like that.

I will, however, answer your question about wanting to be someone else. No, and no. Surprises the hell out of me. I must have grown into myself. In which case I have frig-all need for letters on the Internet.

You can, finally, go to hell with your patronising crap about thinking about me in the dentist. Don't bother your arse.

Darcy

Although she was blind with rage, Darcy, as she always did when she had a Saturday morning dental appointment, gave serious consideration to walking to the O'Connell Street McDonald's and having a Big Breakfast, with scrambled eggs, hash brown potatoes and bacon skating around an oval styrofoam plate on their own oil, before walking to Merrion Square. She decided against it, this time, even though McDonald's was open at seven-thirty. It would mean having to clean her teeth all over again, and anyway, there was a special pleasure in eating after the oral anaesthetic wore off, if you had been starving for the duration of the surgery.

In the middle of her rage over the arbitrary termination, it galled her that she had missed some point Alex had made to her in one of his letters. Sometimes, she thought, it was easier to remember what people communicated to you when you could remember the context: oh, yes that was when we were driving through Carna, or that was at the dinner party where the Attorney General was so funny.

Filled with a sense of virtue over passing up McDonald's Big Breakfast, she picked up the newspapers and then, weakened, drove to Grafton Street and tried to read them in Bewley's with a thick white mug of coffee made on steamed milk (pip, pip, pip, three Canderel sweeteners rather than sugar) and a sticky bun with cherries in it. The Internet typeface kept coming between her and the paper she was trying to read. She must, she decided, shake herself loose from it. She must start reading the political columns that filled the Saturday papers, since the political lobbying division was within her area. Politics bored her. Which probably meant she needed to pay it more attention.

She glanced at her watch – the last present her father had given her, the Christmas before his death. Time to get a move on.

Merrion Square was wonderfully easy for parking on a Saturday morning. She took one of the newspapers with her, and, as she always did, enjoyed turning and gesturing with the tiny remote-control gadget that centrally locked her car and armed the alarm system. The car phone she left under the front seat. If somebody rang her in the next couple of hours she would be in no condition to talk to them. On the other hand, she didn't want to leave the phone in clear sight of any passing thief.

As she strolled along the path towards the dentist's building, she noticed a group of people gathered on the path and on the road ahead of her, looking into a big excavation in the road, which was fenced about in a haphazard way with strung plastic ribboning.

On one side, the plastic ribboning was completely torn away, trailing into the hole as if someone had run along the road to win a race and, breasting the ribbon, leaped into the excavation and taken it with them. In fact, as Darcy found when she got closer to the group, it wasn't a person who had breached the plastic ribboning, but a car. Or rather, two cars. She could barely see past the people, but a glance between two of them showed a small sports car and a bigger car tilted behind it. As if, she thought, the big one was trying to mount the other one.

'Who'd be responsible for that, now?

'Nobody in them. Thanks be to God for small mercies.'

'Still and all. You'd do terrible internal damage to a car in a fall like that.'

'Probably the whole chassis bent?'

'Or the frame.'

'Axle cracked, likely.'

'You've got to be thankful all the same.'

'Could've been worse.'

The comments died away as she ran up the steps and went into the building. Hers was the first appointment.

'Did you see the two cars in the hole outside your door?' she asked, settling into the chair and allowing a plastic bib to be tucked under her chin.

'Yeah,' her dentist said. 'Wonder if the owners know or if they're going to arrive this morning to drive away and think, "Oho, someone stole my little MG".'

He approached her with a syringe, and said what he always said to prepare her for his painless injections.

'Just a little pinch, now, Darcy. Little pinch and then

we'll give you the rest of it. You drive a Honda yourself, don't you? You can't beat the Japanese. I drive a Nissan and I'm really happy with it. Really happy with it. Wouldn't change. How are we doing, now?'

She smiled up at him, lopsided with the anaesthetic. As he worked, he would do a wandering patter which allowed response when his patients were capable of it.

This morning, she wasn't. So she let him expatiate on Japanese cars, the infiltration of the American car market by the Japanese, John Updike's novels as an illustration of the changing patterns of that market, the improvement in car safety and how this, particularly the introduction of air bags, seemed to be generating a less responsible type of driving on the part of people who believed themselves to be completely protected from disaster by the new devices.

Occasionally, she made a response.

For the most part, she listened to him like music, seeing again the tiny slice-picture, carved out between two sets of shoulders, of the two cars in the excavation. One trying to ride the other, she repeated to herself. The big heavy car behind. Blue. The smaller car in front and under. Red. MG, he had said, the man looking in. That would be the small car in the front. The big car at the back would be a Volvo, she decided, even though she wasn't good at identifying cars from their shapes. But the big Volvo was so uncompromisingly blocky, like a brick. Built like a brick shithouse. 'Built like a brick shithouse – ' Greg's voice said it in her head, louder than the dentist's patter, and she swallowed the wrong way and began to choke. The dentist and nurse were all concern. No, it was her fault. Yes, she would sip the bright pink water. No, no, fine. No problem. Seriously. Really. No, carry on. Absolutely.

The wind-drill screamed in her mouth. She could still hear Greg's voice. 'A Volvo's built like a brick shithouse,' he had said when he bought it, and given herself and Sophia a laughing lecture about the Swedes reckoning on having seven

Volvos in their lifetime, because the cars were so well-built, so reliable. A laughing lecture, because he knew they knew he had bought it for show, to underline his position, and because they knew he knew what they knew and were in a triangular joke together. The big reliable new car was blue. Greg had asked Sophia to pick the colour and she picked blue.

The wind-scream died away and the dentist began making small-scale, culinary-type gestures, mixing glues and cements on a tiny white plastic cutting board. What was he talking about? Oh about Just in Time and how the Japanese were now being outpaced by other Pacific Rim countries. He was quite an interesting man, she thought guiltily, knowing that normally she interacted more with him, and that her intervals of silence this morning were misinterpreted by him as residual distress from the choking.

She concentrated on asking him questions and in no time was finished. She took a white card with her next appointment and asked the nurse to ring Neasa on Monday, knowing only too well that she would have lost the card by then. She went down the carpeted stairs slowly, trying to order her thoughts. It was now eleven o'clock, and the crowd around the excavation was four-deep on all sides.

She stood behind the group until people drifting away allowed her to get to the plastic ribbon – she was at the side of the excavation where the plastic ribbons were still intact.

One small red MG was directly below her and, tilted up almost as if to present its number plate to her, was the great blue Volvo belonging to Greg. She apologised her way back out of the crowd and got to her own car, sitting for a long time without turning on the engine until someone looking for a parking space spotted her and beeped interrogatively. Yes, she nodded, she was coming out. Yes. Straight away. Nothing to be achieved here. No, no problem. Pleasure. Any time. Call again. The Honda pulled past the crowd at the side of the road and made a left into Fitzwilliam Street.

Such great old Georgian streets, Darcy thought. Such a splendidly central Dublin location to pick for a disaster. The word 'disaster' rattled her with its finality and she realised that, quite apart from the diminishing bruised numbness in her face, she needed to be in her own home. Her car, animal-like in its knowledge of the road, got her there without conscious involvement on her part.

She made coffee and it drove the numbness ahead of it so that soon her face was throbbing but she was afraid to take even an aspirin, for fear it would confuse her thinking. Not that her thinking was that productive. Perhaps if she wrote it down? She sat at the computer and told it to Alex. Seeking no advice. Just parking the problem in the electronic mailbox in the sky for him to look at whenever he happened upon it. Later she realised that she wasn't speaking to him and shrugged the realisation away. Just typing it out had helped her to focus.

Timing. That's what she could look at. She could not do anything about it at the weekend, because the sisters tried to give each other space at the weekend, encountering each other, if at all, *en passant* on visits to their mother. Otherwise, except in dire emergencies, there was a moratorium on visits and phone calls. Dire this might be, but an emergency? No, the weekend would be allowed to run its course. She would visit her mother and feed her, mouthful by mouthful, because Colette had now lost the connection between food and eating. She could not use a spoon, but when something she liked was put in her mouth, would chew and swallow.

It was late on Sunday night before Darcy checked out her Internet mailbox.

> From: alex@antro.missuni.com
> To: darcy@imagmak.iol.ie
> 13 January 1996

Darcy

    I didn't mean that our correspondence would

cease. I hope it will not. My own career path is moving me into a situation where I can no longer follow all the agreed protocols of the study, that's all. I will explain in greater detail when you have time to hear it. In the meantime, please forgive the infelicity of my announcement.

Alex

Darcy and Sophia were having their first cup of coffee at 8.30 on Monday morning in Sophia's office, when a telephone call came from the Fenton Corporation's Snackattack Factory in County Louth. Snackattack was a very recent client. Darcy was glad she did not work on it, because she had no doubt it would add stones to her weight, supplying, as it did, the snack market with crisps and savoury snacks based on carbohydrate blown into strange shapes, brightly coloured and with flavourings sprayed onto them. Darcy's suggested mission statement for Snackattack was '*Cheaper, fattier, saltier brighter greener junk food for all.*'

The problem was very simple, the CEO explained to Sophia. Their biggest British supermarket customer had just found Foreign Bodies in their product. Foreign Bodies? Fried bird-droppings, to be precise. Not unexpected, he admitted, since there were such big holes in the plant roof. He was taking the Delta flight to Atlanta to discuss emergency action with the corporation's president and would appreciate if Sophia went with him. Sophia picked up the overnight case she always kept packed for such emergencies and departed.

Darcy immediately rang Greg.

'Greg, I need to see you.'

'Sure, Darcy, when?'

'Ten minutes from now.'

'This morning? Oh. Darcy, that would be really difficult. I don't want to sound disobliging, but I have this meeting at – '

'Greg, I don't give a shit about you being obliging or disobliging. I am not asking. I am telling. You are seeing me in ten minutes' time. At your house.'

'Darcy, what on earth is eating you? This is so unlike you?'

'Your house, ten minutes' time?'

'Darcy, I don't think you realise – '

'Your house, ten minutes' time?'

'Darcy, I couldn't physically *get* there in ten minutes. I have – I have car problems.'

'Oh, you have, haven't you?' Darcy's voice was silky. 'OK, call yourself a little taxi and make it twenty minutes' time.'

She put down the phone and briefed Neasa on what to do in the face of various possible exigencies over the next hour or so, given her and Sophia's unreachability.

'I'll be back as soon as I can,' she promised, and drove to Sophia's house, sitting outside in her car even though she had a key to let herself in. After a few moments, Greg arrived, signed a taxi receipt and, nodding curtly to Darcy, opened the front door. She walked in after him towards the kitchen, where she sat, he stood. There was no offer of coffee. He was grey-faced.

'How did you know about my car trouble?'

'My dentist has an office on Merrion Square. I had root canal work on Saturday morning first thing.'

He closed his eyes in silent surrender to her knowledge. She waited.

'You saw it?'

'Them.'

He rubbed his eyes as if he was hung over and walked over to sit at the far end of the kitchen table from where she was sitting.

'What do you want me to say, Darcy?'

'How about the truth? I know you and it only have a glancing relationship but push yourself.'

'Shari's flat is in the basement of the house the roadworks are outside of. On Friday night, I went there to – I went there.'

'Oh, don't spare me, Greg. I'm a woman of the world, remember? You went there to fuck her. As per usual.'

'I didn't, actually,' he said with the simple resignation of a man who didn't expect to be believed.

'Not at all. Purely platonic relationship. You went to help her with ideas for photo opportunities.'

'No. I went to break it off with her.'

The silence shimmered and flattened between them.

'Now I see it,' Darcy said, getting up and going to the window. 'Light dawns. Yes, the TV star's car is mounting the little blonde PA's car in a hole in the middle of Dublin. That's the bad news. But the good news? The good news is it's all over – it was just an aberration. Nobody would ever have –'

'Darcy, shut up and listen, would you?'

Darcy looked at him with a hatred that was wasted because he had his hands over his face.

'Just sit down, shut up and listen. I'm not persuading you of anything, because I'm past caring. I'm way past caring.'

'Such a pity Sophia isn't past caring, too.'

'Darcy, I went to see Shari about eleven. I told Sophia I had to check an edited tape so I'd be gone for an hour, not much more. Because I was that sure I was putting an end to it.'

'To what?'

'I'm a shit, I know.'

'This is true. A shit having a cheapo affair. Bit on the side. With his wife's PA.'

'Cheap word, Dar.'

'My name is Darcy. Darcy.'

'Sorry, I didn't know you minded a pet name.'

'That isn't a pet name. It is a diminutive. Nor are you entitled to pet name me, you shit, with your *Cosmo* magazine affair.'

'That's a cheap word that has nothing to do with the reality of what happened.'

'A fuck fest,' Darcy yelled at him, horrified by her own lack of control.

'You don't understand.'

'You could sing that if you had an air to it.'

'I love her, Darcy.'

'Correction. You couldn't sing it. You can't sing and you can't tell the truth. Under pressure, you can't ever tell the truth, can you, Greg? Nice guy in the good times. War breaks out? Tornado approaches? Pyoo – he's gone. Or he's lying like crazy.'

'I *love* her, Darcy.'

'And Sophia?'

'I love her,' he said in the same voice. 'It wasn't just an affair.'

'Now I get it. Affairs are what other shitty little people do. They cheat on their wives and they run around and fuck other women. But Greg McEnerney? No. He – well, shucks, it's just *deeper*, you know? More *real*?'

'Darcy, this girl isn't sexy. Jesus, she sleeps in a sweatsuit.'

'Oh, excuse me, Greg, I may throw up. I'm not sure I need to be reassured about what she wears in bed.'

'All I'm trying to show you is that she's not the sort of person who would set out to have an affair with the husband of her boss.'

'Greg?'

'Mmmm?'

'You're actually right. You're completely right on that. Shari was never in the seduction business. I picked her, remember?'

Greg looked at her.

'When I picked her, I found out things about her that no doubt you've found out since. About her father. About how she cared for her father. You are a sensitive person, Greg, and she probably told you the story, did she?'

He nodded, relieved.

'It's not a pleasant story. Not a story that someone would

present to make them attractive to someone else. It's a story that someone in mourning, a half-destroyed person, would tell. And if she told it to a man, that man would know she should be cared for, at a distance, not exploited when she was most vulnerable. But you moved right in, didn't you, Greg? You sympathised her straight into bed, didn't you? You bet your ass she didn't set out to be sexy. But now you want brownie points for not screwing an obvious tart. Subtlety makes infidelity OK, does it? God, it probably turns it into a form of social work.'

He absorbed this diatribe in silence.

'So, boy meets blonde, boy fucks blonde – '

'Darcy, what's the point of this?'

'I'm trying to get a feel for the situation. As the bishop said to the actress. I'm afraid I don't have the benefit of *family* experience in this area.'

'Oh, *Darcy*, please. I met this girl, I heard Sophia talking about how wonderful she was, I saw some of her ideas. She had to be in contact with me because she'd often be trying to reach Sophia at home. And then there was the time of the launch, when Sophia ended up in hospital.'

'Needed comfort, did you?'

Greg looked at her in a kind of desperation.

'Yes, Darcy, believe it or not, I did need comfort. I was put through the wringer. The danger was that Sophia might not survive, and then the surgery. Realising that it was very unlikely we would be able to have children without major – major – ' his voice trailed away. 'I was lost, yes. I was grateful for any kind word.'

'Let me just check, here. Who was it had the ectopic pregnancy, you or Sophia?'

She knew the pattern of his behaviour the way she knew the melody of a familiar song. That pattern called, now, for a spurt of profane dismissal. It did not come, she realised, because he saw this conflict as the first stage in some kind of negotiation. She could torture him as much as she wanted and he would stay quiet, his eye on the long-term objective. She could torture him as long as she wanted and because he was a man, the words would slide off him. He would even, later on, admire the way, as he would put it, she had 'stood up for' her twin. Darcy took refuge in contemptuous silence. What the hell is the point in arguing with him, she thought. He'll concede where he needs to, he'll tack and weave, confess and confirm. He'll keep prating love for Sophia, helpless admiring passion for Shari and some kind of concern for the common good, which he'll share with me.

Greg talked on. He talked of Shari and her blunt incapacity to seduce, her raw discomfort with duplicity. Darcy waited for him to let slip an implication that in some way Sophia was to blame, but heard only about her beauty, physical and spiritual, her sweetness of nature and how bad this made the situation.

Every 'how could you?' gasp of outrage Darcy might come up with was met on the rise, every 'so you're saying that' accusation was cut off by a baffled unwillingness to come to any judgements about anything. The monotone went on and on.

'Cut all that,' she said. 'Go back to Friday night.'

He nodded obediently. 'I went to Shari's place to tell her it was over, that for all of our sakes it was time to call a halt. She agreed.'

'So why are we not all living happily ever after?'

'Because she's pregnant.'

'Oh, *please*. She sprang this on you on Friday night?'

'No, I'd known – well, no, I don't know. I'd been told about ten days before, but I didn't really believe it. I asked her to go to see Duggan.'

'Duggan?' Duggan was an obstetrician whose name was known because of his involvement in anti-abortion groups.

'Duggan and my dad are old friends. I asked Duggan to see her. To confirm she was pregnant, if she was – '

'Oh, you sacrificed your marriage to her, but you couldn't

trust her to be pregnant when she said she was?'

' – and I thought, because I had done some background advising of his groups – '

Oh, had you, Darcy thought. Had you indeed? You are supposedly an objective current affairs broadcaster, and all the time you're telling anti-abortionists which angle to hold their posters of the dead foetus at?

' – that if she was pregnant, he might persuade her not to have an abortion.'

'Which she'd decided to do?'

'Which she'd decided to do.'

Greg put his hand to the breast pocket of his jacket and took out a small, already opened envelope, with Shari's name scribbled across the front of it. He handed it to Darcy, who pulled out of it one of those small sheets, half the size of normal notepaper, used by doctors. Duggan's name, qualifications and address were printed on the top. In the middle was a scrawl.

'What's this about?'

'Duggan gave it to her so she would have something to show me.'

Darcy grimaced at the theatrically bad handwriting and eventually worked out what it said.

This patient is pregnant. The foetus is approximately 12 cm long. Its heart is beating.

'So what did Shari say, having shown you this?'

'She said she hoped I was satisfied, having put her through the most humiliating pointless process. That she never wanted to see me again as long as she lived and that she was on a flight to London for the abortion on Saturday. I talked to her for hours to try to persuade her out of it.'

'Why?'

Greg looked at her as if she had asked the question in a language with which he was not familiar.

'*Why?*'

'Yeah. Why did you spend hours trying to prevent her having an abortion?'

His hands came up in bafflement.

'Go on, tell me. Is this a moral issue: abortion is murder. Or is it a fatherhood issue: don't do in my son and heir.'

'Oh, Darcy,' Greg said in agonised distaste.

'Which is it?'

He rubbed his face as if her presence and her accusations had somehow tarnished his skin. Then he told her he no longer cared about her judgements of him. He told her about his need to have a son, a daughter – a child. His horror at abortion. For once, she thought, what she was hearing was the disorganised, unrelated yet mutually supporting prejudices that add up to a personal value system.

'Eventually, I began to think it was hopeless, so I went up the stairs – it's a basement flat – intending to go home. Except, when I came out on to Merrion Square, the cars weren't there, and a Garda told me a drunk had come along in a big van and ploughed into the back of my car. He must have been doing a hell of a lick, or kept trying to get out of it or something, because my car pushed Shari's car in, and then the edge of the excavation apparently caved in and my car went in after hers. I explained to the Garda that I owned one of the two cars and he told me what I'd have to do and which Garda station was in charge of the accident.'

'You tell him Beethoven owned the car?'

'My name is on the log-book and the insurance.'

'Shucks,' said Darcy, snapping her fingers. 'What a missed opportunity.'

Greg sat, long past the point of being reached by her barbs.

'And then?' she prompted.

'And then I went back down to the flat to tell Shari what had happened, and we agreed that we'd both have to get the cars the hell out of there first thing Saturday, or as near first thing as we could manage, because someone would quickly spot the reg on the cars and add two and two together. She wanted to sort it out before going to London.'

'First comes love, then comes marriage, first comes logistics, then comes abortion, that it?'

'I didn't get home till half-three, and Sophia was awake. She hasn't been sleeping well in the last few months.'

'So you told her everything,' Darcy said, waiting for the lies he would have told Sophia and their attendant justification.

'Yes.'

'What?'

'I couldn't think what else to do.'

'So you told her.'

'I told her.'

'And?'

'She was very – sad.'

'Sad?'

He refused to be drawn.

'So where did that get you?'

'I told her I loved her.'

'Always a great consolation, that, for the wife in the situation.'

'I told her I loved her and that I would do whatever she wanted me to do. If she wanted me to go, I would go, but I wanted to continue to be her husband.'

'Not surprised. Best of both worlds.'

Again, he sat mute, this time for so long she feared it might be mutiny.

'She accepted what I was saying . . .'

Silence fell again. Oh, come on, Darcy thought. I'm supposed to be running your wife's company in her absence, and a stack of little pink notes saying X called and Y called is probably the height of Mount St Helen's on my desk. Get on with it.

'She didn't want Shari to have an abortion. She said she

413

would be willing to adopt the baby, if Shari was prepared to carry it to full term.'

If that sonofabitch professor was still in official correspondence with me, Darcy thought, I'd tell him *that*. So my sister is Snow White's Stepmother, is she?

'Did you go back to Shari with that?'

'Yes.'

'And?'

'She sent Sophia a letter of resignation. It came by taxi about an hour later. It said Sophia was the best boss any woman could work for, that Shari owed both you and Sophia more than she could ever repay and that she would regret for the rest of her life the pain she was now causing Sophia. There was a letter to me, as well. It was, it was – it was pretty harsh. She said she couldn't believe that I would have told Sophia, that I had wrecked Sophia's happiness just to get guilt off my chest and that I was a shit to be involved with and a shit to be married to. She told me that I believed in nothing and that my so-called principles about abortion were nothing but . . . It doesn't matter. It was quite a short letter, but it – covered a lot of ground. She said she was gone out of the company and out of Ireland as of this past weekend, that Sophia would be able to say "family reasons" which would be true, and that if I ever, directly or indirectly, tried to make any contact with her, I would be very sorry.'

'So by now the abortion's happened?'

He nodded. They sat in silence in the kitchen and church bells rang in the distance. Church bells? Darcy thought about it, then realised that she was never out of the office at noon and that the parish church in the area must be ringing the Angelus. She had forgotten the Angelus, she realised, and tried saying the prayer in her head. Hail something or other? Is that how it began? Or was she putting words in an angel's mouth on the surmise that a newly arrived angel was likely to announce itself with the contemporary equivalent of 'Hi'?

She looked at him. He was flaccid from emotional excess

and sleepless nights. I can see your life, she thought. A life of easy options and scattered victims. A life of pleasant accomplishment, not towering triumph. Trustworthy only in laziness, in going along. You learned what would get you through exams, but you learned none of the elements of greatness. Decent guy. Nice fella. Good company. They will tell each other, as you approach your fifties, that you would have made a great this or that, but they will be wrong. You are all potential without the possibility of fruition. You are all intelligence and warmth without the possibility of growth or learning. Like a holiday photograph. Sunshine on your shoulders.

Without another word, she left the house.

CHAPTER TWENTY-EIGHT

Whenever she went to Dublin Airport, Darcy made a resolution to write to Aer Lingus about the huggies. 'The Huggies' was her mental title for a piece of sculpture on a grassy island just before the car park: squatted figures head-butted in embrace, mother and babe plumping into each other in trusting closeness. Bonding in bronze.

Always the sculpture reminded her of their mother's readiness to nestle them to her as children. Always it grieved her in its reminder that her mother, now, was passing even that point where embrace was a comfort, was unlearning that human connection, retreating to the reptile brain's rules of swallow, stare and sleep. Always Darcy thought irritably that she must write to Aer Lingus and ask them why, when they had such a lovely piece of work, they didn't keep the flowers from growing so high around it, obscuring the shape of it.

'Aer Rianta,' she would say aloud as she stubbed an index finger at the parking card machine. 'Not Aer Lingus.'

Having sorted out which company she should write to, she would then forget about it until the next time. It was, she reflected, just one of the differences between herself and Sophia. Sophia's mental resolutions were never forgotten.

In the arrivals area, a big TV screen was tuned to a cable news station. She sat behind a man who was giving out to his wife about the screen.

'When we were growing up, you came to the airport to look out,' the man was saying, angrily. 'You looked out. There were things to see.'

Mmm, his wife said.

'There were planes and the runways were shorter, so you could see them all.'

Mmm, his wife said again, as if she were a musical

instrument designed to produce this one minor key note.

'The Dakotas and the Constellations. The Constellation – d'you remember the tail of it? The three sticking-up bits?'

Mmm, his wife said.

'Lovely,' the man said. 'Lovely design, the Constellation. Shot flames out of its engine when it started up, too. And the Viscounts, of course.'

At this point, his wife made a peculiar ghostly singing noise.

'That's right,' the man said, turned good-humoured by the memory. 'Very distinctive noise, the Viscount made.'

The two of them sat in front of Darcy, singing the sound of the Viscount engines in such perfect amity that she nearly missed Sophia, who, having only hand luggage, was the first off the transatlantic flight. For a split second, Darcy wasn't sure that the emerging figure *was* her sister. She looked slighter than usual and had the prison pallor of too many hours breathing re-cycled pressurised air.

Darcy found herself walking parallel to Sophia, almost afraid to approach her. Darcy's business-suited figure, long russet cashmere coat thrown over her shoulders, seemed huge in comparison to her twin.

'Would you stand up straight – you'll be bent over by age soon enough,' Darcy said aloud, in their father's voice.

Sophia started, straightened and searched for the source. 'What on earth are you here for?'

'To pick up my VIP sister from the plane,' Darcy said, still walking towards the escalator, but moving closer to Sophia. 'And feed her.'

'Oh, no, I need to get straight to the office.'

'You don't. You need to talk to me.'

Sophia stopped and looked at her.

'Welcome home,' Darcy said gently, and hugged her as if Darcy were an adult and Sophia a child. Sophia held on to her overnight bag and returned the embrace one-handed. Then Darcy was moving towards the escalator, her coat swinging like a regency dandy's cloak, Sophia trailing.

'You find a table,' Darcy said over her shoulder as they reached the restaurant floor. 'I'll bring the food.'

'I don't want food.'

'Yeah, you do. Probably didn't eat all day yesterday.'

When she arrived at the table Sophia had chosen, Darcy was carrying a tray with a mug of black coffee, a mug of cappuccino and one full Irish breakfast.

'I never eat that kind of food,' Sophia said, examining the sweaty fried tomatoes bursting blowsily out of their wrinkled skins.

'So experiment,' said Darcy, throwing her coat over the back of the third chair and appropriating the cappuccino. 'Learning to manage change is the biggest challenge facing today's managers. It said so in one of yesterday's business supplements.'

Overhead, a voice announced the final call for a flight to London, naming two passengers who were advised that the plane was ready to take off.

'That's why this table was free,' Sophia said, stricken. 'People must know it's under a loudspeaker.'

'Don't worry about it,' Darcy said. 'Think of it as punctuation.'

Darcy drank her coffee. Sophia ate some of her egg. The announcer got testy with the two passengers who had failed to see the error of their ways.

'Hard at it behind the duty free, they are,' Darcy said.

'Who?'

'The two that won't board Flight whatever it is.'

'It's great that there's no mandatory stopover at Shannon any more,' Sophia said, determinedly bright and positive. Hell with this, Darcy thought.

'I know about Greg and Shari.'

Sophia collapsed as if the statement were a blow.

'Good,' she said eventually.

'Why good?'

418

'You'll be able to help me to do the right thing.'

One for sorrow, two for survival. That the new version, Sophia, my sad sister?

'There's a letter of resignation for you from Shari.'

'Greg didn't reach her before she went?'

'Nobody did.'

'Oh dear.'

'Oh dear, nothing. What the hell was wrong with you, Sophia, to offer to adopt the kid?'

'Greg should have children,' Sophia said wearily, 'and I won't be able to have any.'

'That's not definitive.'

'Definitive,' said Sophia, rejecting the word with the disappointment of a drowning swimmer handed a lead weight.

'Why don't you get the hell rid of him?'

'He's my husband.'

'So?'

'I'm committed to him, whatever his flaws are.'

'Oh, Sophia, don't give me that shit.'

The loudspeaker overhead broke into speech again.

Sophia gestured Darcy to silence as the announcement finished, listening to it with hushed attention.

'What's so important about a no-smoking ad?'

'Just the voice.'

'D'you know him?'

Sophia shook her head.

'No. I think it's the guy who used to do the Nuacht. He reminds me of someone, that's all. Connemara Irish.'

Darcy considered pursuing this, then decided against it. Life was complicated enough.

'Darcy, what do you think my alternatives are?' Sophia asked.

'Leave Greg. Kick him into Kingdom Come.'

'And?'

'Start again with someone else.'

'I don't want someone else.'

'Then start again on your own. I can recommend it.'

'I would be lonely.'

'*What?*'

Sophia smiled at her sister.

'I'm a twin, remember? I'm used to having someone around all the time.'

'I'm a twin, too, but I can do a solo performance without panic attacks.'

'You might have to give me lessons.'

'But have you even *looked* at the alternatives to staying with him?'

The minute she had the question asked, Darcy realised how ludicrous it was. Sophia would have – perhaps on paper – listed the pros and cons of each possible course of action. Factored in duty. Counted in obligation. Added idealism and concern that in some way this might affect the future of the company and of her sister. Concern, too for Greg's career. Care for Shari.

'Darcy?'

'Yes, Sophia?'

'Darcy, I spend my life doing the best I know.'

'I've never doubted that.'

'The best I know doesn't seem to work very well. But the best I know is all I can do. I can't decide to do something less.'

The aggressive female announcer filled the space between them as Darcy thought about this, recognising its truth. Most of the time, Darcy did *not* do the best she knew, distracted from her failings by a windmill of rage, reproach or self-mockery, yet she was unscathed. Sophia was scathed. How's that for a new word to learn, Sophia, Darcy thought. As in hurt unfairly, as in scarred and scored by your sunshine boy's defection from what you dreamed him. Like our mother said, you love them when you are young for what they are going to be and you love them when you are old for what they were – or what you thought they were.

The Irish language no-smoking announcement came on again, and Sophia sat looking into space, eyes glazed. Darcy watched her, filled with a great hopelessness. You will not yield to dramatic diatribes as I would, she thought. You will not let anyone know about your suffering. You will surround yourself with the business of each day, my sister, she thought, and a million little obligations and attainments will turn the raw hurt in your soul into a criss-crossing of little scars.

'He will leave me, you know. In time. He will.'

The two of them were transfixed by words one of them should never have said. Because prophecies must be fulfilled, Darcy thought, and now they would both watch for it, and in watching, they would guarantee.

'He will leave me.' The repetition came with certainty but no sadness, no self-pity.

'You're just going to wait for it to happen?'

'I will work hard to prevent it.'

'Jesus, I need more coffee,' Darcy said. 'More coffee for you?'

'No, I'm dehydrated after the flights. I would like a glass of water, though.'

She watched Darcy, standing in line to pay, giggling with a fat schoolgirl about whether they would be wicked and buy flapjacks or behave themselves and drink black coffee. You see, Darcy, Sophia thought, that's the difference between us. You are sunlight bouncing out from behind a cloud, ready to shine on anything, and I'm like a stone. A small, perfect stone shaped by sand into smoothness. But cold and isolated with no internal way of warming. Cold with an illusion, every now and again, of the hope of permanent warmth, when a big sure personality shines on me. Like my father. Like Ruaidhrí. Like Greg. Like you, Darcy. A stone can't shuck its shadow, Sophia thought. You want me to get rid of the things you see restricting me, but I need them, Darcy, I need them. I need the bright circling warmth of Greg.

Until he leaves me, I will absorb the radiant heat of him.

Darcy put a tall paper cup filled with water in front of her and Sophia drank it in silence.

'Being with Greg is like being in Florida in January,' Darcy pronounced. 'It's so warm and sunny, you have the secret conviction that the weather must be good everywhere and that people at home are being sort of hypochondriacal when they whinge on the phone about black ice and downpours. When you're with Greg, it's difficult to imagine – '

'Death. Or loneliness,' Sophia supplied.

'So he just gets away with it?'

'As opposed to what?'

'As opposed to being forced to face up to the consequences of his actions.'

'Gosh, Darcy, you sound like Dad.'

Buffeted by the truth of it, Darcy stood again, her back to Sophia. Her hands were on the railing at the edge of the restaurant.

'Darcy, *you* forced him to face the consequences of his actions in the Volkswagen.'

'What actions?' Darcy asked, not turning around.

'Who knows. What does it matter?'

'It's not the same.'

'Of course it's not the same. But it's probably all of a piece. People change very little,' Sophia said.

'They should.'

'But they don't. You and I haven't.'

Darcy turned at the rail.

'Sophia,' she said slowly. 'I've just realised what you're trying to do. You're trying to make *me* resigned to *your* problem.'

'Well, I already am resigned.'

'How can you be? Why should you be? Jesus, there's nowhere you can't go, nothing you can't do.'

Sophia began to search in her wallet and handed over a credit-card sized piece of cardboard with print on one side.

'It's the alcoholic's prayer. Mam told me about it years ago, and then I came across it in that shape. I thought it would be nice to have it so handy.'

Darcy handed it back as if it were burning her.

'That makes it worse,' she said. 'That makes it worse. Sweet living Christ, you're not thirty and you're saying prayers of fucking resignation because you're married to a fraudulent fart who should be – should be – '

'Punished?'

'Yes, punished. Or got rid of. Instead, you're going to run up white flags and keep prayers in your wallet, letting on to be Miss Dynamic Happiness.'

'And running one of the most successful businesses of its kind in Europe.'

Sophia carefully put the credit card prayer back in her wallet.

'When I compare my life to so many other people's lives, I'm blessed,' Sophia said. 'Nobody has any right to hope for fairytale happiness.'

'You win some, you lose some?'

'Precisely.'

Maybe when I'm older I'll agree with you, Darcy thought. Maybe the decades will teach me the habit of concession, the ritual of dignified retreat. But I'll not learn it from you now, Sophia. I am too young.

'I think I was always older than you,' Sophia said.

'Yeah. By nine minutes.'

'There is a lot to be said for duty and detail,' Sophia said.

'You sound like the bloodywell Seven Dwarfs. Heigh Ho, Heigh Ho, it's off to work we go.'

'What on earth made you think of Snow White?'

Sophia began to gather her belongings and Darcy, reddening with guilt, was happy to assist her. What made me think of it was the fact that my elderly academic called you Snow White's Stepmother before he announced he was pissing off into the wide blue yonder, she thought.

'By the way,' she said as they got on to the escalator, 'Centurion, the film company, have been on. They're insisting on meeting me, I have no idea why. I suppose I have to?'

Go on, Sophia. Back up there into the boss role. Give me orders. Encourage me. Motivate me.

'But that's terrific. Of course you should meet them. They're making a film in Wexford, aren't they?'

'Wicklow.'

'Wicklow. I saw a picture of Michelle Pfeiffer on a sheepskin rug or something like that.'

Darcy found her car without difficulty and paid the parking fee.

'Darcy?' Sophia said.

Sophia, please don't tell me that if I had got a receipt the company would have paid the four quid.

'Sophia?' Darcy said.

'It will be all right,' Sophia said. It was a question pretending to be a statement.

'It will be better than all right,' Darcy said. It was a glowing lie.

'You'll drop me at my house?'

'You might have to pay extra,' Darcy said.

'Sorry?'

'If I'm hobnobbing with film directors, I could start getting uppity,' Darcy said.

'That's true. On the other hand – ' Sophia said.

'Yeah?'

'If I commandeered Neasa, you wouldn't be uppity for long.'

'I wouldn't be able to shagging well find uppity, you're right. McCaw and me would have to fly into the sunset together. McCaw, by the way, is moulting.'

'That makes two of us,' Sophia said.

CHAPTER TWENTY-NINE

To: alex@antro.missuni.com
From: darcy@dub.imagmak.iol.ie
Friday 19 January 1996

Alex

How I have found the time to fill out the
enclosed terminating questionnaire I do not know,
given the awfulness of this week. I cannot understand why there should suddenly be a deadline on
this bloody thing so you must have it this week.
This 'rite of passage' as you call it. You could figure
what I would call it.

It follows. As does an account of the weekend
and of Monday, may I never live through another
such. May Sophia never live through another such.
May Greg get gangrene of the gonads. May he get
halitosis. Tinnitus. Anything which is personally
inconvenient, humiliating and chronic but which
does not turn him into a dependant on Sophia.
Furthermore, now that I think of it, I know damn
well at the time that all your official non-judge-
mentalism when I had the Volkswagen episode with
Greg was concealing your thinking that I was way
over the top in my response. What had he done
but snitch someone else's name to cover his nakedness. Well, *now* you know. Dishonest sex-shittery
is a lifelong ailment like cold sores, just waiting for
the right opportunity to make a comeback, take its
show on the road again. She is right, Sophia is.
When he has a publicly saleable reason, in about
ten years' time, he will grow to believe in that
reason, then persuade her to, then leave her, finally
have kids and probably be a good father.

I, meanwhile, am forced to meet Head-the-Ball from Centurion Films. Darcy doesn't want to meet Head-the-Ball, whoever the nameless fart is who is directing this film out among the Wicklow sheep.

When you come off the study, will you still be on the Internet?

Darcy

> To: darcy@imagmak.iol.ie
> From: alex@antro.missuni.com
> Friday 26 January 1996

Thank you for both documents.

Yes, I will be on the Internet.

Alex

As Darcy turned away from her computer, Sophia came into the room, almost glittering with gaiety.

'You never told me who wanted to see you from Centurion.'

'I didn't pay attention to the name,' Darcy said.

'Brooke Stone,' Sophia supplied.

'What about him?'

'He's the guy you're meeting.'

'I'm meeting the director.'

'He's the director.'

'He's one of the stars.'

'He's directing it too, like Jodie Foster does.'

'And Redford,' Darcy thought, wondering who had first pointed that out to her. Alex, she thought. So many of her references looped back to him, a stitchery of ideas coiled in primary colours through the open-weave canvas of her life. Without the basis for the correspondence, the structure would not hold, Darcy thought. There would be great gaps in the weave, distorting the occasional stitches.

'Imagine meeting Brooke Stone,' her secretary, Neasa, said reverentially, coming into the room behind Sophia.

'Imagine Brooke Stone demanding to meet Darcy,' said Sophia, determined to find a business or personal benefit beyond the imputed pleasure of it. 'Aren't you thrilled to be meeting him?' I must be glad, Darcy thought, because Sophia's bubble is nothing now but drips on the ground, iridescent with might-have-beens, and I must help her in the distraction of herself. As she would with me, if she knew what I have lost. Though what I have lost cannot compare with her loss. Mine is not fleshed and real, familiar-scented in a bed at night. What I have lost is just an electronic penpal, and the loss will be gradual, a tapering off.

She looked at McCaw's vicious small face. The bird was talking to her all the time but she wasn't hearing him.

'I know who I am,' she said to him quietly when the others had gone. 'I know where I'm going. This will get into context.' The breath wobbled out of her in a sob, and she blinked to prevent tears. 'But I'm entitled to a few minutes of great loneliness,' she told the now silent bird. 'Because I have had a companion. A companion. Someone always looking out for me. Someone to try ideas out with. A companion. No more than that. Not even that, probably. I'm twenty-seven years of age and – oh, McCaw, I am bereft. I am bereft. God, isn't this just so stupid.'

To: alex@antro.missuni.com
From: darcy@imagmak.iol.ie
Friday 26 January 1996

Alex

I'm going to say this once, so listen up good. (As you would say yourself.)
1 I don't believe the correspondence will continue.
2 I will miss you. Thank you for your companion-ship over the years.

Now, mark my card about this bloody actor you worked with, Brooke Stone. I have to meet him today. I will hate every minute of this meeting but

427

it would help if I knew where he was coming from. They've put profiles of him and interviews with him in front of me and he sounds a rough intellectually arrogant hardchaw. No sucking-up to journalists – half the time he seems to be stretched by the effort of being merely civil. Jesus.

?

Darcy

To: darcy@imagmak.iol.ie
From: alex@antro.missuni.com
Friday 26 January 1996

Darcy

Sorry not to have come back to you before now – I know you must be just about to go meet him. You'll be fine.

Talk to you.

Alex

'You know what you are, Alex my professor former friend?' Darcy said to her home computer screen, having read this communication at seven that night. 'You are a meat-faced shit-head. That's all there is to it. If I had the time, I would tell you what you could do with yourself in letters a foot high, or as high as they would let me go on the Internet. But I do not have time, so get stuffed.'

The apartment doorbell rang. Darcy gave the finger to the computer, squared her shoulders and opened the door.

He was lying up against the door frame, a tall big-shouldered rangy ease of a man, with an impact to him not vested in good looks, because this was no regular-featured glossy smoothness but a weathered face textured as tree bark.

'Darcy.' Brooke Stone said this as if confirming a Bill of Rights or an international treaty.

Darcy's hand went to her mouth to squash laughter. It spilled out sideways and he waited, eyebrow raised.

'I'm sorry. I'm not often addressed as if I were the United Nations in general assembly. Also you wear a wig on screen. Plus you're a lot taller than I expected.'

He said nothing at all, draped up against the frame of the door, looking at her as if she had to be learned. It was discomfiting and took the fun out of her. In punishment, she didn't invite him in. She stepped past him and locked the door. He ambled after her and pushed the button on the elevator. Stood in easy silence, watching her. She could not, she decided as the elevator arrived, tell him to stop watching her, because that was what people did when they first met. Bad enough to tell a man you noticed his sparse hair without telling him that a quality of attention which probably was very flattering to most women unnerved you completely.

He put a hand under her elbow as they came to the six steps down to the courtyard, and she was minded to be civil about it.

'Thank you,' she said. 'These shoes are difficult.'

'Yeah,' he said. 'Whore's shoes.'

He opened the door of the Mercedes for her, and she got into the car in a state of bemusement. She always described herself in media interviews as wearing tart's or hoor's shoes, but to have them so described by a total stranger was unexpected. He drove, which surprised her (she had expected a film crew driver or a taxi man), and clearly had decided where they were going. She laughed, and he looked at her in question. The pitting in his face was more pronounced than on screen. He looked as if someone had chipped at him with an ice-pick, and then dragged a forefinger to sharpen his temples and cheek-bones.

'I've never had a stranger describe my shoes in that way before,' she said. 'I suppose you don't meet many women who blurt out rude comments about your hair?'

He shook his head and grinned at her, his face no longer severe but lit with humour.

'They usually tell me I'm *more* sexy in real life,' he said, his voice lifting an octave to indicate a woman's tones. 'Took me a while to realise that was PR-speak for Jeez, you're bald, whyncha wear a rug?'

She laughed and imitated his imitation.

'Well, *whyncha* wear a rug?'

'Whyncha wear sneakers?'

'Out to dinner?'

'Or low-heeled pumps?'

'Because I can't stand the shaggers.'

'There you go, Ma'am.'

'You wear a rug in movies, though.'

'Not always. Not in the one I'm making right now.'

'Why not?'

'Because I'm the director, too, and the director doesn't see no reason why my character should have a slew of hair –' he thumped the thin hair above his forehead, ' – so I don't got to wear a rug. Or a slidin' roof.'

'I thought it was only in Ireland we called them sliding roofs.'

To this, he did not respond. There was silence in the big car for several miles.

'Play pretty hard to get, don't you?' he asked then.

'Oh, they told you I was trying to get you to meet my sister?'

The car stayed on the sea road.

'Several times.'

'My sister is the person who's really in charge of *Image Makers*,' Darcy began.

'I've read about her,' he said, and the finality of it, the tone of 'let us not waste time on your sister' rankled with Darcy. She stayed silent as the car drew up to the restaurant and someone came out to park it. Hand under her elbow again, he led her up the steps, past the big potted palm, shook his head when asked if they would like to go first to the bar, and walked her through the restaurant. It was as if he were consciously presenting her to the people in there, his identity on show purely as a device to serve and display her. As if he were a prop. As if she were the famous one. This, she thought, might be because normally he *was* escorting very famous women and had got into the habit of submerging his fame.

The Danegeld was one of the city's best seafood restaurants. It was situated in a series of old terraced houses so to get to the more private areas, you had to walk through other rooms filled with diners. A few greeted Darcy by name and she twinkled her fingers at them, moving faster with each recognition. But as each table was passed, there was a sudden hush in the sparky talk before a rush of conversation flamed up in their wake. Listening hard, she could hear her companion's name in mutters and whispers.

The hostess took their coats and seated them. 'Tonight, Ms King, we have the most splendid scallops and also very good oysters. Oliver will be along in a moment to give you the details.'

She nodded to Brooke Stone and disappeared.

'I know this is going to sound naïve,' Darcy said, opening her menu, which was the size of a children's picture book, 'but I had no idea you were that famous.'

He smiled at her and she was glad that he did not play modest and ask her to define 'that famous'.

'Evidently, my value has gone up here tonight,' she added.

'You don't like that, do you?' he asked.

She put down the menu. 'It's not, actually, that I don't like it. I suppose I've never needed it. We're well known among the people we need as clients. We don't need to socialise with the famous. Mostly, when we go out with the famous, it's because we've made them famous.'

Oliver arrived. Darcy and Oliver were old friends. Oliver's life was an exquisite tension between three things: his emphysema, his weight and his love of his job. The first two, in combination, made him monosyllabic. His utterances were carefully planned and tended to sound like ultimatums, rather than invitations.

'Ms King,' he said now, leaning heavily on the back of the spare chair at their table. 'Mmf,' he added by way of a greeting to Brooke Stone.

'Good evening,' said Brooke Stone respectfully.

Oliver, who had launched himself on his next speech-instalment, stopped and hated Brooke Stone for a moment, having banked on the silent nod he usually got from men.

'Scallops, tonight – excellent.'

Darcy nodded appreciatively.

'Sole – very good.'

Oliver sucked air, his tuxedoed shoulders up around his ears with effort.

'Almandine, or grilled with herbs and butter.'

They waited.

'On or off the bone.'

Darcy nodded. Wisely this time, by way of a variation.

'Superb lobster.'

Darcy glanced at Brooke Stone to see if lobster met his fancy. He was watching Oliver with a peculiar intensity.

'Thermidor. Or – '

Oliver's ruddiness darkened, challenged by his failure to finish a sentence before needing more air.

' – steamed and served with drawn butter.'

The head waiter lifted one hand off the back of the chair and kissed his thumb and first two fingers. Back went the hand. Up went the shoulders. In sucked the breath.

'Also have brill.'

Dispensing with the possessive made sense, Darcy thought. She knew who had the brill. Unless Brooke Stone was dumber than he looked, he, too, could figure out who it was that had the brill.

'Crabs. Small.'

Oliver produced a pad and a pen.

'More time or – ?'

'No, no, I think we're ready to order now,' Darcy said

432

recklessly. She would kill this big American if he made Oliver do another journey. The head waiter looked at the actor. The actor looked back and a strangely collusive smile creased up his uneven face.

'You know something? She's been here before. So if she went first, I could follow her choices slavishly, couldn't I?'

'Indeed you could,' said Oliver, delighted to be asked a question that could be answered in three words.

'Sir,' he added generously, on the next breath.

'OK,' said Darcy, 'In that case, we're starting with the crab salad and then having the sole almandine and we will have a bottle of your 1990 Savennières.'

'Excellent,' Oliver said, slapping his notebook closed. Darcy watched his back view as he walked away, shoulders up, elbows out as if to give his ribs more room to expand.

'You were studying him,' she said dispassionately. 'You were studying him so that you could play someone like that some day.'

'I wasn't, but I could see why you'd think I was,' he said comfortably, filling their water glasses. 'Whatcha want me to do, anyway, form a support group?'

The response was so unexpected and so frank it made her laugh.

'You picked my favourite restaurant in this whole city,' she told him. He seemed unsurprised and unimpressed, and she went back to not liking him.

'OK,' she said, leaning her elbows on the table and nudging the cutlery out of her way. 'Why are we here?'

'To talk. To eat.'

'Well, I didn't think you were overwhelmed by lust for my body.'

'Didn't you?'

'*My* body? With Michelle Pfeiffer starkers, or as near as dammit, on a bearskin on the floor in front of you?'

'Sheep.'

'Sheep what?'

'Sheepskin. Not bearskin.'

'Look, friend, I don't *give* a shit if it was freshly tanned mountain goatskin, let's get back to what we're here to discuss.'

He grinned at her as if what she had said were a compliment to him, and she began to feel that she was at a tilted angle to the communication. That she didn't know the rules of engagement.

The *commis* waiter arrived with their crab and offered different kinds of mayonnaise. Also brown bread. Also hot rolls. Also lemons. Darcy began to get desperate that no matter how decisive she was, this earnest white-faced kid would come up with yet another possibility. As he finally retreated, reversing rather than walking normally, she wrinkled her nose at the actor in dismissive puzzlement and apology.

'Ever strike you he might want a look at me?'

Darcy looked after the boy and discovered him peeping furtively around the kitchen door for one last look at her companion.

'No. Quite honestly. It didn't. D'you get a lot of that?'

'Of course.'

Darcy began to eat the crab, smothered in mayonnaise. The hell with fats for tonight. Her bile ducts were going to encounter a tidal wave of fats. Or was it the gall bladder that was endangered?

'I'm surprised you still notice, then,' Darcy said.

'You must remember I've only been a star for about six, seven years. If that.'

'You must remember,' she said, pointing half a roll at him. 'You must remember that not all of us spend our lives going to the movies.'

'Meaning?'

'Meaning I've only seen you in one film. Maybe two. I saw you in that Kinsale thing and – '

He named the other film she was likely to have seen and she nodded.

'So I'm probably not whelmed enough by having dinner with Ay Star. Ay Megastar.'

'Star. Not megastar. Actor, mostly.'

'Also rough-edged, take no prisoners, obnoxious git to every passing journalist, if the profiles I've been reading are anything to go by.'

He put down his cutlery and laughed. He had an uncomplicated laugh. Not a performer's laugh. Not a see-how-amusing-you-are-to-me laugh. Just a laugh.

'I assume this is a carefully crafted persona?' she asked.

'Like your sister's?'

'Oh, you read profiles before you meet new people too?'

'No, I don't.'

'Read profiles?'

'No. I don't craft my responses to journalists as part of a planned persona. I get impatient being asked the same questions. I guess the impatience shows, so that gives them the angle: arrogant intellectual.'

'You don't seem to have the need to be loved,' Darcy said to him.

'*Loved?* By journalists? Who'd want to be loved by journalists?'

'Most of my sister's clients. Business people. Politicians. Captains of industry. Yeah, they want to see themselves positively interpreted in print, but the first objective is to make this journalist *understand* and like them. You can see them plying the journalist for clues as to what the journalist would like them to be and then setting out to be it.'

The wine was good. The food was good. Darcy was finding this dinner the way she found exercise on the odd occasion she tried it out: much more pleasurable than anticipated, but fraught with a contradictory conviction that she should be doing something more to the point, somehow.

'You already have an image, as is patently obvious. So what are we here to talk about?' she asked him abruptly.

'The truth. Maybe.'

She looked at him. 'Life, the universe and everything?' Her voice was weary. I know these old lines, it said. I know them without ever having heard them before. I know and I resent and there is at least another hour I have to bear before I can get the hell out of here.

'Well,' he said, sounding as awkward as if she had spoken all her thoughts, 'Well, maybe we'll leave the truth for a bit. Tell me, first, how long an image lasts?'

'A person's image?'

He nodded.

'Same as a generation. Seven years. Every seven years you have to reinvent yourself. Image obsolescence in people happens because they think the first image they have is the defining one. So you get a politician who becomes famous when he's an open-faced, uncomplicated, zestful boy-next-door, and fourteen years later, he's still peddling open-faced uncomplicated zestful boy next door and he's dying on his feet. Working hard at the gym, dyeing his hair, using the same little phrases that were so endearing back then. The terrible problem is that not only do people not like the reheated version of what they once liked, but they revise their memories and decide they never thought that much of him in the first place, which means they don't have to feel they've betrayed someone.'

'Revisionism,' he said, nodding. 'The weeks after JFK was shot, a whole generation of American voters revised their personal truth. Decided that they had voted for him in the election against Nixon. Jeez, if he'd had all the votes he was subsequently credited with there'd have been a landslide. Similarly, people afterwards credited themselves with voting for Roosevelt during the Depression, but most of them didn't. Most people's mental health is directly related to how much they can reinterpret themselves to fit changing realities.'

Darcy was silent, thinking about Sophia, who was so resolute in not reinterpreting herself, whose gaze was to a perfect future and whose imperative was self-improvement, in the face of all setbacks to this theme. Brooke Stone watched her tranquilly until she shook herself slightly and tried to rejoin the stream of thoughts.

'The thing is that in real life, you can get away with a lot. Your kids may find you tedious because you sort of wind around and around what you were when you were twenty, but they're *your* kids, so what the hell, they have to at least tolerate you. Or they should, anyway. But if you're very public, if you're a TV personality, you can get locked into a public perception.'

'Do you ever get people who *don't* get locked in?'

'Yes. Unexpected people. People who have no need for a "public" performance at all, so they can grow without being force-grown for display. Or people who are curious. Speculative. Intellectually speculative. People who don't need other people. If you don't need to be liked, you have a freedom that is fantastic. If all you need, at the most, is tolerance – the uninvolved toleration of others – the "kindness of strangers", you are – '

Darcy's hand sketched wind-blown flight in the air and he looked at her without moving. She glanced away from him, eyes narrowing with irritation at herself for how much she was talking, and how much she suddenly wanted to say all the stupid things people tended to say: 'I don't know why I'm telling you all this, I don't usually talk so much.'

'You've talked enough for a while,' he said. The craggy pitted face was serious and filled her with an unexpected dread.

'You're going to talk, and you're going to be *very* serious,' she said, desperate to lighten the mood, unsure whence came its heaviness.

'I am,' he said. A waiter came within five feet of the table and suddenly the actor's hand was raised. Six inches, but a threat, a refusal. Daunted, the waiter retreated. Why am I afraid, Darcy thought. This is ludicrous. This guy isn't a client. I don't know him. I owe him nothing. He has no right to make me fearful and he's probably doing it as some kind of actor's mind-game. She met his gaze with a rage-filled defiance that said, I can walk out of here, right now, try me. Watch me.

'I want you to marry me,' he said, very quietly. 'Darcy.'

Laughter, contempt, fury, humiliation, relief, confusion washed over her and the idea came to her that she would upend the table on him.

There were boxes in front of him, and opening them, he confirmed the feeling she had that this was planned like a Candid Camera nightmare sequence. There would be rings in the boxes. There were. The rage died away and she was not ready to walk out yet, partly because she had kicked off the high-heeled shoes under the table and was trying to find one of them with her toes without making noise.

'What are you doing? Why are you doing this?' she asked in what set out to be casual derision but came out, she realised to her fury, as plaintive. Furious with herself, she added: 'I mean, what the hell is all this about?' The gesture was wildly impatient and the back of her hand collided with the tall jug of iced water, arcing it at him in a sparkling column of water and ice cubes and jug. One-handed, he lifted the chair out from under himself, backing and deflecting the jug with the other hand so that the bulk of the liquid missed him. But enough of it connected to stain the dark trousers from belt to knee, sticking them to his thighs in a sudden sheen, the cold of it sucking his breath into an almost admiring 'Whooo . . . '

For a moment, she expected him to lift the chair and point it legs first at her like a lion-tamer in a circus. She could not imagine what the other guests and the staff in the restaurant thought he was going to do, but all eyes were on him. First he laughed and extended his hand across the swimming table to give her a firm and congratulatory shake. Then he was surrounded by helpers, by napkins and towels and laughter, and within seconds, it seemed to Darcy, the wet tablecloth was removed, the starter plates with it. He had patted off the excess water and indicated he would survive the rest, their main course was in front of them, and the ring boxes were back in the same place. Closed.

'Eat,' he said and proceeded to do so himself. As Darcy began to swallow bits of her sole, the other diners began to get back to the dynamic of their own conversations.

'What are you doing?' she hissed at him, under cover of those conversations.

'I'm tryin' to propose to you,' he said, a touch of ol' boy drawl in his voice, 'and you're makin' it kinda difficult.'

'But what's the purpose?'

'Ma'am, I'm a sociologist by trade, and I can tell you without fear of contradiction that not many men get asked to state their purpose when they propose to a woman.'

'What the hell are you calling me Ma'am for?'

'I was brought up to show respect. Even when a woman tries to drown me on first meeting. My purpose is to persuade you to be my wedded wife. It surely is.'

Apparently in high good humour, in spite of the soaking, he continued to eat with demonstrable appetite.

'And if you don't succeed?'

'Oh, I will succeed. Be in no doubt about that.'

Darcy breathed deeply, controlling her desire to swear at him.

'But if you don't?'

'I suppose I'd just go back to being an elderly academic. Nuthin' else for it.'

All her circuitry closed down. Her mind log-jammed, her mouth dry, she looked at him and the words spun her into dizziness, so that six of him refreshed her six glasses and then his six glasses.

'You OK?'

I've wanted all my life to faint dead away in company, Darcy thought, and now that I have the chance I will fight with all I have not to do it. She lowered her head and looked at her hands until the spinning stopped, then slowly came up and looked at him. There was no humour in his expression, no playfulness, no sentiment, no cleverness, no triumph, no timidity, no confidence.

'Who the hell are you?'

'Alex Carbine Brookestone.'

'You living shit.'

She was halfway out of the seat, avidly watched by the other diners.

'You *wanker*.'

'I've waited half my life to hear you call me that,' he said, a hand around her wrist tugging her down into her chair again.

'You've waited half *my* life, you ageing fart, you're a *hellova* lot older. You misled me – '

'I never misled you. You showed great mental laziness. Once you got me pegged in my stereotype, you weren't gonna let me out of it, no Sir.'

'*You're* –

'That's right, Ma'am. And because I knew I was meeting you this week, I had to tie off the study, because any contact directly between – '

'I know, I know, I know.'

'What's wrong?'

She looked at him in flurry of sudden embarrassment, glad her back was to the rest of the room.

'I'm trying to think of some of the things I've told you.'

'What *haven't* you told me?' he said with such gentleness her bones went soft, and when he put his palm to her cheek she could not slap it away or duck from it, but sat in thrall, in trance, the hand moving over her neck, then down to touch her own clenched hand on the table so the whiteness of her knuckles faded. 'What haven't you told me,' he said again.

Oliver arrived to receive their verdict on the meal, and Alex talked easily to him, mentioning things he knew about him, things Darcy had alluded to down through the years, so that Oliver blossomed and glowed. Darcy used the time to draw back her hand, to distance herself, to fight off the sense she had of welcoming someone home.

'When will you marry me, Darcy?'

'Oh, Alex, don't be silly. Jesus Christ, that's the first time I've ever said your name. I feel completely ridiculous. It's so improbable.'

'A lot of improbable things happen in every ordinary life.'

He watched her as she drank iced water like a Sahara survivor.

'I could not know you better had I lived with you every day of the last ten years,' he said softly. 'I learned the essence of you first, not the externals. I listened to your voice across space and time. You went from innocence and curiosity to knowledge and appetite. All the time I was closer to you than your own twin sister was. Much closer, while you grew into the big heavy magnificent woman you are now.'

No man should tell you that you're heavy, she thought, and if it happens, it should not leave your eyes bruised with the need to close so you could lean into his touch. She looked at the tablecloth, the weave of it glossed by starch, and he moved cutlery to one side and gathered her hands in his own as if it were a habit known to both of them.

'I know you without pretence or – '

The words evaded him and they sat for a moment, the restaurant noises welling up around them.

'Courtship displays,' Darcy said.

'Courtship displays,' he acknowledged. 'I have been far away from you but I have been inside your mind. There were days when I wanted to toss the study, just to come stand between you and endangerment. I have compared every other woman I encountered with you, in laughter and in bed. I have tested every idea out against you, imagining how you would react. I have been learning you these many years, Darcy. Learning you.'

'Distance learning?'

'I have been learning you and you me.'

'I've just had a daft thought,' she said, on a blurt of laughter. 'You must meet McCaw.'

'Before I meet Sophia and Greg?'

'Oh shit.'

'Oh shit, what?'

'This is unexplainable to sane people.'

'Let's not explain it, then. How about we just get married?'

'Alex!'

'Neat name, isn't it?'

'This has been a clever joke and it's a lot of fun to meet you, now that I'm not quite as furious, but let's not build something unreal on it.'

He looked at her through narrowed eyes.

'There is no unreality or strangeness. I'm here to marry you, Darcy. I have loved you for longer than Jacob loved Rachel. I have loved you without telling you. But now, I'm telling you. And I'm marrying you.'

'I get no choices?'

'You get all the choices, Darcy, but you only take one of them, and I'll tell you why.'

The waiter appeared and Alex paid the bill.

'Because you don't play games, Darcy. You're a bright blunt woman and you know when something feels right to you right into the marrow. You know when something feels like it's been there for years but you never noticed it. That's how you feel about this and I know it.'

He took an engagement ring and put it on her hand.

'Do you remember I asked you to draw me your idea of a perfect engagement ring back in the fax days?'

She shook her head, startled. He nodded to the ring.

'Your design.'

Stuffing the ring boxes into his pocket, he rose, took her arm and steered her through the restaurant. The journey was quite different, Darcy thought. Now, there were glances at the two of them followed by knowing looks between the people at the tables.

Then they were out in the chill night air and walking, her hand stuffed into the pocket of his coat where he held it. He was humming, and she tried to make out the melody.

'*Dublin can be heaven,/with coffee at eleven . . .*' he sang in quiet helpfulness.

'Oh, shag off, I might have guessed you'd learn that.'

Now they were on the pier overlooking the harbour and she stood back from him. 'Alex?'

'Yes, Ma'am,' he said, and bowed. As if reporting late for duty.

Then he was kissing her, his strength backing her against a lamppost, leaning in to her, warming her with his body and his hands and then, one hand above her against the lamp post, pulling back and looking at her, telling her she was beautiful.

Through the thin silk knit of her dress there was a clammy coldness.

'You're still damp,' she said, dropping her hand to the fabric at his thigh.

'That, too,' he said, guiding the hand.

'Marry me, Darcy.'

'Jesus, Alex. When?'

'Tomorrow.'

'You can't do it that quick here.'

'How do you know? You've never tried.'

'OK, OK, we'll see.'

He held her face between his hands and told her wonders. She fought not to believe him and lost. There were gaps in time. There was a car journey and then they were pulling up outside her apartment block.

'I have to tell Sophia straight away. Tomorrow, anyway.'

'Two for joy?'

'She'll be so glad for me. If you ever, once you have met her, call her Snow White's Stepmother again, I'll divorce you.'

'You can't. Not in Ireland. You people don't have divorce yet.'

'We'll get it in time for that eventuality.'

They got out of the car and kissed again. He caught her hand and pulled her after him up the steps. She turned him around to look at the river and the sky, alight with moon and stars, reflected and multiplied. She leaned against him, rubbing the fabric of his jacket to make sure of the reality of it, stunned in wonderment.

'Well, fuck me,' Darcy eventually said.

'I surely will, Ma'am,' he replied.